DANGEROUS OFFSPRING

Also by Steph Swainston

No Present Like Time

The Year of Our War

DANGEROUS OFFSPRING

STEPH SWAINSTON

An Imprint of HarperCollins*Publishers*

This book is a work of fiction. The characters, incidents, and dialogue are drawn from the author's imagination and are not to be construed as real. Any resemblance to actual events or persons, living or dead, is entirely coincidental.

This book was originally published under the title *The Modern World* in Great Britain in 2007 by Gollancz, an imprint of the Orion Publishing Group, London.

HarperCollins books may be purchased for educational, business, or sales promotional use. For information please write: Special Markets Department, HarperCollins Publishers, 10 East 53rd Street, New York, NY 10022.

FIRST U.S. EDITION

Library of Congress Cataloging-in-Publication Data is available upon request.

ISBN: 978-0-06-075389-4
ISBN-10: 0-06-075389-7

07 08 09 10 11   ❖/RRD   10 9 8 7 6 5 4 3 2 1

To Brian

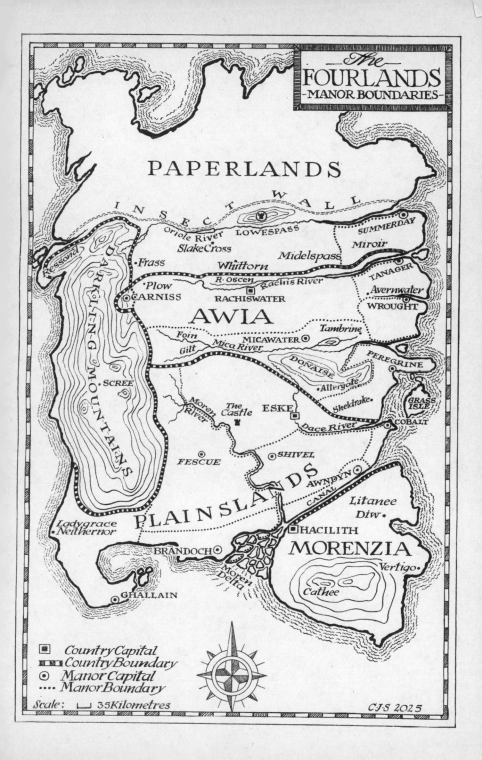

He let go by the things of yesterday
And took the modern world's more spacious way.
Chaucer, *The Canterbury Tales*

I wake, and lie motionless on my camp bed in the dark tent, listening. The wind roars down the gaps between my pavilion and the next, hisses over the guy ropes. Outside, heavy canvas cracks and flaps. The lantern outside my tent door vibrates on its iron stake and sets up a loud humming. When the gust dies back it unmasks the din that woke me. Soldiers are screaming. Men are shouting to each other in the absolute darkness outside. The gale gusts again so loud I can't distinguish anything at all. I can have been asleep for only a couple of hours; it must be one or two in the morning.

I throw my blankets aside and leap off the bed. As my bare feet touch the damp grass the ground shakes so violently I fall to my knees. My bed and the low cane table next to it collapse, spilling my letters and clothes onto the sparse grass. Is it an earthquake?

The tremor surges strongly, a guy rope snaps and in the gloom I see the poles of my fyrd-issue pavilion start to lean to the right. The walls begin to droop, gathering creases.

There is a constant banging, the lantern flame wavers. Its light blows out: suddenly everything is totally black. Its pole hits the ground with a thump.

Wind puffs out the walls then sucks them hollow, drawing in the far-off sound of a desperate, unearthly shrieking, urgent hammering and splintering wood. That isn't human. What's going on? What's happening? I fumble around trying to find my matches, before I realise what it is. Animals are making that noise. Horses. What the fuck would make them scream like that? They're in their stalls at the top of camp; the smashing is their hooves beating the gates where they're trapped. Their noise is solid panic but I can't hear anything else. In a second the power of their agony winds me so tightly on edge that I whimper. I grab my combat trousers off the grass, hop about on a bare foot shoving one leg into them, then the other, pull them up to my waist, button them.

The gale swells and punches the tent walls. The horses' screams die out, one by one. Now I can hear men and women yelling, their shouts come from both sides and from the row of pavilions in front of mine.

'Help!' A man's cry fragments in the wind. Footsteps thump on the duckboard track outside, resounding in both directions. People are running to and from the centre of camp; I can't tell what they're trying to do. Lamps flare outside, far on the other side of the pavilion lines, towards the gate. Their light shines through my walls as yellow dots with fuzzy haloes, outlining the ridges of the surrounding tents.

I thrust my toes without socks into clammy leather boots, shoving them right down to the hard sole and drawing the bucket tops over my knees. I pick up my scale-mail hauberk, hold it up, jangling, over my head and struggle into it as if it is a jumper, leaving the bottom straps loose. Its freezing scales slap against my bare skin but I have no time to put on the undershirt.

I fumble my left arm into my round shield's leather loops. I can't see anything but blackness at ground level. I feel for my ice axe, snatch it up and wriggle its webbing strap over my hand, around my wrist. The canvas ceiling sags down to my head. Its rear wall billows in on a cold blast, carrying the smell of tough grass and wet moss. The ropes stretch to breaking strain, then yank thick pegs out of the ground.

I dart to the entrance, unlacing the flaps from each other with my long, white fingers up in front of my face. A silhouette stumbles past outside, running for its life, then back again in the direction it came. He falters one way then the other, incapable of making a decision, swiping at the air with a broadsword clutched in one muddy hand.

I scrabble out under the cloudy starless sky, onto the planks that serve row fifty-one. I tread on something lumpy and yielding, and look down. It is a severed right hand. I lift my boot toe off its palm and its curled fingers relax slightly.

Abruptly a tremendous noise like a tree trunk breaking crashes through the gale, followed by a running series of snaps starting deep in the night in front of me. It sounds like sailcloth ripping, or a hunter stripping the ribs off a carcass. It approaches louder and closer, peels past me on my right, and ends far behind me with a ear-splitting crack. I crouch wondering what the fuck it was. The wind exalts with twice the strength and splatters water drops from the tent canvas across my face. The palisade must have gone down. Three sides of our square encampment are wide open. The wind roars straight from the high moor with no shelter to break it up and searches out the tiny gaps in my mail shirt. I have a sudden impression of the vast, empty hills. It is five kilometres to our reinforcements at Slake Cross, three to the nearest fortified farm.

This must really be an earthquake if it's strong enough to rip down the palisade. The ground shakes in short spasms. Behind me my whole pavilion collapses with a sigh, blowing air past me. The wind tugs at it, twisting it into a rustling, living form. Torn strips flap past, writhing as they ascend. They fly like flags from the tent next to mine; it has been shredded. Tangled bloodstained clothes roll and wrap themselves around the base of its pole. To my right, towards the centre of camp, the neighbouring tents in the line lie collapsed in the same direction, like trees in a blasted forest. There are more lamps along the track but the ones that aren't dead gutter feebly. I stare into the roaring night but I can't see any further.

A dark-haired man sprints along the duckboard, clutching his crumpled, padded undershirt to his naked chest, the greaves on his otherwise bare legs flashing.

'Stop! What's out there?'

He just disappears against the moors' lightless bulk.

I sense rather than see movement on my right towards the fallen palisade. Maybe men, heading away from the tents. They seem to thin out, are gone. I hear clicking and swing round with a breath to my left. Did something scuttle behind the canvas wreckage? My hand is so tight around my axe haft I feel its tally notches pressing into my palm. I bring it up into guard.

A soldier is squatting to shit in front of the next tent. The tent's walls are patched with blood and it emits a warm cloying smell of viscera. The soldier is looking away from me, so terrified that his bowels let go and he's getting it over with as fast as possible.

Another man runs past, wearing nothing but a coat and pants, his ponytail whisking. I don't know how to stop them fleeing so I yell the rallying cry, 'To me! To me! Minsourai! . . . Wake up! . . . Wake . . .' But there is no one to wake. I can't see inside the laced tents and even if I could I don't want to. I back away; I might be safer at a distance from them.

These are the advance guard, only five thousand men but still too many to rally. Where's Hayl? These pavilions are for his minsourai, mounted scouts who reconnoitre and find routes for the fyrd, locate and mark positions to camp.

I begin to pick my way in the opposite direction towards the centre and the Castle's field headquarters. If we can possibly regroup, the Sun Pavilion will be the best place.

I follow the duckboard raised above the grass that's bruised and pasted down into the mud. The mud is becoming more slimy with blood. Under the boards I see a boot with a lower leg protruding. No sign of the rest of the body. Further on, dismembered limbs scatter the tussocks and track.

The wind batters against me and, somewhere within it, I catch the rasp of an Insect's leg against its shell. I shrink back and stare around. I can't see anything!

Behind me, something the size of a pony but with thin long legs skitters across the track. I glimpse a flash of red-brown shell. They're everywhere! My scalp tingles: at any moment one will lunge out of the night and grab me before I even see it.

Far on the other side of camp, lights are clustering and moving away. I'll try to reach them. If I can trust what I've heard, the palisade's still upright over there.

The wind gusts from every direction carrying the brief sound of mandibles chopping closed, like a whetstone on a scythe blade. Closer to the centre now, the tents on either side are nothing but shreds. Inside one, I hear the sound of bone splintering. In each pavilion, ten men are dispatched by bites before they wake up, their bodies twisted into different postures. Ten men fused together into a slaughterhouse heap so unrecognisable I'll have to use their dog tags to identify them.

The next tent stores the armour consignment that arrived yesterday. I hear crashes as clawed feet skid over the steel, knocking against piles of plate, jostling sheaves of pikes. I smell whiffs and hear scraping from the latrine shack. Insects are in there too, turning over the earth and eating the shit.

The path begins to zigzag. The earthquake has shaken some of its joined sections apart. Then I see it folded into peaks; the boards are still connected but standing on their ends.

Grey eye facets glitter. I glimpse an Insect face-on. It pulls back into the darkness between two pavilions. Its triangular antlike head moves up and down; it is tangled among crossed tent ropes, severing them with bites. Pieces of paper and torn pennons fly through the night, brushing the ground and catching against buckled ridge poles.

I see angular shapes of Insects standing, feeding on the corpses. A brush of air, something rears. Instantly I see jaws like stag beetle mandibles, then it crashes into the shield. Its jaws slide off the curved edge. I yell and swing my axe, feel it connect. I free the axe and bring it down again. It's dead. It's dead! Calm down! Short breaths rush in and out as I feel not think – how many more? I have to get away. I plunge down the track, running blindly. I'm on the verge of completely losing control, then I stop.

The track has ended. There are no more planks.

At the same moment a heavy gust blusters against my face carrying the unmistakable firm burnt copper scent of Insects. When as a child I lost my milk teeth, pulling at a tooth and turning it rushed a salty blood taste into my mouth, and I had a strange sore pleasure from turning a tooth on a flesh thread or biting down the sharp underside onto my gum. That's what Insects smell like, and it's so intense there must be hundreds. How have they appeared inside the camp? My jaw prickles as if I'm about to vomit. I gulp down saliva and I let out a scream to release the fear.

'Jant!' a voice answers, faint on the wind. It is Tornado, bellowing but I think I hear an edge to it as if he's in pain. 'Jant, where are you? Hayl, is that you?'

'Tornado!' I yell with all my strength.

'Jant! Jant!' Tornado sounds desperate. 'Fuck –'

The wind's noise rises higher and higher. If I open my wings, it will smash me into the ground.

Something whizzes past my face, with the gale, and thuds into the duckboard behind me. I crouch down to investigate. An arrow is sticking in the plank at a steep angle, its bodkin point embedded deeply. Its shaft and white fletchings are still quivering. I start to hear, but not see, more arrows hissing down. They pelt from the sky, from somewhere ahead of me, not spent, striking with force.

I raise my shield in front of my face and feel it jar. Arrows come down like hailstones sweeping across the track, thudding into the corpses, into the soldiers who are still alive but wounded, lying on the ground sweating and twitching. All the ground I can see is filling with arrows. Our archers must be a couple of hundred metres away. Why are they shooting at us?

I yell into the night, 'Stop!' and the wind tatters my voice.

Invisible arrows strike the board in front of my toes; one deflects off my shield and drops at my side. They catch in tent fabric. I hear them tap on an Insect shell and the clicking of articulated claws as it scuffles under fallen canvas.

The arrows buzz in well-timed flights, but I can't hear any voice ordering the loosing. Who's out there? Lightning – if it is Lightning – must have concluded that everybody is dead or beyond help. The archers will be terrified. They're protecting themselves and they're never going to stop. I hurry away from them, stumble over a shaft embedded in the track, and break it.

I catch a glimpse of a single flickering light ahead. It illuminates a white tent from inside. All around is dark so the tent, rectangular because it's side-on to me, looks as if it is hanging in the air. The light moves slowly, in jerks, along at floor level. It inches towards the entrance; closer and closer. A sense of dread weighs on me because I know what I am going to witness next will be even worse. Whatever comes out of that tent is the last thing alive this side of camp and I don't want to see it. I don't want to have to deal with wounds so awful. It will be mutilated and driven so insane by agony it won't even be human any more. I fervently hope that it dies before it emerges.

A lean hand clutching a lantern pushes out from the flap and Laverock crawls out on his hands and knees – head, shoulders, chest.

I know him as a minsourai captain, a local with vital knowledge of Lowespass. Digging ramparts made him sinewy, with shorn hair and a face like a weathered leather bag. He was raised with the constant pressures of the Insect threat and Awian ambition.

An arrow snicks into the grass beside him, its flights upright.

'Laverock!' I cry.

He looks in my direction, not recognising me. As he draws his legs from the tent flap I see he doesn't have feet. His feet have been bitten off above the ankle, though not cleanly because sharp tubes of white bone stick out from the severed ends: they look like uncooked macaroni.

Insect antennae flicker after him. Bulbous, faceted eyes follow and the thing strikes forward. Laverock's eyes widen in terror. He pushes himself upright and tries to run on the stumps but his bones sink into the ground like hollow pegs. The Insect seizes his hips low down; its jaws saw over his belly. Laverock knows this is his last second. He snarls in fury as he falls and swings round the iron lantern dangling from his hand. He smashes it over the Insect's head. Yellow-flaming liquid spreads over its brown carapace. I smell scorching chitin, then Laverock's shirt and wings catch fire. His long primary feathers drip and shrink as they burn, as if they're drawing back into his wings. The Insect bites through his body and with a shake of its head throws the top half towards me. The Insect and Laverock's remains sink to the ground, welded together in the fire, vivid against the line of wrecked tents.

By their light I can suddenly see I'm standing at the edge of a vast pit. The flames jump up and shadow its far side, twenty metres away. I stare at it, uncomprehending: this should be the centre of camp. The conical hole gradually, steadily, widens. Turf breaks off under my feet and rolls into it. I step back, seeing that the slope is covered with debris. On the other side, the Sun Pavilion, collapsed down the incline, lies plastered to it like a gigantic wet sheet, trailing ropes still attached at their ends to dirty uprooted pegs. The brass sun bosses that top its main poles glint among its folds. Dead men are splayed out around and underneath it, pale and naked or half-dressed, some still in sleeping bags. As soil rolls down, they slide towards the base of the cone. Their limbs shift position with jerky marionette motions – they look as if they're waving. Swords and broken camp bed frames rattle off stones in the soil as they slide; kitbags spill their contents.

Tornado's voice peals out again, 'Jant!' I look up to see the giant man standing on the far bank beset by seven Insects, five on the slope in front of him and one on his either side. Yet more Insects are running up out of the crater. Tornado backs himself against an empty ambulance cart. It has 1st DIVISION LOWESPASS SELECT roughly stencilled on the side, and its spoked wheels have curved boards nailed to the rims, to widen them and prevent them sinking in the mud.

Tornado's breeches are slashed and blood wells up from red cuts underneath. It flows down his leg from a deep wound in his thigh. His denim shirt is unbuttoned; his big hands curl around the shaft of his double-headed axe. Every second he is taking wounds that would kill me outright.

An Insect below him darts forward but Tornado swings the axe under its mandibles with such force that he decapitates it. He hews down the ones on left and right with a fluid movement. At his feet a mound of carcasses bleeds thick pale yellow haemolymph down the widening pit. Two more Insects run up the slope and over its rim. He deals one a massive blow, cleaving its thorax through. The other seems to brush past him with a movement of its head but it opens a huge streaming gash in the roll of fat over his unfastened belt buckle. Tornado bellows.

He starts to droop forward. He clutches at the cart for support; it rocks on its curved boards. His knees sag and his skin is pallid. He kneels, one knee then the other, head bowed. I can't see his face.

I watch as an Insect climbs the cart from behind, crests the top, appears above Tornado's head as a spiked silhouette, with actions like a jointed puppet. It reaches down to Tornado's rounded shoulders. It starts to feed.

Under their weight, the edge of the pit gives way and they tumble. Tornado rolls, unconscious and arms loose, down the slope. He hits the edge of the mass of debris and lies still, near the bottom. Soil continues to crumble away; the cart's front wheels jolt over the edge. It teeters and then runs straight down the slope. Its wheels' boards slap and leave footprints, its dragging hafts plough furrows. It runs over Tornado's outstretched arm and fractures it, impacts into the duckboards and broken tents, and comes to rest upright on top of him, its four wheels caging him in.

Tornado's down. What chance do I have? The oil is burning off Laverock's Insect and its light is dying down. The shadows shift and I see the base of the pit, where soil has been swept aside from the pale grey bedrock. It has been brushed clean. A wide crack runs across it, separating it into two slabs like deeply buried gravestones. The gap transfixes me – it is pure black – so black that as an illusion it seems to jump and shimmer. I stare at it as arrows still whicker and thud around my feet.

A flash of movement on my left, and an Insect's head with open mandibles lunges at my waist. My elbow's levered up, and before I can stop it, the head is under my shield. I flinch away inside its jaws, with a fast reaction but I can't dodge far enough: it turns and plunges its open left mandible into my stomach like a dagger. I go rigid with the shock of it penetrating. It tosses its head like a bull goring and I feel the razor mandible gouge upwards. My skin parts before it. My loose hauberk rucks up over its head with a metallic rasp. Its cold jaw slits all the way up and hooks under my lowest rib. It tries to continue its carving slice and pulls me onto the tips of my toes. By luck, I stumble backwards and slip off the point.

With my hand clawed I rake over the bastard thing's eye but my nails have no effect and I hate myself for reverting to act like a Rhydanne and scratching, while my ice axe drags on the ground.

My strength fails quickly. I raise the axe and bring it down between its eyes, into its forehead plate studded with three smaller eyes and dimpled antennae sockets. The frons plate cracks across like a nutshell and one side lifts up: I glimpse the base of its compound eye rooted in a damp membrane underneath.

The Insect rears up and shoves me. I topple backwards and fall. I brace myself but I'm surprised to find I'm still falling. My wings open instinctively. The pit's edge tilts up into the sky above me. I hit the slope hard with my left wing under me and – crack! – its bone breaks.

This isn't my camp bed. Where the fuck – ? No: I'm lying on my back on the slope with my wing buckled underneath me and I had better not faint again. My right arm is outstretched, the strap around my wrist is holding me attached to the axe pick still embedded in the Insect's head.

It lies flat; its head moving left and right in its death throes tugs at my arm. Its mandibles open and close. Its flattened forelegs kick back and forth, scooping soil off the top of the slope. Turf chunks and grainy dirt sift down on top of me, covering me lightly all over.

I clutch one hand instinctively across my stomach but the gash is too long to hold together and my fingers sink under the edge of the flap of skin. It is warm and very slick. I feel a loop of gut spill out over my arm. I look down and see it adhering to the ground, picking up pieces of soil and grass blades. Unable to stop it, I watch it uncoil out of my midriff from under the mail shirt. The guts slither over each other; they are different shades of grey and firm to the touch.

All I can see of my wing is the bicep and a sharp shard of broken bone sticking out of the muscle close to my body between the black feathers. As I breathe out, air rushes out of the hollow bone. The air sac inside it inflates slightly out of its pointed end. It is a very thin, moist and silvery membrane. I know that Awians have two air sacs deep in their backs and in their limbs' long bones nearest the body; humerus and femur, but I'd never seen one balloon out before. I breathe in, dizzy from shock and lack of air, and it inflates. I exhale and it flutters where it's ruptured and the air flutes out. Under the feathery skin around it, a blister starts to grow as escaping air is trapped there. Oh, fuck. That's me fucked then if I'm breathing through the bone.

The ground shakes but I don't roll further down the slope because I'm anchored to the dead Insect at the top. I can't muster the energy to turn myself over and crawl. I can't move. I'm going to die here. I have to do something, anything, not just give up. The wind gets under my broken wing and blows it around, grinding as it twirls on the bone. Between gusts it settles down slowly on top of me, then the wind picks it up again. I take my hand from my ripped stomach and reach out to flatten it against the ground but the feather tips still curl up.

The agony begins. It is fiery and sharp, a white-hot blade the length of my side. I lie with my cheek in the cold, uneven soil like a toad's back and scream. Mud grains get into my mouth and coat the back of my tongue. I grit my teeth and they grate against the surfaces. I feel soil filling my nostrils, I retch with the earthworm smell of loam and cut roots. I scream wordlessly with all my strength, trying to relieve the pain. A human or Awian would scream for help, but Rhydanne don't because Rhydanne know there is no help to be had.

I can feel the sweat trickling out of my hairline and a stream of blood running freely out of my side, into the ground. I didn't know I had this much blood.

The uneven piles of dirt close beside me, that I know are tiny, now seem as impassable as mountain ranges, and dark with the organic matter of rotting soldiers . . . whom I will soon join.

The black sky rains arrows. The wind's noise is a great distance above me; it doesn't affect me any more. I feel a warm patch spreading between my legs: I have wet myself. I begin to suffer from an over-bearing sense of shame. What will people say when they find out I've wet myself and my trousers are sticking to my crotch? But I will be long dead by the time they find me, if they find me at all.

I take another mouthful of dirt and scream again, petrified by the thought of leaving the world for ever. I'm twenty-three; I don't want to die. I'm one hundred and thirty years old, I don't want to die. I can't feel my toes or fingers, then feet or hands, then legs or arms. The cold clings to my skin like wet cloth. It permeates my bones and my muscles ache with tension. I can't curl up against it. I am shivering from the freezing air in the wound, it reaches inside my body until I feel as if I am more naked than naked.

I quickly run out of energy and lie exhausted, with my throat raw. The damp ground at last feels comfortable against my cheek. I am as cold as the soil, throughout my body, as if I am already part of it. I start to forget how to breathe. How still I am. I can hear an Insect's claws scraping underground as it pulls itself through the crevice in the rock.

I sink into fatigue and start slipping into warm sleep despite the pain. I am dimly aware of my body shutting down. I fight to stay awake, in furious denial, but why bother? No one is left to help me. Sleep tempts me. I scream at myself – if you sleep you die! Stay awake! The numbness seeps deeper and I have no choice. It steals up inside my core. While my consciousness fights fiercely to stay awake, a part of my mind falls asleep, then another, blocking it in. I can't revive my memory. I can't wake my sense of hearing ... touch ... vision ... I am surrounded by sleeping mind; I die.

CHAPTER 1

I woke. I tried to sit up and banged my head hard on a wooden plank above me. Shit, had they put me in a coffin already?

I was curled up tightly in a tiny space, tense with suppressed panic. I calmed down, relaxed and remembered where I was. It isn't 1925, it is the year 2025, and we are six kilometres south of the Wall in Slake Cross town. I had been sleeping folded up on the lowest shelf of an enormous bookcase. My wings extended, half-spread, taking up metres of the paved stone floor.

Frost, the Architect and owner of the bookcase, was sitting behind her table a few metres away. She glanced down. 'It's nearly nine o'clock, Jant. We only have an hour until the meeting, remember?'

I unpacked my long legs, stood and stretched, attempting to tie my hair back so I could see her.

Frost sounded curious: 'Did you have bad dreams again? Was it the nineteen twenty-five massacre?'

'Yes. I have flashbacks every time I come here. God, I hate this place.'

'I'm not surprised you have bad dreams if you sleep on a shelf. Sometimes I forget you're a Rhydanne but then you do something really bizarre. Tornado and Lightning haven't been bothered by nightmares.'

'They weren't eviscerated, and besides, they remember worse disasters.' I hooked my thumb in the pocket of my jeans and pulled the waistband down to show the old knotty scar that curved up the left side of my stomach.

'Yeuch. Still, you should have got over it by now. Have you been under the influence?'

'No.' Not since that last handful of mushrooms anyway, and whatever I'd washed them down with. 'I'm clean.'

'Well, being "clean" seems to have done wonders for your vanity.'

I had unfolded a little mirror to check the kohl around my eyes. My irises were dark green like bottle glass, the pupils vertical like a cat's,

11

backed with a light-reflecting membrane. It's a Rhydanne trait. So are my silver bangles and a brightly coloured serape shawl wound around my waist, its indigo tassels hanging down. But I am half Awian and at the moment my clothes are too; well-tailored boot-cut riding trousers. The faience beads and broken buzzard feathers in my black hair. Then there was the natty slashed shirt I picked up in Wrought, through which I was windburnt, so now with the sleeves rolled, my arms were brindled and spotted. I had spent the last six months carrying messages for Frost and constant flying had honed me down to bone and muscle. I feel so much better these days and everyone can see how much better I look.

I stretched my wings and Frost watched the workings of the joints, unfortunately not with the eye of a woman who finds them attractive, but as a fascinated engineer. Frost, through and through a Plainslander, was a human without wings. She looked to where the limbs, as thick as thighs, joined to me above the small of my back. The muscles around my sides, attached to the tops of my hips, drive them.

I folded them both neatly so the quills lined up, like organ pipes emerging from delicate, corrugated skin. The limey Lowespass water had dulled my feathers.

Frost sat behind a rough table in the middle of the hall, with a large brass coffee pot at hand. Propped up against it was her small and extremely threadbare soft toy rabbit with one eye. It had been a present from her husband more than three hundred years before. The coffee pot and the rabbit weighted down a stack of papers, a mound of dog-eared textbooks and notes, all in Frost's handwriting but some of the paper was ancient. An enormous chart of the Oriole River valley curled off the table at either end. Fiendish equations were pencilled across it; underscoring, memos and neat, blocky doodles. Her genius calculations were written in lines; tiny numbers and letters. There were all sorts of little triangles there too. I appreciated the little triangles.

Frost presided over this orderly mess, a double-handled glazed mug cradled in her square palms. Her round face was slightly blotchy without any trace of make-up and her nose was red. Dryness lines bunched together around her eyes and two vertical creases between them made her look fearsome, but they were caused by peering into windswept trenches, not by scowling. She had a bulky brown ponytail with a few grey hairs twisted and tethered behind her head with a clip. Wiry strands fizzed out of it, around her broad forehead and the pencil wedged behind her ear.

The arms of Frost's chunky cardigan were rolled back into bunches above her elbows. Its wool was pilled and marred with snags. She had knotted a kerchief around her neck and her big thighs in comfortable trousers fitted into the seat of her camp chair. Frost was not concerned with the niceties of dress and she only ever wore black. Her feet, in thick socks and steel-toed boots, rested alongside a stack of architectural plans on graph paper taped to drawing boards.

The hall was thirty metres long, echoing and austere; its half-round ceiling arched above us like the inside of a barrel. Since Frost had begun to use it as her office, she had covered its trestle tables with samples of masonry; keystones, voussoirs and coping stones milled into interesting shapes. There were metal boxes – dumpy levels for surveying, pattress plates for strengthening brickwork, a basket of red-painted corks to measure water flow and an intricate scale model of the dam. The oil lamps hanging from the brick vault had just been lit as evening was wearing on and, against April's chill, a fire was set in the hearth. Frost's assistants were pulling some benches into rows. I reflected that her world is rather more practical than mine.

She said, 'Lightning and the Queen are out walking on the dam. They've been there since dawn; they said it was the best vantage point to decide how to position the fyrd. Can you fly over there and ask them to join us?'

I mimicked the Queen's decadent voice, 'Oh, my darling, *must* I?'

Frost's mouth twitched. A smile only escaped her when her guard was down. 'You've got her beautifully. Yes, you must. I mean she must. She probably finds it as tiresome as I do.'

'Have you seen any reporters yet?'

'God, no. Most of them are waiting in the Primrose. You know I don't like talking to them. They twist everything I say and I can tell they're not really interested. They wouldn't get even the most basic facts wrong if they were. I don't know why I bother holding press conferences. Everybody apart from journalists finds the dam self-evident, and their waffling questions always lead me away from the point.'

'I'll make sure it goes smoothly.'

She pulled her oversized cardigan closed and sipped her coffee. 'This is the culmination of years of work since I unveiled the model. The dam has occupied my every waking hour ... and my sleep too. But I doubt the reporters care. They look for other stupid stories and then concentrate on the wrong one. They'll chase off after any scandal no matter how momentous the occasion.'

I said, 'It's all right. Don't worry, just leave them to me. I'm used to keeping them in check. If they ask me a question I can't answer, I'll bring you in.' I waved my hand in the air and Frost stared at it. I dug it into my pocket. 'I'll find a quick flight refreshing. The dam breaks up the air in interesting ways. It is a masterpiece.'

'Oh, yes! It really is the most efficient structure! There's never been a dam with the functional strength of this one, there's never been a lake so capacious!' Keen enthusiasm lit her face. She had been boring people on the subject of river engineering for three hundred and fifty years and this was her greatest project. 'It makes Micawater Bridge look like an apprentice piece! Every engineer said I was being over-ambitious, but the figures were sound. So is the actualisation! They said it was impossible. They said, "You might hold the model in your hands but you'll never raise the biggest construction of all time right on the Insects' doorstep." Three years later, I took them for a tour! Since the Wrought blast furnaces are operational again I've had iron for the rack and pinion cast in segments and assembled here, an elegant solution, you must admit, and you should look out for the way I've bridged the walkway above the overflow conduit so –'

'Frost, please . . .'

'I thought you liked it.'

'I do, but you've just asked me to call in Lightning and Eleonora.'

'Oh yes,' she said, chastened. 'So I did.'

I blew her a kiss with both hands that became a mock bow. 'See you in an hour, OK?'

I walked out to the cobbled central courtyard, enclosed on its three other sides by the cookhouse, mess room and tavern. Each was built of limestone blocks and roofed with lauze; thick, heavy slabs that looked shaggy, like the boughs of a fir tree.

The buildings were pierced with arched alleys, three in each side, just wide enough for one man at a time. They were designed to stop all but the smallest Insects reaching this square, a final refuge if the town's outer defences were ever penetrated.

The plain hall had fulfilled many purposes over the years: a hospital, a headquarters for immortals, and it was now Queen Eleonora Tanager's temporary residence and Frost's office. Frost's orange banner ran along the length of the roof: 'Riverworks Company Est. 1692' in bold black letters. Beside it flew Tanager's swan pennant, Micawater's argent mascle on an azure field, and the Awian white eagle on sky blue.

Soldiers had gathered outside the Primrose Tavern opposite. They sat on stools made from barrels to watch two immortals sparring in the middle of the square. The Swordsman, Serein Wrenn, was fighting the Polearms Master, Lourie Hurricane. They had an Eszai competitive edge to their play; they both knew that if they weren't training, somewhere a potential Challenger was.

Lourie Hurricane was a quiet perfectionist, a tall man from Plow who used to be a vavasour cart-driver before he became immortal. Serein Wrenn, on the other hand, was short and stocky and had the silliest haircut of all the Eszai – waxed up into short spikes with bleached tips. His narrow sideburns tapered into a little chinstrap beard.

Wrenn had come forward and beaten the previous Serein in a fair Challenge, according to the Castle's rules, only five years ago. Many still said that his predecessor was the more steadfast fighter, but Wrenn was quick with the desperate gambit. He had frequently been Challenged until word of his flair spread. He had latched on to Lourie; I think he admired Lourie's ascetic, taciturn poise. In the depths of his aplomb Lourie might have been grateful; it is always the case that Eszai lose friends but gain sparring partners. These two were often seen together arguing monomaniacally as to whether glaives or broadswords were the better weapons.

There were both objects of great amusement to the other immortals seated nearby watching them fight: Tornado the Strongman, the Sapper, the Artillerist, and Gayle Holthen the Castle's Lawyer who also acted as provost for the fyrd. She was a smart, cosmopolitan woman who had joined the Circle after a full career as a judge.

Lourie swept his glaive in balletic circling moves, not one millimetre out of the perfect sequence. He dipped the two-metre pole, swept the pointed blade under Wrenn's feet. Wrenn jumped it. Its hook caught behind his shin as he landed. Lourie tugged the pole with a grace that belied his strength. Wrenn hopped and let the hook slip out under his foot.

Gayle laughed and clapped her hands, bringing the Cook out of the tavern to watch.

All fifty immortals were arriving. I had been calling them up one by one, either from the Castle or wherever they'd been pursuing their interests elsewhere. Those involved in advance planning had been here for a month but all would be assembled by the end of the week.

Immortals, called Eszai in the low Awian language, are people proven to be the best in the world at their chosen profession. We all play our parts in the battle, because the Emperor San joins us to the Circle and shares his immortality with us as long as we lead the war. Here at the front we have overall authority, even over governors and the Queen; but elsewhere, or in issues not connected with the war we can do no more than advise them. Likewise, San's word is advice to the world but to us it is law.

Wrenn deflected Lourie's blade. Lourie pulled it back, grinding its rebated edge, and thrust the metal-clad base of the pole. Wrenn parried it with a full-strength clash. The mortals watching gasped, but we Eszai knew Lourie's great skill; we'd seen it a hundred times before.

The Castle saves the very best and improves on it gradually, incrementally; little is ever lost. I've been Comet for two hundred years, the fastest Messenger of all time. I'm a freak, yes, but it means I get to live forever.

I turned to the wall behind me, took a grip on the rough stone and pulled myself up. I climbed swiftly past the doorway and the plaque above it; the only decoration in the town. Its sgraffito red plaster, incised through to the white layer underneath, depicted the Castle's sun-in-splendour standard, surrounded by an inscription: 'In memory of the battle at Slake crossroads, one night in the ongoing war. 4981 Plainslanders, Awians and Morenzians died on the 12th of April 1925.'

As if we need to be reminded, I thought as I pulled myself over the guttering and scrabbled up to the apex of the roof. Balancing there, I looked down on the mortal soldiers outside the pub and I suddenly realised they did need to be reminded. The massacre was three generations in the past, long out of their living memory. It meant nothing to them but a date in a schoolbook. I stepped lightly along the ridge, thinking for the first time that I had more in common with the other Eszai than with the mortals, the Zascai, who had no idea what it was like to stumble through the middle of a massacre. I contemplated with dread that no matter how much effort I put in to knowing every up-to-date trend in Zascai fashion and the developments in their business, the gap between us was steadily widening. Well, I decided, it isn't inevitable that I will become as out of touch as Frost or Lightning. I must simply try harder; it's my profession after all.

From the rooftop I saw the series of concentric squares in which the town was laid out. The buildings around the courtyard formed the first of three rings. Behind them ran a wide road, then another ring comprising the smithy, workshops, food, livery and ammunition stores, since Slake Cross is the supply base for all of western Lowespass. Every junction was staggered to prevent any Insects that might get in running straight to the heart of the town.

The smell of hot iron rose from the blacksmith's shop, mingling with the yellow-hay stink of horse turds on the road and the washy smell of potatoes boiling in the cookhouse adjoining the hall.

Below, the innkeeper thwacked a brass tap with a mallet to drive it into an enormous keg of beer. His blows rang around the square together with the wail of the innkeeper's squab and its mother shushing as she tried to calm it. She held it inside her cream shawl, against her breasts. It flailed one naked pinion with three pointed fingers like the wing of a plucked chicken. 'Squab' is Morenzian slang for Awian babies before they are fledged, and it was probably crying from the itching as its pinfeathers were starting to push through.

The long buildings of the third ring were barracks to billet ten thousand troops. I could see the stone cisterns on the shower blocks' roofs, replenished by recent rainstorms. The Awian soldiers had added a sauna and a talcum bath: conditions are bad enough at the front without suffering from lice in your wings.

Then came the stables and allotments, in shadow at the foot of the curtain wall. Mangy apple and hazelnut trees bowed over cramped, tilled plots with green shoots – hardy runner beans and turnips. The soldiers supplemented their diet by growing vegetables but they were only permitted to do so inside the walls because any kind of plant attracts Insects.

A few metal cages beside them each contained an Insect the size of a warhorse. Their jaws and antennae were bound with wire; they were soon to be sold and carted south to the Rachiswater amphitheatre. Their scent set mastiffs barking on the far side of town.

Towers reinforced the exterior curtain wall at intervals along its length and at all four corners. It was tall, height being more important against the Insects than thickness, and it extended below ground to stop them undermining it. Roofed wooden walkways overhung the tops of the walls along their lengths. The single gate faced north towards the Paperlands. A guard with a jaunty crest on her helmet stared out of the large, square windows in the gatehouse tower.

These military towns – Slake Cross, Frass and Whittorn – had been designed by Frost soon after her initiation to the Circle. She became a great favourite with the troops who no longer had to construct open air camps. Each town was in essence a fort, with a shifting population of fyrd and the people who supply them: quartermasters, fletchers, sutlers and male and female prostitutes.

Slake Cross gave me a sinking feeling like the cold trepidation you feel on returning to a place you knew long ago. All your friends have moved on; their houses have strangers in them now. Even the routes you used to walk have changed, because the pubs you knew have been boarded up and cafés opened where they shouldn't be. The last time I was here I was completely screwed up, living on drug time, time measured by needles and veins, not real time at all, and I scarcely noticed how bleak and utilitarian the place was.

I concentrated on the far end of the roof, breathing calmly like a gymnast on the high bar, arms out for balance. I started running, opened my wings and their fingers spread automatically. They dragged, pulling me back, and I pushed at the tiles to find more speed. I lengthened my stride, faster still. I reached the end of the roof, sprang into the air, pulled my legs up and swept my wings down powerfully.

When I begin to fall I always – because I have the same instinct as everyone – expect to hit the ground immediately as if I've merely tripped. But I keep falling, feeling nothing under my feet but more thin air.

Two more desperate beats, and I strained my body upwards in a graceful curve. My wingtips came together in front of my face, then I pushed away and I was no longer falling. I stretched out my legs, lying horizontally.

The people below saw the soft inside surface of my black sickle wings, the sun shining through their trailing edges. I felt air spilling off every flight feather. Their hard and sharp leading edges rasped louder as I beat harder and gained height. I scraped over the tavern's ridge, pushed off with my palms and started laughing ecstatically as I flapped over the road, the barrack ring, the curtain wall and out of town.

The Lowespass Road ran straight as a rule. Its cobbled, slightly convex surface was crispy with hoof prints in reddish clay mud. Water filled its drains; since the completion of the dam the whole countryside was like a puddle and pools had begun to appear all over the place.

From the air, Slake Cross looked like a square grey archery target lying on the contours of the pale green valley side. I looked back to the gatehouse. The gate, twice my height, was crisscrossed with deep iron strips. Shallow troughs scarred between them where Insect mandibles had reached through to scrape the old timber. On my right stretched the Lowespass Road and ahead the reservoir glimmered, flat and silver. I was heading towards the Insects' Paperlands covering the entire north bank of the river and as far as I could see into the distance, like a white sheet drawn over the land.

Strong gusts kept me flying low, no more than twenty metres from the ground where I could follow a direct path with the minimum effort. I flew over the crossroads with the smaller Glean Road along which troops arrive from western Awia. The Slake Cross monument, a smooth obelisk, stood there on grass scattered with yellow primroses – fragile blooms transplanted from the river bank before the flooding process began. Ointment made from them is a sovereign salve for wounds, and they had become a symbol of the massacre.

The uncompromising hills were always striding along the horizon, their stony summits rose to mid-sky and framed Lowespass valley. Further east at Miroir there were exposed tracts of moorland covered in peat bogs. Pondskaters V-rippled over black gullies of acidic stagnant water and mosquitoes whined over patches of spongy sphagnum moss among the heather. At this end of the valley the soil was thin. Thistles and ragwort sprouted in the clints and grikes of the limestone pavements. Caves riddled the valley floor. For thousands of years the rainwater has been carving faults in the rock into fathomless potholes and massive chambers, where drops precipitate strange and magnificent formations like the Throne Room columns. The Insects' own tunnels join the system; it does no good to think about it.

Slake Cross town itself is built over a resurgence of an underground stream, so it never lacks fresh water. Frost has used dye to investigate the routes of the system. She started messing about with the water table and everyone watched, unnerved, as the level in the deep well rose to its very brim.

The road crossed uneven ground, slicing through the outcrops, and a larger quarry had scarred the side of a big knoll. I glided over its levelled area where carts were parked, completely covered with hardened white lime dust.

I passed some lime kilns in the side of a cutting; room-sized stone ovens with ragged chimneys, now cold and empty, with charcoal heaps growing damp outside their mouths. Frost had constructed them and employed the stokers; as soon as she knew she had enough cement she had moved them to work on the dam itself. A high wall protected a stand of pine trees, which grew relatively quickly and Frost used for building material.

On the north side of the road was the first of a series of static catapults called petraries, set into a concrete platform slick with pools of green algae. Its waxed wooden beam and sturdy foundations glistened, beaded with rain water. Its cable had been removed and the counterweight box was empty. Barbed wire rolls stacked haphazardly beside its pyramid of ammunition stones. Far off I could just see the nearest peel tower, a link in the chain stretching from Frass to Summerday to monitor Insect activity.

At the river I altered my course, heading upstream to the dam. Bulrushes bowed to the water's creased surface as the wind ruffled through reed beds on the south bank. Its other bank was nothing but mud mashed with three-clawed footprints: Insects had stripped the vegetation bare.

Frost's workings began and the ground changed abruptly. Her company had done nothing less than remodel the valley. Cart tracks criss-crossed the bank; water in their ruts reflected the sky. Broken shovels, dirty string and red striped ranging rods littered the ground, with abandoned workmen's huts, empty burlap bags, splays of spilt gravel.

The overturned earth was glutted with beige specks – calcined bone fragments – some recognisable as ribs or skulls; the remains of generations of men and women. There were pieces of archaic armour and broken Insect shells, which don't easily decay but weather to porous shards. The Insects have been creeping or swarming southward over fifteen hundred years. In response, we constantly move men and supplies to the front to stop them, on such a massive scale that I fancy all the Fourlands will eventually erode and end up here as a series of hills.

The river banks straightened, reinforced by walls of metal mesh boxes full of rubble. The river flowed more slowly but its level had hardly dropped. Frost couldn't allow it to dry up because, since Insects can't swim, the Oriole River was our main defence.

I approached the dam from the front, its stone face a gigantic sloping wall. The ends tapered down and curved towards me like horns. The outflow hole at its base looked like a giant blank eye. A fortified winch tower stood on the crest above it, holding the mechanism to raise the gate. The walkway ran through the tower, blocked with formidable portcullises on entry and exit, so Insects could not cross from the Paperlands.

Lightning and Eleonora were two tiny figures beside it, looking down from behind the split-timber fence. The wind's speed was increasing over the smooth outflow platform. Air hit the wall and hurtled up its slanting surface. I lay with my wings outstretched and let it carry me – square blocks and mortar streaked down past my eyes – I could have filed my nails on them.

Along the whole length of the dam the wind went rocketing up the incline faster and faster until it burst vertically from the edge of the walkway around Lightning and Eleonora and up into the sky.

I soared rapidly past them, hearing the last exchange of their conversation, '– This could be the answer.'

'Perhaps. I just wish that we'd thought of it before.'

I found the right balance to hang motionless above their heads. My shadow fell over them and my boot toes dangled at the level of their faces. They drew back and shaded their eyes, seeing me suspended in the middle of six metres of glorious wingspan.

The enormous lake formed from the backed-up Oriole River spread out behind the dam. On its north bank the water lapped and merged into the mazes of Insects' paper cells; irregular, many-sided boxes ranging from the size of a cupboard to that of a house. Passages wound between them, some covered with pointed roofs, the rest open to the air. They looked like ceramic fungi, or geometric papier-mâché termite mounds.

The lake stood cold and mirror-reflective in the fresh morning light. A swathe of ripples dimpled across its middle, broken by white, angular peaks projecting from the surface: the tops of flooded Insect buildings.

Insects had built and abandoned walls five times as the water level rose. Their tops contoured the irregular lake margin like tree rings. Our old camp and the shakehole that destroyed it were somewhere on the lakebed, completely papered over.

I could just see the Insects' new wall on dry ground ten kilometres distant, beyond the marshes. They had instinctively joined the new stretch to the immense Wall that seals them in, protecting their Paperlands from coast to coast of the entire continent.

I let the wind blow me backwards over the walkway. Little by little I flexed my wings closed and descended. I bent my knees, absorbed the shock, and landed in a crouch with my stiff feathers brushing the paved track on my either side.

I stood and bowed to Queen Eleonora Tanager. She kissed me on both cheeks and studied my face at leisure. 'How are you, darling? Oh, Jant, flying makes you so cold.'

Her attar of roses perfume enveloped me, calling to mind the rose-scented letters that she used to send. They were always crinkled and salty, having been written on her most recent lover's sweaty back. Eleonora was arguably the world's most powerful mortal, but she was shod with scandal; she was no good at delicacy and even worse at tact.

I stepped away and looked at the reservoir's breathtaking expanse. 'It's incredible,' I said. 'I admit I had my doubts. But from up here you can see the extent of Frost's vision. I feel privileged to be part of it.'

Lightning, the Castle's Archer, said seriously, 'Well, I hope it is not just the latest of the thousand plans we have tried and had to put aside.'

Eleonora shivered. She was wearing Lightning's long, fur-lined overcoat and, statuesque as she was, it nearly fit her. Her scale armour glittered underneath. Awians sometimes wear full plate, but prefer their traditional scale mail and I can understand why because plate is horribly restrictive.

She had tipped her helmet back from her head and it hung upside down from a strap showing its green satin lining. It had eye holes and a nosepiece in the Awian style. Its copper-pink horsehair crest rustled against her back and nearly touched the ground. Her chain mail coif and scale shirt were copper-coloured too, and damascened with a raised pattern of feathers matching her greaves and vambraces. She had pulled out her satin undershirt a little between each joint.

Eleonora had a wide, prominent face with a delicate, tip-tilted nose. I should say she was good-looking but she had a sly and filthy smile. Her ecru wings were naturally a different colour than her close-cropped dark hair, a phenomenon so rare I had never seen it before.

I said, 'Queen Eleonora, I don't know if you realise the time but you're already late for the press conference and Frost sent me to call you back.'

'Oh, I suppose we must attend,' she said huskily. She set off along the walkway, between the sheer drop on one side and the lapping water on the other. She strode with a slow, shapely-legged pace; from the deliberate way she carried herself it was clear she was used to being looked at.

She continued to enthuse as we joined her. 'If this works we have a way of destroying the Paperlands completely. The effect's there, right before our eyes! The Insects move out of the flooded area, make a new Wall and retreat behind it. Of their own accord, without any resistance!'

'Then we drain the area and in we go!' I said.

'Let us concentrate on clearing this patch first,' said Lightning.

Eleonora smiled. 'It all depends on infantry. We'll position them while Frost empties the lake. Isn't that right?'

'Yes.' Lightning indicated the town squatting in the mid-distance. A constant queue of mules and baggage carts plodded towards it, bringing provisions and tackle in preparation to set up the camp that would soon be surrounding it. Outriders protected the convoy, riding in formation at specified distances from the road as soon as they entered Lowespass. We had not yet mustered the main body of the cavalry, because they consume a tremendous amount of fodder. In the other direction a tumbrel cart of manure was setting out from the stables towards the pine plantation. 'We will position twenty battalions of Select, wielding axes, there ... and there.'

I said, 'It'll be very muddy once they start to march.'

Lightning said, 'That is an understatement. Think what it'll be like for the battalions in the rear after the first ten thousand have walked over it in front of them. We will need a whole division to lay duckboards as they go. We will progress slowly across the drained lakebed, keeping in line, chopping down the Insects' buildings. Without . . .' He savoured the words: 'Without any expectation of casualties at all.'

'I've never been in an Insect cell before,' Eleonora said thoughtfully. 'But they're too close together to take horses through.'

Lightning said, 'When we reach the new Wall, we will secure the area, continue to dismantle the cells and bring up some trebuchets. The Queen's lancers will patrol and act as rearguard.'

The wind was ruffling Lightning's dark blond feathers and making them stand upright. Irritated, he shook his wings out and folded them tightly. I can't believe he gave Eleonora his coat. Doesn't he know her reputation? I looked at him carefully, thinking that even he must be aware of the ribald rumours. Eleonora was the only child of Lord Governor Osprey Tanager, who was killed by Insects twenty years ago, the last of that family. When she was not at the front she held court in Rachiswater Palace, but as soon as she had rebuilt her family's manor house she intended to restore the capital of Awia to Tanager, as it was in 1812 before the Rachiswaters took the throne.

The lake reflected the banded mackerel sky, with thin clouds the grey-purple colour of an artist's paintbrush water. Trochanter, the morning star, was growing fainter. Below, the surface of the river winding east towards Lowespass Fortress had an oily, rainbow scum of old poison washing out from the Wall.

We crossed a bridge over the dry overspill chute and descended to the shore. The two soldiers guarding the access to the walkway uncrossed their spears promptly and we passed between them.

A beacon basket full of twigs and hay stood next to a large bell on a pole and my semaphore device set at neutral. Their metal stands prevented Insects eating them. Eleonora's bodyguard of four Tanager Select lancers sat obediently at attention on their warhorses. She appraised them out of habit: their embossed armour, the woollen cloaks hanging to their stirrups, their helmets with blue and white striped horsehair crests and fluttering muslin streamers. They love ornamentation, do Awians.

Eleonora's horse waited between them. The silver inlaid armour on his head was richer than anything I owned. The chafron plate beaked over his nose came to a point; the crinet covering his neck was steel openwork, scallop-edged like batwings. Lightning's horse was drab in comparison. Eleonora greeted them enthusiastically, 'Hello, Perlino! Hello Balzan!'

Perlino looked skittish at my scent. He put his ears back and flared his nostrils imperiously. 'I don't like you, either,' I told him.

Eleonora patted his neck and he nuzzled her hand.

I said, 'It isn't my fault most horses are afraid that Rhydanne want to chase them down and eat them.'

'Maybe I should take Perlino to Darkling and give him a sniff of pure Rhydanne for comparison. Then he'd appreciate you.' She fitted her toe into a stirrup, swung herself onto the horse. She sat straight, holding the reins loosely. Perlino high-stepped with his strong front legs, in rein-back, then Eleonora made him pirouette.

She leaned from the saddle and prodded my chest, 'Race you!' She tapped Perlino's flank and was away down the track. Her bodyguard looked at each other and followed suit, standing on their stirrups, their lances tilting backwards in their saddle rests.

Lightning hesitated, surprised, then stepped up astride Balzan, drew his reins left, turned and sped after her. They picked up the pace from a gallop to a charge; I watched them disdainfully until they were just dots above clouds of spray. Then I sighed, shook my wings open and ran to take off.

CHAPTER 2

Frost had given me days to prepare a speech but as usual I hadn't bothered; I'm used to speaking ad lib. I stood outside the hall listening to the low hubbub and expectant atmosphere. It reminded me of court.

Everybody looked up as I entered and silence descended over the benches filled with journalists and their assistants, saddle-sore in crumpled clothes.

Frost was sitting on a bench by the front wall, facing them. She fiddled with her river pearl wedding ring, her only jewellery, but she looked meditative rather than nervous; she was probably passing time by working out equations in her head.

A number of architects and engineers sat on the furthest benches. Many were women, watching their role model with expressions of adulation, fountain pens poised to scribble on sheaves of paper on their knees. I scanned the room for familiar faces, thinking: I'll watch out for the Morenzians, they tend to be the least respectful – but I spotted Kestrel Altergate, the exception to the rule.

Frost had taped a schematic drawing of the dam to the chimney breast. I stood in front of it and addressed the audience. 'Good morning, everybody. Welcome to Slake Cross, representatives of the governors and of the press. I know you've made many days' journey and I apologise that the lodgings we have to offer are of necessity fairly basic.

'Tonight is the centenary of the battle of Slake Cross. On this very night, one hundred years ago, thousands of Insects emerged from the cave system under the river, into the middle of a vanguard camp of five battalions. Only thirty mortals survived, all archers who showed incredible courage.

'I was there, and can never forget, but even for those who were not, the date is charged with meaning. We were forced to retreat in this part of the valley. Here and only here, for the first time since the foundations of Lowespass Fortress were laid in the year ten-oh-nine, the Insects extended their Wall on the south side of Oriole River. It is our vulnerable spot. For exactly a century the Castle has been striving to push the Wall back and reclaim our land. A hundred years and – by god – it seems like a long time!'

I waited until the journalists' polite laughter had subsided and then I opened my wing towards Frost. 'The Circle's Architect has taken five years to design and build the dam, the largest construction ever. It is truly the wonder of the modern world.

'Insects may be instinctive architects but they had to run when the river began to expand. I watched from the air, I saw them drowning, curling and twisting. Now, next week we will drain the lake and you are all invited to witness the prodigious sight. It'll be the biggest waterfall you can possibly imagine.'

My enthusiasm made them sit up. I was very excited at the prospect of seeing millions of tonnes of water spurting into the river. 'As the lake level drops, the Insect buildings will gradually emerge, slick and slimy.

'All the immortals will lead the fyrd to secure two hundred square kilometres of land and the north bank of the river. We have battalions already drawn up from coastal Awia – that is to say, the manors of Tanager, Peregrine and Wrought – and Lakeland Awia, the manors of Micawater and Rachiswater. I have also requested battalions from Hacilith and Eske, so you see the Empire's other capitals are participating with good will.'

Kestrel Altergate, on the first row, tried to interrupt me, 'Comet –'

I raised a hand, 'Please wait and I'll take questions at the end. I'd like to hand you over to Frost, who will give some more details of her magnificent achievement.'

I waved her up extravagantly and went to sit down. As we passed each other I clapped her shoulder and leant to mutter in her ear, 'Don't bog them down with technicalities.'

Frost stood behind her table, using it as a barrier between her and the audience, speaking over the top of her papers. She smiled, and a lifetime of looking uptight disappeared from her face. She held her hands apart and expanded the distance between them as she expounded her thoughts. 'I have built the dam where the Insect Wall crossed the river. Its wall is two kilometres long and thirty metres high. It holds back a lake twenty kilometres in length. The dam is an embankment, an earth mound with a core of rubble, faced with protective stone. It is an economical construction – the fyrd are used to building earthworks for our defences and this is no different. It is constructed around piers set into the former river bed.'

Oh god, I thought; here she goes.

'The headwaters – I mean, the lake – is intended to be wide rather than deep to flood the largest possible area. You see, the valley is shallow so the lake spreads out.

'A team of horses will be harnessed to wind a capstan and hoist up the sluice gate. It is so heavy I have used ship's rope for the winch rather than chain, or else the horses won't be able to lift it. However, rope doesn't last for ever in the damp environment and will need to be replaced, so a maintenance shaft accesses the top of the gate.

'The capstan's gears are a new invention and they're fascinating, you see –'

I caught Frost's eye. She dropped her notes, picked them up and shuffled them. 'Um. Well ... Two hundred million cubic metres of water will be released at a hundred and ten kilometres an hour. The waterfall into the stilling basin and the gabionned and canalised reaches of the river will indeed be impressive.'

I let her drone on while I appraised Kestrel. He was the son of the reeve of Altergate. Kestrel always managed to be the first reporter on the scene of any trouble and he was far too astute a commentator for my liking.

I kept half an ear on Frost's speech but I had heard it all before and my attention began to drift. I speak every one of the Fourlands' six current and seven dead languages but I will never be fluent in Frost's engineering jargon. She once tempted me to learn mathematics by telling me it was a language, but I soon found it was only used to describe things that were really dull. Frost was losing the rest of the audience too. Reporters don't thank you for too much information because newspapers are never more than three printed sheets.

I thought about my place on the Castle's tennis ladder. About ways to avoid Eleonora as much as possible. And about the fact that Frost could actually be rather attractive if she made the effort.

Eleonora strode in, waking me from my reverie. The brassy firelight starred her shoulder and waist. Lightning was close behind her, scraping his boots. I leapt to my feet and called, 'Please stand for the Queen of Awia!'

She seated herself on the bench beside me, placed her helm on the floor and tucked her 1910 Sword behind her on the seat. She sat with her hand on the fabulous opal hilt of that finely-tempered blade.

Frost waited for the audience to settle, then continued, 'I believe at long last we have a means of winning the war. I am determined not to stop here. The dam will allow us to control the river for decades to come. We can flood adjoining sectors, from which the Insects will also retreat. I can redirect the river and use additional dams to inundate more and more land. Canals will keep Insects out of cleared areas. Over the next half-millennium we can push them further and further back, until we reclaim the entire Paperlands ... Then my work, and the work of the Castle, will be complete ... Um ... I've finished, I think.'

I said, 'Thank you, Frost. Are there any questions?'

Kestrel raised his hand and shouted over half a dozen other reporters, 'Comet!'

'Yes, Kestrel?'

'A hundred years ago the ground gave way. Am I right?'

'Yes,' I said quietly.

'Why can't it happen again?'

I gestured, allowing Frost to answer. She said, 'No, no. That's not possible. I tested the ground thoroughly and it's solid. The lake has flooded the Insect warren, and the bedding planes and phreatic passages in the karst bedrock – I mean, the caves – are completely full. Slake Master Cave swallowed twice as much water as I first estimated. I admit the tunnels are big. Really big – with a breadth the size of the Throne Room – but there are no Insects left underneath us; foam is pouring out of the resurgence to prove it.'

I said, 'They pose no danger to the advancing troops, wouldn't you say, Lightning?'

Lightning stood up. 'The only difficulty I foresee is an attack from further down the valley. Insects have been pressed back into the Paperlands where there is nothing edible left, so they will be ravenous. But with archers and lancers at all sides, I assure you no Insects will infiltrate our defences nor live to lay a scent trail for the rest.'

Kestrel nodded, and I pointed at another man who had his hand up.

'Smatchet, *Hacilith Post*,' he said. 'Is it true the Trisians are causing difficulties for the Sailor?'

I said, 'We're not discussing Tris now. We're talking about the dam.'

'I hear Trisians are striking because they don't want to be fyrd or sailors.'

'It must have been days since you ran a story on Mist Fulmer,' I said sarcastically. He was beloved of the gutter press, finding as he did a whore in every port and a port in every whore, and only half of them women.

'Is it true there's a garrison in Capharnaum?'

Kestrel turned to Smatchet and said, 'The Trisians have put a chain across the whole harbour mouth to prevent ships entering.'

'Really?'

'Absolutely.'

I glared eloquently at both of them. 'The Senate has asked the Castle for assistance in restoring order and we're complying with Governor Vendace, nothing more. OK?'

Smatchet backed down: 'OK.'

'Any more? Yes, Kestrel?'

'Will draining the dam be safe?'

Frost said, 'Oh, yes. I agree these are immense hydrostatic forces. To novices the interactions between fluctuating pressures would certainly appear frightening. But I will raise the gate very slowly and control the outflow. It will take five days to release a year's accumulation of water. I wish I could be more accurate but I can't, of course, because the reservoir and tunnels are an irregular shape, so we have conditions of flow under varying head. To put it in context ...' She rummaged through the papers on her table and emerged with a sheet covered in a complicated sum. She held it up, then looked frustrated as she realised few people in the room would understand. 'Come and see me afterwards and I'll explain ... Well, I'll try to. You can watch the event from a safe distance. It'll be great – air entrainment and bulking –'

'White water,' I said.

'Whatever.' Frost shrugged.

I said, 'Not only will it be safe, it'll be a sight you can tell the grandchildren about. Are there any more questions? Yes, Smatchet?'

The *Hacilith Post* reporter addressed Lightning, 'My lord, our readers would like to know if you are ready to announce a date for your wedding with Governor Swallow Awndyn?'

'That's not our topic!' I said, exasperated.

Lightning answered mildly, 'I think our engagement needs a little more time.'

I said, 'Well, there's your answer. Any more *relevant* questions?'

Kestrel crossed his legs and nudged his assistant to keep writing. He said, 'With respect, Comet, is Queen Eleonora making the same mistake as King Dunlin?'

Frost panicked but Eleonora stood up and looked at Kestrel impassively. I said, 'I don't understand. What do you mean?'

'Well, ten years ago the campaign of King Dunlin Rachiswater tried to breach the Wall and for our pains all we had was the worst swarm of Insects for centuries and a horrendous death toll. Altergate lost every man in its conscriptable generation, so that now the Castle has exempted it from the draft. Tambrine is also exempt from fyrdinge.

Awndyn manor is in the enviable position of being able to use its Trisian trade profits to pay scutage rather than raise fyrd. Lowespass and Summerday are the only two manors where the Castle can appoint a governor, and both have been given to the Queen's lance captains. Their garrisons have been increased because the threat still remains –'

'Kestrel –' I said.

'– But you are proposing to advance into the Paperlands *again*. What did we gain last time? Nothing! The Wall is still in the same place. Many people think it should be left alone. Don't mess with it. Is your campaign military necessity, or are you rushing ahead too fast?'

Eleonora took a breath. 'Comet, I will answer the man. The offensive of Dunlin Rachiswater was poorly thought out. His was a campaign of muscle not the mind. The Insects' bodies are so much stronger than ours, we can only beat them with our skills and our brains. Dunlin responded to them rather than outwitting them and it was the downfall of his dynasty. Our current attack in no way compares. We're using our knowledge of the Insects' behaviour rather than our soldiers' lives. We will take ten times more land than he did. Our fresh approach uses the Castle's latest innovations – which are, dare I say, watertight? – and the might of my well-trained and experienced Select. The Emperor approves it.'

She hooked her thumb in her sword belt. 'Insects from here devastated the western reaches of my kingdom; I must protect Plow's precious fields. I will not allow Insects to make paper from Awian feathers and bones.

'I am simply first among the governors of Awia. In a time of emergency I took special care of my people and now that things are returning to normal I have made sure of my governors' support' – Lightning nodded in agreement – 'Awia has always had a stoic attitude. The Tanagers never accept defeat. I have fielded all my Select Fyrd because I know this will improve their families' lives.

'Let me tell you that if we are successful we will no longer need to call up the General Fyrd. There will no longer be a need for a general levy of the whole of the people. I know they resent their sixty days' unpaid service per year, and we are aware of desertions during the harvest and midwinter. Well, from now on they may remain at their proper work.

'There is good news for the Select Fyrd too. Their monthly payments will be raised to five pounds a week and an equipment allowance of twenty pounds a year. Commissions will be renewed as usual on godsloss day. I expect that the advance will be over by then. At last we have the means to win the war! In future we will look back on this as a momentous date, not because of nineteen twenty-five but twenty twenty-five, when we at last halted the onslaught and took the first step that led to the death of every last Insect!'

Eleonora gave her grand smile. Kestrel and the other journalists were hunched over, scribbling rapidly. None of them, therefore, was free to meet her eye. Their finished pages dropped, leafed down and slipped under the benches.

I said, 'Are there any more questions ... No? ... Very well. Then on behalf of the Castle I draw this meeting to a close, may it please Your Highness, ladies and gentlemen.' And added informally to the reporters, 'You can get lunch in the pub.'

They still took ten minutes to finish and gather their belongings. The benches scraped on the flagstones and they left the hall. It suddenly seemed very spacious. I rested my backside on the table edge, leant back, arms straight and stretched my legs.

The Architect had disappeared in a crowd of excited students in thick fustian jackets. They were asking her questions and surrounded the table to watch while she sketched an answer to one. She extricated herself by giving them as many figures and equations as they could take in and then we all watched them trickle out of the hall with their minds reeling.

CHAPTER 3

'I think that was successful, if I do say so myself.'

'Red or white?'

'No thanks. I had too much yesterday and I'm still recovering.'

Lightning was now on his second glass. 'The vintage is not as good as the previous year, but still . . .'

'Well, a splash of red then, thank you.'

Frost, Eleonora, Lightning and me were celebrating with lunch in the hall. We were together at the head of the table so we could hear the hubbub of the other immortals further down and occasional voices from the tavern across the square as the journalists entertained themselves. Frost rested her notebook on the table beside her. Woe betide anybody who gets between her and its pages when she has an idea.

She neatened her bone-handled cutlery with precision and began to rub a little butter into her chapped hands. 'Thank you, Jant,' she said. 'I couldn't have done it on my own.'

'No more should you. It is Jant's office and I am glad he is pulling his weight for once.'

'Hey, Archer, what are you drinking? That's not like you.' I grinned at him.

Lightning scowled back. 'At least your Messenger service has become more reliable recently.'

Eleonora, at the head of the table, leant to the side as a boy served trout cooked in verjuice. She said, 'Cloud has surpassed himself, don't you think?'

'It is all right for the front,' said Lightning, who tended to bring good food and a cellar's worth of wine with him. It was his only show of wealth because his clothes were understated, if expensive. You wouldn't know from looking at him that he has millions a year.

Each of Lightning's features taken separately would also seem normal rather than striking, but even if I didn't know he was noble he would impress me as such; he has that confidence that casts a glow and makes a man the centre of attention, because he knows he ought to be. Give his plain grey eyes an imperious look but make them often prone to be cloaked. Dimple his chin, make his mouth firm, used to command but with a twist of sarcasm. Mark that he not only alternates between being ardent and brooding but sometimes manages to be both at once.

Constant training is the only thing that will make men stick fast in a shield wall, and Lightning drills the fyrd until they are less terrified of the Insects than they are of his anger. Since he is the Lord Governor of Micawater manor, as well as an Eszai, he boldly shapes the world but he still welcomes the yearly cycle of harvests, hunting seasons and accounts. He takes the world seriously, because he has no imagination. Because he has no imagination, he is a popular novelist.

The Lowespass wind blustered across the square and howled through the alleys. It never seemed to stop. The Riverworks banner fissled and slapped on the roof.

Frost glanced at me. 'The wind's getting up again.'

I shuddered. I had a sudden vivid image of the soil crumbling over my clothes. I could taste it. I said, 'We're supposed to be celebrating your accomplishment. Don't remind me of the state I was in a hundred years ago.'

Lightning said, 'You survived. Simply take more care next time.'

'*Next* time?'

'Most of us have been bitten. Tornado has been bitten more times than he can count.'

'Do you remember being picked up?' Eleonora asked me.

'Ha! Of course not.'

'He was in a coma,' Lightning said.

'I was moribund.'

'He lay unconscious for fourteen weeks in the field hospital at Whittorn. Rayne moved him to Rachiswater Infirmary, then to her hospital in the Castle. He stayed there for a year.'

I wrapped a strip of fish around my two-pronged fork. 'It was terrible. I'm far too impatient to convalesce in hospital for day after day, with nothing to do but the occasional haemorrhage.'

I had a collapsed lung and pneumonia – which injured Awians are prone to – and a bloody great hole in my side. Sepsis led to organ failure but Rayne knew to let me lie dormant until my body recovered itself. When I came round I screamed solidly, high and eerie like a sick infant until she pumped me full of painkillers. I was in shock; it cocooned and isolated me from reality. I knew I was very badly hurt but could only lie still and trust her. The thought I might never fly again constantly distressed me; if that broken wing had grounded me permanently I would have been vulnerable to Challengers so I made sure Rayne paid it careful attention. I also suffered from a great sense of failure because the mortals who looked to me to lead them had all been killed. I desperately needed to talk but I kept my silence. It was like being in a dark tunnel that very gradually widened and I began to realise what had actually happened to me. I relived it again and again and I grew to understand it. Then I began to talk about it and I healed more quickly.

'He harried us for all the news,' Lightning told Eleonora.

'Four months were missing from my life!' I said.

Eleonora asked Lightning, 'Where were you in that battle? Why weren't you hurt like Jant?'

He shrugged modestly.

'Go on,' she teased. 'Tell me.'

Lightning never needs much encouragement to recount a story. 'In the preceding weeks,' he began, 'everyone seemed tired, overworked and irritable. Little things kept going wrong. We couldn't know then that it was because something so momentous, so awful, was going to happen that it sent ripples back down the flow of time, to disturb us and disrupt our attention.

'I was in the Sun Pavilion, writing. You know the story where an Eszai is Challenged, but he sends an assassin to murder the Challenger before they meet, so San throws him out of the Circle?'

'No,' said Eleonora.

'Doesn't matter,' said Lightning. 'But this is proof that romantic novels can save your life. The ground began to shake and, one by one, the candles guttered out. I could see nothing, not the back of my hand, not the page in front of me. I couldn't grasp what was happening.

'I called the captain and together we walked along the line of tents summoning the archers, getting them kitted up and reassuring them. By the time we had one hundred men the rest had gone. They had fled. The ground was falling away under our feet so fast it brought down the palisade.'

Lightning was staring intently, watching the memory. He sub-consciously dropped a hand to his sword hilt. With eyes bright and the other hand spread, he leant over the table, talking directly to Eleonora. 'You should never meet Insects on open ground. Use fortifications whenever possible. I knew that, but what did we have? Two companies of archers and a handful of arrows.

'We retreated along the stockade until we came to the only corner where it was still upright. I ordered them to form up inside with the fence at their backs. They were breaking down with fear but I made them pull a fallen section in front of us and shoot for all they were worth. We shot straight out over the top, in relays, all night long.'

'For the whole night?' asked Eleonora.

'If we slowed we would die, I knew that full well.' He swept his hand out over the table. 'Fss! Fss! Went the arrows. Every time we paused, stragglers were coming in, some no more than naked, and we lifted them over the defence. Insects scaled it and I had teams to chop them down as they reached the top. After the first hour men started giving up, falling from exhaustion and hypothermia. I dragged them to the back and I kept the rest going. We could see nothing. We knew we were hitting people out there, but they were already lost to the Insects. I could not help them. I did what every Eszai should do in a disaster: cut your losses and save your fyrd.

'When we ran out of ammunition I sent fifty men to bring more. Only ten returned. It was a suicide mission. We had no way of knowing what was happening beyond our palisade. We just kept shooting, holding out against the instant we would be annihilated. I felt the Circle break and I knew Hayl Eske was dead, but I didn't tell the men.' He glanced at me. 'I was waiting for the Circle to break for Comet and Tornado. It was not the first time I have had to leave the battlefield on my own.

'After that first hour I knew everything out there still moving was an Insect. I kept up volleys in pulses for six consecutive hours, until dawn began to resolve.

'The light came up slowly, pale grey, and through the murk we could at last see the utter devastation. The ground in front of us sloped straight into the pit. The middle of the camp had vanished. Only the tents at the far end were left standing, leaning inwards. Around us, the corrugated stockade sagged and twisted like a ribbon. Insects were everywhere, feeding on the bodies. We were helpless, stranded in our corner and tired to death. My vision was dark at the edges with exhaustion but I wrapped my wings around me and I persevered.

'Then came the sound of thunder along the road. Heavy cavalry were riding in. They were armoured head to foot and they poured into the camp with their lances levelled, riding the Insects down. Do you know who was leading them? Rayne. The Doctor. Bundled up in her old cloak on the back of a destrier.

'She had felt the Circle break. She had been here in Slake with the rearguard and at first light she gathered all the cavalry left and set out to find us. We climbed the palisade and hailed her.

'She brought her horse around the lip of the crater. "Bracing morning you have for it, Saker," said she. "Where are the other two?"

'"I don't know,' I said. They were both pulling on the Circle, we could tell that much.

'She said, "You have exposure. Go back to town."

'I did not return to town. I picked my way over the subsiding ground with her, looking for Comet and Tornado. She spotted the sunburst on his shield –' He gestured at me '– through the scattered soil and set her soldiers to dig him out. Finding Tornado was more difficult. She had to bring in some of her trained dogs. But of Hayl Eske we never found a single piece ... Long, drawn-out ordeals are the ones that change us. For me it was just one night. But what a night!'

I said, 'It was my biggest battle.'

'Falling down the hole was not the best thing to do under the circumstances,' Lightning assured me.

'At least I wasn't as useless as Hayl.'

Frost said, 'Everybody remembers where they were when they heard the news.'

Lightning nodded. His face was flushed. He unlaced the strings at the neck of his shirt, downed the dregs of his wine and called, 'Bring some more claret. No, no ... that old bottle ... You'll like this one, Eleonora. I had to sell a house for it.' A servant gave him the bottle and he clinked his intaglio ring against its glass. 'We shall toast Frost's dam with this. There are only six bottles left in the world ... Well, five. But you only live once.'

I made my excuses, left the table and walked out to the washroom block to have a piss. I was just buttoning my fly when a figure loomed behind me. I glanced over my shoulder and saw Eleonora at the doorway. She looked left and right with a pervert's smile. 'Hmm. Interesting in here. Why is it such a mess?'

'Why are you following me?' I asked.

'You have a pert backside.'

'Oh, bugger,' I muttered.

'Don't give me ideas!'

'Eleonora ... *no*.'

She laughed. I was begging and that was good enough for her. She said, 'No, anyway. I want to talk to you about the Archer.'

'What about him?'

'Not here.' She beckoned. 'Come into the church, out of this terrible wind.'

We walked past the stores, stepping over the rail tracks that carry fodder to the stables, through the alleyway and into the church beside the hall.

It was a quiet, white room with beanbags on the floor. Churches are only single rooms but they are often built and funded by governors and sometimes as a display of the sponsor's wealth can be quite ornate. They employ no officials, except a caretaker to look after the building, and they are places in which to think and relax, and reflect on the absence of god. People sit, or walk around admiring the decoration. Travellers are welcome to shelter there for the night. They are for people, not god, since god has left the world on an extended break and has had no impact on anybody's life since the calendar began.

The church was empty so Eleonora spoke openly. 'Do you know what's bothering Lightning?'

'Is something bothering him?'

She blinked in disbelief. 'Yes! Men – you never notice anything, do you? Have you ever seen him so tipsy before?'

I considered it. 'No, not for a long time. Is it his fiancée?'

'Swallow!' Eleonora said contemptuously. 'No. He wouldn't mention it to you, because it isn't connected with the dam. I know how Eszai hide their weaknesses. He told me and, since the weight of responsibility for the advance is on you immortals, I thought I should let you know what has shaken him.'

'He told *you*? What? What did he tell you?'

'Do you remember Cyan, his daughter?'

'Of course I remember Cyan.'

'She has gone missing.' Eleonora paused, dramatically.

I said, 'What, again?'

'Pardon?'

'She was kidnapped once,' I explained. 'While you were busy wresting the throne from Staniel Rachiswater and exiling the poor fool.'

Eleonora tipped her foot and thoughtfully rolled her rowel spur up and down on the floorboards, leaving a line of dents. 'Oh, I see. Well, that explains Lightning's extreme reaction. He jumped to the conclusion that Cyan has been snatched. She is, after all, the future governor of Peregrine and the daughter of Governor Micawater, so she's a target for kidnappers. They know he would give his manor for her safety.'

'Where did she go missing? Awndyn?'

'Hacilith. In the city.'

'Why? What was she doing there?'

'I don't know. I was hoping you'd sort it out. Eszai should bloody well tell each other if something goes wrong instead of moping around and drinking.'

I nodded. 'Maybe I can help.'

I was much more familiar with Hacilith than Lightning was. In fact, I know it like the veins in my arms. I could put the word around and if any hotelier or spa owner had spotted a girl as glitteringly important as Cyan the city would be buzzing.

Eleonora followed me out of the church – and pinched my arse hard as we passed through the door. I sped up to get away from her and returned to the hall.

A servant was moving around the table placidly, collecting plates and glasses, and pouring yet more claret for Lightning. He was talking to Frost but I barged in on their conversation. 'I can't believe you didn't tell me that Cyan's gone missing!'

Lightning looked confused for a second, then narrowed his eyes at Eleonora. 'I . . . Well, I admit I have been a little preoccupied.'

'You can hardly concentrate,' Eleonora told him.

'On the contrary, the planning is taking my mind off the problem.' He took a sip of wine. 'But I can't stand the fact that Cyan's life may be at risk.'

'What are you talking about?' asked Frost.

Lightning sighed. 'I suppose I should tell you. My daughter has contrived to get herself lost while on the Grand Tour. It is an Awian tradition, Frost. I received a letter yesterday morning from my steward, Harrier. He was accompanying her. They'd toured Awia and were stopping once in Morenzia to see the sights of the city. That morning they had visited the Agrimony Campanile, the church at the place where the Emperor was born, and the great bronze façade of Aver-Falconet's palace. Harrier went to sign into the Costrel Hotel and when he turned his back, she vanished.'

'I would, too, with an itinerary that dull,' I said.

Lightning gave me a look with the force of every minute of his fourteen hundred and forty years. He was older than everything in this reclaimed valley, even Lowespass Fortress that you would have thought immutable. I shivered.

'It is not easy to give Harrier Disante the slip. He could have traced her anywhere but in Hacilith.'

'Did he see any kidnappers?' I asked.

'No. When she started the tour I thought it was essential tutoring for her to see the world, but now I am afraid she is learning too much.

I would do anything for Cyan, buy her any present, let her travel anywhere except she must not be alone in the city.'

'I can put your mind at rest,' I said. 'I'll go to Hacilith and see if I can discover news. If I can find Cyan, I'll bring her back.'

Frost stared at me with incredulity. 'You're joking, aren't you?'

'No.'

'On the eve of the advance? Certainly not.'

'It's only four days' flight there and back,' I said blithely. 'You'll scarcely notice I've gone.'

'Of course I will!' Frost snatched her notebook off the table and held it pressed to her chest, her arms folded across it and her eyes round. 'Honestly, Jant. Another of your picaroon ideas! Just because it's Lightning's daughter. Just because it's him! Quite frankly I think all those beads you wear are cutting off the blood supply to your brain. The Emperor asked thee to work for me this year. Thou knowest I need thy help. I need communication and logistics more than anything else!'

I can tell Frost is distraught when she starts to pepper her speech with the remains of her old Brandoch accent. Nobody, not even in the Plainslands, has spoken like that since the seventeenth century.

I said, 'I've already sent out my dispatches. The troops are on their way and no matter how much I chivvy them, they won't march any faster. I want to see you raise the gate as much as the journalists do, but it's eight days from now. Even if I don't find Cyan, I can easily make it back in that time.'

Eleonora said, 'How like an Eszai to take too much on!'

Lightning said, 'Frost is right. When Cyan was kidnapped before, I deserted my duty and went looking for her even though Insects were swarming. The Emperor was unforgiving – and rightly so – because there are still bite marks in the gates of Shivel manor house and paper stains in the parlour of Tanager Hall. San only gave me one more chance and his decrees are set in stone. I do not want to have to crawl to him like that again. He went so far as to say that every one of those thousands of people killed had been worth as much as Cyan.'

'You're afraid of the Emperor.'

'Yes, I am. For myself and for you.'

Frost said, 'How old is this Cyan, anyway?'

'Seventeen,' said Lightning, refilling his glass.

'Seventeen!' Frost exclaimed.

Seventeen ... I thought, and confirmed my decision to go and find her. Mortals seem to age very fast these days. I had been thinking of her as a child but now she must have a mind of her own, and a body too. Her father was born with the silver spoon and could afford to believe the best of human nature. Her mother, who died at Tris five years ago, was a schemer convinced of humanity's worst. How had these traits mixed in Cyan? How had she turned out?

Frost said, 'She's probably just enjoying herself and she'll come back when she's ready. Don't you remember what it was like to be seventeen?'

'Yes. Why do you think I'm worried? I did a lot of stupid things when I was that age ... There was that incident with my father's chariot and the lake ... Anyway, we had a sense of propriety and Cyan, I fear, has none. It is strange. Why should she run away? She can't be angry with me or I would definitely know about it, otherwise she would have wasted the effort. Either she has been untruthful for some time or this was a temporary aberration. I imagine her coming to her senses again and realising she's lost.'

'She's smart enough to get herself found,' I said. 'She hasn't exactly led a sheltered existence.'

Lightning twiddled his glass and gazed at the stationary surface of the wine inside it. 'She has not visited the city before ... Meanwhile I'm supposed to be drilling these archers who seem to think they're here for a stroll by the water stair.'

I thought Lightning was wrong. He had always said Cyan could do what she wanted, but now she chose to exercise that freedom he was up in arms. If she had only just discovered freedom, of course she'd want to know how much she could use it without losing it. She would just drink too much and spew in the street at three in the morning. She'd have gut-rot and a hangover, recover and feel ashamed. Then she would find the sheets rough in the coach house and bedbugs too; cold water in the pitcher and no soap in the bowl. I said, 'Lightning, she'll come home wiser in the ways of the world, with her tail between her legs, and vow not to leave the palace for a long time.'

Lightning passed a hand over his forehead. 'Oh god. You don't understand. Cyan has the blood of a thousand-year-old dynasty. She is the new heir of the house of Micawater ... Why does nobody have the slightest inkling what that means to me?'

I said, 'Blood doesn't matter any more.'

'It matters. It matters to me. Oh, I know what you're thinking. That I'm some sort of relic of the seventh century. Well, let me tell you, it was the golden age of Awia – hic! – (excuse me). The genealogies of every other family twisted and turned and snuffed out. But Micawater comes straight down through the centuries: me. And now Cyan. She is the heir to Esmerillion's crown. And she's also my daughter and I love her and I want to see her safe.'

'The old money of the country even then,' Eleonora murmured.

I said, 'All this past is just like a millstone around your neck. Can't you forget about it for once?'

Lightning said, 'That would be forgetting history.'

'I do forget history.'

'You would. You're a Rhydanne. But the history of my family is the history of my country, and even if Insects take our land they won't take what we are.'

'Hear, hear!' said Eleonora.

Lightning nodded, warming to his subject. 'When in four-fifteen the Insects first appeared in Awia, the chaos they caused led to the collapse of the governments in every country. The Insects extended their Paperlands and Awian families began moving south to escape them. Everyone knows that account, but my ancestors were among them. Our records don't stretch back that far; we were not notable then. We were unplanned settlers but we had courage and intelligence. We settled Pentadrican land. They were in anarchy and grateful for the order we brought. We also brought the knowledge of how to fight Insects. We lived in harmony with the Pentradricans who remained. Soon King Murrelet made a decision to shift the boundaries of Awia south. All the land from the rivers Moren to Rachis was Pentadrican land back then. If you know what you're looking for, Eleonora, you can still see vestiges of the Pentadrica today – the Dace River, that was one of their fish names, like the Trisians still use. Awia stretched from the Rachis river to the north coast of the continent, all under paper now.

'My family staked a claim on bountiful land in Mica River valley. We founded the manor and took the river's name for our family name. Then gold was discovered in Gilt River, my family started to mine it and we flourished. We married into the Sheldrake family and gained all the land south of the river mouth. Our rise in influence seemed unstoppable.'

'Look,' I said. 'We know all this.'

Eleonora said, 'Shut up, Jant. He's talking to me'

She gave Lightning an encouraging nod and he continued, unfortunately: 'The Murrelets held the throne for centuries. They had claimed the Rachis Valley, but they died out in five four nine and we inherited the throne. Queen Esmerillion was the first of our dynasty – her charm was legendary. She moved the capital from Murrelet to Micawater town. She built the palace, away from the best land, obviously, but she gave it the best vista.

'Ninety years passed. Then my grandfather, King Gadwall, married Minivet Donaise and we gained her manor – the whole of the Donaise hills were added to Micawater. Gadwall and Minivet had two daughters, the firstborn being Teale. Teale Micawater married a warrior called Garganey Planisher and, though their children – my siblings and me – numbered nine, we were the last generation . . . until Cyan was born.' Lightning sighed and folded his arms.

I drained my glass noisily and declared, 'God, I needed that.'

'I understand, even if Jant doesn't,' said Eleonora. 'We live forever through our descendants.'

'I prefer to live forever through being the fastest messenger in the world,' I said. 'Lightning, do you want some more wine?'

'Thank you. But, you know, I was only fourth in line for the throne and I was never expected to inherit so I was not brought up knowing how to run the manor as were my brothers Peregrine, Gyr and Shryke. I made many mistakes in the first few years.

'Peregrine knew he was dying of cancer. He speculated that I would live longer than a whole mortal dynasty so he placed the manor in my hands, but Gyr should have inherited. Gyr was the last of my brothers left alive but he was the black sheep of the family; he had been embittered by the death of his sister decades before. We quarrelled . . . I handled it badly. You see, the Castle had made me a soldier not a statesman. I beat him around the Great Hall and I threw him out. Every harsh word is still burnt into me.

'That was in the year six eighty-seven and it was the end of our dynasty. Gyr wanted to put some distance between us, so he married bloody Korhaan Allerion. He wanted to change his name but the process was the same then as now; the name of the wealthier parents' family was passed on to the children. The Allerions could never be wealthier than the Micawaters, so Gyr changed his name completely. He called his dynasty after the river that flowed through the lands he carved off from my manor. His lack of originality was the final insult.

'Eventually the Avernwaters yielded the throne to the Piculets and I knew there was not a drop of my family's blood left in the world, apart from me . . .' His forehead creased, then he shrugged and sipped claret.

'I try to trace my line as far as the Rachiswaters, but I am only fooling myself,' he added. 'So, when I say the seventh century was our golden age, I mean it. I have managed to keep my manor preserved at the peak of my dynasty's expansion and achievement. We brought stability to our manor, then the whole of Awia, and we stopped the Insects coming further southward. I have always thought that's the reason why San let me keep the land when I became Eszai. It also meant that Awia couldn't expand its borders any further into the Plainslands. Adventurous dynasties like the Tanagers beat north against the Insects instead, and the Rachiswaters pushed west.'

Frost had been talking to Gayle on her other side, but she caught a fragment of our conversation and smiled. 'No one can better Lightning on the ebb and flow of featherback dynasties. He remembers them all.'

Lightning raised a finger shrewdly and drunkenly. 'I knowed . . . I mean . . . I knew them all.'

'We realise. Why don't you have some of this?' I said, offering him a slice of fudge cake which would be well-nigh impossible to talk through.

Lightning refused it for the chance to show Eleonora his knowledge. 'Our court was in power from five forty-nine until six eighty-seven. My mother held the throne at the time of the Games. The Avernwaters followed, from six eighty-seven to the year one thousand; they held out a long time but their town is now only a Tanager muster. The Piculets rose in power, from the year one thousand until ten eighty-one. Then the Pardalotes were very successful, ten eighty-one to thirteen twenty-six, when Insects killed the last. The Piculets returned from thirteen twenty-six to thirteen ninety-eight. I liked them, but I didn't think much of the Fulvetta dynasty (thirteen ninety-eight to fifteen sixteen), very debauched in the fifteenth century. The exhilarating times of new Awia had long gone. They used to tell me, "Be decadent while you still can. The Insects will destroy us too." Well, the last one, Lanare Fulvetta, poisoned her family and was imprisoned for patricide. Then rose the Scoters (fifteen sixteen to fifteen thirty-six) until a flu epidemic put an end to them and tens of thousands more. They were followed by an interregnum and I was champing at the bit then, let me tell you. The Falconets were merchant arrivistes – with sporadic insanity – who filled the vacuum from fifteen thirty-eight to sixteen forty-one. I had to sit through that; they were all quite mad. There was a schism in the family and poor Petronia Falconet went to Hacilith, but his son did well as the first Aver-Falconet. Then the Tanagers appeared, a famous warrior family –' He smiled at Eleonora '– and succeeded to the throne. They restored some of the wonderful original vigour from sixteen fifteen until eighteen twelve . . .'

'Financial problems,' put in Eleonora graciously.

'Financial problems,' Lightning concurred. 'The Rachiswaters rose to power (eighteen twelve to twenty fifteen). They founded Carniss but an Insect swarm ended them, and back came the Tanagers ... twenty fifteen until who knows when?'

Eleonora said, 'That's the way you see mortals, isn't it? Just offshoots of family lines, just the latest kings or servants or soldiers.'

Lightning prodded a finger at the table top. 'That is a very involved question. So in simplest yes and no terms, let me just say, perhaps.'

'I expect you think there's no point in getting to know them personally.'

The smile spread over his face again. 'You, Eleonora, are an *excellent* personification of the Tanagers.'

'We may have been good warriors but we weren't so successful in peaceful times. My forebears didn't care as much about money as yours must have done.'

Lightning said, 'Nevertheless, I think you'll last. Pass the wine, please.'

'You've drunk enough.'

'I ... have drunk enough claret in my life to fill Micawater lake. 'S true. I worked it out. A whole damn lake of calret. Claret.'

'Only Awia has such royal splendour,' Eleonora continued. 'I feel sorry for the other countries.'

I felt sorry for Lightning's daughter. He seemed to want her to begin his dynasty once more, so this time he could watch over it properly, but evidently he couldn't even look after her. I said, 'If I find Cyan, I'll explain all this to her. Besides, I've been at the front for a long time; I'd welcome a change of scene.'

'You all have your priorities wrong!' Frost wailed.

Lightning said to her, 'I wouldn't let Jant go if I didn't think he could do it. Cyan knows and likes him. She listens to him.'

'I know the underworld, too,' I said.

'Oh, god ... Good luck.'

'What do you want me to do if I find her?'

Lightning propped his head on his hand. 'Hmm. Send her to the palace. No, on second thoughts, bring her here. I can keep an eye on her. Otherwise she might run away again. Harrier may be growing too long in the tooth to keep up with her.'

'She can watch us drawing up the troops,' Eleonora suggested.

'Yes. It might do the uncouth young lady good to see the fyrd in action. She needs a firm hand. She calls herself Cyan Peregrine, as she should, because she will inherit the manor when she's twenty-one. I am glad she accepts it, but everything else she does these days seems designed to cause me pain. If ... If the worst has happened and you need constables, or horses, ask Aver-Falconet. Cyan was supposed to be meeting him anyway . . . Harrier had to make all kinds of excuses.'

Frost shook her head and clasped her hands around her coffee cup. 'I don't like it. I'm busy with my speciality as San wants us to be. I don't branch out. I don't have pastimes; I work all the time. But, Lightning, when you're not playing geopolitics you're playing family history!'

He asked her, 'Will you be able to work without Jant?'

She bristled. 'Yes, of course! I coped for hundreds of years before *he* flew in!'

'Use my couriers,' I said.

'Typical. Everything to be done at the pace of a nag rather than the pace of an eagle.'

Lightning said, 'Give him six days, Frost. You never give anybody enough time off. Including yourself, I suspect.'

'How else would I have built the dam?' she asked, then turned to Eleonora. 'Your Highness, be my witness that I object to this ridiculous errand.'

Eleonora shrugged. 'As you wish, but we're at the front so I can't intervene in an argument between Eszai.'

Frost could see she was outnumbered and I felt a twist of guilt because the advance is supposed to be our priority. However, I can manage both and she's probably just annoyed that I'm more busy than her. She said, 'Jant, when you return, report straight to me. I'll have a stack of letters for you by then.'

I picked my jacket off the back of the chair, leant over the table and gathered some cheese rolls.

Lightning said, 'Wait a minute.' He struggled to his feet and threw an arm around my shoulders. He was taller than my one metre eighty-five and nearly twice as broad as I am. He accompanied me to the door with a confidential air, saying, 'Jant, you must know that . . . Um . . . I have my own doubts. Um . . . Oh, god knows I have always tried to show you the right way but you are far too easily tempted . . .'

'What?'

'Cyan is a very attractive girl.'

'Good,' I said.

He rubbed the tips of his fingers over the scar on his right hand. 'I'm not sure if . . . if she pretty how knows she is. Knows how pretty she is. It might have an effect on certain men . . . On certain men who have volunteered to find her.'

'What!' I said indignantly. 'I promise I won't touch her!'

'You never know what you are going to do, Jant, so don't bother promising. I wish for once you would plan ahead rather than living in the instant and rushing into things. I remember how you were when you first joined the Circle, eagerly looking for ways to destroy yourself. You still pride yourself on being dangerous.'

It took him some time to say this and I waited patiently. 'Lightning, you have old-fashioned ideas.'

'With time you'll learn they're the safest. If you ... If you take advantage of Cyan I'll have your guts for bowstring. I will do you more damage than that battle did ... I'll break every one of your weird-looking fingers.'

'God. You really know how to get through to a Rhydanne. There's no need to worry, trust me; I told Cyan to think of me as her brother.'

He nodded, mollified. 'Well, my town house and hunting lodges are at your disposal, as usual. Oh, and Jant, if you can't find her in the six days, you must return. Don't let your tremendous energy tempt you to ridiculous feats. The Emperor would dismiss us both.'

CHAPTER 4

I found my pace and the wind was with me; I flew over the convoys coming in to Slake Cross. I was glad to be flying in the opposite direction, against the flow, at right angles to society. I was enjoying myself; I live for flight. I felt light and ethereal.

The wind buffeted my wings. I exerted my strength and held them steady, like struts. I respect the winds, because at a touch some gales could snap my bones and tear my muscle, so to be weather-wise I study the clouds.

Flying long distances is a very fulfilling challenge, because it has taken me all my life to learn the rules of the sky. It is always laid out like a chessboard halfway through a game, a confusion of risks and potentials. Flying puts the minutiae of life into perspective – I was concentrating so hard playing out the moves, I didn't dwell on any of the daily worries.

I looked for the small, fluffy white clouds that sit on top of thermals. They had been forming all morning and were drifting with the wind to make an archipelago, each cloud a signpost in a corridor of updraughts that would carry me south.

I entered the first thermal and felt a jolt of lift. I turned and circled close to its centre, the tips of my wings spread wide to catch the rising air. The moorland spun under me as I rose smoothly, and all the time I was looking around, trying to predict the next source of lift. After a few minutes the warm air bubble faded and no longer bore me up, but I had already gained so much height I could glide out towards the next one.

This is the best way of flying. From birds I learnt the trick is not to flap all the time but glide as much as possible to save effort. It's a game of wits for me, though. When I was on drugs, I took the overfamiliar countryside for granted; flying around in a daze, delivering letters or failing to. No longer – I was seeing it with new eyes, full of gladness that I'm clean at last. The excitement of the real world made me high – the sky was more vivid than a trip – how could I have forgotten the scenery's intense beauty when in love with all the Shift worlds to which cat could take me? The Fourlands was so much better.

I pulled my little round sunglasses down from my forehead and looked out far in advance. The shape and colour of the ground influences the wind currents and spots where thermals form.

As I left Lowespass the lines of trenches fell behind, but pillboxes and platform towers dotted the border of Awia – places to seek refuge from Insects. I could tell I had crossed into northwest Awia when I went over the Rachis River, a thin silver thread shining like flax unspooling through flower-spotted water meadows.

I was flying over the upper Rachis valley, patchwork farmland thickly and evenly spangled with villages. This was the muster of Plow. All manors are divided into musters of roughly equal population, with the original purpose of marshalling fyrd. Each muster is administered by a reeve who is appointed by the manor lord. The reeve's family change their surname to match the muster, a system created in the distant past, probably to make it easier for us immortals to remember them.

I caressed the air over Plow, the largest town in its muster, but still not much more than the reeve's moated farm around which gathered stone granges with red-tiled roofs and courtyards. They belonged to the tenant farmers who work the land under the reeve, and the vavasours who sub-rent from the tenant farmers.

All the barns were empty of hay and the cattle turned out into the fields. Men and women looked up and pointed me out, pausing from their work bent double pulling up weeds from between shoots of wheat and barley. I waved and motion flourished all over the fields as hundreds of people simultaneously waved back.

No wonder Plow muster is called 'the bread basket of Awia'. Rock dust ground by glaciers in the mountains blows down in the high air streams and settles across the area, where the rivers add loam and make the most fertile land in the Empire. Awia is fortunate that the country is so fruitful; it would otherwise soon be ruined since it bears the brunt of the Insect incursion while the rest of the Fourlands can prosper free of any fighting.

I passed over Toft town, built of ivy-clad marble tracery salvaged from old palaces. It was once famous for being the seat of the Fulvetta dynasty, and now famous for nothing but its ruins.

The land started to bump up into grassy slopes. The last thermal failed me and I had to ascend by flapping. I beat strongly, breathing deeply to quell the pain in my wings and stomach muscles. When I fly long distance I try to dissociate from the pain by counting off the landmarks and seeing how soon I can pass them. It's just like running a marathon; it gets harder and harder until a certain point. If I can break past that point I feel I can go on for ever.

I crested Irksdale, the heather grouse moor, into Micawater manor. The land dropped steeply in limestone bands and escarpments, leaving me gliding high above fresh beech and old oak woods. This was no wild wood but Lightning's carefully managed purlieu, a hunting ground popular for the revels of ladies and gentlemen. They come up from the Awian palaces and the summer homes of Hacilith businessmen further down the valley. Every time I fly over it brings home to me how rich Lightning is, with all these thousands of people paying rent to him. His manor alone was probably worth half the Plainslands. Long accustomed to immortality, he plans far ahead and his people profit from his vast experience. He looks after them well; in fact, nobody lives as a cottar in Micawater.

Lightning would be even richer now his investment in Trisian trade is starting to pay off. But I'm not envious. What would I do with all that cash, hey? I have twenty primary feathers and the blue dome of the sky!

A herd of fallow deer caught sight of me and panicked. They were so far below, they looked to be the size of hares; they bounded beneath the trees, white tails flashing. I could only see them occasionally, grey-brown backs and the stags' antlers in velvet, but I drove them along in front with glee. They reached the edge of the woods and waded out into the shallow Foin River, where I left them standing in the fast current. The Foin is fordable along its length, giving rise to the proverb, 'When there are two bridges over the Foin'; that is, never.

I looked directly down and found myself staring into the ground – a rocky chasm. I was over the fuming torrent of the Gilt River in a breath and above the trees again. The Gilt cascades down from Darkling where it rises in the mountains' black granite and schist, from which it abrades tiny translucent flakes. They sparkle in the water all the way downstream and embed themselves in the plashers of waterwheels from Kettleholes to Micawater town that glitter as they turn.

The shadows were lengthening and already the evening was drawing in. It was better to cut my journey short today and enjoy Lightning's hospitality, than to press on, gain a few more kilometres but have to spend the night in a grim Fescue coaching inn. I leant my weight and swung left, to follow the river down to the next village, Chalybeate. A long skein of geese straggled into view, a few hundred metres below me. Their honking and whirring wings awoke my ingrained hunting lust. I let them pass under me, then swung into a standing position, folded my wings and fell, feet first. I hit the last bird in the line with the soles of my boots and knocked it stone dead. It dropped out of the air and crashed through the branches.

I landed, picked it up then ran to find the path, kicking up clouds of spores from puffball fungi. The stalks of bluebells on the bank were invisible; their flowers hung in the air like fine eye-shadow dust. Silky beech leaves were unfolding like fans from the buds, ferns uncurled like green question marks, up from the ground covering of dog's mercury and herb robyn.

I knocked on the door of Chalybeate Chase, one of Lightning's picturesque and immaculate hunting lodges. I have a delightful privilege as Messenger: I can ask for lodging anywhere. It always amuses me to see great lords scrambling to give their best suites to a junkie ex-street kid. The caretaker's surprised face appeared in the doorway.

I held up the goose and he broke into a grin.

Every centimetre of Chalybeate Chase's inside walls was crammed with hunting trophies. The table, where I was sitting to eat my roast goose dinner, was a glass-fronted cabinet containing a display of stuffed wildfowl. Hundreds of deer heads surrounded me, mounted looking left and right to fit their antlers into every available space. Pink and orange paper chains draped all over them – the debris left by Lightning's last party hadn't been cleared up yet. He has a habit of announcing that it is his birthday at random intervals. Sometimes he has two or three in a year, sometimes none for a decade. The first time he asked me to deliver invitations I thought it really was his birthday until Rayne explained it was nothing but an excuse for a party and no one knows when his real birthday is. According to Lightning, immortals' birthdays don't count.

Next morning I headed out of Awia, flying south and watching the Plainslands expand. It was fantastic, so refreshing! If one day I crash and die flying, then it will all be worth it. Look at me, the Emperor's Messenger! I hold all the rights of passage. My strength, my speed, the scars of Slake Cross Battle seemed to burn in my flesh. God, but it was good to be alive, in the chill exhilarating air!

I waved my arms from sheer exuberance but that didn't seem to help dissipate it. All I need now is my old guitar, so I can coax 'The Frozen Hound Hotel' out of it while I ride.

I glanced up to another layer of fine, thin cloud thousands of metres above. I have tried, but it's impossible to fly that high. I can't breathe up there and I come down covered in ice. I usually travel long-distance at about one and a half thousand metres and never higher than five thousand, much lower than the valley where I once lived in Darkling.

In such fine conditions I can glide a hundred kilometres without flapping once, but I could no longer see much detail. Navigation was easy; all I had to do now was follow the Moren to Hacilith. The river was speckled with barges sailing upstream to the mining villages. Their sails were angled and they had white mounds on their decks, probably sacks of coal being shipped in from the collieries of Avernwater and Fusain muster in Wrought. As the terrain flattened, the Moren began to meander lazily back and forth. Fescue manor continued on its south side, all poor sandy heath interlaced with dirt-track drove roads. Little more than gorse grew in central Fescue.

By early afternoon I passed over the Castle itself. From this altitude the grey octagonal walls, corner towers and the Emperor's palace fitted inside looked as if they could sit on the palm of my hand. I couldn't distinguish the elaborate buildings but I saw sunlight reflecting with a flash on the gold sun finial topping the Throne Room spire. A spur from the river fed the gleaming double moat. On the smooth glacis lawn grass I recognized various outbuildings; the oval amphitheatre adjoining the square gymnasium and the stables' courtyard. The archery fields and jousting lists looked like green tiles.

It was strange to think the Emperor was sitting on his throne directly beneath me, not knowing I was gliding thousands of metres above his head. I unpacked my sandwiches and let the paper fall. It tumbled away and dropped behind me amazingly quickly, suddenly giving me something to judge my speed against. I hoped the Emperor was standing on his balcony and it fluttered down onto his head.

The Castle's curtain wall dwarfed Demesne village just west of it, past the series of mirror-like fishponds. The Castle's servants live in Demesne village and it is the only land the Castle has ever owned. The land on which it and the Castle stands is independent of any manor but much smaller than any muster. Its fields can only sustain the village itself and not the Castle, which is dependent on the good will of the Empire; San's deliberate wish, to symbolise that the Castle is the Empire's servant.

Pinchbeck town crowded into a bend in the river. Open, blunt-prowed barges no bigger than apple pips nosed onto its jetties. Timber-framed cranes were swinging sacks onto their decks. Here was the first sign of the city – Hacilith sucks in a vast amount of produce – the whole Plainslands and the rest of Morenzia can't match the quantities its markets buy and sell. My excitement began to grow – even out here in Shivel you can feel the pull of Hacilith.

Heavier barges sat low in the water, carrying millstones and masonry from the Heshcam quarries. Felled logs butted among them, floating in huge rope corrals, to be drifted downstream to the hungry capital.

Pinchbeck diminished and I flashed by plain farmland; all beehives, tariff barns, cow sheds, pigsties, duck ponds, threshing sheds, oil-presses. Before me, Shivel, the second-largest Plainslands town, spread out from the river, flat over the land like lichen.

Shivel manor house was just outside the town on the main road. I contemplated how unlike most Awian manor houses that was. They're usually at a distance from town in their own parkland, but the Plains-slands governors live near their citizens. That may encourage their people, but I'm dubious, because for all their physical proximity the Plainslands aristocracies are even more distant from their tenants than are those of Awia – and the corrupt oligarchy of Hacilith, living in the same streets as their citizens, may as well be in a different world.

Further on, I passed over a scatter of reed-thatched, run-down hovels, the dwellings of cottars who scrape their existence by hiring themselves to the tenant farmers at sowing and harvest, at little more than subsistence levels. In the months between, they labour at any odd job available – women were pegging linen on lines to dry. All the men seemed to be busy building another hovel from clay cob. Kids ran about barefoot and chickens scratched around under their ladders; the cottars let their scrawny livestock live in their own houses.

I lifted my wings a touch from the horizontal to glide efficiently. They cut the air; it forced over their hard, smooth upper surfaces with a swish like sword blades. I was having to fly faster now, to get enough lift, and I had neck ache from keeping my head up and looking forwards.

A squad of archers were marching along the road, just dots with long shadows stretching before them – probably a patrol returning from the downs – all governors use them to keep the main roads clear of highwaymen. The horse jumps in the next field looked no bigger than matchsticks and dainty trotting palfreys were like models. I felt I could reach down and move them about.

The land began to look crumpled, like a sheet that had been shaken and left rucked and folded. I was rising up over the tail of the Awndyn Downs. I went over Coutille town in its muster, all uncobbled roads and self-consciously traditional half-timbered homes. The walls of the oldest buckled outwards so they looked as if they were about to collapse and concertina down in a pile of thick thatch.

More signs of the city dotted the south Awndyn Downs: the handsome private houses of Hacilith industrialists or lawyers; litigious and venal merchants, shipmen, and businessmen. They were not interested in owning land because it's more respectable to be a merchant in Hacilith, but they were eager to display their wealth.

All along the horizon white figures cut into the chalk hills were turning pink in the twilight. They were miniscule in the distance but just distinguishable as the badges of the adjoining manors, the dolphin of Awndyn, Eske plough, Hacilith fist and Shivel star, cut and maintained by their fyrds.

Hacilith cast an upwards glow on low cloud base; the pale yellow of cannel coal fires in thousands of homes. I could smell the coal tar already. Closer, and the larger buildings loomed into familiarity; I could name every one. The field of vision narrowed, the roofs increased in size, and the suburban tatter of the Pityme district opened out beneath me. It extended in a ribbon along both canal banks and for a shorter distance up the Camber Road as if stuck to it.

I cruised at the rate of two beats a minute, my legs straight and pressed together in quick accipitrine flight, above the road as it ran across the single, flint-faced span of Pityme Bridge, the oldest on the canal, carrying the Camber Road into the city of Hacilith and the republic of Morenzia.

The Moren River was silted and sluggish, seemingly a solid bulk. It reflected dully, as if shellac varnished, the lights glimmering on its far bank – the Marenna Dock piers and waterfront way over in Brandoch manor.

The Moren is tidal as far as Hacilith and its banks are brackish. I saw a dismal grazier wandering on the marsh, looking after emaciated sheep. Then the huge iron lock gates at the end of the Hacilith–Awndyn canal hove into view and the marsh ended in a continuous stretch of wharves.

This immense canal was Frost's grand waterway; it took her fifty years to complete and it ensured the rise to prominence of the Wrought armouries. The canal made Awndyn's fortune too, but it turned Diw harbour into a ghost town, as ships no longer needed to risk rounding Cape Brattice.

Below me, the rough Galt district docks sprawled along the whole east bank of the Moren, surrounded by refuse tips and the shacks of 'mudlarks' who scrape an existence by beachcombing the mudflats. The paddletrams had been decommissioned decades ago, and their waterwheels had been dismantled, but the decaying supports reared like spires out of the river.

Fat chimneys, squat chimneys of pottery and slate. All the mucky house backs with alleys hung with washing and piled with so much refuse it was turning into soil.

I made very sharp turns and fell steeply with my wings fanned out and my legs dangling. My descent and angle of vision became more acute: the shop fronts too sheer to see, just lines and lines of roofs running in the same direction. I seemed to be going faster the lower I dropped, because I could measure my speed against every ridge and gutter. Landing is the most hazardous time and I concentrated completely on finding a safe place. It was impossible. I couldn't glide down any of the roads without hitting a shop front.

I turned and the exclusive Fiennafor district tilted into view ahead. The tall eighteenth-century town houses were regimented in quarter-circle curved terraces. Aver-Falconet's bronze-clad palace front glowed dully in the street lights. Puddles glinted among the cobbles on its wide parade.

Here was the arc closest to the palace, all double sash windows, Neo-Tealean white fronts with plain columns flat against the walls. The gates in their iron railings gave onto the parade, around an immaculate oval lawn with a spreading plane tree. It was The Crescent, and Lightning's house was number one.

I descended in front of it. I thrust my wings forward and the feathers spread flat automatically to stop me stalling. Wings' fingers open, legs down: my boot toes skimmed over the surface of a puddle leaving two long ripples. I stepped down out of the air and began walking without a pause, folding my wings behind me.

The yellow wheels of a glossy coach rolled past an arm's length away. I let it pass, crossed the road and walked up the steps to the black painted door.

The door knocker was so highly polished it looked unreal. I rapped it and looked around as I waited for the major-domo to answer. The sky was heavy with more rain and the evening still.

The major-domo showed me a room. She laid out a dressing gown of the best Awian silk and took my clothes to be cleaned and pressed. She spread the table with hot coffee and pancakes. When I had eaten I stripped all the covers off the bed and slept on the floor.

CHAPTER 5

I began searching for Cyan and thought it best to try the fashionable district first. I walked around Fiennafor and looked in Aver-Falconet's palace, then Lorimer Street with The Moren Grand Theatre, The Bourse and The Old Almshouse Café. I found no sign of Lightning's daughter anywhere.

I hired a carriage and drove east to Moren Wells, a very upmarket spa town recently swallowed by the fringe of the city. I searched for Cyan in the Sinter Spa and Calandra Park, but no one there had heard any news.

The next morning I wondered what to do. I only had one day left and I doubted I could find her. I decided to work my way south through Galt into Old Town. That way I could visit Rayne at the university before leaving. I made sure my wallet was safe, buttoned my coat pockets tight, and submerged myself in Galt, the largest of the five districts.

The further I walked, the more I realised that I would never find Cyan but, ever hopeful, I walked slowly and looked around carefully, especially at the girls, as I passed the:

Scuttlebutt Casino
Cockfighting pits
Prize-fighters' boxing booths
Clutchfut Vintners
Inglenook Hostel
The bull ring
The paper mill
The brass hammer mill
The denim mill
The cartwheel lathes
The markets:
The cattle market
The hides and skins' market
The broadcloth Furbelows Market

The woodwork Treen Market
The glass and pots Frit Market
The fish and salt Gabelle Market
The Meal Market, where shiploads of corn change hands
The Meat Market, its drains running with blood
The Mop Market, where job seekers sell their own services
The Crimp Market for mountains of coal
The Whispering Market for perfumes and objets d'art – a covered
arcade where the stalls are packed so closely together that business
is done at a whisper in case anybody hears the deals
Past the butterstone at the markets' end
Past the Cooper's yard
Past the Atilliator's yard
Past the rope walk
Past East Sea Customs House
Past the dry dock, where ships were repaired
To the wet dock where goods were being unloaded.

I paused there and looked out over the river, a solid mass of inshore galleys, barges, tugs and flyboats; waiting to load, register, enter the canal or extricate themselves from the chaos. Upriver, a single armed caravel watched the teeming industry with a constable's eye.

The incredible number of wagons, drovers' turkeys with pitch on their feet, grain storehouses full to the roof, the stink of coal tar and the hubbub of the markets reminded me of the queues coming into the battlefront. I didn't stand any chance of finding Cyan if she was lost in these crowds.

I bought a kebab on a stick, and a copy of *Lammergeier* fashion magazine to see what my wife, Tern Wrought, was doing this season. I scanned her column, called 'Ageless Taste', but it had nothing about me. I had not seen Tern this happy since last century; she had paid off most of her debts with the booty from Tris and was supervising the rebuilding and redecorating of her manor house. Wrought isn't called the fashion capital of Awia for nothing; Tern was working hard, from party to party, trailing people without noticing them, except for when they itched.

It began to drizzle and the damp Hacilith chill sank into everything. I turned away from the river and walked deeper into Galt, heading towards Old Town. The houses here were all back-to-backs with alleys between them; no yards but one outside toilet shared by each alley.

Rainwater chuckled along the gutter, washing over some rotting pamphlets from the recent elections.

The poverty was obvious here; many lived in the streets. Everyone wore hats, endless designs of cloth caps and liripipes. A beggar was shouting, 'Fists and daffodils! Swans and shells!' I riffled through my wallet and dropped him a couple of ten-penny notes with the Summerday shell.

I glanced over to the shield factory's covered courtyard. Boys from the workhouse were laying out unpainted shields for their glue to dry. I could just see onto the factory floor where craftsmen were making them by hand.

I stopped and looked around. I knew I was still heading towards Old Town because the university's tower, with turrets at each of its four corners, projected above the shambling roofs. I was deep in Galt now but I felt weirdly disorientated. I had expected to recognise my old haunt, but it bore no resemblance to the Galt I knew. There was no ground plan left of the streets, no trace whatsoever of the old docks. It's been two hundred years, Jant, I told myself; what do you expect? It was unfamiliar ... no, so *nearly* familiar, that it was giving me the creeps.

A cart laden with rubbish went past; the whiskery driver bellowing, 'Raag and Bo-one! Raag and Bo-one!'

What was that about? Where were all the wharves? All this used to be open ground – it seemed impossible – how could so many houses have been fitted into it?

I was sure I should have passed the Bird in the Hand Awian strip joint, but there were just more houses. Either I was completely in the wrong place or the very roads had changed. Well, I thought, the chemist's shop where I used to work would have been over there. I'll walk down and see if I'm right.

When I lived here, the city way of thinking trapped me, narrowing my horizons just as the factories block out the sky. I didn't even want to leave. I put all my energy into misguided actions and negative reactions until I couldn't pull myself from the mire. Back then, the roads out of Galt led in two directions. To the left, the streets thinned out and one road wound over Pityme Bridge into the beginning of grassy hills in the distance. I could have taken that road and escaped, but I never did; not until I was forced out. That road may as well have not existed. Every night I went right, down the other alley to the strip joint with a sign promising 'Great Tits!' in the window. I convinced myself that I'd had enough of travelling, should stay in the shop and read books, and visit whores. It never even crossed my mind that the Castle would want my talent, until my life in Hacilith was in ruins.

I had liked working in Dotterel's chemist shop, it was dim and quiet; the gang's fear of employment made it a safe refuge. With the shutters down, every customer who entered saw me, a boy slouching on the counter who had already looked them over, a freak perhaps, tall and skinny even for adolescence, but a perfect confidant.

My time looking for Cyan was nearly up. It's hopeless, I thought – I'll go and see Rayne instead, if she hasn't already left for Slake, and then I'll head back. At least I'll be able to tell the others when Rayne should be arriving.

I reached an open plaza and stopped. This should be Cinder Street. Maybe . . . that row of shops was along the same line. I looked around. If this was Cinder Street, then the Kentledge pub would have been at the far end . . . And my chemist's shop would have been . . . there. And the Campion Vaudeville! That should be on the next street over! I ran quickly towards it, remembering the peeling playbills fluttering on its boards, the shards of glass that topped the walls around it, the masks and scrolls around the windows in its leaking mansard roof.

The street ended at an empty plaza with a row of smart boutiques and some sort of trendy wine bar. The Campion Vaudeville had totally gone.

They've redeveloped my street! How dare they? Yes, it had been run down but I had liked it! There was no trace of the second-hand shops full of individual texture I had loved so much. That corner was where I busked with Babbitt – and now it had all been swept away.

The new shops had no character; time hadn't given them any unique pattern of wear. They blocked my view of the canal towpath, pressed up tall and narrow against each other as if someone had put a hand at each end of the plaza and squeezed them together. Their colour-washed fronts were rose pink, yellow, pale blue, chalky green and grey. They proudly announced they'd passed inspection, with firemark, ratmark and lousemark tin badges tacked to their walls.

I walked along the row, half whited-out by drizzle. Streams of water dripped from the sign of the horrendous new bar at the far end and pattered into concentric rings on the paving stones. That bar would be more or less on the place where the Kentledge pub used to be, where our gang leader carved the Wheel scar into my shoulder. The power of the memory made me shudder: I outlast whole *streets*, and now Cinder Street and everything I remembered was no more.

*

This must have been exactly where Dotterel the chemist picked me up; when he made me his apprentice. I stood and stared at the row of shops until I could call up an image of the Campion two hundred years ago. It seemed larger in memory, closer and brighter than the shops it overlaid. Its smoke-stained stone had flaked off here and there showing clean, biscuity spots.

I heard a whir, a paddletram! – It sounded like it could be . . . but it wasn't. Simply flocks of starlings screaming and swirling in to roost.

A vision of my younger self jumped down from the Campion's portico and ran past me, soundlessly though his footsteps should have splashed. He vanishes. He reappears again in the alley by the Kentledge; transparent – then solid – a lanky fifteen-year-old in a filthy parka. He ducks his head and wipes his nose on his sleeve.

Lines of coaches are waiting outside the Campion Vaudeville, and wisps of smog are curling through and around their wheels. Oil lamps are guttering out with gin-blue flames since it is three in the morning and the late show is just ending. The act closes to half-hearted acclaim and people begin to stagger out into the street. Linkboys hang around in a curious cloud, their tapers scribbling lines of smoke into the air above them. The Rhydanne boy hates them, because they understand each other. They know how to buy bustard burgers and tablet fudge. They swagger with the all-encompassing importance of their job.

From the end of the street there are raised voices, lads shouting to each other about the can-can dancers. Paddletrams groan past in the background, grinding cabbage leaves and hawked-up chewing tobacco into a black sludge between the rails. The boy is faster than sight; he pauses to draw breath and ducks behind the frame of a waiting coach. The nearest human moves on and the boy relaxes.

He moves in quick bursts, waiting behind lamp post and coach wheel, doorway and alley. He crooks his elbow and tears the Insect wing windows of all the coaches along the line.

'I saw you!' calls a voice from somewhere in the fog. Quick as a rat the boy leaps onto the top of the carriage, which hardly rocks at all on its flat springs. He crouches, nose streaming, piercing eyes in a grimy face.

An old man emerges from the porch of the Campion. His head is bowed and his face is in shadow. This is a trick the boy very much admires. The man looks up; his face is padded, deeply wrinkled and his nose veined cranberry red. Wisps of hair too white for Galt adhere to his bald head. He is wearing a long, grey coat and carrying a cane with a silver handle, which he points at the boy. The boy simply crouches further on thin haunches and spreads his wings.

The man knows that if he takes a step or even stares too hard, the boy will run. Very querulously he says, 'Who are you?' but he says it in Scree.

'You speak Scree? How? At last! What is this place? Er ... I haven't spoken to anyone since last melt season. I'm ill all the time. I've never been this ill before. I have to hunt for myself! And I c-can't make any one understand! No one –'

'Sh! Slower, boy; don't gabble. You're alone?'

'You're observant!'

'Why did you break the windows?'

The boy shrugged. What else could he do to show his anger or make his presence felt? He sat cross-legged on the coach roof, reached a hand down through the torn window and brought out an apple. He began to examine it with the delicacy of mime.

'They don't belong to you, Dara.'

'I'm a Shira. That could be the reason why I am finding it so entertaining to break them.'

'You're quick,' said the old man, smiling.

'I'm the quickest,' said the boy.

The man took a tight grip on his cane and tapped the cobbles for a while in thought. The boy, seeing this, threw down his apple which rolled under the folds of the man's long coat. Enthralled, the boy watched it, head on one side. His instincts were to bolt, but this man was the first person he had spoken to in a year. Indecision rooted him to the spot. He swore in Scree, but all those insults about goats didn't seem too relevant in Hacilith.

The man gave a rustle of coughing laughter. 'Well, I need an assistant, but I never thought I would have to tame one ... I will turn now and walk away,' he continued slowly. 'You can follow me if you want. No one will hurt you. No one will force you, but it will be best for you if you come.'

The man walked on and did not look back, and gradually disappeared into the smog. He did not seem to be a threat; indeed, he could be a saviour. The boy watched from his precarious perch, then fluttered down and sauntered after him, still prepared to run.

Dotterel and the boy walked through the wall of the bar and disappeared. I sighed. Any Rhydanne would have been naïve in the city, but I had been naïve even by Rhydanne standards. I was quite the little foreigner; it's a wonder I survived at all.

I need a drink after seeing that, and besides, the rain was running down my neck. I investigated the bar, plated with brushed and burnished bronze along its whole front. Smooth almost featureless metal statues with folded arms and stylised wings like blades stood with heavy elegance on either side of its doorway. It was done up to look like Aver-Falconet's square palace, in the new Decorative Art. Its sign said: The Jacamar Club. An Awian pub, then, the sort popular with the few tourists who came out this way from Fiennafor. As if to prove my thought, some frightful shrieking laughter resounded from inside. I have never understood why travellers and expats feel the need to go to a pub mocked up with all the features of a bar of their homeland to drink wine at ten times the price. There were any number of Morenzian inns nearby where they could drink beer, eat boar pie and hear the citizens speaking their own language.

I went inside, flapping my half-closed wings to dry them and flicking drops everywhere. A couple of students at a nearby table yelled, but when they looked up and saw me, they shut up abruptly.

The pub's fittings were the most up-to-date design but the floor was sticky with spilt drinks. Square columns were bolted to the walls, all painted black but with gold lightning flashes and pointed feathers on the tops. A strikingly graceful fresco of a deer chased by hundreds of hounds fled along the walls. All the way to the rear wall the hind ran with the hounds ever at her throat and, below her outstretched legs, on a leather sofa stained with nicotine, sat Cyan.

CHAPTER 6

Oh, no. I could hear Cyan's voice from the doorway. She was too conspicuous, blissfully unaware she could be attracting every thief and rapist in Galt. She was recounting an anecdote at the top of her voice to a group of students and she hadn't noticed me, so I approached slowly, watching.

Cyan was no longer a child. Her blonde hair hung perfectly straight to the level of her bodice top. Its straps and laces showed and so did her armpit hair. Her short skirt kept riding up and she kept pulling it down. Her stockings plunged into huge black boots. She didn't have wings, she took after her mother, and she was willowy; slighter and more hourglass-shaped than an Awian woman.

At her hip hung a dagger, tied into its scabbard as city law dictated, and the most impressive little compound bow I have ever seen hung off the chair arm in a lacquer holster. Under the table a waxed cotton quiver held enough arrows to depopulate the whole bar. Didn't she know it was illegal to carry a bow openly in the city?

I hadn't seen Cyan since her mother's funeral. Her very poise seemed to have changed; a vehemence had taken root in her previously innocent adventurousness. This was the girl I used to tickle until she was helpless with giggling. This was the girl I picked up off the shipwreck years ago – but of course she wouldn't remember. I watched covertly, feeling special, slightly dizzy having flown such a great distance and having walked into the city-dwellers' trivial little world. There was no way they could understand or even acknowledge my effort. To them I just appear.

As she talked animatedly an enormous ruby pendant on a gold chain rolled back and forth above her flattened breasts. Fortunately some of the other women's glass costume jewellery was just as ostentatious, but you didn't have to look closely to tell that Cyan's ruby was real.

She was surrounded by lots of girls, who must mistakenly think she could arrange a rendezvous with Lightning. They started to notice me and one by one slunk or darted back to their tables. She didn't look up until I was directly opposite her and the last of her court sloughed away leaving just one rugged-looking fyrdsman.

Cyan jumped nearly clear of the cushions in surprise. 'Jant! Come here, come here and sit down! Why have you come all this way? Never mind; the coolest Eszai will make my night complete!'

I sank into an armchair on the other side of the table. Everyone's eyes were prickling from the corners of the room. Cyan was overjoyed. 'Let me introduce you. Rawney, this is *the* Comet Jant Shira. He flies in from the Castle to see me. Sometimes he carries ice down from Darkling for our drinks . . . Jant, this is Rawney.'

'Rawney what?'

'No. Rawney Carron.'

'Very Morenzian. Pleased to meet you.' Rawney Carron ignored the hand I offered him and glowered at me. He seemed to have claimed ownership of Cyan. He was not tall so I guessed he was city born and bred. He wore fyrd fatigues with the murrey fist blazon of Hacilith sewn on the breast and he also had it tattooed on his arm. He had a weightlifter's build and he clearly fancied himself.

'He's a corporal,' said Cyan. 'And this . . . er . . . that *was* Sharny. He seems to have gone. Well, never mind. What are you doing here? Did Daddy send you? And why do you have soot on your eyes? Oh, it's make-up.'

Rawney sniggered.

'Shut it,' I told him. I was not prepared to take any cheek from a fyrdsman. 'Cyan, this time I'm here to bring you home.'

'She wants to stay,' said Rawney.

'Go and join the rest of your squad,' I told him.

'I haven't got one yet. I have to press a General Fyrd squad tonight.'

'Are you going to the front?'

'Yes. I'm looking forward to it. It's better than working in the docks. It's an adventure.'

'Good.' I gave him a grin.

Only the musters of Hacilith pressgang fyrd, and I knew Rawney must be professional Select Fyrd because only Select can be officers of any rank in either fyrd. He leant back on the couch and put his arm behind Cyan. I shuffled forward, as if to protect her.

'Did Daddy send you?' she repeated.

'As a matter of fact I suggested it to him. Are you all right?'

'I'm having a great time!'

'Do you have lodgings?'

'Yes.'

'And money?'

'Yes, of course. Daddy gave me pocket money for the tour, and I can always draw on my account. He fills it up now and again. He's loaded.'

'In that case I'll have a double whisky,' I said.

'Fine.' Cyan shook a five-pound coin from her purse.

'Ask him to fetch them.' I nodded and smiled at Rawney, and pushed the coin towards him.

'Rawney, go and bring some whisky, another wallop for me and get yourself a jug of beer. They don't take orders at your table here,' she added to me. 'It isn't that Awian.'

Rawney lumbered off to the bar. I called after him, 'And a couple of baskets of chips!'

'I wonder where you put it all, you're so thin.'

'I fly,' I said shortly. 'Cyan, why did you run away? Lightning's worried sick. And don't you know it's illegal to carry bows in the city?' I took it off the chair arm and slipped it under the couch. 'What are you doing here? You have to come home.'

She looked me over. 'There's no such thing as "have to". I am not going back to Micawater or Awndyn. Not ever. No way. You can't make me.'

'Yes, I can, actually. What are you doing with that hulk?'

'Rawney? He's gorgeous.'

'He's dim. Lightning wants you to come to the front. We're about to advance at Frost's lake.'

'That old eel-eater. I don't want to go to the damn dam. I want to stay here.'

'You're not lodging with that Morenzian meathead, are you?'

'That's none of your business! Hmm ... I don't think I'll tell you, because you'll just flutter off back to Daddy and spill the beans. I know what I'm doing.'

'Do you really?'

'I was fed up with dull old Awndyn.' She sighed. 'I had to get away. Away from obligation! I want to stay here and live it up for a few months. I have a freedom here I never had with Swallow, with Daddy; they're all living in a dream world. They have no idea how the real world works. This is the real world –' Her gesture took in the bar and what little of East Bank was visible through the window '– This is where the real people are.' She lit a cigarette and narrowed her eyes against the smoke. 'I know I'm lucky and I can do anything, but I just haven't made my mind up yet.'

'Please come back.'

'Don't be crap, goat-breath. You do what you want, you always told me that. Why shouldn't I?'

I was frustrated that I had to spell this out: 'Hacilith is dangerous.'

'Yeah!'

'You can't be Rawney's girlfriend. You might pretend but you'll never really understand him.'

She smiled sweetly. 'I can play him along for kicks. He worships the ground I walk on.'

I hissed, 'No. You might think that, but he reckons you're his girl. If you try to leave him, he might hurt you.'

'Whatever gave you that idea?' she said, shocked.

'Oh, Cyan. Please be careful. You might find it hard to get rid of the likes of him. He knows he can't really have you, so instead he could try to make your life misery. He could blame you for the fact that he's Insect fodder and you're glittering with rubies.'

'I don't think so.'

'Oh, yes. Worse still, if he believes you're something you're not, he could chase you unto the last of his energy and be prepared to die for what his imagination makes you into. He'd love to marry the heir to Peregrine.'

I glanced over to the bar but fortunately Rawney was taking a long time. He was chatting with a skinny, wasted-looking guy. I took a sip of Cyan's 'wallop' – ginger beer that was more beer than it was ginger – and went on; 'You'll never understand what Hacilith is like under the surface. It's impossible, but try to grasp that I'm telling you this from my own experience. My image isn't just an image, Cyan; I witnessed the last days of the East Bank gangs.' I pushed my coat off my shoulder so she could see the circle with six spokes that our gang leader had carved there. 'The other gang, the Bowyers, had arrowheads scarred on their forearms. We used to flay them off and stick them to the door of our warehouse.'

'Wow.'

'Yes. Well, I suppose I should never have tried to encroach on their patch. When they caught any of us, they dumped us in the canal lock. When we caught any of them, we nailed them to the struts of a waterwheel. Hence the Wheel.' I took her hand and traced the furrows of my scar with her finger.

'I can feel it.'

'That's right.'

She didn't know whether to believe me or not. 'Didn't the constables do anything?'

'Oh, I always tipped off the constables. But they left them revolving round and round for a few hours before they took them down ... The Bowyers eventually traced where I lived. I came home one night and found my shop on fire. I ran in, trying to find my master ...' I continued sadly as I put my coat back on. 'He was called Dotterel. I tried to run upstairs but the steps were burning through. I expect – I hope – he died of smoke suffocation long before the flames reached the second floor ...'

Cyan said, 'I'm sorry.'

'I couldn't feel grief back then, only despair. It was the next inevitable avalanche to happen to me. What sort of life was Hacilith, anyway? My girlfriend pulled me out of the shop as it rose in flames about me and, right then, we determined to leave Galt. We took the road that went left over Pityme Bridge and we realised that even the Castle was possible.'

I never tell Zascai that I used to be a drug dealer, but I let them know my unfortunate adventures. It makes me seem so much more talented for having escaped them.

Cyan said, 'Hacilith must have changed.'

'Yes, it's different now. The underworld is more inconspicuous and a damn sight more complicated, but it hasn't gone away.'

She took a sip of her drink and rolled her eyes. 'Oh god. If that's your advice, I don't need it. I don't want Daddy's advice either, and I certainly don't want Swallow the mad diva's homespun instruction. I thought better of you. Let me make my own mistakes!'

'You don't want Lightning's advice? Fourteen hundred years of it?'

'Fourteen hundred years of boredom, more like!'

'You'll inherit Peregrine when you're twenty-one,' I said.

'That's what I'm running away from! My true place in life, huh. How can I be an Awian lady when I don't feel Awian at all? Not that being wingless matters; Awians will accept me and anyway, they don't have a choice. But I don't feel I belong anywhere. Daddy gave me this –' She hooked her fingers under the chain of her ruby pendant as if she was about to rip it off and throw it away. 'He says it's an heirloom. But I don't belong in Micawater either. "Come home," you tell me, but just where home is, I can't say. Morenzia is the only country that's free.'

'Don't say that in front of Lightning.'

'Just five families in Awia own eighty per cent of the land. Morenzians don't have such a silly aristocracy. They don't have to bow and scrape. You don't know what it's like to be a girl stuck in Awndyn.'

I nodded. That much was true.

'Hacilith is so big! There are so many people my age! I never had friends in Awndyn. But, god, Jant, what does that mean to you? You're bloody ancient. The Castle protects you, just like Daddy.'

'You should have seen me at Slake Cross trying to hold my guts in with one hand.'

'Oh, yeah. Sorry.' She pinched her cheek and wiggled it. 'You think you see a girl but looking out of these eyes is a very experienced woman, in experience terms at least as old as you are. Well, nearly. I've travelled all over the place.'

'Did you go or were you taken?'

Her eyebrows drew together. I continued, 'You haven't been south of Awndyn before and you haven't been north of Micawater.'

'I'm here of my own accord *now*. So don't misunderestimate me. Take Rawney, I only met him four days ago and he says he will do anything for me. He can get anything for me, even jook. He helped me move onto the Tumblehome.'

'Is that where you're staying?'

'Oh ... Yeah, it is, actually. So let me express myself. I'm not going to be cooped up in Awndyn with the mad diva.'

Rawney returned with the drinks but without any food. He didn't give Cyan her change either but she didn't notice. He put a whole bottle of cheap whisky down in front of me. 'There! Get your talons round that!'

'I don't have talons,' I said indignantly, but he continued to stare rudely while I poured a glass. I stared back, and he looked away.

People naturally resent anybody who gives them orders and Zascai are especially resentful of good-looking immortals who can fly. Rawney was trying to find something to feel superior about and, as usual for such people, he was concentrating on my Rhydanne heritage. There is not much in my appearance and bearing for Morenzians to identify with; all that is human in me, I have learnt. They characterise Rhydanne as a bunch of hopeless drunks; the fact that one might flap down from the mountains and start giving them commands is a further affront to their dignity. Also, if he is like most Zascai, he will think of me as the voice of the Emperor and be doubly afraid. Mortals often assume that because I have the Emperor's ear I am somehow closer to him than other immortals. That isn't true, and anyway why would San send me to spy on someone like Rawney?

Cyan gave an embarrassed giggle. 'It's so strange to be talking to one of Daddy's workmates.'

I said, 'As the future Governor of Peregrine, you'll get used to it.'

'How many times have I got to tell you? I don't want to be governor! I hate feeling the weight of Daddy's expectations on me all the time!

It's all right for you, flying around and never counting the cost. I'm not impressed with his plans for me. I have different plans. How dare he assume my tastes are the same as his? He doesn't even know me!'

'But you used to love hunting in Peregrine,' I said.

'Yes, I know. Weird, isn't it? It became overfamiliar, I suppose. It disappointed me. I don't want to see all those same faces again.' She turned to Rawney. 'Jant used to frustrate the fuck out of me with all his exciting plans I wasn't allowed to realise. I loved his tales of faraway places. Now I'm in one!'

That made me smile. 'Lightning would be furious if he knew you were sitting in a bar.'

'Huh. Him. He doesn't understand what's real in life. He's stuck with his sense of honour. I think we should feel first and act on our feelings instead. I wanted someone to know my mind, Jant. No one in Awndyn could, so it's me who has to change. I thought: if I don't change, I'll die. But now the future has opened up wide!'

I poured more whisky. Every spoilt teenager talks like this, and Cyan was in full flow. 'I've got my enthusiasm back. I used to feel dormant, as if I was waiting to start my own life. I was breathless and apprehensive, but I was ready and now things are starting to happen! My hatred of Awndyn wound me up like a spring and shot me out to Hacilith. I'm not stopping now.'

I said, 'You might find the front just as refreshing. Have you ever seen a live Insect? No? Well, I can show you things even more exciting than Hacilith.'

She glanced at Rawney. 'Bring him, too,' I said. 'Lightning will love him.'

She said slowly, 'Hacilith is more cleansing. I can get lost here. Nobody knows who I am.'

'I think they do!'

'Bollocks, Jant. Bollocks. Listen. There are three sorts of people: the ones in Awndyn or Micawater don't have to ask who one's father is, because they know and they take it for granted. Then I travelled a bit and met the sort, like in Aver-Falconet's household, who do think it's important to ask who one's father is. They're surprised and a bit scared when I tell them, because they don't really know what to say. They think they should treat me with kid gloves. I hate them. Then there are the real people, like these Morenzians. It never occurs to them to ask; as far as they're concerned it's a meaningless question. They treat me the same as any other girl.'

'That's the problem.'

Rawney said nothing but became gradually redder and redder in the face until he burst. 'You know fuck all, immortal! You left this town! You hit the big time. Yeah, you went away and won immortality and married money. So what are you doing here? Why have you come here? Go fuck off back to the Castle. Go on – get out! You don't belong here with your fucking smart comments and your weird old-fashioned clothes!'

I tilted my head and gave him a good look with my cheekbones. If he wanted a fight I could shove my axe up his arse in three moves. 'I swear,' I said softly. 'If we didn't send the people of Hacilith to fight Insects, they'd be fighting each other.'

Rawney flinched, glanced at Cyan and rallied. 'Look, babe, we're talking to a madman. A real creep. He's two hundred years old and he's not going to die so he must be mad compared to us mortals. He has nothing to do with us.'

Cyan pursed her lips. 'It *is* off-putting that he always looks the same. It reminds me of when I was small.'

I sighed, sick of invective. 'Please, Cyan. I don't want to leave you here. I can't tell Lightning this.'

'I can't believe you're on Daddy's side!'

'I'm not. I agree that you shouldn't sweetly follow the life he's planned for you. Forget the governorship, if you want. That's fine by me. But I think you're a bit vulnerable and –'

'I can look after myself!' She grabbed the bow from under the sofa and before I could stop her, she slid it out of its holster.

The bar suddenly went very quiet. Every face turned towards us, but Rawney stood up and called, 'Do you want to see another trick?'

To my astonishment they all began to applaud. Nobody slipped out to call the constables. Cyan acknowledged them with a wave. She held her bow across her knee and ran her hands over it to warm it, then carefully bent its limbs back and strung it. They were tapered, surprisingly whippy for a reflex bow. She slipped a horn ring on her thumb and pulled two arrows, shorter than fyrd standard arrows, from the quiver. She pressed ginger beer bottle corks onto their sharp bodkin points, saying, 'I'll show you my trick.'

'I've seen this. It's one of Lightning's stunts.'

'No, it's *my* trick.' She lost none of the emphasis the second time round, so I decided to let her win. 'Go on, then.'

She did not bother to stand up. She nocked an arrow and drew it to her cheek with a pinch grip. She aimed and let fly.

A bottle on the furthest table jumped into the air, clattered down and started spinning round, flashing its empty neck and base.

Cyan shot the second arrow and it recorked the spinning bottle. The force of its impact sent it off the edge of the table. It skidded across the floor bounced off a young man's foot. He held it up, the cork firmly fixed and the arrow protruding.

Cyan's impromptu audience gave her another round of applause. She stretched up her arm and raised her three middle fingers, her thumb holding her little finger down. It was the archers' salute, long ago, and now it's a very filthy gesture.

'See!' she said to me. 'All these new friends!' And louder: 'Let's show Comet a good time. All the drinks are on me!'

There was a cheer and the sound of a general rush to the bar. Much impressed, I said, 'You're very accurate. And that's a glorious bow.'

'Thanks. It's one of Daddy's own designs.'

'Don't ever use it in Hacilith again when I'm not here! Why don't you come to the front, if you're keen on shooting? You can practise on Insects every day.'

'I am *not* going to Daddy. There'll be two bridges over the Foin before I do! The Emperor will leave the Castle, god will return and the world will end before I talk to him!'

'He did his best. He brought you up as well as he could.' I indicated the bow as an example of Lightning's largesse.

'Huh. It was his fault my mother was killed. He could have saved her but he let her die.'

I put the bottle down. 'What? Who told you that?'

'Carmine Dei. One of my stepsisters.'

'She's lying. Lightning did all he could to save your mother. I know; I was there.' Cyan's stepsister was as big a bitch as their mother, Ata, had been. After she died, some of her huge family remained in contact, a large clandestine organisation, and these days Carmine has the whole suspect network well under her hand. She was the city's harbourmaster; she had failed in the last competition for Sailor, and being Sailor manqué had made her even more poisonous.

I said, 'You mustn't listen to anything Carmine says. Are you staying with her?'

'No. Not quite. Carmine told me a lot of Daddy's secrets and I know some of them must be true. After all he abandoned me with Governor Swallow Fatarse. She made me learn silly musical instruments I wasn't the slightest bit interested in. Once, when I was little, I pretended to be an Insect under her dumb piano and I accidentally scratched it. She went totally crazy. After that being an Insect was out of the question. Silly cow. And she plays Daddy better then she plays any instrument! I visit Micawater now and then, but he doesn't realise how long the gaps are between visits. What is he doing that's so damn important I had to fend for myself?'

Cyan has never had to fend for herself. Everywhere she goes, servants hover to accommodate her every whim. I tilted the glass back and swilled whisky. I didn't want any more hassle. Cyan had used up my quota of patience and I had far too much on my mind. I wasn't sure if I was becoming wise with age, or simply exhausted; but then, if wisdom is a more prudent use of one's time, maybe it's exhaustion that forces us to be wise.

I shook my head. 'Whatever. Oh, what it is to be seventeen and open to rumour. Believe what you like. I won't tell Lightning that I found you. But when you tire of gallivanting around the city, join us at the front, all right?'

'Great!' She lit another cigarette and offered me one, leaning forward to light it with her own.

Rawney glanced at her jealously, but he slopped some more whisky into my glass. Maybe he wasn't so bad after all. He shook the bottle, then looked at me oddly. 'Damn. All the tales I've heard about Rhydanne are true.'

'Another cretinous comment from you and I'll post you to Ressond. Anyway, Rhydanne live above five thousand metres. We need to drink alcohol so our blood doesn't freeze.'

'Oh, yeah,' he said sarcastically.

'All true,' I said. 'No word of a lie. Would I lie to you? No. We have to drink alcohol constantly. And it takes Rhydanne minds off their awful food. There's no time for cuisine between the hunting and the hangovers; I think they only bother to cook because they can't eat it raw.'

Cyan said, 'It can't be true you're the only mix of Awian and Rhydanne.'

I shrugged. 'I'm sure there were others, and there will be others in future, for as long as Awians keep trying to conquer peaks ... I keep pulling their stupid flags off and sending them back. Some Awian–Rhydanne children might have been unviable and didn't survive. Maybe some never made it out of Darkling or weren't able to fly, either not strong or not clever enough to learn. It took me ten years, after all. I should imagine most half-breed babies were thrown over cliffs. I would have been if it wasn't for Eilean. A Rhydanne single mother will kill an unwanted baby that slows her down.'

Rawney said, 'That's brutal. Animals.'

'No. It's a matter of her own survival. And anyway, look who's talking.' I turned to Cyan. 'Maybe we are similar. I've left my heritage behind me and you're trying to.'

'Rubbish,' she teased. 'You love being different. You keep turning your head so your eyes reflect.'

'I do not!'

'You do. And you read fortune cards. You carry them around everywhere.'

'Only for a party trick.' I dug in my inside jacket pocket for the battered sheaf of twenty-five squares of leather and, with a flick of one hand, spread them out. I offered them to her and she leant forward to pick one. She examined it closely, turning it over. 'Look, Rawney. Jant has these Rhydanne fortune cards.'

'Give me a break,' he said. 'Come on, babe, we ought to be going.'

'I keep telling you to stop calling me "babe"!'

He grasped her wrist and I tensed, but Cyan twisted herself free. I saw her blood rise and for the first time I could actually believe I was talking to Lightning's daughter. She made the most of her accent: 'If you do that again, fyrdsman, I will leave with Comet.' Then she said to me, as if to cover up, 'Will you read the cards for me, Jant?'

'All right.' I wiped whisky off the tabletop with my sleeve. I tapped the pack to neaten them and arranged them face down.

'How does it work?'

'The cards ...' I swigged my drink. 'The cards don't tell the future. How could they? The future isn't set. These cards tell you about yourself in the present. All you need to know, to predict the future as accurately as possible ... all you *can* ever know, is yourself right now. Most people don't know their own character well and these cards help you reflect. Then for the future, you extrapolate. Go ahead and make the future up – your character will be the main factor.'

'They're cards for the *present*?'

'Rhydanne live in the present. They don't think ahead to the future much; it's just another present to them. You have to do the reading yourself. You're best placed to interpret your own character.'

'But I don't know what the pictures mean!'

I waved my cigarette around. 'They're just pictures. They don't have defined meanings. They mean whatever you think they mean. That's how it works.'

Cyan looked daunted. 'I think I'm too drunk for this.'

'There are five suits: ice, rock, alcohol, goats and eagles.' I turned over the lowest in the ice suit, the snow hole shelter. 'That one, for example, can mean: remember to maintain your equipment or you'll starve. This one, the goat's kid, can mean: don't chase a woman you're not married to. Or don't marry some slow-running slut whose children are all Shiras. It depends on your circumstances, you see. Pick five cards ...'

Cyan did so. She set them precisely in line and turned over the first. 'Boulders,' I said.

'I beg your pardon?'

'That's from the rock suit: grit, pebbles, boulders, cliffs and mountains. Make of it what you like.'

She pondered the square of hide. 'It means something that blocks your way, doesn't it? An insurmountable problem. Like Daddy. You know his palace? Did you know that all the keyholes in the doors along the Long Corridor line up so well you can look down them from one end of the palace to the other? That's how infuriating it is. It's so finicky and stultifying it makes me sick. Every time I visited I was terrified of breaking something. I think I scare him, because he's been trying hard to cultivate a friendly fatherly image. I hate Micawater. Boulders all right; it's so heavy and stagnant.'

She turned the next card, and exclaimed, 'What in the Empire is that?'

I peered at it. 'It's the dead goat. From the goat suit: dead goat, pastured goat, randy goat, mother goat, kid.'

'You have got to be joking.' She looked from the card to me. 'It's to do with mortality. These cards really do work, don't they? I'm mortal and Daddy isn't ... Everyone knows that at some time in the future their parents will die. They wonder how it'll happen. What will it be like to hear the news? How will they bury him? If they're the eldest, they can't help but think about the inheritance. I don't have that. I can't speculate. That's one of the things I can't stand – Daddy will always be there, exactly the same. In fact, I know that the day he buries me in a tomb on his stupid island, he'll look just the same as he does now. The palace will be no different. I'll never be rid of him! It makes me feel heavy ... I think it's dread.'

She opened another bottle of beer. She had not inherited Lightning's connoisseurship but she had his ability to discourse at length. Beer begets beer, as you know, but she wasn't as drunk as I was. I sipped the whisky appreciatively. 'This was shit at the beginning but it's all right now ... All the nice whisky must sink to the bottom.'

Cyan turned the next card, the soaring eagle. 'Well, that's easy. That's me escaping, trying to fly free of the flock and find some clear air, trying to do something different. It's a wild animal, symbolic of freedom like my name. I'm glad I didn't bring any belongings. I've stranded myself here deliberately with no past, nothing to prove I exist. I have myself, that's all; I'm content with that . . .'

I waited, indulgently.

'. . . I feel awkward in the city, big and clumsy. I pull at doors I'm supposed to push, push at doors that open by pulling. But I'll get used to the city soon. I'm alone, scattered in the multitude – just as I want.'

'To be scattered in the multitude, hey?'

She glowered at me and flicked over another card. 'What's this one?'

'The nesting eagle.'

'A nesting eagle . . . That must stand for domesticity, marriage. Marriage . . . oh, yuk, did I tell you about all the men Daddy introduced me to? They're horrible.'

Rawney smirked. 'Don't the suitors suit you?'

'They're so superficial! They make all these unfounded assumptions!' Cyan slipped into High Awian, which was good for talking of art, society and its insults, but not much else. 'This is their repertoire: "You are Lightning's daughter, really? When do you come of age?" "Oh, are you acquainted with Cyan Peregrine? Such a well-groomed blonde." I grew up with all that small talk, it's maddening. Their conversations revolve around themselves, they never talk about anything outside their own heads. I hated every last battalion warden of them. I didn't bother to convey myself, I let them slip through my fingers – and I don't care that they've gone.'

She looked at the window, now a mirror backed by darkness. 'In the palace the days seemed to last forever. I went to bed an entirely different person from when I woke up. I rattled around inside that bloody great building like a piddock in a rock.'

'Like a what?'

'Sorry. Awndyn slang. I tried to continue from habit but I couldn't attend to my tutor. An inertia came over me. I kept excusing myself from the dinners and going to my room. I lay on my bed and wondered why I felt such confused dislike. I goaded and rebuked myself. I turned my thoughts over until they were a thick, boiling mass. I needed someone to talk to or I would have cracked. Swallow puts a dampener on everything and she's happy to be of no use whatsoever. So I ran.'

I folded my arms on the table and put my head down. I was at the point of drunkenness where any further drink tasted like puke. I felt my brain shrinking and my thoughts drying up.

Rawney put his big, hairy arm around Cyan's shoulders and whispered in her ear. She nodded, preoccupied with the cards. 'I keep toying with ideas of the future. What will happen to me? I keep imagining myself in future scenarios but I can't see myself as Governor of Peregrine no matter how hard I try.'

'I'm not shurprised you're afraid of telling Saker,' I slurred.

'Saker? Who? Oh, you mean Daddy.' She giggled. 'Weird . . . I never think of his real name . . . Yes. He's been alive forever. It's scary to argue with him. Maybe I am conceited to disagree with him. He has an answer for everything, tried and tested, and he's always right! He knows everything and he never gets angry, he's so bloody patient. He just gives me more boring answers! It's so infuriating! I want to try something new, even if it's wrong!'

She turned the last card in the line.

'That one . . . thatsh the jug of beer.'

Rawney said, 'Well, that has to be a lucky card for Rhydanne.'

'Mm.'

'So everything will turn out well,' Cyan exclaimed, getting carried away. 'I'll be successful in making my own way in the world. It's beer not Micawater wine!'

'There isn't a card for wine,' I murmured.

'I'll learn who I am. If it really did depend on blood, Lightning would know me better, wouldn't he? I might have inherited one or two family traits, but I'll rediscover them myself!'

So you should, I thought. My mind's sky had thoroughly clouded over. I closed my eyes.

Cyan leant and whispered in my ear, 'I'm living my own life from now on, where and how I choose to. Tell Daddy to forget about me. In a couple of hundred years, he will. It's the only way.'

I woke up. The pub was unlit and deserted. An uneasy lamplight shining under the landlord's door illuminated the shapes of chairs placed on the tables and textured lines drawn by the broom in the stickier patches on the floor. Towels hung over the pump handles.

Shit. I am absolutely pissed . . . and I've lost Cyan. She's given me the slip. Oh, shit, I had her, and I . . . she . . . Rawney got me drunk! The bastard, and I fell for it!

I staggered over to the bar and stuck my head under a tap, pumped water into my face. The landlord must have left me sleeping there while he closed up the bar around me. Of course, he wouldn't have dared to wake an Eszai.

I wrestled with the door bolts. Outside, the misty drizzle gave everything a slick sheen. I turned my coat collar up, but it soaked through the denim, wetting me as effectively as pouring rain.

Galt was very dark, none of the lamps were lit and the shops' upper stories had closed their shutters. All I had to see by were occasional chinks of light between them.

Now I was back to playing hide and seek with the little cow across the entire city.

CHAPTER 7

All the oil lamps stood disused, their glasses fly-spotted and filthy. Whale oil was scarce these days, reserved for lighting homes, not streets. It had soared in price since some enormous sea snakes had taken up residency in the ocean. Their main source of food seemed to be whales.

The paving of the plaza outside the bar was covered in a sheen of water, mixed with mud trekked in from the towpath. I looked down, at the palimpsest of footprints spreading out from the door. Could it be possible to track Cyan? I searched around and found the fine mud drawn into a distinctive print of a thick-soled boot, too small for a man. Those are Cyan's expensive boots. I followed them slowly, careful not to miss any. They were few and far between, but if they were hers she seemed to have walked along the towpath.

I carried on, beside the dark canal, shunning the varicose hookers and their crisp pimps revealed by the night. The mud squashed under my boot soles. I was heading east towards Old Town, but I wasn't out of Galt yet, and horrible sights loomed in alleys and alcoves. I passed quickly by a whore with bare breasts and ragged shorts, her razor ribs showing through the stretch marks on her sides.

I lost the trail under furrowed bike ruts and glanced all around, overly aware of how Rhydanne I looked. I learnt how to track on visits to the mountains. Veering towards the canal, a smooth leather imprint with a firm, mannish step could be Rawney's. Yes, there was one partially obscuring Cyan's smudged trace. I continued, thinking; I really tried not to be like a Rhydanne in Hacilith but other people's expectations kept throwing me back on it. I often found myself playing out the solitary self-centred flightiness they expected. But what the fuck, it meant they gave me leeway. They might be patronising but they also didn't expect too much, and they left me free to do what I liked.

There was a strong smell of fried food grease, as if every citizen had scoffed a newspaper-full of chips, then belched simultaneously. I passed out of Galt into Old Town. The canal basin has obliterated most of it, but the remaining buildings, replaced many times over, are still so close together there isn't room to fit one more between them. Awian towns are sometimes destroyed by Insects and rebuilt in one go, but here old buildings persist, with a mishmash of modern styles between them. New houses spring up in the wake of fires and the residents continually improve their city so much of Old Town was quite new. I ran under the merchants' tall houses. Their baroque gables sprouted pulleys and platforms to bring in goods they store in their own attics. I walked by the mooring of the River Bus that shuttles to Marenna Dock on the west bank. I passed a roast chestnut stand littered with paper bags and dripping with rain. I cut past Inhock Stables, making the rum-sellers' pannier donkeys bray uneasily. Horses were tethered here, since they weren't allowed in Old Town's narrow streets.

I passed the wharfinger's office and came to a deserted part of the navigation, heading towards a footbridge. I swore as I walked; the whisky was smearing all my thoughts together and the rain was getting worse. All storms arrive first in Hacilith from the sea, all seasons seemed to start here too, and the spring rain fell with a vengeance.

The gutters drained into the soupy canal basin where timber narrow boats were moored. Some were impossibly shiny, others rotting hulks. Several were a full thirty metres, others no more than boxes. Their curtains were closed and they were silent. The darkness muted their paint to different shades of grey.

I went under the bridge, lit by the lamps of a narrow boat moored on its own. The tracks ran into a mass of scuffed ground, so many other prints I couldn't tell what had happened at all. Some led back towards Galt; Rawney's was among them but Cyan's weren't. She had stopped here – or the men had carried her.

I searched for her tracks further away, my task made easier by the lights on the boat. In fact, the rotund lamps at its prow and stern were glowing as brightly as if there was a party on board, but it was quiet. Who would desert a boat and leave its lamps burning?

The small barge was bottle green with red panels and brass trim. Its tiller was polished with use and wound with ribbons, and by it hung a bell to sound instructions to the locksmen. I casually looked down to its bow, just above the level of the quayside paving stones. Red and white diamonds like sweets decorated the top of its transom, either side of the nameplate that read: *Tumblehome*. Underneath in small white capitals: Carmine Dei. Registered: Old Town.

I crouched down to the leaded windows. A rug had been tacked over them on the inside. I tapped the glass and called, 'Cyan! Hey, Cyan? Rawney?' Silence.

I listened, aware of all the sounds of the night – at a distance the noise of Old Town had merged into a low murmur. Ducklings were cheeping, somewhere in the undergrowth on the far bank. I called, questioningly, cheerfully, politely, and finally with a firm demand, but it only produced more silence.

I'm the Emperor's Messenger and I'm not standing for this! I grabbed the rail on its roof and jumped onto the flat ledge running all the way round the boat. It bobbed slightly and I felt its keel bump off the fetid slime of the canal bed. I really cannot stand boats. I could all too easily imagine it turning turtle, pitching me into the black water. I edged towards the stern, feeling my boots grip on the grit embedded in its paint.

I stepped down onto the stern deck, ducked under the tiller, and pushed open the varnished, cupboard-like doors. I wedged into the little entrance. The air inside was warm and stuffy.

I looked down into a long rectangular room. A draught of wind blew in past me and started tinkling some capiz shell mobiles. Discs of coloured glass clattered against the windows. A hanging lantern with moons and stars cut out of its sides sent their projections spinning round the walls.

From a futon, which was a piled mess of quilts and sheepskins, projected a slender blue-white arm, and a limp hand hanging down. I gasped. Cyan!

She sat upright among cushions, her head lolled back and away from me, her legs apart and her skirt rucked up. A thin man lay on the floor at her feet, head back and foam dried into a crust around his mouth. He was stone dead.

OK. This is nothing to do with me.

Yes, it is. She's *Lightning's daughter*!

I stretched a leg down the steps and shuffled in on my backside. The dead man was lying wedged between the wall and the futon. He must have had a fit and thrashed around because he'd kicked a potbellied stove free of its tin flue. It stood at an angle on its platform. I turned him over; he was so stiff that when I propped him on his side, his arm stuck up in the air. His blank eyes no longer stared at the ceiling but at me instead. I checked his dog tag – his name was Sharny. As I did so, something fell to the floor and rolled across the rag-rug. I leant down and felt around until my fingers closed on a glass hypodermic. Sharny's sleeves were unbuttoned; I pushed one up. His arm was covered in red pinpoints, packed so densely his veins had collapsed, looking like they were open to the air. The skin inside his elbow was juicy with infection.

Shit, shit, shit. Not *cat*, surely? Not *Cyan*? When I use, I try to space out the tracks so that they can't be seen when I'm at the podium, to keep the veins fat and easy to hit. Sharny, on the other hand, had sunk lower than the dregs.

I turned Cyan's face towards me gently. Her eyes were rolled back, only showing white slivers under half-closed lids. Her lips were blue, she was hardly breathing; just a little sigh every so often. Two sips of the air, another ragged sigh with a high-pitched whistling sound. From elbow to shoulder her right arm was a solid bruise. I loosened the tourniquet above her elbow, hooked my thumbnail in it and pushed it down. I could only see one needle mark in the crook of her arm but that didn't necessarily mean this was her first time.

I tried to ignore the thought of her fast dropping into unconsciousness, helplessly watching Sharny's avid experimentation with the needle in the back of his cold hand.

I pressed my finger inside her fingers, waiting for a grasp response but nothing happened. 'Cyan, can you hear me? Breathe. Breathe in. And out. Again. Keep going. Can you squeeze my finger? No? OK ...'

I must get her outside, into fresh air. I lifted her; she folded like silk, gave every impression of being dead. I laid her completely relaxed body on the bedspread and wrapped it around her.

A table beside the stove caught my attention. It carried a decanter of water, a spoon, a razor and an unfolded paper of fine white powder standing in a peak. Some had been nicked away.

I recognised it immediately. It called me like a lover and the next second I was down on my hands and knees. Don't look at it! I thought; steady! Turn away. If I so much as touch it I'll be hooked again. I'll be hooked before I know it! Where did Cyan get cat? Where the fuck did she get so *much*? I felt sick and giddy. I knew I was going to pick it up. I moved with no volition of my own; the drug there on the table had more control over my limbs than I did.

Let me explain what craving is. Craving is when your friend manages to talk you out of the corner and gets you to put the knife down. Craving is when you ask to be locked in, because otherwise you'd fly all night from the court to score. Craving is when you wear your fingernails to bloody stumps trying to pick the lock.

What was she doing, playing with cat? But they hadn't called it cat or scolopendium. What was their word? Jook? *Jook, don't you know, it's the latest thing, all the rage.* If I just take a little bit no one will mind. The Emperor won't be able to tell. Shut up and help Cyan. I realised I had been holding my breath for so long my ribs were hurting. I swallowed hard, then stood up. Very slowly and judiciously I refolded the fat wrap of cat and dropped it into my pocket, where it burned.

I bundled Cyan out of the double door, hoisted her onto my shoulder and jumped onto the bank in a bound that set the pool of lamplight lapping up and down. It slid up the inside of the bridge's brick arch, then quickly down to the mooring loops. Viscid water sloshed around the *Tumblehome*'s ridged hull.

I lay her on the ground and checked her. She had stopped breathing. Her eyes had receded into round hollows as if her skull was rising to the surface. Shit. This isn't just a dead faint, it's respiratory failure. I tilted her head back, fingered her mouth open, pinched her nose and blew into her mouth. Her chest rose. I rocked back on my heels watching it fall gently, then blew again.

Her lips were soft, but her mouth was rank with beer, smoke and the metallic taste of death. I had to blow hard to overcome the resistance from the air inside her; my cheeks prickled and my jaw started aching. Her hair brushed my cheek every time I put my head down, but it stank of stale cigarettes. She was only a child, just as when I saved her from the shipwreck. Her chest rose, I looked sideways down the length of her body, between her breasts falling back from the bodice collar as she exhaled.

She twitched, but it must have been nerves, because she definitely wasn't anywhere near consciousness. She gasped and began to breathe for herself again. Thank fuck. 'Well done, girl,' I said as I wrapped her up. 'Keep breathing.'

I had been working so hard keeping her alive that I hadn't been aware of my surroundings. Footsteps were running over the bridge. A boot ground on the path in front of me. I realised I'd seem like a mugger hunched over his victim, so I looked up – into the baby-blue eyes of Rawney Carron.

Two men I hadn't seen before stood either side of him. Movement at the edges of my vision told me three more had closed in behind me. They held naked broadswords, their hair was tied back into tarred pigtails. They couldn't be sailors, because sailors, doctors and armourers are professions safe from the draft. Ex-dock workers, then, and probably owlers, a very dedicated breed of nocturnal smuggler.

'Is this your fyrd squad?' I asked Rawney, calmly keeping anger out of my voice. 'Were you coming back to check on her or to collect your payment?'

Rawney spat, 'Comet, don't you just know everything?'

'Let me go, quick – she's dying!'

'We won't let you arrest us.'

'Look. I don't care if you're dealing. I won't report you. Even though you've done this.'

Rawney shook his head. They knew that to be caught in Morenzia would be their end. One by one they'd be carted to the scaffold, bound to a cart wheel and every bone in their body, ending with their skulls, systematically broken by blows from a mace. What they don't know is I never turn dealers in. The only time I confiscate cat from soldiers is when I'm in short supply myself.

I stood up, palming the flick knife from my boot. 'This is an emergency!'

'No!'

Exasperated, I said, 'I know two cartels that run "Ladygrace Fine" in from Brandoch. I know Emmer Rye fences everything coming into Galt. I don't know you, so you must be kids.'

'Fuck you. You're one man against six. And you're not much of a man anyway!'

'Don't mess about.'

The legs of one soldier were starting to bend with fear. He never thought he'd see an Eszai so close in his lifetime, let alone face one with drawn sword. I could see Rawney trying to balance this against the fact I was obviously drunk and apparently unarmed. He jerked his head and said, 'Kill him.'

I whooshed my wings open, yelled, 'In San's name, with god's will – get out of my way!'

The man on Rawney's left and the three behind me turned and ran.

Rawney snarled and drew his dagger. I flicked my knife. The big man next to him chopped with his sword but I was already inside his reach and up against him. I hugged my arm round him, pulled him close and drove my knife deep into his heart. Blood forced thickly up the runnel, like rising mercury.

Before it reached the handle he became a dead weight. I stepped back and let him crumple.

Rawney was running, putting ground between us as fast as he could. I sprang over the dead soldier. I pounced – caught a fistful of Rawney's hair at the nape of his neck. He cried out. I dragged his head back and pushed my knife's point alongside his windpipe. He stumbled to his knees and I followed him down, my arm tense against his snatching hands, careful not to sever the artery. When the knife was in deep enough I levered it to the horizontal and pulled it towards me. I cut neatly through his windpipe from behind.

Rawney worked his mouth but had no air to scream. He put his hands to his throat, ducked his chin. Blood sprang out like red lips. The ends of the tube snicked as they rubbed together. He drew his next breath through the cut and it whistled.

I booted him in the solar plexus and he doubled up. He turned his head away and the stretched skin parted, laying bare more of the cords in his neck, slick gleam of a vein and the rings of cartilage above and below his severed windpipe.

I hissed, 'You're to blame! You fucking killed Cyan! You can't be her boyfriend. You're scum. Like me. See? Eszai don't do this ...' I crouched and leant onto him, weighting him down. With four quick slashes I drew a square around his fyrd tattoo. I sunk my fingernails under one edge, peeled the skin off, and I stuck it to the ground in front of his frantic eyes. 'But gangsters do. *Never push cat on my turf!*'

Rawney bubbled. His lungs were filling with blood. Huge amounts of bright pink aerated foam frothed between his fingers clutching his throat, and bearded him down to the waist.

I lifted Cyan and jumped up fluidly into a sprint down the towpath. Behind me I heard the strangled liquid gargle, gargle, gargle, of Rawney trying to breathe through his slit throat.

I ran. I ran along the slippery pavements, over the open drains. Above the roofs the moon gave a sick light through the clouds. I swear, anyone who ever bared his teeth at me has had them kicked in, and anyone who ever bared his neck to me has had his throat bitten out.

I sped south, away from the canal, passing a sign pointing to the Church of the Emperor's Birthplace. I ran beside the tiny portion of the original town wall that still remains – because no one had yet built over it. I passed through Watchersgate, the one surviving town gate, useless in its broken piece of north wall, with grooves where its portcullis had been. Life-sized statues with raised arms stood on top. They once held spears as if defending the town, but the spears were removed a hundred years ago after one fell off and, dropping twenty metres, transfixed both the Awian ambassador and his horse.

The venerable astrolabe clock high in Watchersgate's tower was called 'The Waites'. Its iron rods started to grind as I passed and it querulously struck two. The damn thing was attached to a mechanical organ that played automatically at dawn to wake the town's workers. If they didn't pay their taxes it was left tinkling continually to remind them. It only had one hand, because back when Hacilith was a walled town, the hour was all you needed to know.

Cyan was still locked off deep in a tiny, animal part of her brain. I didn't know if she would ever come out, or if what crept back out would still be Cyan. I was terrified for her – and for myself – how the fuck was I going to explain this to Lightning?

'Cyan, scolopendium is powerful shit. Nobody knows better than me on this subject, nobody! When I overdosed the Circle always bailed me out. I based my life round that cycle of "feel good, feel bad". But you can't shrug it off like I can. I've seen what it does to Zascai who don't respect it. I've seen too many die. Stupid girl! What did you do it for? You've got to be already screwed up if you're taking to drugs. Some people need it but what pain could you have?

'Oh, god, oh god. Don't worry, Cyan, I won't let you die. I'm the one who's good at becoming addicted, not you. I'm the one who leaves used needles around the place. I wake up junk sick. I punish myself for taking it by taking more. I'm the one who shoots enough to kill a destrier, not you. You'll be fine . . . Nearly there . . . keep breathing . . . please keep breathing . . . Oh, god. Why did you come here in the first place? The city is a cess pool, where the same shit goes round and round and round!'

I continued blethering in low and high Awian, then in Morenzian and its old and middle forms, Plainslands and its Ghallain and Ressond dialects, ancient pre-vowel-shift Awian, Trisian and Scree. I could tell I was closing in on the university, because the number of brothels was increasing.

Five minutes and eleven languages later I reached the south end of Old Town, and the curlicued gates of Hacilith University, the oldest university in the world.

The university's gates were always open, just as the Castle's gates are always open. Its red oriflamme pennant flew from a pole beside them, representing the light of knowledge. I sped through the gates, ignoring the porters shouting behind me.

I flitted into the shadow of a residential hall and quietly along the path, leaning sideways to counteract Cyan's weight. Her stockinged feet jutted out in front from the end of the bedspread roll.

The university buildings were older as I neared its centre. Joss stick smoke caught at the back of my throat. Student poverty everywhere smells of cheap incense and burnt toast. Light diffused from oilcloth windows, each of which gave onto a different student's room. They were silent – not tranquil – ominously dead quiet so I feverishly envisioned every undergraduate inside had been murdered in a different way. But worse still – they were cramming for exams. My imagination removed the outer wall, so each square room was suddenly visible in a cutaway like pigeonholes. Each room has a lamp, a book-laden table, a chair, a scholar sitting pen in hand. One lies on the bed, one sits on the floor. Each one works by himself, no one talks to another. Hundreds of individual student's lives are separated in tiny rooms in a huge building; they reminded me of polyps in a coral.

I clattered through a courtyard, past a marble statue of the founder, so ancient it wore a doublet and hose. An old professor stood in its shadow with two prostitutes, male and female, on the plinth in front of him. They were stroking his bald head and I heard their silky voices, 'You're sexy . . . you're so sexy . . .' The don was shaking but I couldn't tell whether it was from fear or excitement. They didn't look up as I hurtled past.

Now in the very centre of the university I came to an unsurfaced track. I slowed my pace in awe, feeling as if I had walked back in time. Stony and yellow in the lamplight the track ran for a few hundred metres and stopped at the perimeter fence. It did not join nor bear any resemblance to any road in the modern Hacilith street plan. The city I knew had been built around it and the university's buildings now hemmed it in. It was sixteen hundred years old – a road when Old Town was all of Hacilith, the only town in Morenzia, and the country was ruled by a king from a palace god-knows-where in Litanee. The wattle-and-daub houses along the track had decayed over a millennium ago, but the College of Surgeons survived.

I walked across and jumped the remains of a deep stone gutter. It once drained stinking effluent from the boilers that had reduced cadavers of paupers and rarities to skeletons for teaching aids. I hammered with my free hand at a nail-studded door. 'Rayne! Rayne! Help!'

Cyan's body convulsed and she vomited down my back. 'Oh, god! Well, better out than in, I suppose . . . Ella Rayne! Open up!'

Rayne's squat, square tower was once the College of Surgeons. Other faculties, refectories and dorms had gradually aggregated around its revered centre of learning – the university formed in much the same way as flowstone in a Lowespass cave. It was officially founded in the fifteenth century, only because it was no longer convenient for the faculties to ignore each other.

The tower's sixteen hundred years gave it a serious gravity. The newer buildings would have overshadowed it if the university had not built them at a respectful distance. Small bifora windows let meagre light into its upper level where a three-tiered lecture hall, now disused, once doubled as a dissecting room and operating theatre. Its roof was flat and its walls unmasoned stone, apart from the deep arch around the door decorated with several bands of zigzag carving. Ironically, given Rayne's origins, the university had presented the building to her, and when she was not at the Castle or the front she lived here among her cabinet of curiosities.

A shutter slid open and Rayne peered out through its iron grille. 'Comet!' She clanged the shutter and creaked the door open. 'Wha' are you doing here?'

'Thank fuck!' I pushed past her into the room, seeing stacks of chests and medicine boxes packed ready for removal.

Rayne said, 'You're supposed t' be a' th' dam. My carriage is on i's way. Wha' – you're covered in blood!'

She grasped her brown skirts and hurried after me, as I loped through the museum and a doorway leading to her bedroom. Her pudgy, purplish feet bulged out between her sandal straps. She had been seventy-eight for fourteen hundred and five years, the oldest Eszai, and the oldest person in the world apart from the Emperor himself.

I strode to her box-bed, set into a deep niche in the wall hidden by a curtain. I laid Cyan down gently inside it, on the crochet blanket, and unwrapped her. Rayne saw a patient and immediately hastened to examine her with quick, expert movements, while she bombarded me with questions: 'She's no' bleeding. Whose blood is i' then? Wha's happened t' th' lass?'

'She's Lightning's daughter,' I said, swaying.

Rayne stopped and looked up at me. 'Cyan Dei?'

'Cyan Peregrine.'

'Has she been mugged? No. There's no concussion. I's drugs, isn' i', Jant?'

'Cat.'

She knelt and turned Cyan on her side to prevent her swallowing her tongue. She observed the girl's violet-grey face, her clicking, shallow breathing. She pressed her dimpled fingers against Cyan's neck for her pulse. 'Obstruc'ed air passages. Bradycardia. Classic scolopendium poisoning. Wha' have you done t' her?'

'It's not my fault.'

'Yes, i' is. Of course i' is! How did you give her i'?'

'It wasn't me!'

'You're a born liar! You're tot'ring, yourself! Oh, Jant, I hoped you wouldn' take i' again. I hoped you'd learned your lesson. You can' be bored, you should be occupied wi' t' dam.'

'I haven't touched cat for five years!'

'You haven' made t' decade. You're no' truly cured.'

'Please,' I begged Rayne. 'Don't jump to conclusions.' The appeal to objectivity quietened her long enough for me to shoehorn a word in. 'Cyan did it to herself. I wasn't there. She bought it from a Zascai, cocktailed with alcohol and god knows what else. A knackered old junkie showed her how to shoot it and for all I know they shared a needle. At any rate, it was back-flushed. I found her already under. I gave her the kiss of life and I'm still trying to get her taste out of my mouth! I killed the dealer –' I tugged my shirt demonstratively, pulling the material, hard with clotting blood, from where it had stuck to my chest.

'You murdered a Zascai?'

'I never murdered a Zascai who wasn't the better for it.'

'Shi'. If t' Emperor finds ou', he'll ...'

'Nobody is going to find anything out. Are they?'

'I –'

'*Are* they, Rayne?'

'No.'

'He was a corporal and he'd turned his whole squad into a gang. They probably were, before they were recruited. Fuck ... Select Fyrd pressganging street scum. If I catch any of them again I'll pump them full of twenty poisons ... Anyway, they didn't know that I'm twice as fast as a human. Well, nearly, 'cause I *am* the worse for drink but I'm not stoned.'

'No. You're replacing one drug with another.' Rayne had her back to me but I saw her expression reflected in the mirror by the bed. She was preoccupied with Cyan.

In Rayne's white bedroom, the eye slid along arrangements of objects as smoothly as a scale of music. Models used for teaching stood on the mantelpiece; large anatomical figures of a man and woman, accurate and to scale. There were painted clastic models of torsos with removable organs like a jigsaw, and a 'wound man' demonstrating various injuries.

Mice were carved seamlessly onto the furniture, scurrying up the chair legs and nibbling the table edge. But netting held the far wall together: ancient goat hair and wood laths showed through the flaking plaster. A bookcase dominated the corner – the books she had written – and it was buckling under the sheer weight of paper.

Cyan wants experience. She'll run headlong into ordeals like this and each one will chop a bit off her teenage enthusiasm until it's down to adult size. I looked at her slack face and burned with fury. 'Is this what you bloody want? Tell me, does it make your party go with a swing? People like Rawney don't want you. He wants to be *like* you! I know, I always did! Did you think it was funny? Well, it's really fucking hilarious. Look at me; I'm laughing!'

'Jant . . .' Rayne said.

'It's fine to be an outsider by choice, but if you get addicted you'll be an outsider by necessity! Then you'll be the loneliest posh minx in the world!'

'Calm down! OK, Jant, you're no' t' blame. I believe you.'

I pulled up a three-legged stool and sat down heavily, legs apart, wings splayed to the floor. I stripped my vomit-covered shirt off and scratched at the bald spots in the pits of my wings. 'Can you bring her round?'

'We may jus' have t' wai'.' Rayne rang a small hand bell. She asked her servant to go across to the medical faculty and bring atropine, and some clean clothes for me.

'I'll do it,' I offered. 'I'm faster.'

'She knows her way through t' complex. And I don' trus' you wi' th' key t' th' vaul's.' Rayne filled a glass of water, took a dropper from the drawer and began to drip water onto Cyan's lips. 'I used t' do this for you, when you had i' bad.'

I huffed. The last time I fell asleep under the influence, Wrenn and Tornado shaved my head and painted me blue. I woke up shackled to the prow railings of the Sute Ferry. I haven't taken cat since. You can face down death, by choosing the harder alternative. Not that I'm overly brave or more than usually lucky; I simply never believed death was an option so I never took it. 'You can't begrudge me a little escape now and again. I'm immortal, I need to lose track of time.'

'You risk losing too much.'

'Yeah, well, the only excitement in immortality is a possibility of loss.'

Rayne grunted vaguely.

I indicated the anatomical male carving. 'He's well-endowed, isn't he?'

She looked up. 'No, tha's t' average size.'

I was never any good at waiting. I paced through to the museum and stood blinking until my eyes adjusted. Rayne's museum, representing her workshop through the ages, was a vast collection so tightly packed together it overwhelmed. Candlelight reflected on the curved surfaces of glass jars, thousands of different sizes, and on the sliding door of a *materia medica* cabinet with tiny square drawers for herbs. What to look at first? Here and there I noticed an object because of its special rarity: a two-headed foetus floating in a jar; or its great size: a broken sea krait tooth; or its beauty: a baby vanished to nothing but a three-dimensional plexus of red and blue veins and arteries to show the dissector's skill; or its ghastliness: the preserved face of a child who died of smallpox. Some objects caught my eye because they were illustrated in the etched plates of books I'd read.

I stepped back, trying to perceive an order to the collection. In the centre a grey stone fireplace housed a copper alembic with a spout, resting on a little earthenware furnace with a bellows handle projecting. It was for fraction-distilling aromatic oils. The lintel above it bore the deeply incised and gilded legend: 'Observe nature, your only teacher.'

I looked at the anatomical preparations: dense white shapes in jars, organs folded, wrinkled or bulging, or feathery and delicate like branching lungs. Alcohol preserved specimens like paperweights, of this or that organ in sagittal or cross section. Living with these, Rayne must see people as machines, nothing but arrangements of tissues and liquids, interesting puzzles to solve. She also knows that individuality is mostly skin-deep because, inside, people are all the same. Rayne and Frost, I reflected, had many traits in common.

Her reference collection was ordered by pathology. Some samples were hundreds of years old – the only immortality available to Zascai by virtue of their interesting ailments. The sufferers usually readily agree to be preserved; it's all one to them whether their useless remains are placed in the ground or in a jar. The only exception are Awians, who prefer to be interred in tombs as florid as they can afford, as if they want to take up space forever.

A glass case housed a collection of surgical instruments past and present – steel bone saws and silver catheters, water baths for small dissections. Rayne kept some – like cylindrical saw-edged trepanning drills and equipment for cupping and blood letting – to remind the world of the doctors' disgusting practices to which she put an end when she joined the Circle.

A six-fingered hand, a flaky syphilitic skull. A hydrocephalic one five times normal size, and the skeleton of a man with four wings growing out of his chest.

Rayne uses me in demonstrations when I'm available. I pose at the front of the auditorium while she lectures the students on how weird I am, or on her great achievement in healing my Slake Cross injuries. One day my skeleton might stand here to be prodded by subsequent generations, my strong, gracile fingers adapted for climbing, my curve-boned wings articulated to stretch full length to their pointed phalanges.

Beside the door I'd come in by stood a large showcase of chipped stone arrowheads, which Rayne had arranged into an attractive pattern. She buys them for a few pence each from boys who pick them up on the Awndyn Downs. There was also a 'piece of iron that fell from the sky onto Shivel'. On the other side of the door a skeleton inhabited a tall cabinet; its label said: 'Ancient Awian, from a cave in Brobuxen, Ressond'.

Over two thousand years the grey smell of old bone and neat alcohol had saturated the tower's very fabric. It was a haze of carbolic and formalin. Spicy volatile notes of orange and clove must be the essential oils Rayne had most recently prepared.

I examined the labelled majolica jars: oenomel, rodomel and hippocras; storax, orchis and sumac. Patent medicines crusted or deliquesced in slipware pots. Their names skipped off the tongue like a schoolyard rhyme: Coucal's Carminiative Embrocation; Popinjay Pills for Pale People; Ms Twite's Soothing Syrup; Cornstock Electuary; Emulsion Lung Tonic; World-Famed Blood Mixture; Dr Whinchat of Brandoch's Swamp-root Kidney Cure; Fruit Salt; Spa Mud; Abortion Lotion; Concentrated Essence of Cinnamon for Toothache; Confection of Cod Livers; Balsamic Elixir for Inflamed Nipples; Bezon & Bro. Best Beet Juice. A pot with a spout: Goosander Lewin's Improved Inhaler. Preparation of Bone Marrow: an Ideal Fat Food for Children and Invalids; Odiferous Macassar for Embellishing the Feathers and Preventing Them Falling Out.

'I' doesn' work,' Rayne said.

'What, any of it?' I asked, but I turned and saw she was referring to the atropine, which her servant had brought, and she had mixed a miniscule amount with the water drops she was squeezing into Cyan's mouth. 'This should work. Why doesn' i'?' she said, annoyed. 'I' brings you round, on t' times I try i' wi' you. I daren' give her more than this. Do you know how much she took?'

'No...' I suddenly remembered I had the wrap in my pocket. I stopped moping around the museum and joined her in the bedroom. 'But I can assay it. I picked up her scolopendium from the barge.'

'Of course, you would.'

I sighed. 'Just don't let me put my fingers in my mouth.' I cautiously brought out the wrap – the sight of it triggered my craving and damp sprang up on the palms of my hands. Truly we are nothing but chemicals.

'Don' give in,' said Rayne, over her shoulder.

I pinched the bridge of my nose. 'I . . . I can't . . .'

'So you'll give in? Think of t' disadvantages – look a' her! Remember how bad you feel for six months after kicking. You're doing well now; each time you ge' clean i's for slightly longer. The balance has tipped.'

I calmed myself, thinking; no one is asking me to do without it permanently. I said, 'It's cooked at source somewhere in Ladygrace. But is it cut?'

The rounded hills of Ladygrace, where scolopendium fern grows, have that name because as you approach from a distance their profile looks like a voluptuous woman lying on her back with her knees in the air. The most difficult part of the route is shipping the finished product across the Moren estuary. It never occurred to me, when I was ripping off Dotterel's shop and selling at the wharves, how much more money I could have made smuggling by air.

I poured water into another glass and delicately shook the paper over it. Grains fell out and dissolved on impact with the surface, leaving no residue. Even the largest had gone before it fell half a centimetre through the water column.

'Shit, it's pure. Maybe eighty to ninety per cent . . . If I hadn't used for a while I wouldn't shoot this.'

Rayne said, 'If Cyan was buying, I think she could prob'ly afford pure.'

'That's what killed Sharny. He wouldn't have been used to it. He didn't even have time to take the tourniquet off . . .' I imagined him thinking – some bastard's cut this – then the fact it isn't cut hits with full strength. His hands clench, he struggles for breath but it's clear there won't be a next one.

Feeling suddenly nauseous I dumped it in the fire and wiped my hands. 'It'd lay *me* out.'

'For how long?'

'A day and a half. Is she likely to die?'

'I can' tell. But if she does i's no' my faul'.'

'I'm fucked. What will Saker do when I tell him his only daughter is in a coma from a massive overdose? I'm the only junky he knows. He'll shoot me!'

'Mmm.'

'When I first saw her I drooled like a dog on a feast day. I thought she was feek! She was a mink!' I ran out of slang and just scooped a feminine body out of the air with a couple of hand movements. 'But now she looks like a corpse! They called it jook, not cat, or I would have known!'

We called the stuff cat because it makes you act like one, roaming all night on the buzz at first, then languid and prone to lying around.

'Did you jus' throw i' *all* away?'

'Yes.'

The night wore on, mercilessly. I put on the clothes the servant had found for me, though they were not svelte enough to fit – I have to have clothes made to measure – and the shirt was red. Red is not my colour at all. I ate some bread, but it didn't cure my hangover. The liquor settled in my gut, leaching water from my body and diluting it. The water I drank turned straight into piss and I was still so dehydrated my tongue clacked on the roof of my mouth like a leather strap. I felt as if my skin was drying; my fingertips were wrinkled and a headache like a steel band tightened round my temples. My heartbeat shook my whole body, and I scarcely knew what to do with my hands.

Pit.

I looked up. 'What's that noise?'

'I don' hear any noise,' Rayne said.

'That noise like water drops?'

'Look around,' she said. 'My collections are valuable.'

I did so and noticed a movement on the first turn of the spiral steps where the staircase rose into the gloom. A worm was crawling there. As I watched, another one fell from the upper floor. It wriggled to the edge of the step, tumbled over and dropped onto the step below. *Pit.* Another one fell. *Pit, pit.* The worms began descending the steps with a determination I could only attribute to one thing. They were dropping faster now, like the first giant drops of a rainstorm. *Pit-pitpitplopplopplopplopplop*, in ones and twos, linked together. The austere steps began to disappear under their pink flesh.

Rayne yelled, 'Worms? Where are they coming from? An infesta' ion?'

'It's worse than that,' I said.

'I had t' theatre cleaned this morning!' She glanced from them to her patient.

I said, 'It's from the Shift. It's called the Vermiform.'

'Is i' safe?'

'No . . .' I giggled. 'It's not safe.'

With a sound like flesh tearing, a curtain of worms appeared over the top of the spiral stair. It started to tatter as individuals fell from it. Large holes appeared, a rent, the curtain swung sideways and fell with a slap onto the steps then began to undulate as it slithered down them.

A flake of plaster fell off the wall, leaving a round hole. Something that looked like the end of a twined rope spewed out, then all of a sudden swelled to the thickness of an arm, and a mouth formed on the end. Under the plaster, flesh seemed to continue in all directions. The mouth bobbed closer to me, then back, as the mass undulated. It said, 'Go to the door.'

'Go to the door!'

A crack ran from the hole and raced splintering along the wall, then forced out another flake of plaster. A thin cord, rolled like a butterfly's tongue, unspooled from the hole and hung, dangling, a mouth on a flesh tube. 'Go to the door.'

It touched the floor and dissociated into long worms that went crawling out in all directions. More mouths started sprouting from the bases of beams, the corners of the room, 'Go to the door! Go to the door!'

Rayne's face was set with fear but she didn't back off. She went to the grate and picked up the coal shovel. 'Wha' is i'?'

'Don't bother. Even if you hit it you can't harm it. It's a colony of worms and it's sentient.'

The Doctor nodded sagely. 'I'll le' you handle i'.' She went to stand next to Cyan, still holding the shovel. As far as she was concerned, her most important task was to protect her patient.

The handle of the outside door turned. Rayne and I glanced at each other. The door burst open and the Vermiform woman flowed in. Ten arms appeared from all over her, waved at me, then sucked back into her. She was much larger than last time I saw her; her worms must have bred, and though her shape and features were pretty her skin was a padded, pulsating mass. Added to the pink tide toppling down the stairs and falling from the ceiling the Vermiform must be huge, and this time I could hear it. Its worms made a rasping noise as they stretched, contracted, slid, with invisibly small bristles. They seethed and pressed like maggots and gave off a stink like urine-ridden sawdust, like old piss.

Through the open door I saw that the statue of the university's founder had gone. That was even more horrific – I couldn't stand the thought of the statue wandering around out there. I stared at the empty plinth until I realised that must have been the place where the Vermiform Shifted through and it had crumbled the marble into rubble.

More worms were pouring through the plaster as if Rayne's room was moving. They twitched out of the ceiling and wound down the wall. They knocked her models onto their sides, and swept them off the mantelpiece. From her shelves a stack of tiles on which pills were made fell and shattered. A flask smashed, spilling heavy mercury. Its curved shards rocked like giant fingernails. A jar tipped over and ovate white pills cascaded onto the floor.

Rayne flinched. 'Hey! Stop destroying my house!'

The worm-woman created two more beautiful female heads on stalks from somewhere in its belly and raised them to the level of the first one. It moved them about in front of my face. I couldn't choose which to focus on and I felt myself going cross-eyed.

'Are you the same Vermiform as before?' I asked it.

'We are always the same.'

'Well, you've grown.'

'We were asked to find you, Comet, although we do not appreciate being a Messenger's messenger. Cyan is in Osseous – for the moment. She is in deadly danger. She is trapped in the Gabbleratchet.'

The Vermiform paused, as if it expected me to know what the fuck it was talking about. Its surface covering the walls smoothed and stilled, lowering slightly as the worms packed closer together. It became denser and more solid, and the shapes of the furniture buried under it bulged out more clearly. I had the impression it was deeply afraid.

Rayne asked, 'Gabbleratche'? Wha's tha'?'

'Why are you frightened?' I added.

The layers of worms blistered as individuals stretched up indignantly. They looked like fibres fraying from a flesh-coloured tapestry. The necks bent and the heads swayed. Their lips moved simultaneously, and its voice chorused like thousands of people speaking at once: 'The eternal hunt. It is travelling through Osseous at the moment. We must try to intercept it before it veers into another world carrying Cyan away for good. We cannot predict it. No one can pursue it. Time is of the essence.' The worms around my feet reached up thin strands and spun around my legs.

I tried to wipe them off. 'What do you mean, "we"? I can't Shift. If I take an overdose the Emperor would feel it. He promised he would cut my link to the Circle and let me die.'

At the other end of the room the worm tentacles were picking Rayne's clothes out of the wardrobe, filling them, and making them dance about. Rayne folded her arms. 'Tell us more.'

This vexed the Vermiform. 'Dunlin asked me to fetch Comet, not an old woman.'

'An old woman! Do you know . . . ! Dunlin? . . . Jant, why is i' talking abou' Dunlin? Does i' mean t' former King?'

'Yes. He's still alive, in the Shift.'

'*Jant!* Wha' have you done?'

'I'll tell you later.' I addressed the Vermiform: 'Did Dunlin see Cyan?'

'Yes. He saw the Gabbleratchet snatch her. Dunlin was advising Membury, the Equinne's leader, how to wage war against the Insects when the hunt appeared. We saw it cut a swathe through the Equinne troops. Those who survived have taken shelter in their barns.'

'Can't Dunlin command these eternal hunters?'

'No. The Gabbleratchet is unfixed in time and space. It was ancient even before the Somatopolis achieved consciousness. We do not pretend to understand it. It never separates and nothing controls it. It eats what it rides down. Cyan mounted a horse when the hunt was still and it ran with her. Like the others it has abducted she will fly until she dies of starvation.'

'*Fly*?'

'Yes. Be careful the instant you arrive. We are easy prey. If it catches us, it will tear us apart.' The Vermiform's three heads on long necks danced about on the surface of the worm quilt like droplets of water on a hot stove. 'We will take you through bodily, without causing a separation of mind and body. It will not strain the circle that suspends time for you, so none of your co-immortals will feel the effect of it labouring to keep you together.'

I shook my head. 'I don't like the sound of this. So I won't be a tourist in the Shift but actually there in the flesh? So this 'Ratchet thing can eat me? No way, it's too dangerous.'

The Vermiform washed up around my legs and bound them together. 'Make haste. Be ready.'

I wasn't ready at all! The room started shrinking: the ceiling was lowering. It drooped in the middle, sagged down, brushed my head. The corners of the walls and the right angles where they met the ceiling smoothed into curves, making the room an oval. I saw Rayne protecting Cyan with her coal shovel raised, then the walls pressed in and obliterated my view. They came closer and closer, dimming the light.

From the box-bed Rayne must have seen worms hanging down from the ceiling, bulging out from the walls, passing her; closing in and leaving the furniture clear until they tightened around me in a flesh-coloured cocoon.

I struggled but the Vermiform held my legs tight. The meshed worms masked my face. I closed my eyes but I felt them squirming against the lids. They let me take a deep breath, then pressed firmly over my lips. Worms closed tightly around my head, all over my body, seething upon my bare skin. I pushed against its firm surface but had no effect. It was like one great muscle.

I couldn't move, panicked. I was bundled tight! Hard worms gagged me. My chest was hurting, every muscle between every rib was screaming to exhale. I was light-headed and dizzy. I lost the sensation in my fingers, my arms. The curved muscle under my lungs burned. I held my breath, knowing there was nothing to inhale but worms.

I couldn't stand it any more. I gulped the stale air back into my mouth and exhaled it all at once. I sucked on the worms and my lungs stayed small, no air to fill them. I started panting tiny breaths. My legs were weak, my whole body felt light. I started blacking out.

The next breath, the worms peeled away and cold fresh air rushed into my lungs. I collapsed to my knees, coughing. The Vermiform extended grotesque tendrils and hauled me upright.

CHAPTER 8

I was standing on the cold Osseous steppe, where the horse people come from. It was twilight and silent; the sky darkening blue with few stars. Around me stretched a flat jadeite plain of featureless grass. A marsh with dwarf willow trees surrounded a shallow river; deep clumps of moss soaking with murky water and haunted by midges. Far on the other side of the river a silhouette line of hazy, scarcely visible hills marked the end of the plain.

In the distance I saw a village of the Equinnes' black and red corrugated metal barns, looking like plain blocks. Between them was one of their large communal barbecues, a stand on a blackened patch of earth where they roast vegetables. A freezing mist oozed out between the barns to lie low over the grassy tundra.

I couldn't see any Equinnes, ominously because they spend most of their time outdoors and only sleep in their barns. They're so friendly they normally race to greet strangers.

The Vermiform had reassembled – she stood a head taller than me. She said, 'We told Membury and the Equinnes that even when the Gabbleratchet vanishes they must not come out for a few hours.'

'Where is it now?' I asked. The Vermiform pointed up to the sky above the hills. I strained to make out a faint grey fleck, moving under the stars at great speed. It turned and seemed to lengthen into a column. I gasped, seeing creatures chasing wildly through the air, weaving around each other.

'It has already seen us,' the Vermiform chorused. Worms began to slough off her randomly and burrow into the grass. 'When I say run, run. It won't be able to stop. Don't run too soon or it will change course. Be swift. Nothing survives it. If it catches you we won't find one drop of blood left. Beware, it also draws people in.'

'What do you mean?'

'Don't look at it for too long. It will mesmerise you.'

It was an indistinguishable, broiling crowd, a long train of specks racing along, weaving stitches in and out of the sky. Their movement was absolutely chaotic. They vanished, reappeared a few kilometres on, for the length of three hundred or so metres, and vanished again. I blinked, thinking my eyes were tricking me.

'It is Shifting between here and some other world,' said the Vermiform, whose lower worms were increasingly questing about in the grass.

The hunt turned towards us in a curve; its trail receded into the distance. Closer, at its fore, individual dots resolved as jet-black horses and hounds. The horses were larger than the greatest destriers and between, around, in front of their flying hooves ran hounds bigger than wolves. Black manes and tails streamed and tattered, unnaturally long. The dogs' eyes burned, reflecting starlight, the horses' coats shone. There were countless animals – or what looked like animals – acting as one being, possessed of only one sense: to kill. Hooves scraped the air, claws raked as they flew. They reared like the froth on a wave, and behind them the arc of identical horses and hounds stretched in their wake.

They were shrieking like a myriad newborn babies. Dulled by distance it sounded almost plaintive. Closer, their size grew, their screaming swelled. As I stared at them, they changed. Yellow-white flickers showed here and there in the tight pack. All at different rates but quickly, their hides were rotting and peeling away. Some were already skeletons, empty ribs and bone legs. The hounds' slobbering mouths decayed to black void maws and sharp teeth curving back to the ears. Above them, the horses transformed between articulated skeletons and full-fleshed beasts. Their skulls nodded on vertebral columns as they ran. Closer, their high, empty eyesockets drew me in. As I watched, the skeleton rebuilt to a stallion – rotten white eyes; glazed recently dead eyes; aware and living eyes rolled to focus on us.

The horse's flanks dulled and festered; strips dropped off its forelegs and vanished. Bones galloped, then sinews appeared binding them, muscle plumped, veins sprang forth, branching over them. Skin regrew; it was whole again, red-stained hooves gleaming. The hounds' tongues lolled, their ears flapped as they rushed through hissing displaced air. All cycled randomly from flesh to bone. Tails lashed like whips, the wind whistled through their rib cages, claws flexed on paw bones like dice. Then fur patched them over and the loose skin under their bellies again rippled in the slipstream. Horses' tails billowed. Their skulls' empty gaps between front and back teeth turned blindly in the air. The Gabbleratchet charged headlong.

I shouted, 'They're rotting into skeletons and back!'

'We *said* they're not stable in time!'

'Fucking – what are they? What are they doing?'

'We wish we knew.' The Vermiform sank down into the ground until just her head was visible, like a toadstool, and then only the top half of her head, her eyes turned up to the sky. Her worms were grubbing between the icy soil grains and leaving me. They kept talking, but their voices were fewer, so faint I could scarcely hear. 'The Gabbleratchet was old before the first brick was laid in Epsilon, or Vista or even Hacilith; aeons ago when Rhydanne were human and Awian precursors could fly –'

'Stop! Please! I don't understand! You've seen it before, haven't you?'

'Our first glimpse of the Gabbleratchet was as long before the dawn of life on your world as the dawn of life on your world is before the present moment.'

Never dying, never tiring, gorged with bloodlust, chasing day and night. The Gabbleratchet surged on, faster than anything I had ever seen. 'How do you think I can outrun *that*?'

'You can't. But you are more nimble; you must outmanoeuvre it.'

I saw Cyan on one of the leading horses! She rode its broad back, decaying ribs. Her blonde hair tussled. Her fingers clutched the prongs of its vertebrae, her arms stiff. She looked sick and worn with terror and exhilaration. I tried to focus on her horse; its withers were straps of dark pink muscle and its globe eyes set tight in pitted flesh. The hounds jumped and jostled each other running around its plunging hooves.

On the backs of many other horses rode skeletons human and non-human, and corpses of various ages. They were long dead of fear or hunger but still riding, held astride by their wind-dried hands. Some horses had many sets of finger-bones entwined in their manes; some carried arms bumping from tangled hands, but the rest of the body had fallen away. They had abducted hundreds over the millennia.

The Gabbleratchet arced straight above me and plunged down vertically. White flashes in the seething storm were the teeth of those in the lead. The moonlight caught eyes and hooves in tiny pulses of reflection.

I had never seen anything fly vertically downward. It shouldn't be able to. It wasn't obeying any physical rules.

Cyan clung on. I wondered if she was still sane.

'Run!' shouted the Vermiform.

The Gabbleratchet's wild joy seized me. I wanted to chase and catch. I wanted the bursting pride of success, the thrill of killing! Their power transfixed me. I loved them! I hated them! I wanted to be one! I tasted blood in my mouth and I accepted it eagerly. My open smile became a snarl.

The dogs' muzzles salivated and their baying tongues curled. They were just above my head. I saw the undersides of the hooves striking down.

'Run!' screamed the Vermiform.

I jumped forward, sprinting at full pelt. The hunt's howling burst the air. Its gale blew my hair over my eyes and I glanced back, into the wind to clear it.

The lead beasts plunged into the ground behind me, and *through* it. The air and ground surface distorted out around them in a double ripple, as if it was gelatinous. The whole hunt trammelled straight down into the earth and forked sparks leapt up around it, crackling out among the grass. It was a solid crush of animal bodies and bone. I saw flashes of detail: fur between paw pads, dirty scapulae, suppurating viscera. The corpses the horses were carrying hit the ground and stayed on top. They broke up, some fell to dust and the creatures following went through them too. Cyan's horse was next; it plunged headfirst into the earth, throwing her against the ground hard. She lay lifeless. The stampede of manes and buttocks continued through her. The column shrank; the last few plummeted at the ground and disappeared into it. Two final violet sparks sidewound across the plain, ceased. All was eerily quiet.

The Vermiform emerged beside me but its voices were awed. 'It'll take a minute to turn around. Quick!'

I ran to the area the Gabbleratchet had passed through, expecting to see a dent in the frozen soil but not one of the grass blades had been bent; the only marks were my own footprints. The hairs on my arms stood up and the air smelt chemical, the same as when I once visited a peel tower that had been struck by lightning. There was no reek of corruption or animals, just the tang of spark-split air.

I turned Cyan over carefully. She had been flung against the ground at high speed – faster than I could fly – and I thought she was dead, but she was breathing.

'I can't see any broken bones. Not that it matters if that thing's driven her mad.'

'Pick her up,' said the Vermiform.

I did so and she jolted awake, gasped, open-mouthed. 'Jant? What are you doing here?'

'Just keep still.' The Vermiform sprang up from under my feet and wrapped around us. More worms appeared, adding to the thread, beginning at my ankles then up to my waist, binding us tightly together.

Cyan waggled her head at the deserted tundra. She screamed, 'Do you have to follow me everywhere? Even into my nightmares?'

The worms nearest her face grouped together into a hand and slapped her.

Cyan spluttered, 'How dare –!'

The hand slapped her again, harder.

'Thanks,' I said.

A horse burst from the ground, bent forelegs first. It pawed the grass without touching it. Its enormous rear hooves paced apart. Long hair feathered over them; its fetlock bones swayed as it put its weight on them and reared.

Cyan wailed, 'What does it want?'

Its fore hooves gouged the air, its long head turned from side to side. It couldn't understand what we were. It sensed us, with whatever senses it had, and it shrieked at us. It could not know its own power nor regulate its voice to our level. It gave us its full unearthly scream, right into my face.

The Vermiform tightened around my legs.

Its tongue curled, its jaw widened, it was bone; no tongue but the jaw dotted with holes for blood vessels and peaks for ligament connections. Its incisors clamped together, the veins appeared running into the bone, the muscles flowered and rotting horseflesh became a whole beast again. It turned its mad, rolling eye on me. Sparks crackled over us, tingling. Hounds and horses began springing up around us. No soil stuck to them; they had treated the earth as if it was another form of air.

The horse arched its neck. I looked up into the convoluted rolled cartilage in its nasal passages. Its jutting nose bones thrust towards me, its jaw wide to bite my face. Slab teeth in living gums came down –

– The Vermiform snatched us away –

Its coils withdrew and dropped me on a hard surface. I sat up and crowed like a cock, 'Hoo-hoo! That was a neat move, Worm-fest!'

Beside me Cyan crawled and spat. I helped her up: 'Are you all right?'

'Jant, what are you *doing* here?'

'I've come to rescue you.'

'*Rescue* me? Sod off! What just happened? Did you see those horse things? ... Argh! Worms! ... What the fuck are these worms?'

'Allow me to introduce you to the Vermiform,' I said. It was writhing around my feet in a shapeless mass. If it had been human, it would have been panting.

'We must keep going,' it chorused.

Cyan said, 'A horse was lying down and it seemed friendly. I climbed on its back. I didn't know *that* was going to happen . . . Oh, god, what *is* this place?'

A water drop landed on my head. Good question. I looked around and realised we were in a gigantic cavern, so vast I could not clearly see the other side.

The sound of a bustling market broke all around us. The stone walls rucked and soared up a hundred metres in the gloom, latticed with ledges from which bats dangled like plums. I gazed up to the roof, into vaults and rifts and wedding-cake tumbles of flowstone arching into darkness. The ceiling dazzled with circular gold and purple jewels, so lambent I was tempted to climb up and collect them until I realised they weren't gems embedded in the stone but water droplets hanging from it. They reflected the cool, blue light from the bulbous tails of Neon Bugs clinging to great trunks of suspended stalactites, bathing the whole chamber in their glow.

Market stalls were laid out in disorderly lines on the uneven floor, filling the cave, and up into a circular tunnel climbing slowly to the surface. Slake Cross town in all its entirety would fit into that passage. Stalls tangled along both sides of it like a thread of commerce linking the cave to Epsilon city's immense market a kilometre or more above us.

'It's Epsilon bazaar!' I said. I'd known it extended underground but I had always turned down invitations to visit. I envisaged a dirty crawl with my head caught and pressed between two planes of rock, my feathers wet and muddied, and my knees popped from kneeling on stony nubs in a stinking stream passage all the way. But this was wonderful!

At the distant end of the tunnel its entrance shone with white sunlight like a disc. Shafts of light angled in, picking out a faint haze in the air. Reflections arced the tunnel walls, showing their smooth and even bore.

I began, 'Well, Cyan, this –'

The Vermiform seethed urgently. 'Explain when we have more time! The Gabbleratchet could be here any second!'

'What?'

'It could be chasing us. If it can still sense us, it will pursue us.'

Cyan said, 'This is weird. In dreams you're not normally able to choose what you say.' She crawled to her feet and wandered off between the stalls.

The Vermiform heaved limply. 'Come back!'

Cyan was looking at the gley men browsing in the aisles. Gley men are completely blind, just a plate of smooth bone where their eyes should be. They feel their way with very long, thin fingers like antennae, touching, touching, searching. They are naked and hairless with milky, translucent, waterproof skin; but underneath it is another skin covered with thick fur, to keep them warm in the deep abyss. You can see through their upper skin to the fur layer pressing and wiping against it.

Cyan didn't seem as repelled by them as I was. She seemed entranced. One of them, by a refreshment stand, was picking cave ferns off the wall and putting them in sandwiches. He had beer bottles, brown and frothy, labelled 'sump water'. He sold white mousse made from the twiggy foam that clings to the roofs of flooded passages. He had boxes of immature stalagmite bumps that looked like fried eggs, breccia cake, talus cones, and crunchy tufa toffee.

Cyan paused at a jewellery stall and examined the cave pearls for sale. She put on a necklace made from broken straw stalactites and looked at her reflection in the mirror-polished shell of a moleusk – one of the metre-long shellfish that burrow far underground.

She didn't know that, as a visitor to the Shift, she could project herself as any image she wanted, so she appeared the way she imagined herself. Like most female Shift tourists Cyan's self-image was nothing like her real body. She was a bit taller, more muscular and plumper, and she wore casual clothes. She looked like a young, unattached fyrd recruit spending her day off in any Hacilith bar. She was slightly less pretty here than in the Fourlands; I suppose that meant she lacked confidence in her looks.

For once, I couldn't alter my appearance. I was here in the body and I planned to take it home intact.

Some stalls sold stencils and crayons for cave paintings. Some displayed everyday objects that 'petrifying water' had turned into stone. Mice with three legs (called trice) ran under the rows and cats very good at catching trice (called trousers) ran after them.

Neon Bugs illuminated beautiful constructions of silk. Replete Spiders hung from the ceiling on spindly, hairless legs, their huge, round abdomens full of treacly slime. It dripped, now and then, on the awnings of the stalls and the tops of our heads. The noisome things lived suspended all the time, and other bugs and centipedes as long as my arm swarmed over the cave walls to bring them morsels and feed them in return for the taste of the sweet gunge they exuded.

The smell of wet pebbles rose from the cavern floor, which descended in a series of dented ripplestone steps to a pool so neatly circular it looked like a hand basin. A waterfall cascaded down a slippery chute, gushing into it. Its roar echoed to us across the immense chamber as a quiet susurration.

Naked gley children were sliding down the chute and splashing into the water where Living Fossil fish swam; the play of their luminous eyes lit up the pool. It was screened by thick, lumpy tallow-yellow stalactites so long they reached the ground and were creeping out over it like wax over a candleholder. Between them chambers and passages led off, descending in different directions into the depths. Most were natural but some were like mine shafts, with timber props and iron rails.

Tortuoise with huge shells crawled frustratingly slowly up and down between the stalls, towing baskets on wheels. There were Silvans, child-shaped shadows who live only in the shade of cave mouths and tree-throws in the forest. At the furthest end of the cavern, where the subterranean denizens who prefer to stay away from the light shop and sell their wares, hibernating Cave Elephants had worn hollows in the velvet sediment.

'Call her back!' the Vermiform chorused. 'The Gabbleratchet could be here any second!'

I glanced at the cave mouth.

The Vermiform said, 'It doesn't need an entrance. It can go any-where! It can go places you can't, where the atmosphere is poisonous: hydrogen, phosphorus, baked beans. You saw that solid rock is nothing to it. It can run straight through a planet without noticing.'

A big, lumpen Vadose was standing by a stall. Cyan realised that the man was made of clay. She sank her fingers into his thigh, pulled out a handful and started moulding it into a ball. The Vadose turned round. 'Excuse me, would you return that, please?'

'It's my dream and I can do what I want!'

'Dream?' articulated the Vadose. 'I assure you, poppet, this is no oneiric episode.'

The ball of clay in Cyan's hands puffed up into a tiny version of the Vadose – it tittered and waved at her. She yelped and dropped it. It ran on little feet to one of the Vadose's thick legs and merged smoothly with it. Cyan slapped his round belly, leaving a palm imprint.

He cried out bashfully and caught the attention of a Doggerel guard stalking past. It was a big bloodhound, bipedal on its hock-kneed back legs, wearing a constable's coat and the helmet of a market guard, black with a gold spike on top. The chin strap was lost in its drooping jowls. It rhymed:

'Shall I remove this silly lass

Who seems to be doing no sort of good?

In fact, you seem in some impasse.'

The Vadose said, 'Yes, if you would.'

It placed its paw on Cyan's shoulder but she wasn't perturbed. She gave it a kick. Its hackles raised; it picked her up, tucked her under one arm and carried her to us. It set Cyan down in front of me:

'Here is your rowdy friend,

Please keep her close.

Otherwise she may offend

One more dangerous than Vadose.'

'Thanks,' I said.

'Talk in rhyme

All the time,' insisted the Doggerel.

'First we are chased, then we are irritated,' the Vermiform complained.

'No, wait,' I said. 'I can do it . . . Thanks for being so lenient

For my friend is no deviant

She's a tourist here for the first time

From now on she'll behave just fine.'

The Doggerel sniggered. 'Only a tourist and she looks so boring?

I'll leave in case she has me snoring.' It strode away with dignity, sturdy tail waving.

Cyan said, 'If this is a jook dream I'm going to do it all the time.' She set off towards the pool but the Vermiform snared her round the waist. She beat her fists at the worms reeling her in. 'Hey! Get off me!'

A small black puppy was trailing her. When she stopped, it sat down on its haunches and looked at her intently. It had pointed ears and alert, intelligent eyes. 'It's following me,' she said. 'It's cute. Makes a change from everything else in here.'

'It's just a Yirn Hound,' the Vermiform said dismissively and pushed it out of the way. It took a couple of steps to the side, resumed staring at Cyan.

'Can I pick it up?' she asked, and as she was speaking another dog padded towards her from under the nearest stall. It sat down and regarded her. She looked puzzled. Another two followed it, clustered close and stared up plaintively. Three more materialised from behind the corner of the next row and joined them.

The Vermiform's surface rippled in a sigh. 'They're desire made manifest. For every want or desire that a young woman has, a Yirn Hound pops into existence. If you stay in this world you won't be able to get rid of them. They will follow you around forever, watching you. Most girls grow accustomed to them, but otherwise Yirn Hounds drive them mad, because until you grow old they'll do nothing but stare at you. You could kill them, but more will appear to fill the space.'

At least twenty little terriers had arrived while the Vermiform was talking. They sat in a rough circle around Cyan's feet and continued to regard her.

'Well, I like them,' she said, bent down to the nearest one and caressed its ears. It allowed itself to be stroked and waggled its head with pleasure. Their crowd thickened, but I couldn't tell where they were coming from – just trotting in from nowhere and taking their places at the edge of the pack.

Their inevitable steady increase repulsed me. I said, 'God, girl, you have a lot of wants.'

'Compared to you? I bet you'd be buried in a pile by now!'

Sparks began to crackle in the tunnels at the far end. I caught a glimpse of the Gabbleratchet thundering in their depths. It more than filled every passage and morphing beasts charged half-in, half-out of the bedrock. Their backs and the tips of their ears projected from the floors: for them, the rock didn't exist. Skeleton horses, rotting horses, horses glowing with rude health reached the tunnel mouths. Paws and pasterns projected from the wall – they burst out! The front of the screeching column came down the cavern in a red and black wave.

'The 'Ratchet!'

I couldn't look away. Their screaming was so deafening Cyan and I clamped our hands to our ears. They tore everybody in their path to shreds – obliterated the Neon Bugs on the walls as they passed, and the lights went out.

The Vermiform wrenched us backwards –

– Bright sunlight burst upon us. I squeezed my eyes shut, blinked, and tasted clean, fresh air. A warm breeze buffed my skin . . . We were on a beach. Cyan yelled, disorientated.

'Precambria!' said the Vermiform. We tumbled out of its grasp onto the yielding sand.

'Good Shift,' I said.

'The Gabbleratchet *is* chasing us!' It quivered. 'We doubt we have thrown it off. We will take you on again.' It pooled down around us, its worms moving fitfully, trying to summon up the energy.

A barren spit curved away into the distance. The aquamarine sea

washed on the outside edge, moulding the compact sand into cor-
rugations. Low, green stromatolite mounds made a marsh all along its
inside. Behind us, on an expanse of featureless dunes, nothing grew
at all. I looked down the spit, out to sea.

A splashing started within its curve. The water began to froth as if
it was boiling. Creatures like lobsters were jumping out and falling
back, lobes along their sides flapping. They had huge black eyes like
doorknobs. One flipped up, and in an instant I saw ranked gills and
an iris-diaphragm mouth whisk open and gnash shut.

Hundreds of crab-things scuttled out of the waters' edge; their
pointed feet stepping from under blue-grey shells with arthropod
finesse. There were long, spiny worms too, undulating on seven pairs
of tentacle-legs.

'Something's chasing them,' said the Vermiform. 'Oh no. No! It's
here already!'

The patch of frothing water surged closer. Cyan and I stared but the
Vermiform started knitting itself around us frantically. Different parts
of it were gabbling different things at once: 'Eat the damn trilobites –
hallucigenia – eat the anomalocaris – but LEAVE US ALONE!'

Straight out of the froth the Gabbleratchet rode, without disturbing
the water's surface by so much as a ripple. Dry hooves flying, the
stream of hunters arced up against the sun. Red eyes and empty
sockets turned to us –

– Endless salt flats. The vast ruins of a city stood on the horizon, its
precarious tower blocks and sand-choked streets little more than
rearing rock formations in the crusted desert that was once the ocean
bed.

'I've been here before,' I said. 'It's Vista.'

'What's that in the distance?' Cyan said, pointing at a bright flash.

'Probably a Bacchante tribe.'

'They're coming closer.'

'They doubtless want to know what the fuck we are.'

After Vista Marchan fell to the Insects, its society transformed again
and again and eventually collapsed completely. At first the people
inhabited the city's ruins, but little by little they left in search of food,
surviving as nomads in the desert. Bacchante tribes are either all male
or all female and they meet together only once a year in a great festivity.
The desert can't sustain them and their numbers are dwindling, but
they roam in and out of Epsilon over the great Insect bridge to survive.

I remembered the only Bacchante I had met. 'Is Mimosa still fighting
the Insects?'

'Yes, with Dunlin,' The Vermiform concurred.

'*King* Dunlin,' I said.

The Vermiform produced its woman's head, and shook it.

'No. Just Dunlin. He has renounced being king. He now presents himself as simply a travelling wise man. He advises many worlds in their struggle against the Insects.'

'Oh.'

'It seems to be a phase he's going through. He is growing very sagacious, but he hasn't yet realised the true extent of his power.'

'Their horses are *shiny*,' said Cyan.

The Bacchantes galloped closer. The four polished legs of each mount flickered, moving much faster than destriers with a chillingly smooth movement and no noise but a distant hum.

'They're horse-shaped machines,' I said. 'They don't have real heads, and no tails at all. They're made of metal.'

'They're made of solar panels,' the Vermiform said.

High over the ruined city, the Gabbleratchet burst through.

The Bacchantes halted in confusion. The black hunters were so much worse against the bright sky. They cast no shadow. Dull, cream-yellow jaws gaped, sewn with white molars. The Bacchantes stared, hypnotised.

The Vermiform screamed at the riders, 'Run!'

The Gabbleratchet plunged down and –

– Splash! Splash!

Freezing muddy water swirled up around me. I sank in a chaos of bubbles. Something tugged me and I broke the surface, spluttering. Up came Cyan, and the Vermiform held us above the algae of a stinking, misty swamp.

The sky was monochrome grey, filled with cloud and a hazy halo where the sun was trying to break through.

'Infusoria Swamp.'

Cyan wiped slime off her face and hair. 'Hey! This is my dream and I want to go somewhere nice!'

'Shut up!' The Vermiform seethed in fury. 'All for you, little girl! We don't see why we have to do this and now we're being chased! We don't know how to get rid of it. We don't know where to go next that won't kill you!'

She shrieked in frustration, grabbed handfuls of worms and tried to squash them but they forced her fists open and crawled out.

'Shifting is sapping our strength,' said the worms.

'Come on!' I shouted at it. 'Let's go.'

'It's my dream so get off me!'

'Stop squeezing us.'

'Piss off and keep pissing off, piss-worms!'

A colossal blob of gel flowed towards us on the water's surface. Flecks and granules churned inside it as if it was a denser portion of the swamp; it extended pseudopodia and started to wrap around the outlying worms.

'What's that?' said Cyan.

'Amoeba.' The Vermiform pulled its worms out and hoisted us up higher with a sucking noise.

'Isn't it rather large?'

'We're very small here.'

'Look at the sky!' said Cyan.

The bright patch was growing in size. Violet forks of lightning cracked the sky in two, leapt to the swamp, hissed and jumped between the reeds. The Gabbleratchet arced out.

The Vermiform gave one completely inhuman scream with all its strength and jerked us out –

– A hot plain with cycads and a volcano on the horizon. Giant lizards were stalking, two-legged, across it towards a huge empty sea urchin shell with a sign saying 'The Echinodome – Sauria's Best Bars'.

A flash of green on the scorched sands before us. The Gabbleratchet burst towards –

– Cyan screamed and we both fell onto a cold floor, knocking the breath out of us. We were in an enclosed space; we Shifted so fast my eyes didn't have time to focus.

The Vermiform parted from us in one great curtain. Its exhausted worms crawled around with Sauria sand and Infusoria gel trickling from between them. I stamped my feet, feeling water squeeze out of my boot lacings.

'We must have thrown it by now,' the worms moaned. 'We must have ... We think ...'

Cyan and I looked up and down the corridor. It was unpainted metal and very dull. 'That's more steel than a whole fyrd of lancers.'

The Vermiform started sending thin runners around the curve of the corridor. 'We're above Plennish,' it said.

'Wow,' said Cyan. 'What an imagination I have.'

I found a tiny, steel-framed window. I stood on tiptoe and tried to peer through the thick glass. 'It must be night time. Look at all the stars.' There certainly were an awful lot of stars out there, filling the whole sky and – the ground! 'Cyan, look at this – there's no ground! There's nothing under us but stars!' I looked up. 'Oh . . . wow . . .'

'Let me see,' she said.

I refused to let her take my place at the little window. I pressed my face to the glass, gazing intently. 'The grey moon fills the whole sky!'

'It isn't a moon,' said the Vermiform. 'It's Plennish. It's grey because it's completely covered in Insect paper.'

'Ah . . . shit . . . All that is Paperlands?'

'Yes.' It sighed. 'The Freezers once tried to bomb it. Now radioactive Insects come from there to infest many other worlds.'

'I'd like to fly around outside. There's so much space.' I looked down again – or up – to the stars. A little one was racing along in relation to the rest, travelling smoothly towards us. It was so faint it was difficult to see. I said, 'A star is moving. It's coming closer fast. Shift us out of here.'

A shiver of apprehension flowed over the Vermiform. 'We can't keep going. We're exhausted.'

'You have to!'

'We can't . . . We can't! Anyway, this is a refuelling dock. If any ship tries to land without the protocol the Triskele Corporation will blow it to cinders.'

I glanced out the window, and saw them from above. Horse skulls like beaks, pinched withers falling to bone. Their long backs carried no corpses now. Sparks crawled around them, flicked up to the window glass; they ploughed straight into and through the metal wall.

'It's the Gabbleratchet!'

Human screams broke out directly underneath us. The Vermiform threw a net of worms around Cyan and myself. Sparks crackled out of the floor beside us. The muzzle of a hound appeared –

Rushing air. I was falling. I turned over, once, and the black bulk of the ground swung up into the sky. The air was very thin, hard to breathe. I fell faster, faster every second.

I forced open my wings, brought them up and buffered as hard as possible against the rushing air. I slowed down instantly, swung out in a curve and suddenly I was flying forwards. I rocketed over the dark landscape. Where was I? And why the fuck had the Vermiform dropped me in the air?

And where was Cyan? Had it separated us? I looked down and searched for her – saw a tiny speck plummeting far below me, shrinking with distance. I folded my wings back, beat hard and dived. She was falling as fast as I could fly. She was spinning head over arse, so all I could see was a tangle of arms and legs, with a flash of white panties every two seconds and nowhere to grab hold of her.

'Stretch out!' I yelled. 'Stretch your arms out!'

No answer – she was semi-conscious. She wouldn't be able to breathe at this altitude. I reached out and grabbed her arm. The speed she was falling dragged it away from me.

She rotated again and I seized a handful of her jumper. I started flapping twice the speed, panting and cursing, the strain in my back and my wings too much. Too much! We were still falling, but slower. My wings shuddered with every great desperate sweep down – and when I raised them for the next beat, we started falling at full speed again.

'Can't you lift her?' said a surprised voice, faint in the slipstream. A wide scarf wafted in front of my face, its ends streaming up above me. It was the Vermiform: it had knitted some worms around my neck!

'Of course I can't!' I yelled. 'I can barely hold my own weight!'

'Oh.'

The scarf began spinning around us, binding us together. More worms appeared and its bulk thickened, sheltering Cyan but her head bobbled against my chest.

We fell for so long we reached a steady speed. I half-closed my eyes, trying to see what sort of land was below us. I could barely distinguish between the ground and the scarcely fainter sky. There were miniscule stars and, low against the far horizon, two sallow moons glossed the tilting flat mountaintops of a mesa landscape with a pallid light.

The ends of the scarf swept in front of my face as they searched the ground. 'I'll lower you.'

It shot out a thick tentacle towards the table-topped mountain. The tentacle dived faster than we were falling, worms unspooling from us and adding to it. It reached the crunchy rubble and anchored there. We slowed; the wind ceased. It began lowering us smoothly, millions of individual worms drawing over each other and taking the strain. They coiled in a pile on the ground. We came down gently on top of them and toppled over in a heap.

The Vermiform uncoiled and stood us on the very edge of an escarpment that fell away sheer to a level lake. Other plateaux cut the clear night sky. In places, their edges had eroded and slipped down into stepped, crumbling cliffs. Deep gorges carved dry and lifeless valleys between them. They gave onto a vast plain cracked across with sheer-sided canyons. The bottom of each, if they had floors at all, were as far below the surface as we were above it.

A series of lakes were so still, without any ripples, they looked heavy and ominous, somehow fake. It was difficult to believe they were water at all, but the stars reflected in their murky depths. The landscape looked as if it was nothing but a thin black sheet punched out with hollow-sided mountains, with great rents torn in it, through which I was looking to starry space beneath. There were no plants, no buildings; the grit lay evenly untouched by any wind.

The Vermiform threw out expansive tendrils. 'How do you like our own world?'

'Is this the Somatopolis?' I said. 'It's empty.'

'It is long dead. We were the Somatopolis, when we lived here. Once our flesh city was the whole world. We covered it up to twice the height of these mountains. We filled those chasms. Now it's bare. We are all that is left of the Somatopolis.'

The pinkish-white moonlight shone on the desolate escarpments. I imagined the whole landscape covered in nothing but worms, kilometres deep. Their surface constantly writhed, filled and reformed. I imagined them sending up meshed towers topped with high parapets loosely tangled together. Their bulk would pull out from continents into isthmuses, into islands; then contract back together, throwing up entire annelid mountain ranges. Caverns would yawn deep in the mass as worms separated, dripping worm stalactites, then would close up again with the horribly meaty pressure of their weight.

'Let's go,' I said. 'The Gabbleratchet will appear any second.'

'Wait until it does,' said the Vermiform. 'We are bringing it here deliberately. We have an idea.'

'The air's so stale,' said Cyan.

'It is used up. The Insects took our world.'

I said, 'Look, Cyan; this is what happens to a world that loses against the Insects.'

The Vermiform raised a tentacle that transformed into a hand, pointing to a plain of familiar grey roofs – the beginning of the Insects' Paperlands. Their raised front arced towards us like a stationary tidal wave and their full extent was lost to view over the unnervingly distant horizon. The cells were cracked and weathered – they were extremely old. They were darker in colour than the Paperlands in our world, but patched with pale regions where Insects had reworked them hundreds of times.

'They bring in material from other places to build with,' said the Vermiform. 'There is nothing left for them to use on my entire planet.'

As we grew accustomed to the distance, we began to distinguish them: tiny specks scurrying over the plain, around the lakes and along the summits. It was like looking down into an enormous ant's nest. I stared, forgetting this was a whole world, and imagined the mountains as tiny undulations in the soil and the Insects the size of ants, busy among them. There were single Insects, groups of a few or crowds of several thousands, questing over the grit from which everything organic had been leached. They swarmed in and out of their hooded tunnels.

The Paperlands bulged up in one or two places and paper bridges emerged, rose up and vanished at their apex. In other places the continuous surface of the roofs sank into deep pits with enormous tunnel openings; places where Insects had found ways through to other worlds. They were carrying food through – a bizarre variety of pieces of plants and animals: legosaurs, Brick Bats, humans, mar-zipalms. Countless millions bustled down there, pausing to stroke antennae together or layering spit onto the edges of the Paperlands with an endless industry and a contented mien. Their sheer numbers dumbfounded and depressed me. I said, 'We'll never be able to beat them.'

'We could have defeated them,' the Vermiform choired. 'We were winning our war. We fought them for hundreds of years. We forced inside their shells, we wrapped around their legs and pulled them apart. We even brought parasites and diseases in from other worlds and infected them, but the Insects chewed the mites off each other and evolved immunity to the diseases, as they eventually do in all the worlds of their range.'

'They're tough,' I said.

'They become so, over many worlds, yes. We turned the battle when lack of air started to slow them down. We gained ground. We forced them back to their original tunnel and they built a final wall. One more strike and we could have driven them through and sealed their route. But then Vista's world collapsed and its colossal ocean drained through. See those lakes? It was their larvae that did for us.'

'Their young?' I asked.

'Once the Insects started to breed in their millions. Their growing larvae are far more ravenous than adults. They scooped up mandibles-full of worms and ate the city.'

Cyan shrieked, 'Look out! There's one coming!'

Twirling antennae appeared over the escarpment edge and an Insect charged towards us. Cyan and I turned to run but the Vermiform shot out two tentacles and grabbed the Insect around its thorax, jerking it to a halt.

The tentacles snaked around the Insect, forced its mandibles wide –

then its serrated mouthparts. The Insect ducked its head and tried to back off, but a third stream of worms began to pour into its mouth, keeping the mandibles open all the time. Worms streamed up from the ground and vanished down its throat.

The rest of the Vermiform still pooled at our feet waited. For a couple of seconds, nothing happened. Then the Insect exploded. Its carapace burst open and flew apart. Its innards splattered against us. Its plates fell in a metre radius leaving six legs and a head lying with a huge knot of worms in the middle where its body had been. They moved like a monstrous ball of string, covered in haemolymph, and reformed into the beautiful woman. The worms of her face moved into a smile. 'We love doing that. Wish they would line up so we can burst them one by one.'

'Ugh,' said Cyan.

I said to her, 'Keep watching for more Insects.'

Cyan said, 'I hate this place. I want to go. I want to see the cave.'

'The market was destroyed.'

'No. This is my dream and I say it wasn't. Take me back; there are too many bugs here.'

'Why do you think I dropped you in the air?' the Vermiform said bitterly.

It was easier to speak to the worm-woman than the amorphous bunch of annelids. I asked her, 'What has the collapse of Vista got to do with you losing the war? Did Vista's sea drown you, or something?'

'It drowned billions of us.' She pointed down to the lake. 'The Somatopolis was dry before that, very hot and arid. That is how we like it; in fact we brought you here during the night because otherwise the sun would roast you. The waterspout surged from an Insect tunnel beneath us and forced up between us. It erupted a kilometre high and Vista's whole ocean thundered out. We fled – how could we cope with running water? Still, it was salt water and we might have survived ... But the ocean began to evaporate, clouds began to form and, for the first time ever in the Somatopolis, we had rain.'

The worm-woman indicated the pools. 'Freshwater lakes formed deep among us. We recoiled from the water and erroneously left it open to the air. And the Insects began to breed. We tried to stop them. We kept fighting but, as our numbers diminished, we found it harder to cover the ground. Generations after generations of larvae decimated us, so we sought shelter under the surface. From there we Shifted to find a new world to colonise ... as many worlds as possible from the construction of the Insect's nest.'

The Vermiform woman dissolved into a snake and slithered to

rejoin the main mass. 'We hope the Gabbleratchet might destroy some Insects,' it added. 'Brace yourselves. We will try to shake it once and for all by retracing our steps.'

We looked around for the Gabbleratchet, in the cloudless sky, against the rounds of the moons, among the peaks of the Paperlands and directly down to the lake.

I thought I saw something moving in it! I blinked and stared. Something was swimming in its murky abyss. It became darker and clearer as it rose close to the surface. It moved with a quick straight jet, then turned head over tail along its length and disappeared into the depths.

'What the fuck? What was that?'

A flash of green on the sheer rock face below us. The Gabbleratchet hurtled straight out of it. Empty white pelvic girdles and scooping paws reflected in the lake.

Cyan screamed. The Gabbleratchet turned; it knew where we were.

'Now!' The Vermiform lifted us off our feet, through –

– Plennish –

– Infusoria Swamp –

– Sauria –

– Precambria –

– Epsilon Market –

– Somewhere dark ... ?

Somewhere dark! Cyan cried, 'Are you there?'

'I'm here, I'm here!' I felt for her hand. I opened my eyes wide, just to be sure, but there was not one shred of light. Then, seemingly in a vast remoteness I saw a faint glow, a thin vertical white beam seemed to ... *walk* past us. It stopped, turned around and began to hurry back again with the motion of a human being, though it was nothing but a single line.

'Where are we?' I demanded. 'You said we were going back to the Fourlands!'

'Stupid creature! This *is* your world. We want to hide for a while in case the Gabbleratchet comes.'

'But ...'

The Vermiform said, 'This is Rayne's room. That is Rayne.'

I think the Vermiform was pointing but I couldn't see anything.

'She is pacing back and forth. She's anxious; in fact, she's panicking. Can't you feel it?'

Curiously enough, I could. The intense emotions were radiating from the white ray and putting me on edge. 'But what's happened to her? That's just a thin line!'

'Hush. If we see the Gabbleratchet's sparks, we will have to leave fast. This is the Fourlands, the fifth to the eighth dimensions. You occupy those as well as the ones you're familiar with, seeing as you've evolved in a world with ten. You can't see them with your usual senses, but you do operate in them. We are amazed that you never consciously realise it.'

Close by, Cyan shouted, 'It's talking crap! Tell it so, Jant.'

'Hey, it's interesting.'

The Vermiform harped on: 'Emotions impress on the fifth dimension, which is why you can sometimes sense a strong emotion or see an image of the person who suffered it, in the same place years later. What other examples can we give? Acupuncture works on the part of you that operates in the sixth dimension, so you'll never be able to understand how it works with the senses you have. And the seventh, if only you knew of that one –'

Cyan screamed, 'Take me home! Take me home *now*! Now! Now! Now!' I could hear her thrashing and kicking at the flaccid worms.

'Think of it as a shadow world,' I told her.

'You goatfucking son of a bastard's bastard's bastard!'

We waited for a long time. The Vermiform eventually said, 'I think we've thrown off the Gabbleratchet. Let's go.'

It gave us a small jolt and our worm-bonds dropped to the floor. Off balance I stumbled forward – into Rayne's bedroom.

CHAPTER 9

Rayne was staring at me, still holding the coal shovel, standing beside the bed where Cyan lay unconscious. I turned to see the cluster of worms behind me, like a tall mould – the back of my head and my folded wings were imprinted in it.

They tumbled to the floor in an inert, exhausted mass; then began to ebb away, slowly and fitfully. Their pool diminished in size as they invisibly poured back into the Shift. When it was about the size of my palm it split into three and dribbled away to the coal scuttle, under the door and between my feet under the rocking chair. I tilted the chair back, but they had gone.

Rayne, with a speed that belied her years, headed off the worms crawling towards the coal scuttle and shovelled them up. She took an empty jar from the shelf and tipped them into it. Then she pressed on the metal lid, held the jar to the light and shook it experimentally. The dollop of worms remained inert at the base.

'T' Vermiform, you say?' she asked.

'That's right.'

'This is a priceless sample. Are t' worms still sentien' when they're separa'ed?'

'I think so. At least, they act independently. I think they're just exhausted.'

She put the jar on the mantelpiece. The worms inside rose up in a wave and pushed against the glass. The jar tipped up, teetered on its edge and clattered back down. The worms collected themselves for another push, so Rayne picked up the jar and wedged it safely between the cushions on the rocking chair.

Cyan jolted awake with a gasp – fell back on the bed. Her eyes were glazed and confused, sockcted with deep purple shadows. Her pale lips were set in a grimace, far from her nonchalant expression of earlier. She was still breathing more shallowly than a fish in the Shift and her limbs were enervated, motionless. She turned her head to one side and vomited over the pillow.

'Cat is addictive!' I shouted at her. 'Don't do it again!'

'Quie', Jant,' said Rayne.

'How could you have even wanted to try it? It's a cure-all for slum kids not stupid rich girls!'

'Quie'! Look, Jant, you can help me. Gelsemium and salicin for her aches. Henbane for her tremors. Hamamelis for her bruising. Go and fetch me all these, and some cotton t' dab in the ointmen'.'

I did, and when Rayne was concentrating on Cyan, I also slipped the jar of worms into the pocket of my new coat.

At length Rayne said, 'I think she will take days t' recover.'

'She can't stay here for days.'

'No.' Rayne glanced at a casement clock, then at the piles of packed equipment. 'Especially no' as my coach will be here within t' hour, and I mus' go t' Slake Cross.'

'Lightning did say to bring her to the front.'

'Wha', like tha'?' We looked at Cyan dubiously. She lay quite still, slowly testing her relaxed body, trying to wake up without throwing up. 'I wouldn' wan' t' move her ...'

'Think of it as another leg of the Grand Tour.'

'I'll "Grand Tour" you! Bloody Awians.'

If we left Cyan, she would go straight back to Galt with a story in her repertoire to add to her growing collection of cool credentials. Rayne seemed to realise this. 'All righ'. I'll take her.'

'Thanks.'

'She migh' benefi' from some advice on t' journey. I'll make sure she's well by t' time she meets Ligh'ning.'

'Don't tell him,' I said.

Rayne pursed her smooth lips. 'I can' promise tha'.'

A faint voice whispered from the direction of the box-bed. 'Help ...'

'Oh, so you've found your voice. You are by far the most stupid girl who ever crossed paths with mine. Jook! Is that what you call it? What did you do it for? Did you think it was a laugh?'

With her eyes shut, she asked quietly, 'Is Sharny dead?'

'Maybe,' I said angrily.

'He is,' she said, resigned. 'He's dead.'

She turned over and slipped out of the bed onto weak legs, staggered, and I caught her. I knew she would be seeing the room as a single flat picture and the objects as shapes. She wouldn't be able to distinguish their depths and the light would create confusing patches of bright and shade that would seem more real and significant than the objects themselves. I delineated a chair for her from the other shapes and made her sit down.

Cyan slurred, 'That trip . . .'

'It's over now.' I spoke slowly and calmly to reassure her, although I knew she'd hear a scrambled version of my words, if she could hear me at all over the roar of her own pulse and breathing.

'Pu' her back in t' bed,' Rayne said.

Cyan's eyes cleared briefly to an avid violent look. 'I had visions.'

'It was real,' I said.

'Now is no' t' time,' Rayne told me warningly.

'I dreamed about *you*.'

'I was there,' I found myself saying. 'I saw it too. Trust me; I used to live with this.'

'No!' She grabbed the nearest object on the dresser – a bamboo birdcage. Her thin fingers sank between the bars. She hefted the cage at an angle, spilling seed and water all over the floor, and the finches inside fluttered madly. She was about to throw it at me, but she gave a little sigh, her eyes rolled up and she toppled out of the chair in a faint, the birdcage still grasped in one hand.

Rayne looked at me with a horrified expression.

'I'll put her in the coach,' I said.

I watched Rayne leave at full speed in a smart coach-and-four. She would change horses at Wichert in Shivel, Shivel town, Slaughterbridge in Eske, Eske town, Carse, Clobest in Micawater, the Rachis valley coaching inns at Merebrigg village, Oscen town, Spraint, Floret and Plow.

I flew.

CHAPTER 10

On the second day I headed towards Awia, passing over the bleak hills of upper Fescue, where the Brome stream meets the Rill and the Foss and becomes the Moren River. Rayne should have reached the Shivel coach stop by now. I hoped Cyan still didn't look two days dead when she arrives at Slake Cross or Rayne is going to have a hard time explaining it to Lightning. I just hope he doesn't connect me with Cyan's condition.

The air was sluggish so I concentrated on its changing shapes as I flew past the quarries at Heshcam and Garron on the Brome stream. The Brome's peaty water, the colour of beer, tumbled out of ghylls between rounded hills topped with millstone grit crags like pie crusts.

Cyan needs to learn who she is. She's as confusing as a shot of pure cat in fourth-day withdrawal. I just hope her experience has taught her not to take the stuff again.

Tapering black chimneys poked up from a cleft between two hills. That's my next landmark – Marram mining town. I flapped towards it tiredly, noticing my shadow on the hillside far to my right.

Marram was tucked in a valley and the roofs and chimneys of the lead and stannary furnaces seemed to take up most of it. I came in very low over the surrounding grey-purple slag heaps. A massive lead crushing wheel turned slowly in an overshot sluice, around which spots of red and yellow were the woollen shawls, head scarves and wide trousers of women picking ore fragments from the machine's trays.

I flapped overhead and they all looked up, began shoving each other and pointing me out. The women seemed glad of a break; they started leering and catcalling. One or two had wings but most were human and they were all very raucous.

One spread her arms and yelled, 'Hey, Comet, where are you sleeping tonight?'

'Wherever they leave me, lover!'

They doubled up with laughter. God, I thought, I can tell this is Fescue.

I couldn't gain height and I flapped around low, making a complete fool of myself until I remembered the smelting furnaces. I circled the tall chimneys and went up like a kite on their updraught.

The roofs of Marram began to spin under me; the smoke-stained houses built in close terraces, the steep narrow roads with ridged cobbles so horses could find purchase. At the edge of town I went over the long, bronze-green roofs of the communal latrines which, by law, all the townspeople had to use. Marram villagers save everything; even barrels of urine for use in alum extraction and the nightsoil to spread as fertiliser on their sparse oat fields.

Higher on the rock face planks and girders shored up a five-metre-wide mine mouth. A dirty piebald pony walked round and round, tethered to a pump capstan at the pit head. The men were all underground already, rooting out copper, tin and lead. These Marram villagers were hollow-eyed and blue-toothed from shale dust and lead fumes, but they were wealthier than the farmers of the Plainslands. Everyone here could own his own house: Lord Governor Darne! Fescue keeps the trade for metals fair.

I was covering distance extremely quickly now, about a hundred kilometres an hour, and in a straight line. On the twisting dirt track roads below, people take a day to travel as far as I can in thirty minutes. I passed into Awia and over Cushat Cote village on Micawater manor's southern border. I flew past Cushat's 'naming court' house, a courtroom where an Awian marriage judiciary meet. They settle disputes as to which of the two married couples' families is the wealthier – a hot topic for status-obsessed featherbacks as the richest bequeaths its name to the children.

The Circle broke.

I blacked out – for a second – came to so quickly I was still gliding, fifty metres lower in a steep dive. The ground filled my vision. I straightened my flight, brought the horizon level, wondering what the fuck had happened.

It had been the Circle, surely? The Circle had just stopped. One of my colleagues had died – I couldn't tell which one. Or maybe – shit – maybe the Emperor has found out I've been in the Shift and that jolt was him dropping *me* from the Circle. Could I be mortal again?

I held my arms out and looked at my hands. Could time be passing for me? I had no way of telling. I can't feel the Circle like the most experienced Eszai sometimes do. I was shaking but I pulled on the air and began to ascend.

The Circle broke.

A second time. It reformed promptly and I spun out of my fall yet lower in the sky. I yelled, 'What's happening?'

The Circle broke.

With a slow sense of void so horribly vacant I screamed. I blanked out for a few seconds and found myself descending still lower. My wingtips touched treetops on each down beat.

I gained height, bracing myself in trepidation of it happening again. Three times! Who'd been killed? Which of us – Lightning? Serein? Frost? The last one had died horribly slowly.

What could injure three Eszai in close succession so badly that the Circle couldn't hold them? In what circumstances could the skill and strength of three of my friends be useless? They were surrounded by troops and fortifications. Could it be a fyrd revolt?

Perhaps I was lucky not to be there. I found myself sobbing, feeling light and drifting. A second of time had passed for me, for all of us, before San reformed the connections. It felt awful, much like the shock on hearing the news that someone you love has died – which is not fair considering that few Eszai love anyone apart from their spouses.

I examined myself. Did I feel tired? Could anyone badly hurt be pulling on the Circle? I couldn't tell.

Shit, shit, shit. Another disaster at Slake Cross and I'm not there. The Emperor will have felt it and he'll be expecting me to come and tell him why – and I don't know! He'll find out I wasn't at the front!

I was cold with rising panic but I forced myself to concentrate. I'm in deep trouble – and so is Lightning – assuming he's still alive. I spoke aloud: 'There's no time to hesitate. I must reach Slake, find out what's happening, then race back to the Castle and take San the news. I'll have to outpace all the dispatch riders and reach the Castle before them, because if any beat me there and tell the Emperor I was absent, he'll have my balls.'

Where the fuck was I, anyway? I looked down on the valley. The oblique morning light cast a shadow of one valley side across the other and the stone buildings of Cushat Cote village at the bottom were still in darkness. The border of Awia. Having got my bearings, I turned sharply. I must steel myself to be prepared for anything. I beat my wings powerfully and flew my fastest towards Slake Cross.

CHAPTER 11

I came upon the baggage train along the Glean Road. It was decimated – nothing was moving down there.

I descended and let the road stream along under me. It was solid with dismembered bodies of men and women, severed heads and limbs. Between the shafts of overturned carts lay the white or chestnut flanks of the hitched horses. Ragged green vegetables and leather-fletched crossbow bolts spilt from the barrels. Dead Insects lay among them, each two metres long. The devastation stretched into the distance along the road. If a swarm has reached this far, what's happening at Slake?

I skimmed over them – the horses and mules were no more than jumbles of bloody hide and entrails, a semi-digested green-shit stench. I could see no sign of the attack having come from any direction – the people lay in equal numbers on both verges as if they didn't know which way to flee. Few were armed. Horses had bolted dragging their carts off the road; they lay on the grass further off, their black hooves raised and rigid.

It didn't make any sense. Where were the live Insects? Once they were out of danger they would always stop and feed but few bodies showed any signs of damage beyond the wounds that had killed them. It was as if a great force had swept through and torn them apart instantaneously.

Here was one of the armoured wagons – steel plate riveted to its wooden sides – designed to be a temporary refuge in case of attack. The worst Insects could do was eat the wheels off and cause it to tumble to the ground. Its doors were firmly shut. As they had to be bolted from inside, somebody must be in there. I landed squarely beside it. On the ground the silence was terrifying. The pools of blood between the carts had dried to brown but the corpses still smelt salty, like fresh meat.

I looked all around, drew my ice axe and banged the haft on the door. I called through an air hole, 'Anyone in here?'

'Just me,' said a young man's voice.

'This is Comet. What happened?'

'Comet!' The voice degenerated into sobs. 'Everything's gone.'

'Open the door. The Insects have left.'

'No!' screamed the man. 'I'm not coming out! Leave me! Leave me here!'

I peered through the air hole but could see only blackness. What would I do with one man crazy with terror in the middle of the Lowespass countryside? 'OK,' I said calmly, 'I'll fly to Slake and send lancers. They'll get you out; you'll be safe.'

'Fly? Safe?' The man started laughing with a horrible high-pitched tone.

I took off and flew as high as I could trying to catch a first glimpse of the town. Beneath me, both sides of the road were 'trap fields' where iron traps had been set. Yellow signposts warned travellers not to leave the highway. The pressure of an Insect's foot on the trigger plate will spring a trap shut and bite the claw off. Now I started to see them, maimed but still alive, moving slowly or spasming on the ground.

I went over the valley head and the moorland pass dropped away – reddish spots were Insects roaming randomly on the slopes. I hastened on, frightened for my friends. This reminded me far too much of 1925.

Slake Cross town sat in the distance, the lake beyond it. A massive misty funnel of black spots was rising high and thin in the air above the lake. It was drifting slightly with the breeze but twisting with a slowness unlike any whirlwind I'd seen. And there was scarcely a wind anyway. I couldn't tell what it was; I stared at it until my eyes hurt. The great spiral towered over the lake and specks cascaded from it like water drops or debris. They rose and fell like soot specks coming off a fire, but they must be huge if I could see them at this distance.

Below me another defence – a 'field of holes' – was full of struggling Insects. Pits had been dug close together over the whole valley floor. Each was two metres square and five deep, straight-sided, concrete-lined with sharp, tar-painted stakes fixed upright in the bottom. I looked directly down into them; some were half-full of Insects skewered on the stakes, in the base of others lone Insects raised their heads, convergent compound eyes glittering. They would try to dig their way out until they wore their claws to stubs.

Further still and I was over the zigzag trenches running parallel with the river. The trenches were square-based, cut in chevrons, so that trapped Insects could be more easily dispatched as they slowed down to scurry round the corners. The trenches trimmed across my field of vision and Insects looking no bigger than ants scuttled up and down them, bristling.

I approached, with a feeling of trepidation like facing the cold wind that precedes a storm. The swirling flurry in the sky was more than five hundred metres tall. The whole sky was mottled with specks bumbling around each other, some over the town, some now between it and me. I concentrated on these, and as I came nearer the space between them seemed to increase. From looking at lots of motes plastered against a blank grey sky I was soon aware of them as individuals hanging in the air. I picked one and closed in on it.

The dot resolved into a dark crescent moving at my altitude with both points facing downwards. Closer still, I could see the crescent had three segments. It was bulky, not streamlined like a bird and I couldn't understand what was keeping it up. Then it turned towards me and I saw its bulbous eyes. It was an Insect! An Insect flying!

I yelled, pulled my wings closed and fell below it just as it swept over my head. Its buzzing nearly deafened me even above the sudden roar of the air stream as I went into freefall. I forced open my wings, looked around, saw I hadn't fallen more than twenty metres, and performed a slow roll so I could look down the length of my body and see it behind me.

A *flying* Insect?

I couldn't believe it was real! It was heading away and starting to turn. I could see its ten bronze-brown abdomen plates, its tail curved and hooked under like a gigantic wasp. Its legs were bunched up under its body, the knee joints sticking out. Above its thorax was a continuous flickering – one, no *two* pairs of long translucent wings, beating so fast they blurred! They protruded from under its thorax's first lamina, attached by a narrow joint that seemed flexible, like a hinge. What *were* these things?

Another one underneath me altered its path, rising up diagonally, but I jinked to one side and it missed. I looked forward, realising what the rising funnel above the reservoir was – a flight of Insects. Thousands upon thousands of winged Insects.

Their massed humming caused the sky to vibrate as if struck, resounding from all directions like the sound of flies on a corpse. It drowned out my own beats.

I have fought ground-bound Insects for so long I was bewildered; I couldn't believe they were doing something different. Are these the same animals? Insects have always had tiny wings. Where have they suddenly got long wings from? And why now? One struck my foot a glancing blow – I dived hastily.

Below me, normal Insects swarmed over the whole valley bottom. They floated dead in the moat, scurried on the road, tore tents down and dragged them over the heather. Trebuchets stood abandoned. Warning beacons blazed on all the peel towers but I could see no other sign of life. A convoy of wagons by the town wall had been chained together to form a laager but every soldier inside the enclosure was dead. The Insects were raining down from above, bypassing our defences, overwhelming everything on the ground.

Arrows pulsed out of the towers' overhanging belfries and irregularly from the covered walkways along the walls of Slake Cross. I thought of Lightning – surely he must be alive, directing the archers? I had to find out what was going on.

I passed over the town and towards the Insect flight. Like a single being, it threw off graceful wisps as myriads tumbled from the apex. Its base was russet with them ascending from their side of the lake.

Every sense was alive as I dodged past the Insects hurtling towards me. I flew low, dropping underneath the main concentrations. I would never see down through the flight if I went above it. I stared out towards the Wall and what I saw took my breath away. On the far side of the lake, against the panorama of the muddy valley bottom, thousands of Insects, no, tens of thousands, were crawling out from irregularly spaced breaches in the white Wall. They blanketed the ground, scuttling slowly and purposefully over the bare earth before the lake. Ranks and ranks of Insects were flowing out. Each had four transparent wings, so long that their wider rounded ends overlapped each one's abdomen and dragged on the ground behind it like a bride's train.

They stopped on the bank. I picked one and focused on it. Its elbowed antennae twirled, even more active than usual, and its head was raised, alertly tasting the air. It turned its head, separated its drooping wings with a mandible and a stretched back leg. It began to twist them up and down with beats. The wings beat faster into a blur and the Insect's back began to arch. It was being tugged up. I could see its feet shifting position and rising until just the tips of its claws touched the ground, then they lifted off and with a tremendous birring the Insect slowly took off from standing, rose into the air and joined lines, skeins, then great clouds of them spiralling up above the Wall.

Hundreds of metres above, the multitudes were converging. Insects clung together in clusters; enormous aggregations of chitin plates and thrumming wings. They were tussling to touch the tips of their abdomens together. They rolled as they fell, losing height rapidly and separating again. When their abdomens retracted I saw sticky strands of mucus stretched between them. They reminded me of ants in . . . in a mating flight!

With this chill realisation I flew a circuit around the rising funnel, risking being attacked, but the insects paid me no attention at all, totally intent on each other. Their numbers seemed to increase and ebb in waves. Individuals in the spiral rose and fell, dropped height and struggled up again, as if with fatigue.

I glided and watched spent Insects tumble out of the spiral, still trailing strands of slime. They righted themselves and descended, drifting south with the wind, around the town and over it. They fell into the town, onto the wreck of canvas outside the walls, onto the glacis between the walls and moat. The moat was completely full of thrashing, hopelessly tangled brown legs and abdomens.

Some landed in the reservoir, or in the river, where they didn't resurface, and I saw the current turning them over and over as it swept them downstream.

Those that survived were suddenly free of their wings, running rapidly back towards the Wall. Whole wings were scattered all over the ground like glinting shards. The Insects trampled them heedlessly. I concentrated on one Insect alone on the river bank. It settled, took hold of its wings with its nearest pair of legs and pulled them off. They didn't leave a wound or a scar, or any sign of the enormous muscles that must surely be driving them.

When the newly grounded Insects reached the lake they joined thousands of others all along the south shore, gathered so densely they were clambering over each other. Many were turning around, dipping their abdomens into the water. What appeared to be streams of froth drifted away from them. All around the lake margin the Insects' tails were pushing out lines of white foam, which lazily tangled with other streams into an irregular lace, drifted towards the lake centre and became indistinct as it slowly sank in the depths.

I put some distance between myself and the chaos of the mating flight to gain a clearer picture of what was happening. Were these different Insects altogether?

The fresh perspective simply brought new questions. More Insects were swarming over the Wall and their saliva was melting the paper as if it was wax. They were working hard to pull out darker lumps from within the liquefying spit. I glided closer to see what was happening – then wished I hadn't. The lumps were cadavers, the remains of soldiers. Free of the spit that had formed the Wall and preserved them, some were so rotten that they began to fall apart. There were horse limbs and heads, whole sheep from Lowespass farms, the feral mastiffs of the forts, and some chunks of matter I couldn't recognise, all covered with the white paste.

The Insects carried them directly to the lake. All along its shores they were wading into the water as deep as their middle leg joint and dropping their burdens. They lowered their heads and nudged the ancient carcasses further in; I could see them bobbing, leaving ripples.

The reservoir edges were filling up with a putrid mass of sodden rotting meat. Chunks washing at the surface and at the water's edge were releasing a thick, dark brown and oily scum that started to resemble broth. They were turning the entire lake into a waterlogged charnel pit. The amount of matter being dumped was displacing the water and the dam's spillway glistened as shallow pulses ran down over its cobbles.

'Oh shit,' I said, for want of a better word. I had never seen Insects do something so complicated. What if they were sentient after all?

The rank smell of rotting fat and skin rose on the breeze, making me retch. I folded an arm over my face and gained height above it, but I knew it would stick in my sinuses for days. I took a last look at the gruesome mess and skimmed away from the lake. More Insects were beginning to build a new Wall around it.

They were ranging freely over the whole countryside, scurrying on the road, feeding on dead men and horses – and carrying fresh pieces, still dripping, back to join the corruption they had made of the lake.

I couldn't stay there, not so close to the stench. It seemed to cling to my feathers no matter how high I flew. I winged towards the town.

High above the gatehouse I saw an Insect buzz through the hail of arrows. They found their mark and it suddenly bloomed with white flights. Shafts stuck out all over it as it passed underneath me. It went into a steep descent, wings beating furiously, and crashed into the roof of the tavern buckling all its legs. Its wings flickered; the time between each vibration lengthened until it died.

I took this as a warning – the steel crossbows mounted on the ramparts have an awesome seven-hundred-metre range – so when I was about a kilometre away from town I climbed high and came in above them.

I looked down into complete confusion. The outermost road of the three concentric squares was totally infested. Soldiers were shooting Insects from the safety of the curtain wall, the large square shutters all hooked back. Archers stood on every available rampart, crossbowmen leant out of windows, rocks and boiling water issued through the machicolations of the hoardings, bombarding the Insects directly underneath. I even saw civilians hurling roof slates into the seething mass.

From the window in the first ring of barracks, spearmen jabbed frenziedly at any Insects getting too close.

In the inner two roads and the central square, smaller numbers of Insects ran at random, claws skittering on the cobbles. Bodies littered the streets. Most of the iron paling gates had been shut across the roads. Others were barricaded with heaps of furniture, anything men could lay their hands on in the panic. Slake Cross was designed so that if a road ring was taken, we could pull back to the next one, and so on, to the middle – but that design depended on Insects attacking on the ground, from outside. The Architect could never have envisaged them dropping in from the sky.

I banked, turning in a shallow glide towards the intense throng continuing to rise into the air above the lake. Their opaque buzzing made it difficult to think and the sweeping movements of the flight were so ultimate, so terrible, it drew my gaze and I watched, hypnotised.

A shout rose over the buzzing: 'Hahay!'

Surprised to hear an Awian hunting cry I glanced down towards the source and saw an Insect pacing me, only a hundred metres below. As I saw it, an arrow storm poured from the walkways. Enfilade shooting from the tower tops caught it in cross-volleys. It twisted in the air. Arrows slashed its wings to ribbons – it seemed to fold up and dropped like a stone, straight down, its abdomen writhing with a blind life of its own. The Insect hit the ground by the moat and splattered – great splits opened up in its carapace and its insides began to seep out, pooling yellow on the grass.

I slewed left and right in acknowledgement at the favour although in reality I was far more alarmed by the prospect of being riddled with arrows than being bitten by the Insect.

Time to show them I didn't need their help. From what I had seen of the Insects' manoeuvrability I was definitely the stronger flyer. I put my hand behind me, unfastened a stud and drew my ice axe from its holster fastened horizontally on my belt. I went into a glide and tapped its steel head thoughtfully against my palm as I circled the town.

I stripped off my bangles and shoved them into my coat, and buttoned my sunglasses into my inside pocket. I positioned myself above the nearest Insect, my shadow covering it. Its dragonfly-like head swivelled: it could see three hundred and sixty degrees around it. It saw me and tried to climb to my altitude, but I was far more agile. I stood on one wing and turned, soared directly over, and gave its rapidly beating wings a good solid kick as I passed. The Insect rocked, righted itself in the air and dived.

I whooped and dived after it. It wouldn't let me stay above its head. I saw dark patches on its compound eyes that looked almost like pupils, one pair on the top, another pair facing forwards. At first I thought they were reflections, then I realised they were areas of smaller facets, set closely together. Perhaps the eyes of these mating Insects are different too; it seemed to see well directly above it. I decided to attack by coming in fast and from the side. I swerved away, turned so steeply the ground and all its towers swung up to my left. I beat with my wings close to my body and bore down on it with full speed.

The Insect saw me too late, jinked, but I rammed into its thorax, grappling so it couldn't turn to grab me. We whirled together, losing height, and the wind stream roared up past us. The ground rotated and spun crazily. I didn't look down, I have a sense of how close I can fall, how big the buildings can grow before I seriously start to panic. I hefted my axe and chopped through its neck. The Insect's head detached and I let it fall but the body flew on thirty metres before tumbling to the ground.

I wheeled away, plastered in yellow blood, yelling in triumph. 'Get out of my sky! Back on the ground, you fuckers!'

I spotted another on the far side of town. I beat upwards, climbing to approach it, then swooped. Its wings whirred beneath me and their wind streamed out my ponytail. I hacked with the axe, missed and collided with its shell back, pushing it downwards in the air. My axe fell free, jerking on its lanyard. My hands were next to the bases of its front wings. They were moving so fast I didn't dare touch them. The great, glassy wings flicked back and forth on either side of me – dry black veins around clear cells – I saw the moorland distorted through their transparent surfaces. I matched its pace, hanging on to the top of it while I recovered my axe and chopped through the base of one wing. The Insect jerked away erratically. Spines on top of its abdomen grazed my hands. It began to fall. Its antennae with ends like strings of beads flicked frantically. Its other wing started beating twice as fast. It spun violently, spiralling tighter and tighter until it hit the road and exploded into a thousand shards.

'Great!' I shouted, and swung into a long turn looking around for more. One was buzzing in a straight path from the mating flight, at around seventy kilometres an hour. I can do twice that. I let it pass overhead, beat hard to come up behind it. Its very thin waist and haze of wings passed beneath me an arm's length away. I tilted, slowed down. The Insect beat faster and it knocked up underneath me, hitting me along the length of my body. I gasped a breath, frightened, then swung my axe and cut through a wing stem. It plummeted away, curling into a ball so tight the pointed tip of its abdomen was over its mandibles. It spun; the brown hunch of its thorax, smooth rounded abdomen, goggle compound eyes.

On the ground, I saw upturned faces and men pointing at me. I grinned and pressed the fingers of my wings together like paddles, pulled the air past me more strongly with the right than the left, rotated as I rose steeply showing them the soles of my boots. Then I fanned out my wings' fingers, came to a standstill for a second, levelled my flight and sped swiftly towards the next Insect, wondering if this is how a peregrine feels.

I ran rings around them. I had no real impact on their numbers but I was more effective than the arrows. I sparred with them for the next three hours until sunset. The swarm above the reservoir was starting to falter and disperse; fewer Insects were crawling out from the Wall. Below me, troops were being marched out of the buildings of the two outermost rings, in an attempt to clear the centre. Civilians packed the hall and church to capacity. I could still see clearly, my eyes had attuned to the dusk and the red-gold smudge of sunset over the hills in the distance. The town's floodlights were abandoned but lamps glowed along the concentric roads and the square. I was exhausted and losing concentration but a few Insects were bombilating in from the flight.

I cut the wings off one and swept on to the next. I soared over and tore a wing, stalled deliberately in front and cracked its head with my boot heels. I glided towards another and dealt it a blow that smashed both antennae roots, knocking it sideways. It turned over and I felt a strong tug above my belt. I looked down – the Insect's back right foot had caught my shirt, its claw had closed and now as it turned away from me it was winding the material around its foot. I pulled frantically at my shirt but I couldn't free it. I yelled and flapped madly – then we plummeted together.

The Insect kicked its extended leg, struggling frantically, and every movement just wound my shirt tighter into a knot around its three claws. I grabbed the hard ankle joint and pulled at it.

The Insect and I began to spin around each other, centripetal force pulling us away from each other the length of its leg. Airflow rushed past faster and faster. I flared my wings, desperately braking, but lying on my side I couldn't gain any purchase on the air. The Insect's underside faced me, the ball and socket joints of its legs under its thorax. Its five other legs razored past as it kicked and it bent at the waist bringing its tail close to my legs. The roaring airstream tore its wings along their length and the loose strips started fluttering around us.

Relative to the Insect I seemed to be stationary but the ground below us swept round faster and faster. I sipped at the rushing air through gritted teeth. The horizon climbed up the sky and the awful gusts buffeted us, blowing my ponytail upwards. The end of it tangled with the Insect's other back foot.

My axe dangled. I grasped its shaft back into my hand and swiped down at the leg projecting from my shirt. I missed. Tried again, and missed. Panicking, I reached down and tapped with little cuts but the angle was impossible. The narrow blade kept chipping past the smooth leg on both sides. I couldn't put any force behind it so even when I did strike the tubular chitin, flattened to barbs on the back, I couldn't sever it. Fuck, fuck, fuck, why do I never carry a sword?

The town blossomed up beneath me. The stone rings opened up; widened; then I lost sight of the outer wall and all beneath me were barracks roofs and the square. I've only got seconds.

I folded my wings in and bent my legs arching my back concave so my feet were almost behind my head. I scrabbled in my boot top for my flick knife. With less drag, we whirled round each other faster – the Insect pulled my shirt and the tight material cut into my waist, restricting me further. I flicked the blade and swept it behind my head, cutting the end of my ponytail free. Then with swift cuts I slashed through my stretched shirt feeling it open up around my sides and tear of its own accord over my stomach. The claw ripped free.

I snapped one wing closed, raised the other and stalled – slipped sideways away from the Insect.

It turned over in the air, legs uppermost, mandibles snapping and antennae whipping. A long bronze line of light reflected from the sunset along the length of its body.

I braked as hard as I could. I spread my feathers wide and flat, fighting against the airflow forcing them up. They hissed and jiggled, bending like bows. I splayed my legs trying to counteract the spin. The distance between me and the Insect increased. It shrank below me. I saw it, still rotating along its length, fall towards a messy impact with the barracks roof.

I did not have enough distance left to stop. I was braking as hard as I could but the spinning roofs were too large, too near. Well, this is it, I thought. This is how it ends. At least it'll be over quickly. I had an image of Tern in my mind like a portrait. I spun as I fell, every couple of seconds, trailing my foot in the corner of my vision. The barracks ring flashed away. I levelled with the towers; they shot above me. I glimpsed soldiers on the ground, their mouths round Os. Detail leapt out: the flags, the cracks between hall roof slabs, grit in the drainpipes. I hugged my arms and legs in tight. I closed my eyes and my mind was already dissociating, awaiting the impact.

Thumpf! I hit something elastic and jolted. I seemed to arc out in a slow trajectory. I almost stopped, then – *crack! crack!* – I tumbled head over feet straight down and hit the ground heavily, backside, wings, and my head jerked back and hit the stone.

Oof. I skidded to a halt feeling my skin burning. I opened my eyes and looked around. I was loosely wrapped in voluminous folds of canvas, through which the lamplights shone orange. The stuff around my face blew in and out with my panting. All right, I thought; I'm alive. I'm on the ground and alive. Ooh, my head. I pressed a hand to it with Eszai stoicism but nothing gave way. I rolled around, winded, and scrabbled at the material but I couldn't find an opening. I stabbed my axe into it, cut a rent and crawled out, onto the cobbles of the central square.

Acres of orange canvas seemed to curl away from me on both sides. I looked at it and saw the massive letters, backwards and upside down: 'Riverworks Company Est. 1692'. A glance up to the roof of the hall told me I had snapped the flagpoles holding Frost's banner. They hung down, trailing it between them.

I hugged my head, rolled over and moaned. My right arm and shoulder were skinned and bleeding profusely. Sliding on the cobbles had worn a hole in the banner, through my jeans' denim as if it was tissue, and blood was trickling down my right leg. My shirt was laddered and my axe scabbard reduced to leather shreds.

I rotated my shoulder, gasping at the pain.

A jangle of chain mail and the flash of plate armour – Tornado was running towards me out of the hall. The front of his helmet was featureless and forbidding. He hooked the visor back and I saw his shocked face. 'Jant, are you all right?'

'I think so . . . I mean, I'm bleeding . . . Shit, I'm bleeding!'

'You lucky bastard.' Tornado pointed at the broken banner. I shrugged lopsidedly at him.

He slipped his shield from his arm and stuck it upright with its spike between the cobbles. It had a printed street map and the horn blast codes pasted on the inside. He hung his axe on top.

Tornado, I'm so glad it's you. I would have wasted hours trying to explain my ordeal to someone with more imagination. Now the nightmare faded rapidly when faced with this bloodstained mail-coiffed frontiersman smiling like a maniac behind a blade I would have been unable to lift.

I said faintly, 'Who's dead? ... I felt the Circle break. Who did we lose?'

'The Lawyer.'

'Gayle? Damn ...'

'Thunder.'

'Thought so.'

'And Hayl.'

'Gayle, Hayl and Thunder ... That's one fuck of a storm ...'

Tornado wiped the edge of the padded hood drawn over his forehead and the thick stubble on his cheeks. 'Come inside.'

I took a couple of steps and stumbled, but he supported me. He said, 'When all this started Hayl rode out to the dam to close the winch tower portcullises. We didn't want Insects to crawl through. Then they started flying! He shut the gates but he, like, never made it back. Thunder was covering him with bombardment from the trebuchets, but the first Insects came down and swamped his crew. He didn't stand a chance, either. Gayle's men tried to stop the artillerists fleeing and she got killed with 'em. Lightning made everyone else stay inside. Flying Insects – I haven't, like, seen anything like this before. We need to tell San. We need Rayne too.'

'She's on her way.' I sighed. Concussion was greying-out my thinking, and I could do nothing more. Tornado walked me into the hall and we pressed through the crowd of civilians and armoured soldiers. Vowing to pretend it was only a hangover I climbed the stairs to my room, still feline but not in as much that cats walk in straight lines. I dressed my skinned arm and leg myself and collapsed on the bed.

CHAPTER 12

The clatter of hooves in the street roused me. I lay with a terrible pain in my arm and a stiff ache in my wings, feeling like death – fast-thawing like a corpse out of the Ilbhinn glacier. I wondered why I was always doing this to myself, until I remembered I came by this pain in the line of duty rather than pleasure.

The sound of hooves intensified, with the jingling of bells. There must be a whole company outside. I tried to get out of bed and gasped as the ache fired into a streak of agony. I slipped a T-shirt on and looked out of the window. It gave onto the second ring; the road below was full of horses, and lancers riding in full plate, holding their lances point down. Their line, two abreast, wound around the corner. The noise of bells on their bridles might reassure the horses, but it put my nerves on edge.

High over the barracks roof, a few Insects were twisting up into the air.

The lancers passed by and the street emptied. On the cobbles a dispersed smear of brown fur and pink bone was all that remained of the Eske fyrd's grizzly bear mascot. Behind it, a door to the barracks block was open and two soldiers with crossbow bandoliers stood on its step. One leant forward to light a cigarette, then straightened up and blew out smoke.

A quick movement caught my attention. An Insect ran round the corner and hurtled down the street. The smokers slammed their door shut. The Insect dashed beneath my window, then seemed to lose its footing with all six legs at once. It fell and bowled tail over forelegs with its own momentum, crashed into the wall and lay still, with a red-fledged arrow sticking out of it.

Lightning will be awake, then.

The door was ajar and I heard Tornado's voice counting to ten three times as he ascended the stairs. He reached the top and knocked so powerfully that the door swung wide.

I called, 'Yes!'

He continued knocking.

'It's bloody open; you can bloody come in if you bloody have to!'

He entered, still in filthy armour, and a scowl. 'You're looking good this morning.'

'The flight is starting again. What time is it?'

'Six a.m. There aren't as many, yet, but the ones that came down yesterday are still clogging the roads. Wrenn's clearing the middle road with a company of hastai, and I'm going to relieve him soon. Lightning says where are you? Lourie sent me because Lightning bawled at him to come and fetch you. He said, "Get that lanky Rhydanne git down here now!"'

'Lourie said that?'

'No. Lightning.'

'Ah.' I tried to comb my hair and gave up, made the mistake of consulting the mirror. Blood and iodine had seeped through the bandage on my shoulder and dried, sticking it to my skin.

Tornado bent to peer out of the window. 'I've never seen the like of Insects in the air. I bet it pisses featherbacks off to find that Insects can use their wings.'

I agreed. 'There we were, happily taking wings as trophies and using them to glaze windows, never thinking they could grow them and use them to fly.'

'I wouldn't have believed it.'

'They're heavy, graceless fliers. They seem glad when they touch down.'

Tornado shrugged. 'You were pretty impressive.'

'Up until the point I crashed. Look how badly skinned I am.' I glanced at my scale mail hauberk and gambeson, which I hang upright on crossed poles like a scarecrow. My helm sat angled on top, the rust-stained tail of its white horsehair crest hanging down.

'At least you're not mad.'

I paused in lacing my boots and blinked at him. 'Mad? Why should I be mad?'

'You should see Frost.'

We descended the stairs into the hall full of soldiers and townspeople, not crushed together like last night but running about in panic, shouting over the distant buzzing. Zascai came and went from the doorway, crowding around Lightning, who stood leaning against the doorjamb, scribbling a note. He had his bow on his shoulder and, standing at his heel, his favourite deerhound, Lymer the-two-hundred-and-tenth, watched the street attentively.

He folded the paper and handed it to a runner, who raced out of the hall. I pushed to his side but he didn't notice me.

Immediately a fyrdsman vied for my attention: 'Comet, what do I do if –'

'Wait,' I said.

'But how can they be *flying*?'

'Just wait!'

The same was happening to Tornado, who was dealing out orders for an infantry company. Eszai are equal in status and there is no hierarchy among us, meaning there is no final authority in a crisis and, if we have no pre-planned strategy, it causes problems. Lightning tended to dominate and I usually deferred to him, knowing he was the best of us at envisaging the whole battlefield. He could remember where every company was at any given time.

'Snow sent me, Lightning,' a woman said in pidgin Awian. 'He said the flamethrowers now are working.'

'At last. Have you any infantry to fend off Insects? No? I'll send for a squad. You – who are you?' He was pointing at an approaching longbow man.

'Warden of the first battalion Rachiswater archers.'

'You are? Since when? What happened to Cirl?'

'He's dead, my lord. We can't get into the barrack attics to shoot from the windows because people are hiding inside and they've locked the door.'

'Can you not reason with them?'

'They won't reason.'

'Break the door down, but make sure you guard them back to their houses. Ensure the houses are free of Insects and for god's sake make them stay there. Then take up your position.'

'Yes, my lord.'

'Lightning . . .' I spoke up, but he was too harassed to hear.

A warden crowded into the doorframe. I guessed from his stainless accent that he was one of Eleonora's cousins appointed to her lancers. He said, 'I believe we should –'

Lightning interrupted, 'I asked you to tell me where Hayl's husband has gone.'

The captain said, 'He is bereaved. He is as furious as he is demented with grief. He has taken a company of lancers to rescue people from the armoured carts and peel towers.'

'Outside town?'

'Yes.'

'I told him not to!'

'He said it was his revenge on the Insects. He said he will ride them down, unless the flight intensifies. The horses are even more terrified of Insects above them, especially the noise, and they can't hear our orders. Becard only has one company from the third battalion Eske lancers.'

'I thought you said the first battalion?'

'Third, Lightning.'

'Third. Third. Well, take the first, then. Put your armour on and venture out. Give him support but order him back as soon as you can. Tell him I said so, in the Emperor's name.'

The hound's hackles prickled; it started barking furiously. Lightning peered out around the doorjamb, unslung his bow, drew and loosed. An Insect charging down the street skidded to a halt in front of us, in death throes. Lightning lowered his bow and noticed me. 'Jant, don't just stand there!'

The fyrdsmen crowded around us. Lightning looked from face to frightened face. 'You will all damn well wait while I speak with Comet ... Jant, what's happening? How can they fly? They never have, before. Never! Have you discovered anything?'

'I think it's a mating flight.'

'A what flight? It's chaos. Come and see Frost.' We turned away from the crowd and his dog padded after us. Lightning continued, 'We've lost seven hundred men and I would say twice that number are too afraid to leave the barracks. I need you to bring me more information. Tornado, please take over and by god tell the second Rachiswater archers to stop dropping stray arrows on the pyre crew.'

'I'm going to report to the Emperor,' I said.

'Yes, of course.'

I heard a soldier mutter to his mate, 'Fody said that Insects are carrying men off and drowning them in the lake. Picking them up and flying away with them!'

I rounded on him. 'That's false! Fyrdsman, don't spread rumours! Insects are weak fliers, and they can't lift anything. On the ground, they return to being normal Insects. Bear that in mind, all of you!'

As we crossed to Frost's table Lightning continued quietly, 'It's not true, is it? They are not normal.'

'No. Their behaviour has completely changed. The ones in the streets are trying to run back to the lake. They all return to the water, and I think they're laying eggs in it.'

'They're *what*?'

'They put their tails in and a sort of froth comes out. Then they range over the whole valley. They drag the people they've killed to the lake. They're dissolving the Wall and pulling all kinds of dead shit out.' I explained how they were making a splanchnic swamp of the lake and were agglutinating a wall to enclose it. It was as if they had claimed it as their own.

Lightning looked shocked. 'Take care how you speak to Frost.'

'Why?'

'She hasn't slept for three days. She is near breaking point. If she worsens I will send her to Whittorn, Eszai or not.'

'No, Lightning. Zascai stress casualties are kept at the front, so we should do the same for Eszai. People recover much faster with their dignity intact.'

'Well, she's having a bad effect on the Zascai.'

'We need her to work the dam.'

Frost had arranged four tables into a square, with no opening, and she was hidden by a high wall of folders, books and stacks of paper piled on top. We walked around two sides, seeing that when she had run out of books she had continued building with tool boxes. Only the far side was clear, facing away from the crowd, with her coffee pot and a pile of nuts and raisins on the surface. Frost was sitting, shoulders hunched, and her head on her hand. She swayed very slightly as she spoke to one of her engineers in emphatic, low tones. 'So Insects are flying again? I need to know.'

'Yes,' he said.

'Go and man the telescope. Watch the dam. If they start papering over any part of it, come and tell me.'

'Yes, Frost.'

'I want all the barrels of limestone-cutting acid under lock and key. I want fifty draught horses ready to ride to the dam at a second's notice. I want weather reports four times a day. If a drop of rain falls I want to know.'

'Yes.' The engineer glanced at me and rolled his eyes.

'Bring me the spillway capacity calculations. If they block the spillway, it's goodbye, Lowespass.'

Lightning cleared his throat. The foreman saw his chance to escape and dashed away.

Frost had dirt under her fingernails and white salt crusted at the edges of her eyes. Her hair, dry with neglect, was tied back but the ends straggled on her shoulders. She shoved her sleeves up her broad forearms with a gesture like a washerwoman, and said, 'Tell me the figures.'

'What figures?'

'How many men have died? How many injured? How many people have I killed?'

'It's not your fault,' Lightning said.

'Come on, Saker, what else can it be?' Her voice took on a hard edge. 'There's no record of Insects ever flying. Thou knowest that more than anyone, thou hast been around almost as long as they have. My lake is the only thing that's new. The Insects are reacting to my action. To my dam – to water.'

'Water?' Lightning said. 'There has always been a river.'

'Standing water.'

'It could be population pressures,' I suggested. 'Maybe they only swarm every two thousand years.'

'They are flying to reproduce,' Frost stated.

Lightning rubbed the scar on his palm. 'Don't be awkward ... If Insects reproduce in the air we would have seen it before. Besides, Rayne dissects them and she says they have no male and female forms.'

'They had no wings, either, before I built the dam.'

'They had very small wings,' Lightning said.

'Oh, yes. We thought their wings were vestigial, but it turns out they were just immature.'

I said, 'Having wings isn't enough. They've also somehow gained the instinct to fly. It isn't easy, it took me years to learn.' I pulled my T-shirt neck down so they could see my collar bones which had been broken so many times they were gnarled.

Frost murmured, 'Two, four, sixteen, two hundred and fifty-six ...' She grabbed papers and started screwing them up. 'It's my fault! I brought it on us! I renounce it!'

I said, 'Why not have some breakfast?'

'Eat? I've no time! The milk in my coffee is all the breakfast I need!'

I sat down on the edge of the table and she indicated her fortification of books and tool boxes. 'This is my office. I am in charge of the dam.'

'Of course,' I said soothingly.

'Even if everything else fails, my project won't!'

'Cool it.'

She put the handfuls of paper down slowly. 'Oh, Jant. Why are we engineers always hoist with our own blocks?'

'We need you. You're the smartest of us,' I said.

'It gets thee nowhere. Being smart just gets people killed.' She poured another coffee.

'Maybe you should stop drinking that,' I added.

'It's just a cup of coffee.'

'It's not a cup of coffee, it's a state of mind.'

Doubt masked Lightning's usually stately face. He said, 'I don't know why the Insects have changed . . . Rayne once suggested that they bred underground or in cells behind the Wall. Why have we never seen a flight before?'

I said, 'I told you they were coming from the Shift.'

'Shut up about your drug fantasies!'

'Don't you remember the bridge?' I asked. 'Where do you think it led?'

Lightning blanked me out, and said, 'Maybe there are lakes out of view in the north.'

I sighed. 'If you want. But I circled their flight and I saw them coupling in a big, slimy orgy up there.'

Frost squeezed her eyes shut. Her body jerked upright, rigid in a long shudder. In a second she was back. 'A . . . another white flash. It's the pressure. Bad tension. I – I didn't know this would happen. How could I?'

Lightning said, 'We can't be sure –'

'Oh yes,' I said. 'I'm sure.' The sights I had seen in the Somatopolis began to make sense: the obscure shape swimming in the pool, and how the water that had spouted through from Vista had triggered the Insects' instinct to breed.

I said, 'They're dropping food in the lake. The Wall is not just their means of protecting the Paperlands but also a way to store food.'

'Food?' Lightning grimaced. 'Why?'

'Because whatever comes out of those eggs will want to eat.'

Frost buried her head in her hands and started murmuring, 'I only wanted to be immortal because of Zaza . . . Two hundred and fifty-six; two hundred and sixty-five thousand, five hundred and thirty-six; four billion, two hundred and ninety-four million –'

'Please stop doing that,' said Lightning.

I wondered how to help Frost. Asking her to relax would be like trying to convince a shark to stop swimming. If they stop, they drown, so I'm told. She habitually imposes so much stress on herself that this additional stress was more than she could cope with. The very qualities that had helped her gain immortality – remarkable self-discipline and a drive to work herself to the bone – were now impediments.

She is addicted to work and buries herself in it so deeply she's surprised when her actions affect anyone else. Let me give her a task, a purpose, another dose of work to calm her mind.

I picked up a scrap from the tide of paper on her desk, folded it into a glider and threw it past her. She looked up resentfully, selected another sheet and made a glider of far better design. She creased the edge of one wing and tossed it. It described a circle around me, turned on its side and flew back to her.

I said, 'Do you know that water is running down the spillway?'

'Ha! A little overtopping; I'd expect it to be displaced by all that detritus. The culvert is adequate.' She sobbed and wiped her nose.

Lightning sighed, looking at the mortals lingering just out of earshot awaiting our command. 'Try to put a better front on for the Zascai.'

'She's in shock,' I said.

'We're all in shock.' Lightning added, 'There are not so many today. The flight could be dying down of its own accord.'

'I hope so,' I said.

Frost began to stutter, 'D-don't you see? That's the point. My lake affected all the Insects in in in the area. When they've all ... mated ... the flight w-will stop. Then what? Then what?'

Now did not seem to be the right time to tell her and Lightning about the death of the Somatopolis. The Vermiform had implied that Insects don't lay eggs in sea water. I asked, 'Can we make the lake saline?'

Frost's arms tensed. 'W-we don't have enough s-salt here.'

'Well, order some up.'

Lightning shook his head. 'Not a hope. How would you take it to the lake? There are too many Insects running free outside. With thousands over such an open area, they would slaughter us even if we had three times the number of troops.'

A commotion in the doorway interrupted us. Wrenn entered the hall, in full armour, dragging an Insect by its two antennae bundled together in one gauntleted hand. He had hacked off all its legs at the first joint, leaving stumps. Its antlike body squirmed, bending at the neck and waist, and it rotated from side to side as he pulled it over the straw-strewn floor to us.

He had caught it before it detached its wings. The long, hyaline membranes surrounded it completely, shredded into ribbons on one side, rattling and clattering together. It reared up its front femurs threateningly and yellow paste oozed out of the severed joints.

Frost stood up. 'Serein Wrenn Culmish, that is absolutely disgusting. Take it outside!'

'Morning, all. Think of it as one less Insect. I want to show you something.' He let go of the antennae and the Insect rocked on its back until it rolled the right way up. It was constantly trying to get to its feet, regardless of the fact that it didn't have any. The loss of a leg or mandible isn't a serious injury for an Insect because it can regenerate them in subsequent moults. This one was missing all six legs but it was still wriggling. It squirmed around and grabbed Wrenn's ankle.

He drew his broadsword with a flourish. As its jaws closed on the greave plate he swept its head off, leaving it dangling from his leg.

Its body slowly stopped moving. Wrenn kicked his foot free, and the head rolled to rest, compound eyes downward. 'I picked this one up on the road. Do you see it's fatter than usual?' He poked its abdomen with the tip of his sword. Pressing with both hands on the hilt, he punctured the softer sclerites under its abdomen at the waist and sliced it open to the tail. He turned his blade to widen the cut and a mass of white capsules the size of my palm suspended in clear jelly splodged out.

'Eggs. Lots of them. Do you see?' He stirred them with his sword point, cutting their cuticles, whereupon they leaked a milky liquid.

I slipped my hand into the cold, gelatinous spawn, picked up one egg and squeezed it. It was the size of a tennis ball and very slimy, with a tough, sclerotic skin. It slipped between my fingers like a bar of soap, and bounced on the floor.

'Ugh,' said Frost.

'Sorry.'

'Thank you, Wrenn,' Lightning said. 'No less than your usual brilliance.'

'So why do they drop their wings off when they could keep flying and attacking us?'

'They're working on instinct,' I told him. 'They're interested in the lake. It's just coincidence that we're here at all.'

'But why fly? Why do they have to fly to shag?'

'Ask it,' I said.

Wrenn took the point. 'Fair enough.'

He sat down on a bench end, removed his helmet and padded cap and ruffled his flattened hair to make the spikes stick up. He called to Tornado, 'It's your shift, Tawny. I've been at it since five. Give me half an hour for breakfast then I'll come back out.'

Tornado picked up the Insect by the tip of its abdomen and dragged it, still dripping transparent gel, out of the hall.

*

Frost had knelt down and was counting the eggs, picking them up with gluey strands and piling them on one side. 'There are upwards of a hundred in here. Tens of thousands of Insects are laying. If they all hatch, there'll be millions of offspring in my lake . . .'

She brushed her hair back, leaving a trail of slime stuck to it, sat on her heels and looked at us, wide-eyed. 'I have to drain the lake – as quickly as possible.'

'How long will it take?' I said.

'I expected it to take days. I can't just reel the gate wide open; it would flood everything from here to Summerday. The breakwave would be . . . well, maximum outflow could easily wash the levee away, and then . . . I don't like to speculate.'

'How fast can you open the gate safely? What do you need? Tell us, so we can make plans.'

She jumped up and dashed to her desk. She whipped a sheet of paper towards her, grabbed two pencils, shoved one behind her ear and poised the other. 'If Q is the flow rate and dt is the time . . . Hum! Could the debris block the gate? No, its compressive stress is tissue to that force of water . . . You there! Yes, you. Bring me some more coffee! Where's my foreman? Asleep? *Why?* We have work to do! Oh, if Zaza were here we could do this in a couple of days!'

Lightning and I backed off. 'Thank you,' he said gratefully.

'I'm just trying to keep her occupied. We don't have sufficient troops to reach the winch tower anyway.'

He nodded. 'I know. We're stranded here, Jant, for now. But at least we're stranded with the largest store of arrows in western Lowespass.'

I noticed Kestrel Altergate at the far end of the room, trying to help a field surgeon without actually touching his patient. 'Just make sure Frost sleeps at some point, and keep those bloody reporters away from her.'

One of Lightning's wardens called from the spiral stairs. Lightning raised a hand in acknowledgement and said, 'I have to organise the archers on the towers. Please bring us some instruction from the Emperor.'

'I will.'

'I hope San knows what to do, because I fear I don't . . . Jant, did you find Cyan in Hacilith?'

'Er. Yes.'

'Wonderful! Well?' Lightning glanced to the Zascai clamouring for his attention. The bolder ones were beginning to approach. 'Is she safe?'

'She's safe now,' I said.

'Now? She wasn't safe before?'

'She was safe before and she's safe now.' But not during the time in between, I thought. Lightning gave me an urgent look, but I met his gaze. 'Rayne is bringing her here. They'll arrive in a couple of days.'

'Good. Thank you, Jant . . .' I could see Lightning wanted to ask me more but the Zascai were waiting. He fidgeted with the scar on his palm, then he nodded and went back to issuing commands.

Wrenn beckoned to me. 'When you see the Emperor, tell him that all our fyrd are knackered and scared stiff. The Cook said that he'll try to resume the wagon train, with extra outriders for protection, or we'll soon run out of food. I don't want to have to chew gum and tighten my belt until new supplies arrive.'

Wrenn pressed the clips to release his plates with a click; gorget, breastplate, faulds, and placed them on the floor. He was so hot his feathers stood up like needles on a pine branch, to let the heat escape. A few detached ones floated down. Wings don't perspire, but everywhere else his undershirt had brown tide marks and with the sweat of his latest exertion it stank.

He said, 'These clips don't last long. I have to keep threading on new ones. God, that's better. I feel much lighter now.'

His armour was state of the art, top of the range. I cast an envious eye over it. 'Nice gear.'

'Isn't it? Check out Sanguin.' He passed me his broadsword.

'Very nice.'

'You can see the temper line and everything.'

I tilted the blade to see its etched arabesques and the name in a flowing Awian script.

Wrenn took his helmet on his knee and picked at the lining, then undid the finger-screws that held its bedraggled crest in place. He slid the crest out of its runners and began to wipe mud off it with his sleeve. 'It's a quagmire out there. And my arms are covered in bruises from lugging those fucking shields.' He looked at my bandages. 'What happened to you?'

'I crash-landed.'

'Did you? Armour, Jant; get yourself some of this.'

'I can't fly in harness.'

'Wear something on your arms at least.' He grinned. 'What do you think you are, bloody immortal?'

I picked up one of his mirror-finish arm plates from the floor and turned it over. Its canvas straps were hidden underneath it and woven through with steel wire resistant to Insect jaws. The straps had metal spring clips – they could be unfastened in a second if something did go wrong, and they were all easily reachable. Wrenn could don full harness in minutes.

He nodded at it. 'You should ask Sleat to make you some. It's much better than that old crap scale you wear.'

'Show me,' I said.

He took off a greave and ran his finger inside it. 'Well, it's lightweight. Feel that. My breast and back plates are thinner than the ones for my arms and legs. Chain mail strips sit under every joint – elbows, waist, knees – they don't add much weight but no claw is going to find its way in there. And see the little holes?' He ran his finger along a line of perforations. 'They make it lighter still, but they're to let the air breathe. It doesn't collect sweat and rust and I can wear it all day without overheating. Not like old lancers' armour.'

It was the highest-quality steel with the sunburst inlaid in orpiment yellow. I ran my thumb over the smooth embossing and Wrenn chuckled. 'Decoration won't save your life. Look here – all the plates are straight-edged and tapered. Mandibles won't find purchase on that. There's deep fluting along every plate – no jaws will be strong enough to crush that much reinforcement. Sleat's proved it in trials. Best of all, there are no small pieces for the bastards to grab – the elbow couters are attached to the vambraces and the besagews aren't discs hanging loose, they're part of the breastplate, see?'

'Is this Morenzian?' All human armour was adaptable to Awians these days but sometimes the added pieces were unreliable.

'Sleat extended the pauldrons for me and I tuck my wings under them. He can do the same for you. He took my measurements when I joined the Circle. He made exactly what I wanted.'

'Sleat custom-forges armour for every new Eszai,' I said.

'He made me a whole garniture suite.'

'Really?'

'Yes. All interchangeable plates, for all purposes and the decoration matches. I wear this to joust; I just change the breastplate for one with a lance stop, and I have a closed-visor bascinet with a crest instead of this light casque.'

'Clever.'

'Oh, and I have a matching surcoat too. I don't want to joust in bare Insect-fighting steel when there are ladies watching.'

'Frost is a keen jousting supporter,' I said. 'You should talk to her about it and help calm her a little. She remembers all Hayl's scores.'

'At the moment I'd rather not.' He began unhooking the leather spats stretched over his feet to prevent mud working in between the joints. 'These are the only thing I have a problem with. Leather never lasts long in a bout with an Insect – I might as well wrap myself in bacon.'

Lightning yelled from across the hall, 'Jant! Are you going to the Castle or are you going to wait until we've all been eaten?'

'Damn,' I said. 'I'd better go. See you in a few days.'

'Bye.' Wrenn attended to replacing the madder-red crest on his helmet. His plumes were an Awian symbol of bravery and he must have bought them at market, moulted by a girl whose feathers were so beautiful she could sell them. They couldn't have been keepsakes from lovers, because Wrenn was enjoying being single far too much. Only one clever lass has come close to snaring him; she was an ardent swordswoman and applied to be taught by him, but when their conversation never turned on anything but swordplay even her patience wore thin.

I walked out to the square and climbed up to the hall roof, dwelling enviously on Wrenn's armour. I wanted some. I thought, we have come a long way since the year 430 when Morenzians started sewing thick metal plates onto clothes. Insects' carapaces are the optimal natural armour and we have learnt from them how to give ourselves the best possible exoskeletons.

I stood on the ridge, watching Insects descending on the town. I ducked as one buzzed overhead, blotting out the rising sun, and waited for a clear space when it would be safe to take off.

In the square, Hurricane was forming up a company of shield lines; five lines deep, ten men in each, standing shoulder to shoulder. They wore thick gauntlets, and padding on their left arms.

Along their lines the heavy rectangular shields reached down to the ground with little space under them; their ground spikes had been unscrewed. Each had one flat edge and the other edge curved into a hook along its length, so they clipped together loosely into a flexible continuous wall without gaps or overlaps that an Insect claw can pin together.

At the far side of the square, under the direction of the Macer, squads of infantry were dispatching dying Insects with heavy lead mallets, their handles one and a half metres long. They looked as if they were breaking rocks or knocking in tent pegs, but I heard the awful cracking as Insect limbs and heads gave way.

*

Three men with shields, one at the front and two beside him on his either side formed a triangle, running towards the gatehouse tower. A young man, sheltering between them, dragged a tiny limber cart loaded with arrow sheaves. They ran as fast as they could, reminding me of servants under umbrellas dashing across the Castle's courtyards in heavy rain. An Insect descended towards them and the three shield men raised their shields into a roof.

The Insect landed squarely on the shields – which angled in different directions under its scrabbling feet. It slid off and the whole thing collapsed – the Insect came down in the middle, tangled in the cart and spilling arrows everywhere. Before it could right itself, the men crowded around and I saw their swords flashing as they rose and fell.

I looked down the road, seeing Tornado's shield lines coming around the corner. They were clearing Insects before them, pushing them forwards. Insects were bracing their powerful legs on the shields' rims, tearing at the spears, trying to crawl up the sides of the buildings, slipping over discarded wings and backing, backing, backing, as the shield wall advanced.

Tornado was walking in the gap between the first and second lines. His company was also five deep. Each line was of shield bearers and spearmen arranged alternately to thrust their spears over the tops of the shields. Those in the last line walked backwards to deal with Insects running up behind them.

Five lines isn't many. I've seen this formation twenty deep when we were clearing Insects from Awian towns.

Tornado's lines were approaching one of the radial roads. Tornado boomed, 'Cover right junction!'

The men who heard him repeated it at a shout. It made them focus, it bound them together and those at the back heard the concerted yell. They pulled their shields in and advanced towards the street corner. Tornado called, 'Line one, continue! Line two, stack to right!'

Behind the first line, line two began to dissolve their line across the road and instead queued up behind the right end of the first line. As they approached the junction, the men in the first line looked down the side road, saw it was crawling with Insects, and called, 'Ten Insects, right!'

The queue of shield bearers and spearmen together dashed out from behind the first line and ran across the side road, turning as they ran to face the Insects in it. They filled the side road wall-to-wall, spacing themselves out. They slammed their shields together. 'Ho!'

The Insects forced against the shield wall but the spearmen had them under control so quickly Tornado didn't have to detach another line to stand behind them. He left them blocking the road and all the other lines marched across the junction.

The shield wall was left defending the junction, a vital position for the overall strategy. They shifted their weight from foot to foot, rubbed their bruised arms and hands and stared up at me. When more Insects hove into view they shouted to steady their nerves. Insects are deaf so our shouts mean nothing to them, but the men needed to reassure themselves over the unearthly buzzing.

A hiatus in the Insect storm, and I was aloft. I flew over the camp and saw the extent of the devastation. The tents outside the town wall were flattened, plastered in mud. Their drainage ditches had collapsed into brooks of sludge. Shining carapaces bobbed in the moat's coffee-coloured water.

Around twenty soldiers were constructing a pyre outside the gate. Bodies were laid side by side next to the woodpile to be cremated. No one buries corpses in Lowespass because Insects simply unearth them.

A squad of ten women were stripping armour, belts, boots and identification tags from the bodies, leaving only the clothes on. A girl crouched, entering the details in a ledger, because armour and weapons are reissued to new fyrd and she would send any money and jewellery to the family of the deceased.

Men were looping ropes around dead Insects and dragging them out of the gate, hefting them onto a pile beyond the pyre.

A fireman was unwinding the leather pipe from his flamethrower, a cart carrying a metal cylinder of neat alcohol and rape oil. He directed the nozzle while his mate pumped the handle. They sprayed liquid flame onto the Insect carcasses. Insects are supposed to be deterred by the smell of burning chitin but I've never seen any evidence of it.

I hastened south to the Castle for the rest of the day and all night, rehearsing in my head what I was going to say to the Emperor. I couldn't see the horizon, so I tried to keep the strain on both wings the same and maintained a straight line. I navigated south carefully, checking the sultry stars by my compass.

Their constellations reflected like scattered salt on my oiled wings. I have always been convinced that stars are an illusion, just like rainbows, because no matter how high I fly they never seem any nearer. The spaces between them mesmerised me and I flew on, composing my report to the Emperor in my head. I wondered what to do if Frost's madness worsened. I couldn't think of any way to ease the pressure on her, because she was the only one of us who really understood the dam.

I didn't know Frost's pre-Castle name but I have heard how she joined the Circle. She won her Challenge in 1703. She had lived all her life in Brandoch, where she founded the Riverworks Company in partnership with her husband.

Brandoch town is built on a little rise so low as to be almost indistinguishable from the rest of the drowned fenland. In Frost's day it flourished because it overlooked the only passage through the Moren Delta deep enough for carracks. Frost and her husband laboured in the manorship's tradition of reclaiming low-lying land from the sea which often flooded it: every one of its polder fields are man-made. They worked as a brilliant team, draining and shoring the marshy levels with dykes and long, raised roads.

Frost only sought the Castle when her husband fell ill with malaria. She realised that if she could make him immortal she had a chance of saving him. She is the most selfless of us all.

Her predecessor, Frost Pasquin, set her the Challenge of moving a fyrd division across the Oriole River using nothing but their own manpower and the materials to hand in Lowespass. Pasquin had been working at the front for too long and had lost touch with the rest of the world. He had not been aware of his Challenger's area of expertise and he was surprised at how gladly she accepted the competition.

Pasquin took eight days to build an ingenious pontoon bridge of pine and cowhide, with a load-bearing weight enough for the five hundred men. Then it was the Challenger's turn.

She moved the river. She surveyed it, dug a short channel and ran it into an old meander. Her husband lay on a stretcher and watched her silently, growing ever weaker while she worked day and night for five days solid. He was forbidden to help her by the Castle's rules even if he had been well enough. The river altered its course and flowed a little south of the camp of fyrdsmen. They didn't have to walk a step; Pasquin's bridge was left high and dry.

The Emperor asked Pasquin if he could return the river to its original course. But Pasquin couldn't, and had to admit he was beaten.

Frost's husband died the same night. She won her place in the Circle but all she would say was that she had failed to save him. She became locked in mourning and refused herself any pleasure.

The changes in people's characters cannot be divorced from the changes in their bodies. An adolescent is passionate and changeable because of his changing body, not just his lack of experience. An octogenarian is fatalistic since he can feel his body failing, and knows it prefigures his death, not solely because he has seen friends die. Middle-aged mortals change more slowly than the very young and very old, so their characters are more stable. And we Eszai never age at all, so aspects of our characters are also fixed.

Moreover, I doubt any Eszai really grows up while the Emperor San is our immortal father. They preserve their identities against the grind of long centuries, and by their quirks they distance themselves from the crowds. So, Frost still retains the attitude of mourning. She lives for her work but complains she can't achieve as much working alone. She leaves the fruits of genius scattered through the Fourlands, like the tidal mills of Marenna Dock, the Anga Shore breakwater on the Brandoch coast, and a hundred six-sailed wind pumps along Miredike and Atterdike that drain the malaria swamp.

Frost is, without doubt, a genius. The traits of genius often coincide with madness, but that isn't strange, because if genius is an infinite capacity for taking pains, then you tell me what madness is.

CHAPTER 13

I flew out of the dawn, into the Castle, my heart racing. I soared in over the curtain wall, bleeding off my downwind speed, and all the Castle's quadrangles opened up as I passed over. Hidden inside and between its buildings, they revealed themselves to me.

I ignored the confusing levels of the roofs slipping away under me; the shallow lead cones of the six Dace Gate towers ascending in size from the bastions in the moat to the enormous barbican. I focused on the spire of the Throne Room as I glided over the Berm Lawns. The spire filled my vision – I flared my wings, swept up close to its wall and landed on a gargoyle projecting from halfway up.

The wind gusted; I steadied myself against the stone, turned around on my narrow perch and braced myself with one foot either side of the drainage channel. It was blocked with moss, pigeon shit and the grit weathered out of the stone. I kicked it clear with my toe and the black water spattered down onto the Throne Room's sheet lead roof. I looked out down its length towards the North Façade; pinnacles and the tops of flying buttresses emerged at intervals around its edges.

Every gargoyle was different, arcing out to my left and right in a ring around the spire, with bulbous human faces and lolling tongues. The one I was standing on had a round, white pigeon's egg in a nest of twigs amassed in the joint of its wing swept back to the wall. I always felt as if their flamboyant features had been carved for me. It seems too much effort to craft such inventive expressions, when the only people who will ever see them are me and the steeplejacks. Still, if a stone mason with carte blanche can't have fun, who can?

I shook out my wings, hopped off the gargoyle and spiralled steeply down to the Berm Lawns.

The door at the end of the Simurgh Wing was locked. Typical. I can't be expected to carry keys to all of the damn doors. I hammered on it but no one was within corridors' distance.

I sprinted around the side of the building, on the grass between it and the Harcourt Barracks, past the armoury, the hospital and its herb garden. I sped onto the avenue bordered with tall poplars and ran down it, automatically avoiding the few uneven flagstones. The magnificent fronts of the Breckan and Simurgh Wings grew before me, with cool, modern open arches. I hastened through the space between them, taking the formal entrance through the Starglass Quadrangle.

I rushed past astronomical and horological instruments, on the main path between their large, square enclosures. The dew made the flint cobbles set in concrete at the edge of the path as shiny and slippery as ice.

The gleaming Starglass Clock struck ten as I passed. I counted its chimes almost subconsciously. The last one remained hovering in the air and seemed to grow louder, with a note of defiance, before fading.

Kings and governors and their retinues sometimes process along this route to the Throne Room when seeking the Emperor's counsel. I hurtled through the massive portal. Its deeply carved tympanum panel showed San entering the Castle to stay for all perpetuity. I crossed into the narrow passage around the Throne Room.

Two guards with halberds stood always by its entrance. They took one look at me, unshaven and panting manically, 'The Messenger!'

'The Messenger!'

'Let me through!' I cried.

They pushed the doors wide across their polished arcs of stone.

The Emperor was sitting in the sunburst throne, and all was quiet behind the screen. He has resided in the Castle, seeing no more of the outside world than is visible from the walls, for fifteen hundred years.

I paused for breath, insignificant in size beside the column of the first arch. I leant forward, hands on knees, to catch my breath, and I was still trying to formulate what to say.

Diagonal shafts of sunlight so bright they looked solid, shone down from the east wall's Gothic windows, high above the arcade of arches and the balcony where ten Imperial Fyrd bowmen stood in silence. Motes of dust and old incense in the air enjoyed brief fame, transformed to flecks of gold as they floated through the beams.

Without looking up or giving any indication that he had noticed my presence, the Emperor said, 'Come here, Comet.'

I shuddered. I strode down the scarlet carpet to the dais, so quickly through strips of light and shade that they flickered red in my eyes. I passed haughty Awian eagles, rearing Plainslands horses and Hacilith fists between the arches. All the Fourlands' heraldry was bold in the stained-glass windows behind the Emperor.

The sunburst, a solid electrum screen behind the marble throne, was polished to a mirror radiance and its rays haloed the throne for a metre on all sides. It rested on its lowest two points and, since the Emperor was sitting, his head was in the exact centre of the sun disc. Every beam extending out around him reflected me indistinctly as I approached.

'My lord Emperor!' I knelt at the foot of the dais, peppered with yellow light from the rose window. I was panting too much to continue.

The Emperor said calmly, 'The Circle broke. Hayl, Thunder and Gayle are dead. Do you know what killed them?'

'My lord, something awful's happening. They were all at Slake Cross – and Insects are *flying*!'

'Flying?'

'Yes, my lord. A gigantic mating flight, over the lake and the town.'

I looked up, but the light was in my eyes and I couldn't see the Emperor's face. He sat in the shade under an octagonal marble vault that stretched high above him into the traceried interior of the spire, like the inside of a gigantic lantern. The white marble throne was imposing, but not so big that it diminished his form. His ancient broadsword and shield hung on its back. I was very glad I couldn't read his expression.

His knurled hands, raised bone covered with ancient thin skin like batwings, uncurled from the scrolled armrests as he stood up. He came to the edge of the dais. 'Tell me all.'

I recounted everything, and ended, 'If the flight has stopped, the others will have cleared the town by now. There must be millions of Insect eggs in the lake . . .' I hesitated, nervously. 'Have I made sense, my lord? Have I been completely clear?'

'This is unprecedented,' the Emperor said.

I bowed my head, frightened. Could this be new even to San?

The Emperor said nothing. He stood in thought, tall and gaunt, with perfect stature, his hands clasped behind his back. His white hair hung straight to the level of his shoulders, his sarcenet robes hung straight to the floor. His clothes were the style of the time he founded the First Circle and was proclaimed Emperor. He wore no crown, never anything but plain white, apart from the robe's wide embroidered collar with panels of colourless jewels.

*

San looked up to the gallery and called, 'Summon the captain of the Imperial Fyrd!'

He unfastened his cloak at the shoulder, took it off and placed it on the cushion of the throne. He lifted the broadsword from the back of the throne and wrapped its belt around his waist.

I gasped – my hand covered my mouth – I couldn't believe I was seeing this. He had never so much as touched the sword before, and now he really was buckling it on. He tucked the strap end through and the sword hung at his side, in the folds of his robe.

The Imperial Fyrd captain ran in, down the side aisle. I waited in stunned silence, hearing his footsteps approach behind the piers of the arches. He knelt beside me. He was shaking, staring, and so pale I thought he was going to faint.

The Emperor took his round sunburst shield from the back of the throne and slipped his arm through it. He stood with the shield held fittingly. 'Is my horse ready?'

The captain was too terrified to speak, but he gave an obeisant nod.

The Emperor said, 'The people need my direction. Assemble all the Imperial Fyrd on the Berm Lawns. Fetch my armour and the locked chest from the treasury. Make haste! I will lead you to the front. Bring the fastest horses; for speed we will overnight at manor houses and we ride without pause. Comet?'

'My lord?' I managed, dry-mouthed.

'Call up the fyrds. All of them, from every manor. Every battalion, every division, every company, every squad. Signal Slake Cross to warn them of our arrival. Then you will meet us at the town.'

San stepped down from the dais, passed us, walked through the first arch to the small door to his private apartments. He shut the door behind him.

Noises began to resound from up on the balcony; a crash as one of the archers fainted. The others dropped their bows and turned to each other open-mouthed, seeking an explanation – as if they could ever begin to explain San's actions.

My insides seemed to liquefy. I risked a glance sideways; the captain's eyes were shut, his jowly face hung forwards. He whispered, 'San is leaving the Castle. It's the end of the world.'

Commotion on the balcony as the archers started gabbling hysterically, mouthing reassurances, anticipating the imminent arrival of god. They rattled down the turret stairs and sped out to spread the news.

I slowly rose to my feet. The captain turned dark blue eyes up to me. 'Why Slake Cross? Is that where god –?'

I was brusque, since I was just as scared. 'You have your orders. Put nonsensical myths out of your mind and do what the Emperor said.'

'Is it the end of the world?'

'We can't change what's happening. Do your job and I'll do mine; it's all we'll be remembered for.'

The Castle suddenly seemed very empty; the archers had gone and the Throne Room was deserted for the first time since the Pentadrica fell. I glanced at the five columns in the apse behind the throne: an azurite column for Awia, jade for the Plainslands, porphyry for Morenzia, haematite for Darkling, and a new, solid gold column for Tris.

I ran to Lisade, the Castle's library. It takes all the books and journals of the Fourlands – the Emperor is believed to read every one. I ran past the Lawyer's vacant rooms, up to the semaphore tower recently built for me on the roof. I had brought the idea of the semaphore back from Tris, figuring that if I didn't then someone else would Challenge me with it later. I had employed several Trisians to handle the network which is being installed across the Fourlands. Its instant communication posed no real threat to my position since the Messenger must be at least as much a diplomat as an errand runner.

I left my messages with the Trisian semaphore operator, and he began pulling the levers which would swing the white planks on their post to send the news out across the Empire. I sped to the other side of the Castle and grabbed some food from the kitchens, called in at the treasury in Carillon Court building and picked up a bag of coin.

The Starglass struck eleven as I sped out to the Berm Lawns, to take off. Had it only been an hour since I landed? The Castle had broken into a whirlwind of activity. Servants raced from building to building, hollering the news before them. The gaudy-liveried Imperial Fyrd were lugging saddle bags out of Harcourt Barracks; halberds and armour gleamed as they were jostled out of the armoury behind it. Stable hands were leading horses in through the Dace Gate five at a time. A few grey-haired Imperial Fyrd guardsmen were piling up equipment between the Throne Room's buttresses.

The preparation gave me a vivid image of the Pentadrican Queen a millennium ago, leading her court to view the newly arrived Insects; a flower-decked procession out of the Throne Room's very building straight into their jaws.

A trainer dashed past, dashed back and valiantly tried to attract my attention. 'Messenger! I brought Alezane.' He indicated a flawless black warhorse. I cast an eye over its splendid tack. I had always seen Alezane kept in the stables or out exercising, always ready for the Emperor, but I never had the slightest inkling I would see San riding it.

The boy put a finger in his mouth. 'I saddled Alezane for the Emperor *himself*! Is he really leaving?'

I said, 'The Emperor isn't abandoning us. He's leading. To Slake Cross – where every one of us is going.'

The boy tried to fit all his fingers into his mouth. 'Is god coming back?'

'I don't know. But within the hour the Emperor will lead the Imperial Fyrd out of the Castle –' I pointed at the Dace Gate. I spoke with growing confidence and a sense of surprise at the back of my mind that I did not need to act. My own self-belief overcame me and gave my voice strength. The grooms began to gather around me, warming themselves on my reassurance. '– Help them to leave as fast as they can. Then all of you, follow on behind to Slake Cross. We'll need you at the other end.'

The semaphore doesn't yet extend to the outposts of the Empire, so I would have to fly to the most distant manors and to those with the most obstructive governors. Brandoch was my first stop. I clapped my hands briskly. 'Right! Let's be *organised* about this!'

I took to the air. As I flew I recalled San going through the non-descript little door of his private apartments. I itched to know what was in there. No one has ever been inside; no servants are allowed to enter. The Cook told me he brings the Emperor's meal to the door every night, after the closing of the Throne Room session. As far as we know, the Emperor only eats one simple meal a day.

Perhaps when San has departed, I could peek inside. No, I didn't dare; not unless I could put at least the length of the continent between him and me. I wouldn't mind trying the sunburst throne, though.

I rode the wind, lost in my thoughts. The Emperor remained an enigma to us all, even those Eszai who had known him longest. He was old before god stopped time affecting him, two thousand years ago in Hacilith. His centuries as sage to the ancient kings, then warrior against the Insects and finally as advisor for the Fourlands, have given him an understanding of people so profound it seems inhuman.

San leaving the Castle signifies the end of the world. Everyone knows that myth. It has been embedded in the Empire since the Circle was founded. But it didn't specify how the world was supposed to end, or the means of god's return.

There's no evidence, one side of me said; you've studied it long enough and you know it's no more than a fable. My other side replied: how long do we have? Days?

CHAPTER 14

I called the lancers of Rachiswater, the longbow men of Micawater, the swords of Peregrine. I called the famed cavalry of Eske. I called the Cathee axe men, the spears of Brandoch, the Litanee pikemen and Awndyn halberdiers. The brave Fescue shield fyrd I called, the Hacilith crossbow men, the horse archers of Ghallain. I called the General and Select Fyrd of every manor. The governors heard the emphasis in my voice and saw the panic in my eye, and took up their arms.

By the time I returned from Carniss, the Select of Awia was already packed on the roads, marching under the manors' colours. Ahead of them, great trebuchets and espringals were trundling from Lowespass Fortress, escorted by the hard-bitten troops of the garrison. The roads from the Avernwater workshops were clogged with flamethrower carts, and barrels of tar were en route from the Lacksheen tar pits. Every troop-carrying caravel in Diw and Cobalt weighed her anchor and stretched her sails.

It was a full mobilisation. Two people from each family, male or female, from the ages of sixteen to fifty, must answer the call. I spoke to the governors, who spoke to their stewards, who spoke to their reeves; who spoke to farmhands and cottars, so that by the day following my visit, everyone had heard my news.

In the city, desks were set up in factory halls and under awnings in the market place. People of every walk of life soaked from the streets towards them, frightened by the urgency of Aver-Falconet's announcements. He sent couriers galloping out across Morenzia to the townships at the coast.

As I glided over the Plains I saw queues of men mustering to the General Fyrd in manor hall courtyards, the porches of reeves' houses and the village greens. Every man realised there was nothing for it but to join the queue and, at the front, sign your name and pick up a shield and sword or poleaxe from the mounds unloaded from the carts from Wrought. Or if you're Select Fyrd, take down your heirloom breastplate and broadsword from the bedroom cupboard. A night's work with sand and oil will restore it to service.

The sheer number of people moving took my breath away. The storehouses of Wrought were turning out crates of weapons by the neat ten thousand into a seemingly endless coming-and-going of covered wagons. Horses and carts appeared singly from scattered farms, convened by the thousand to fill whole fields, then each rank decanted out onto the road. Anything could happen. Everything was happening! The scale of the effort astounded me. Carnival girls turned entrepreneurs walked up and down the long queues of traffic dammed up outside Shivel, selling food and drink.

I have put all these people in motion myself! The power of my words filled me with exhilaration. I dropped from the sky onto a different manor each day, and people upwelled in my wake and channelled out to fill the highways all the way to Slake Cross.

CHAPTER 15

When I returned to Slake Cross, we gathered in the hall. The Insect flights had ceased but the valley was swarming with them. Rayne and Cyan had managed to ride through and had been here two weeks. I heard that Cyan was already antagonising her father and had offended nearly every Eszai.

Lightning crouched down and held a wooden taper in the hearth. Shielding it with his cupped hand he crossed to the table and touched the taper to the rope wick of an oil lamp. He turned down the wick until the smoky flame stopped fluttering, then stubbed out the taper and sat down next to Tornado and myself.

The yellow glow illuminated our faces and Tornado's front as he hunched over a pint of beer with a glum expression. Wrenn paced up and down in the darkness between the table and the fireplace, more restless than a rat on a stove, his hand on his sword hilt. Nobody spoke. Cyan was sitting on the hearth step, reading one of Rayne's books. She looked a lot healthier now. She was poking her thumb through a hole in her jumper, making a woollen glove, and paint was flaking from the designs on her riding boots.

A heavy, insistent hammering came from outside; the Sapper was keeping soldiers working long into the night, building palisades to enclose the canvas city growing outside the town.

The fire took some of the dampness out of the air. The first week of May had ended but the cold night rain still permeated everything. It flattened the grass on the moor and sent ripples down the dam's overflow chute. Pools in the mud along the Lowespass Road deepened and coalesced. Many carts mired to the tops of their wheels were abandoned haphazardly on the verges.

Frost had fallen asleep sitting at her table, her head down on a sheaf of calculations. Lightning went to her and put a hand under her rounded shoulder. He gently tipped her backwards, her head lolling. He caught her with his other hand in the small of her back, put his arm under her knees and lifted her up. He carried her to her camp bed and laid her down carefully.

'Is she all right?'

Lightning shook his head. 'She's been awake seventy-two hours. Every noise and shadow has her on her toes. She forgets that if you keep a bow strung all the time it will warp – and then when you need it, you won't be able to use it. She is tillering the string of her mind so taut I wonder it hasn't already snapped. Tell us the news, Comet.'

I said, 'The Imperial Fyrd are on their way and so are all the manors. I've never seen anything like it – a hundred and fifty thousand soldiers and nearly the same in auxiliaries. All the inns and camp clearings are full, they're filling churches with straw sacks to sleep on. They strip the depots clean as they pass. It's as if all the towns are moving – the roads are just like long, thin towns. When I tell the governors that San has left the Castle, they don't give me any problems raising fyrd. I haven't even had any resistance from Eske or Hacilith. I think that's why San is coming – to demonstrate how important this is.'

Tornado folded his arms. 'When will the Emperor arrive?'

'I saw his entourage this morning. They're passing the troops already coming in on the Calamus Road. It's taking them longer to get here than I expected because half of Awia and the Plainslands is ahead of them. At that rate they'll take a couple more days.'

Lightning said, 'I have ensured billeting for the Imperial Fyrd. The quartermasters and armourers are checking our stocks, and we're carting in more fodder as fast as we can.'

The sleeves of Tornado's leather jacket were pushed up to his elbows, so I could see the faded red sunburst tattoo under the hairs on his massive forearm. He said, 'I'll send troops to clear the way. There are too many Insects running around out there. I don't like it. I don't like it one bit. That Insect flight was not, like, natural. It creeps me out. We're the Emperor's bodyguard so I'll go and take charge of the Imperial Fyrd. Half of them hardly ever leave the demesne. They're like, only the Castle's guard.'

'They train very hard,' said Lightning.

'They only bloody parade! They never campaign together, at least not as a single division.'

Lightning said, 'Most of them are veteran Select. If they weren't good they wouldn't have got the job. But yes, I agree theirs is an honorary position and you should go out to meet San. He will have this hall as a centre of operations.'

'Where will his private quarters be?' I asked.

'Your room.'

'Oh, thanks.'

'Well, you weren't here and we thought you wouldn't mind ... After all, you can sleep on a bookshelf.'

I picked up a bottle and poured some wine, hoping it would ease my nerves. Wrenn paced around the table and said to the room in general, 'The boss is coming. What have we done wrong?'

'I wonder whose head is on the block first?'

Wrenn pressed me: 'Doesn't San leaving the Castle mean the end of the world? I was taught he would leave to prepare the way for god. Is god returning? What will it do?'

I had met with this question in every manor and it was really starting to annoy me. I said tiredly, 'Shut the fuck up about god.'

Lightning said, 'Don't swear in front of Cyan.'

I glanced across to Cyan, who smiled innocently.

Tornado spoke up: 'I hope god returns. It's what I've been waiting for all these years.'

I gave a frustrated shriek and waved my hands in the air. 'Hundreds of thousands of troops are coming and we have no space! Let's concentrate!'

Tornado ignored me and addressed Wrenn: 'I know I'm prepared for god. To me it's the whole point of being immortal – I get a ringside seat when it shows up. San knows everything I do is for the Castle so I'm damn sure he'll give me a good report.'

'God is an inhuman power,' Lightning said quietly.

'Still, I like to think it'll be refreshed and in a good mood.'

Lightning said, 'Please can we keep to the point?'

'This is the point!'

He shook his head. 'No, Tornado. In my experience stories are rarely as old as people say; and traditions are never as time-honoured as they like to believe. The idea that San never leaves the Castle originated about a hundred years after the Games. I don't remember him announcing that he would never leave. Many opinions sprang up around that time; they became stories and then the centuries twisted them into legends. Please do not be distracted by myths of the world ending because the truth is much worse. We all know the original version deep down. Cyan, Wrenn; when San leaves the Castle it logically means the end of the *Circle* not the end of the world. We have failed him and he needs to take command again himself. I think – I fear – that he will disband the Circle.'

'He took charge of the Imperial Fyrd just like a warrior,' I said with wonder.

'Yes. San the warrior is not so strange to me. I remember him leading the First Circle. I was introduced to him once, in the field at Murrelet, where Rachiswater is now. When I was a boy he would stop at the palace on his expeditions from the Castle to the front. Could we be redundant?'

'No,' I said quickly. 'San asked for every fighter we can field. Who'll lead them? He needs us more than ever.'

'I cannot begin to predict what he plans.'

Tornado said, 'I still think god might appear.'

'Well, you are from a more religious era,' Lightning said airily.

'And you're full of bullshit!'

'What will god look like?' Wrenn asked Tornado.

The giant man's voice sparked with interest. 'Dunno. I asked San to, like, describe it, but he wouldn't. San says god made us, so it's more powerful than us, so it can't be Awian or human. It wouldn't have made us anything like itself, either in looks or the extent of its power, because then we'd be able to rebel and of course god wouldn't chance that. That's why god is an "it". Most books I've read say it can look like whatever it wants to. It, like, creates stuff. That's what it does. So it can create forms for itself. If god was speaking to you, then I guess it might choose to look like an Awian.'

'You're making this worse,' I complained.

Wrenn glanced at Lightning for support. 'Do you believe in god?'

Lightning said, 'I see no reason not to, because San does not lie. No one has ever given me a more convincing alternative. Besides, we are immortal. God must be behind it somewhere, or how could San have immortality to share?'

Wrenn gave a great worried sigh. He unbuckled his belt and laid his sword on the table. He ran his fingers through his hair and set off pacing to the fireplace again.

I was suddenly furious. I couldn't believe we were talking about this crap! 'Tornado, you're wasting our time! Are we credulous Zascai? Are we Trisians, to be sitting here pontificating? Is this the Buncombe Beach Young Philosophers On The Brink Of Disaster Club?'

'Don't speak Plainslands,' said Lightning. 'I can't follow you if you go that fast.'

'Sorry. I'm just telling him that we're in this together and god is not going to help us. Nothing is going to come and save us. We have no one to run crying to, nothing to rely on. We must stand on our own two feet. Can we just grow up, please? Why do you think San told me to muster everyone from Frass to Vertigo? The strength and resources in each of us is all we have!'

'You used to believe,' Tornado said. 'I remember when you joined the Circle. You weren't so cynical then.'

I shrugged. When I was an apprentice in Hacilith I saw how seriously my seniors took the story. What other conclusion can a child draw from the sayings of adults? I grew more experienced and I realised that adults don't have all the answers, and in many cases they're even more credulous and confused than children. Then I saw the Shift, then I saw the Somatopolis, and I realised how truly alone we are – not only in this world, but in all of them.

'All right,' I said. 'I have no proof. But if we don't know whether god is real, we can't depend on it. If we can't prove anything either way, and if we'll never know the answer, we should shut up about it and do something more practical. Instead of talking we should save ourselves! God might return and make everyone immortal, or us mortal. It could alter and revoke the laws of physics at will and leave us with a terrifying disorder. God might already have come back – remember the posteventualist heresy? Maybe San is god, watching and chuckling to himself. Maybe the Insects are god; they appeared, didn't they? Or maybe god intended them to be the next phase of creation, more perfect and far hardier than us men.'

'Fuck that!' Tornado thundered. He stood up, so I did too, but I foolhardily kept going: 'San is coming to see something new to him, that's all.'

He patted me on the shoulders – and I sat down heavily on the bench.

'Please!' Lightning said.

Tornado said simply, 'If Jant picks holes in my belief, it will shine still brighter through them.'

I sighed. 'God coming back is nothing but a story. I've lived everywhere; I know a tale when I hear one. From Darkling to Hacilith to the Castle I've had to don and doff beliefs so many times I've realised stories are only ever about the people who make them up ...'

'Have you quite finished?' said Lightning coldly.

'I think he's crazy,' said Tornado.

'No, I'm not crazy. I've just been around. Let me show you what I mean. Tales of god from different countries would seem as outlandish to you, as yours would to them.'

'I have had my fill of outlandish countries,' Lightning remarked quietly, stroking the scar on his palm.

'You find Rhydanne strange, don't you?' I asked Tornado.

'I find you strange,' he said.

'Rhydane think of god as looking like a Rhydanne.'

He sniggered.

I said, 'Listen to the Rhydanne version. God the hunter made the world, the mountains, the plains, the sky; but it was empty of animals. So god made an animal to chase, and the animal she made was enormous, as if every single creature of the Fourlands, dumb and rational, had been joined together in one giant form. It had feathers and scales, skin and fur, hands, claws, wings and tails. It had hundreds of heads and thousands of eyes. It was both male and female. The beast sat on Scree Plateau and used the Plainslands as its footstool. Its heads towered above the peaks in the highest mountain clouds.

'God chased the beast all over the Fourlands. She twirled her bolas, the stones of which were as large as the glacial boulders on the slopes of Tarneilear, tied to leather strings as long and as wide as the Turbary Track. Eventually the creature tired and god caught up with it. She cast her bolas and brought it down on the summit of Great Fheadain.

'God killed the beast and its blood flowed down the gullies of Fheadain and created the first waterfalls. Then god skinned it and carved up its flesh. She kindled a fire and placed the cuts of meat on flat stones near the hearth. The warmth of the fire brought all the pieces of meat to life. They jumped up and ran off, all over the Fourlands and became the people and animals of the world.

'The Rhydanne were quickest; they ran away first, before the fire could cook them. The humans were closer to the fire, and got burnt, which is why they are not as pale as Rhydanne and they need a warmer climate. Some cuts of meat had stuck together – humans and eagles – so now we have Awians. The Rhydanne had already populated the mountains, so humans and Awians must perforce live in the lowlands. God saw this had happened accidentally and decided to get drunk. She drank and drank and eventually fell asleep. One day she will wake up, with the heaviest hangover of all time. Rhydanne live in dread of having to pacify her with more alcohol on that day, I can tell you –'

'Jant . . .' Lightning cut me off with a calm voice.

Tornado said, 'That's the biggest load of rubbish I ever heard.'

'Eilean told me it when I was small, back when I assumed Darkling valley was the whole world.'

Cyan brushed her silky hair back with her jumper sleeve and turned up her face. Rather self-consciously, she said, 'If god is coming back, wouldn't San have told Jant?'

'Maybe even San doesn't know,' Tornado said.

'Why don't you ask him?'

Everybody looked at Tornado, who said, 'Um, no ... I can tell you haven't, like, met the Emperor, girl.'

I said, 'If San wants us to know, he'll tell us. But the Insects are a more pressing consideration.'

'You know what your problem is?' asked Tornado.

'No. But I know what you think my problem is.'

The veins stood out on his bull neck. 'Oh, I'm sick of your smartarse comments, you flying streak of piss! Why don't you step outside?'

I bridled. 'Gladly!'

Lightning said, 'Jant, wait until the Circle's disbanded before starting a new career as a quintain for Tornado.'

'If we don't know what will happen,' I repeated, 'it's sensible not to waste time arguing about it but continue with our plans.'

'Hear, hear!' Frost's crackly, desiccated voice came from the direction of her camp bed. My outburst had woken her and she lay propped on one elbow watching us. She said, 'I will use science to fix the problem that science has caused.'

She reclaimed the reeking coffee pot from her desk, poured herself a cup and scooped powdered milk into it. 'Only scummy powder left, damn it ... Can't Snow stop that hammering?'

Her voice was faint, as if coming from kilometres away. She rubbed a bloodshot eye and watched wrinkled skin forming on the surface of her coffee. She appeared less like herself and more like an actress adept at pretending to be Frost. She was like a deserted mill relentlessly grinding grain because its mechanism can do nothing else, although nobody is inside to tend it.

She fingered a raisin out of the pile on her desk and ate it. Then she returned to her calculations.

'Now, as to the Imperial Fyrd,' said Lightning. 'I don't trust them if things get tough —'

'Dad ...' Cyan interrupted. She was bored to be stranded here, while her father talked with his workmates above her head. The fact she was a minor, helpless in front of the world's best warriors, embarrassed her even more.

'Dad.'

'Eszai should provide San's bodyguard instead —'

'Dad ...'

'I'll do it,' said Tornado.

'Why not me?' said Wrenn.

'Because I'm the strongest. Officially, like.'

'Da-aad.'

'*What?*' said Lightning.

'Nothing. Can I go to the tavern?'

'No. Stay here where I can see you, young lady.'

'I have enough money.'

'I know you have. But there is nothing left in the tavern to buy.'

'I'm going, so tough!'

Tornado said, 'Lightning, will you keep your daughter under control?'

'Oh, she won't be any trouble.' He gave her such a warm, conspiratorial smile that it made the whole place seem homely; for a second it shrank the room, but she did not return it. 'Come sit down by me,' he added.

Cyan scudded over and slumped onto the bench. She said, 'You're all scared, aren't you? You are, you're all terrified, you just don't want to admit it.'

'Hush,' said Lightning. 'We must simply let San see the overall strategy. He will direct us.'

'God might,' said Tornado.

I pushed the heels of my hands into my closed eyes until grey-green patterns kaleidoscoped. I had only been back on the ground for two hours and I was on edge already.

'Are you all right?' Wrenn asked me.

'Hmm? Yes. All it is, is ... I've been on drugs for a very long time and now I'm not and I'm finding it a bit difficult, that's all. Especially at night ...'

Wrenn looked as if he was going to make a remark, but decided against it. Stranded on the other side of the age gulf, all he could do was start pacing again. The lanterns were flickering outside in the square and darkness was trailing in, with the sound of the innkeeper's baby crying. 'You know,' he said. 'It wouldn't be so terrible if civilian women and children weren't trapped here too.'

Tornado stood up. 'Can you hear the watchman's bell? Someone's at the gates.'

'It's probably god!' I glared.

'I hope so,' he said casually. 'Only god can stop your nonsense.'

Lightning said, 'It must be another fyrd troop.'

A minute later the watchman sent a runner in, who stood open-mouthed until I beckoned him to the table. I recognised him as one of the Castle's servants; I know them all by name. 'Yes, Eider; what is it?'

'Carniss manor has arrived, Messenger. We opened the gates because Insects were harrying them – they've been fighting off Insects all the way from the mountains. The governor says he's recruited everybody he can; he has a whole battalion but they lost most of their mules. He requests orders to billet his men.'

Lightning said to me, 'I'll greet Carniss. I expect that manor holds unpleasant memories for you.'

'More likely those bastards will be uneasy taking orders from a Rhydanne.'

'Do they only have one battalion?' Wrenn asked. 'Well, I suppose every little helps.'

Lightning picked his coat off the back of the chair, thrust one arm into it and felt about for the other. He said, 'Carniss may be a small manor but their archers are superb marksmen. They earn their living hunting.'

I glanced at the ceiling. 'They're bastards to a man.'

'Jant, I know you don't like Carniss, but we're very crowded and strained here, so don't sow discord. Even their General Fyrd bring their own fine bows. We can give them horses; I know they fight better as skirmishers than in formation.'

Frost added, 'They have excellent master miners too, from the silver mines. They're tough and they work hard.'

Tornado nodded. 'I like Carniss. They have a decent attitude for featherbacks; they're very down-to-earth. Frontiersmen make good garrisons. They're used to danger, so they stay alert and observant, which is more than you can say for the city fyrds.'

I said, 'They're a lot of grubby unmanageable trappers who take deep revenge for slight offences.'

Cyan said, 'Cool. Can I come and see them?'

'No,' Lightning told her. 'Stay here. Jant, would you look after ... *No*, don't give her the wine! Bloody stop drinking! And, Wrenn, can you ... Oh, forget it. I can't believe what's happening to the Circle these days!' Lightning swung his quiver on his shoulder and stormed out after the servant.

Cyan looked up at me. 'I want to watch Governor Carniss's men come in.'

Wrenn said, 'Let's go, then.'

She glowered at him. 'Not with you! And don't look at me like that!'

'I wasn't looking at you like anything.'

'You've been staring at my tits all night, you syphilitic Miroir bog-trotter!'

Wrenn's face split in a grin. 'Well, they are nice tits. You must be very sporty. I've heard you can shoot straight.'

'Now you're leering!'

'I'm not leering. I'm smiling. Don't you want a smile from the world's best swordsman?'

'The only weapon you handle is your own dick . . . mangy wanker.'

'I don't think she's feeling the fun of the day,' Wrenn said to me.

She stuck her nose in the air. 'No, because a short-arsed whore-monger keeps asking if I want to see his sword.'

'Come on, Cyan,' I said hastily.

Sheets of rain hissed down on us as we walked out to the gate. I cupped my tall wing around her to give her some shelter and I felt her warmth. We stood in the archway under the lanterns and watched a line of horses moving above their amorphous rain-pocked reflections. The men's heads bowed, greasy rivulets ran down their waxed cotton hoods and tent-like cloaks they had stretched over their saddles. Bow cases projected from bundles and panniers on their cruppers. The nearest horse's ankle flexed, its unshod hoof splashed down shattering the reflection.

Most men were on foot, carrying spears over their shoulders. They walked past wearily, in a worn and handed-down, or looted, assortment of armour; threadbare brigandines with steel scales showing through the rents. Their cuirasses were flecked orange with recent rust, fur scarves tucked into their metal necklines. Mud had rubbed up their boots between their legs to the thighs.

Their standard bearer dipped the Carniss crescent flag under the archway as he passed us. I thought the outpost's association with the rest of the kingdom was a thin veneer; the slightest battle tension scratched it and showed their harsh settlers' identity. Their greatest loyalty was to each other.

Cyan breathed, 'Wow. I haven't seen anything like this before. Awndyn fyrd never go anywhere.'

'Wait till the Eske heavy cavalry turn up. Then you'll have something to stare at. See the man who looks like his mare? That's Governor Veery Carniss.'

Veery was dismounting to greet Lightning. His teeth were so horsey his voice whinnied. His ears were like bracket fungus and, though he frowned, a duelling scar lifted one corner of his mouth, permanently changing his expression for the better.

Cyan said, 'Oh no, look at Daddy being bloody effusive.'

I wondered what to say to her. I wanted her to stop making Lightning's life so difficult, but on the other hand I didn't want her to end up stuck in a palace all her life, even more jaded than she already was.

I said, 'Lightning's torn between his duty to the Emperor and to you. Ten years ago he put his love for you first and it cost him severely. I know in the past he hasn't given you the attention you deserve. But he's incredibly busy now and your attention-seeking is distracting him. Have you told him about your brush with jook?'

'No.'

'Well, Rayne knows. If you took it again, she would definitely tell him.'

'God, no. I don't want to see those *things* again.'

'The Gabbleratchet?'

Cyan shot me a look. 'How did you know?'

'I was there.'

'It was just a dream. It wasn't real.'

'Oh, the Shift is real, all right. San ordered me to keep it secret from Zascai. I suppose he doesn't want mortals trying to reach it and dying in the process.'

Her quick temper ignited. 'You pansy boy! That's bullshit – all bullshit!'

'I was there, Cyan.'

'As a trick of my imagination!'

'The Gabbleratchet is not a trick of your imagination.'

'Gabbleratchet.' She rolled the name over her tongue and scowled. 'I once longed to fly like you can. I used to dream of the smell of clouds and the thin air, the way you smell. Now I have nightmares of rotting hounds. I woke up screaming last night. Daddy wanted to know what was the matter, but I told him that being lost in Hacilith had frightened me. You're not joking, are you?'

'No. There are more worlds than we visited but the distance to Shift would kill us. The Insects' own domain cuts through thousands of worlds; I meant it when I said they make us look inferior.'

'God might be in the Shift.'

I laughed. 'Oh, don't you start.'

'God is on a break. Why not in the Shift?'

'Sure,' I said sarcastically. 'San keeps it prisoner in Epsilon and feeds it chocolate biscuits.'

'Are you the only person to know?'

'No. Rayne has also been to Vista, when she was your age . . .'

'What a scary thought.'

'Yes. She was young once . . . so she says. Your father has seen a Shift creature but he wouldn't discuss it with me afterwards. He won't say a word about the Insect bridge too, even though he burned it down. It's too weird for him.'

'Typical of Daddy to ignore an adventure so important!'

'He's denied it, filed it away in the same part of his mind that he'd use if you told him you'd taken jook. He treats me with a bit more suspicion, though; as if I'm having a disordering effect on the world.'

'I think he blames me for a sea change too,' Cyan said. 'But if he can't deal with it, it isn't my fault.'

'Maybe in twenty years I'll drop the Shift into the conversation and see if he responds.'

The Carniss troops filed in past us. Those on horseback were mainly women, with crossbows slung on both sides of their saddles – two crossbows, to work in duo with their reloaders. They were pulling bolts from bandoliers around their bodies and slipping them point first into the depleted racks attached upright on their saddlebows.

The crossbow bolts' points gleamed – hard steel moulded to soft iron sockets, which cushion the shaft so it doesn't split on impact with Insect shell but drives straight through.

Cyan stared at the division captain, who wore a rain-darkened leather apron over her lap on which a hook from her pulley belt rested. She had been spanning her crossbow in the skirmishes. Insect mandibles had slashed her boots and the metal toecaps shone brightly through the cut leather. Her sallet helmet was not as shiny; it had a golden-brown patina from being polished with sheep fat every night.

She bowed her head to me as she passed. She trailed a leash from the saddle, attached to the muzzle of the division's mascot. It padded beside her on big paws like snowshoes, pasted with mud. Its deep, pure white fur was flattened by the rain, but its galena-grey eyes were keen.

'What's that?' said Cyan.

'A Darkling white wolf.'

Wrenn appeared beside us. 'Don't mind me standing here?' he asked, risking death by dirty look from Cyan. 'The others, they . . . Well, I just feel better to be around you two.'

I understood. He's only thirty, and the average age of our colleagues in the hall was about eight hundred.

'It's good to see Veery again now I'm Eszai,' he said. 'I gave him that scar but he seems OK about it.'

'After all, you did turn out to be Eszai-good,' I said.

He hopped from foot to foot. 'The Emperor, coming here! We're in for it, aren't we?'

I nodded. We stood there for a while, watching the seemingly endless procession. Sporadic hammering still echoed in the background; rain drove through the spotlights around the palisade. The carpenters, proficient Peregrine shipbuilders drafted to the fyrd, were continuing through the night.

Eventually Cyan said, 'That captain was a woman.'

'Yes,' I said.

'Not much older than me.'

'That's right. Come inside.'

'I want to watch.' She stood, stubbornly, and descended into her thoughts again.

I drew my wing closer around her. I don't know about her, or Wrenn, but I wished I was a very, very long way from here, sitting in a bar.

OUR BRAVE BOYS ARRIVE SAFELY

The Hacilith General Fyrd began arriving at Slake Cross today. The pals from Galt and Old Town marched in with a smart step and big smiles, after 900 km by cart. The Captain of the Ninth Division, Connel, 22, said, 'We're raring to have a go at these flying bugs. The people have been great as we came through Awia. The Awians have a spotless record, but now the Hacilith lads are here those bugs haven't got a chance.'

They are the best that Morenzia has, strong, keen and selfless. We wish them the best!

Smatchet, with the troops at Slake Cross fort
Hacilith Post 27.05.25

CHAPTER 16

Lightning reluctantly agreed to let Cyan leave town. Since I was welcoming the governors and wardens while Lightning was holding Insects off from attacking the arriving troops, he asked me to look after her. I took her to the armoury and got her kitted up.

'Here's a brigandine jacket.' I passed it to her and she let it drop dramatically almost to the floor. 'It's heavy!'

I helped her buckle it on. 'It fits very well, though. Here are some greaves for your legs, made for a woman about your size.' I showed her how to fasten them. Even if she was strong enough, I thought it too risky to give her plate armour made for another person, which wouldn't fit properly or might have unseen deterioration. The fyrd who wear the mass-produced stuff that comes in three sizes only do so because they can't afford better. I found her an open-faced sallet helmet with a tapered tail to protect the nape of her neck.

Then we went to the stables but Cyan didn't want to go in. 'I don't know ...' she said. 'Since the ... since the Gabbleratchet ... I don't really like horses.'

It took me half an hour to convince her to enter the stables and she walked close behind me holding my hand. We passed the stalls of a hundred other mounts until I found her an exceptional piebald palfrey that in no way resembled the horses of the Gabbleratchet.

Cyan examined its hooves uncertainly. She still needed some coaxing. 'The eternal hunt won't come here,' I said. 'The Shift is so big that the chances of it reaching our world are minute. To be honest I've always got the impression we're a bit of a backwater. Besides, those things weren't horses. You know that, Cyan; you've been riding since you could walk.'

'I couldn't control that black horse. It was the only time I've never been able to manage one.'

'Because it wasn't one. The Gabbleratchet is just itself. It's inexplicable but we left it behind.'

The stable boy brought me my sleek racehorse. Pangare butted her buff, suedy muzzle into my hands and shook her head, flopping the neat knots of her short, hogged mane from side to side.

'What a peculiar animal,' Cyan said. 'I didn't know you had a horse.'

'Well, now you do.' I held Pangare's halter. 'These Ghallain duns have unbelievable stamina. She might not be a thoroughbred but she can outlast anything your Awian stables have to offer.'

It always takes me a long time to find a mount who can both tolerate carrying a Rhydanne and is fast enough for me. I had heard of Pangare, a seventeen hands high courser winning every race on the Ghallain pampas, and she had cost the Castle a fortune.

While the boy fitted Pangare's bridle and buckled the wide strap of the saddle under her taut belly, I corded my satchel to the cantle through rough-cut holes and clipped my crossbow to it. 'Come on, then.'

Cyan swung up into her saddle, ducking under the beams. 'I'm brave, aren't I? I got back on.'

'Yes, you are very brave.'

'Just like that fyrd captain? I'm as brave as she is.'

'Of course, you could be.'

We walked our horses out of the stable and rode slowly through the commotion of the growing camp. Smoke from cooking fires rose into a pall above the lines of cream tents.

We rode off the road – it was completely packed with carts, horses, and men marching quickly – now that town was in sight they wanted to reach it as soon as possible. It was a river of humanity, and lancer escorts formed other streams on either side.

Cyan leant forward, sped to a gallop and hurtled past me. I gave Pangare rein; she loped exuberantly, kicking out with her forelegs, and caught up with the girl at once. 'Hey! What are you doing?'

'I'm just glad to be outside,' she said, free for the moment of her usual ennui. 'I've been cooped up since Hacilith. I think without a doubt this is the worst place I've ever been dragged to.'

'I'm inclined to agree. Where would you rather be?'

'In the city, of course. All the places I've lived are dreadful compared to Old Town. Where would you rather be?'

'Up there.' I pointed to where, far behind the town, the cliff-topped hills stretched along the horizon.

'In the mountains?'

'Those are just the foothills,' I said. 'You should see the high summits – there are so many pinnacles and valleys that a hundred Rhydanne could live there for a hundred years and never meet each other.'

'Sounds awful.'

'Let me show you what Pangare can do. Come on!'

We galloped beside the road. In the fresh air, it was almost as fulfilling as flying. The sky was a uniform white, with blue-grey round the edges like milk in a dish. The sun, a burnished silver coin, blazed ineffectually at its zenith. An infuriating, unsettled breeze stirred the few grass stalks still upstanding between drying, churned-up clods of mud. Higher on the hillside, bunches of heather hooped and shivered, clustered around the white rocks that looked like the moors' uncovered bones.

Cyan kept looking down the road with a twinge of wanderlust. I would have to watch her carefully or she would try to escape again.

'How many thousands of people?' she asked emphatically. 'Their line goes on into the distance.'

I checked my notebook. 'This is just the Cobalt baggage train. The Peregrine archers should be next.'

'Peregrine?' she said. 'You mean – my manor? I have fyrd?'

'Of course! When you come of age you'll have a fyrd of more than twenty thousand men. That's more than we can see to the horizon.'

'Like the Carniss men the other day?'

'Pah. Carniss only has one muster. Cobalt here, only has two: Cobalt and Grass Isle, and their governor is too old to lead them. You have four musters. The baggage train for Peregrine is twelve hundred wagons.'

'Can we see them?'

'If you want.'

We rode to the end of the Cobalt carts but there was still no sign of Peregrine's sleeping falcon standard. 'They're probably delayed by the traffic jam,' I said. 'We'll have to stop here. I don't want to take you too far from town.'

Cyan reined in her palfrey, halted and gazed at two standard bearers with vertical gonfalon pennants covered in knot-work. It was the Morenzian dexter red hand banner, rendered completely in interlaced lines. The standard bearers, riding wearing nothing but purple or grey singlets and breeches, were so covered in tattoos that their outlines looked blurred. The ingeniously entwined bands, alaunts biting their own legs, elongated horses and spiralling sea snakes in every colour covered them so confusingly that it was difficult to tell where their tattoos ended and their clothes and knot-work jewellery began. Old tattoos had been interlinked with new ones, storiated over their whole bodies apart from their faces.

The battalion they led marched to the beat of similarly decorated drums on their saddlebows. Thickly accented voices burred among them.

Cyan said, 'Wow. Who are they?'

'The first of the Litanee cavalry.'

'Such beautiful designs . . . They're so weird.'

'You'll have seen their designs on the pottery and glass Litanee exports. The Plainslands esteems their work highly. Well, these are the richer craftsmen – most of Litanee's battalions are infantry and they'll be coming in by ship. Let's have a closer look.'

We cantered to meet the head of the column and I greeted the warden and took his name. He let Cyan look at his panoply, all covered in knot-work; stencilled on his brigandine from Hacilith, his helmet adorned with twisting, intertwining Insects. Tooled on his saddlebag and belt, painted on the sides of their carts; every surface was filled with interwoven designs.

'To us they're just pictures,' I told Cyan. 'But the Litanee can read them like biographies. They encode the stories of their lives. He's covered in his memories, so to speak; no one from the Litanee region is ever short of a topic of conversation.'

'I've crossed the canal into Morenzia but I never saw anyone like this.'

'You probably didn't go far south enough. See the pictures of grey wolves, beavers and boars? They're extinct everywhere but the Morenzian forest. And the dogs on their muster flags? Their hunting hounds are considered the best. Your father loves them. See – there's one.' A huge mastiff loped alongside one of the horses. 'Litanee brings them for guard dogs, but I've seen a pack take an Insect down.'

I was cut short by the rumble of hooves behind me. A shrill whistle made the nearest men stop abruptly, and those following stumbled into them. I looked around; a body of Awian lancers were bearing down on us. Metal strips like blunt fingers, riveted in splays to the backs of their saddles, screeched as they cut through the air.

The eagle banner unfurled above them; it was Queen Eleonora and her bodyguard.

The Litanee humans, most of whom had probably never seen such a behemoth of steel and horseflesh, slowed down to squint at the Awians' ostentatious armour.

The Queen raised her hand and the others, with their lances like semaphore poles upright in their rests, slowed and spread out in a semicircle around us. She cantered up to us alone.

She had pulled the chrome tubes of her saddle back out of their housing and it projected higher than her shoulders, a padded support.

The saddle's faring almost enclosed her legs; with her feet in long stirrups she was practically standing up in it. It provided cushioning against the impact when the speed and weight of her horse drove her lance through an Insect. It was splashed with haemolymph.

She tilted her helmet to the back of her head. 'Comet? What are you doing on the ground? Enjoying a good ride?'

I made the introductions: 'Your Highness, I present Lightning's daughter, Cyan Peregrine ... Cyan, your Queen; Her Royal Highness Eleonora Tanager.'

'So this is Lightning's daughter. What a pretty girl.' She looked Cyan over, narrowed her eyes at me and said to her confidentially, 'I'd watch that one, if I were you. He moves faster than rumour in a morai.'

I said, 'Eleonora ...'

Cyan closed her mouth and gulped. All the etiquette she had been taught didn't seem to fit this situation. She tried, 'I am at your command.'

'Of course you are.' Eleonora made her horse high-step sideways. She spread her long, aristocratic wings and gave me and the Litanee men a flap. 'Don't let him be a bad Rhydanne now.'

She wore the 1910 Sword, one of the classic, bejewelled masterpieces made, about once a decade, by the Wrought blacksmiths. All the craftsmen must agree on whether a sword is good enough to be 'dated' and they sell at a very high price.

She put a hand on the hilt and tilted the sword back, pivoting where it hung at her waist, until the scabbard stuck up in front of her like an erect cock. She grasped the hilt and drew the sword little by little, and its soft scabbard flopped flaccidly from the tip downwards. All the lancers guffawed loudly.

'You wicked bitch,' I muttered.

'You wicked bitch, Your Highness,' she corrected with a smile.

She turned, and all the lancers fell in behind her, wheeling away over the open land towards the Wall to resume their patrol.

'What was that about?' Cyan gaped.

'Nothing,' I said, and in silence we watched the Litanee men go by.

I remember Eleonora's costume masquerade in 2017 at Rachiswater Palace. I recall it with extreme clarity; it still sends a shiver through me. I was sitting on the high balcony that curved around the exterior of the circular, spotless hall. Below me, a servant carried a tray of sparkling wine out to the geometrical gardens. All was quiet, compared to the riotous clamour of Eleonora's birthday ball.

She had only recently been crowned, and to emphasise her reign this lavish party had drawn in all the nobility. I had come as an Insect, having half-heartedly pierced holes in real sclerites and laced them over my usual clothes. I picked up my glass of wine and took a sip, sighed and lay back along the top of the balustrade. My wife had a few moments ago taken Tornado's arm and walked him out to the spiral maze for a 'breath of fresh air'.

Music slid luminescent from the hall; I looked down into its white drum filled with laughing, cotillion-ing figures.

Eleonora stepped out onto the balcony, her bronze mask in front of her face. She pulled her metallic silk skirts away from the threshold and shut the casement door. She tilted the mask away, raised her eyebrows and half-shrugged, meaning: What are we doing here, two sensible people like us?

I spidered a bow. 'Happy birthday, Your Highness. Looks like you've passed me at last.'

'Never ask a lady's age, Jant. I'm three years older now.'

'Your beauty increases.'

Eleonora strode towards me with hauteur. Her gloves covered her arms up to the shoulder and the level of her bulging breasts. Her voice was fleshy; 'It will look better if you join the party.'

'I like it out here.'

'Why do you always sit near sheer drops?'

'They attract me.'

She turned from the gardens and looked at the palace front. On both sides of us, its crescent wings curled forward, clasping the gardens' falcate terraces between them. 'It looks like a snail shell.'

'I think it's spectacular. The Rachiswaters had taste.'

My snub didn't bother her. 'Yes. They're almost legend already – but we're still here, making history.'

'You've achieved a lot.'

'Oh, there's still so much remaining.'

I drained my glass and picked another from the tray on the floor. The rumours about Eleonora had piqued my interest. (Why, oh why, did I drink so much that night?) I'd heard that she likes to watch maids tie each other up, that she spends afternoons arranging footmen in interesting patterns for her pleasure, or she calls up gladiators three at a time, two to hold her legs open and the most well-endowed to fuck her.

I'd have to sleep with her, of course; or at least try – the Queen of Awia would be the biggest notch on my bedpost.

She said, 'Did you receive my letter? I mentioned I always noticed you.'

I contrived to look nonplussed. 'I always noticed you, too.'

'You always notice everybody.'

'But I notice you more.'

She said, 'Jant – be careful or you'll appear desperate.'

'I thought I appeared like an Insect.'

She eyed my skew-whiff antennae. 'Where's your wife?'

'In the –' I gestured at the maze.

'Oh. With someone?' She suddenly sounded predatory. She leant over the balustrade and shouted down to the water terrace, 'Let it spray!'

A footman dressed as a ship's captain turned a silver wheel on a polished pipeline and all the fountains sprang up in the gardens. Shrieks from the maze as its water jets spurted. They latticed across its annular marble entrance, trapping everyone inside.

Eleonora laughed. 'Now, feline-with-feathers . . .' She studied every part of my body, imperiously spinning her mask. 'Such long wings. Such a sculpted back. I bet you fuck so athletically . . . you can make me come so hard I see gold flashes . . . Can you?'

I didn't meet her eye. 'Eleonora, I'm the Messenger at your beck and call but I'm not your call boy.'

'Pity. Still, there are others. Merganser's here but he's not as good as you're said to be.' She turned away.

'No!' I said. 'Wait.'

She gave a sidelong glance. 'Go to the Onyx Room . . . no, that's occupied. Go to the Topaz Room, remove your clothes and fold them on the chair. Then kneel on the bed. Await me there.' And she was gone, like a caravel in full sail back into the party.

Eszai have seen most things but I'd never encountered anyone like Eleonora before. (My curiosity will be the death of me.) Some Awians were starting to object to her hedonistic rule, for all that she saved them from the Insects two years before. If the previous King, now exiled in Summerday, living in a garret and writing bad poetry, ever had offspring who could claim the throne, then Eleonora would need to spend even more on guards and spies.

I turned a handstand and walked on my hands through the party, and I ran up to the room. A bottle of wine was already opened for me.

The warm summer evening backlit the curtains drawn over open windows. Eleonora kept me waiting. When she entered, she seemed pleased that I was kneeling. She swung the door shut behind her and fiddled with her skirt. It fell to the ground, revealing her bodice and some riding boots extending over her knees, tight to the shape of her legs.

I could only see her silhouette as she crossed in front of the curtains, tapping the stem of her mask on her gloved hand.

She started to lick my feathers; she ran them through her mouth and tongued between them until I was in ecstasy.

'Put your hands on the bedpost.'

'Why – hey!' She grabbed my balls.

'Put your hands on the bedpost!'

I followed her command. 'Why? Bloody let go!' Before I had finished protesting she whisked a cord around my wrists, tied an ingenious knot and bound my hands to the post.

I struggled, but I couldn't free them. I leant forward and bit the cord – but she was pulling another one from under the pillow. She looped it around my wings, leant back and pulled it tight.

I gasped, beginning to lose the feeling in my wings' fingers. 'What are you doing?'

'Now you can't cover your pretty backside with your wings, when I sodomise you with my riding crop.'

'*What*? – Ow!' She cracked me across the backside. It wasn't her mask – she was holding a whip! She passed it over my mouth and I tasted the leather, and felt the little gold ferrule on the end. Suddenly I was dangerously sober. 'Let me go!'

'Please let me go, *my lady.*'

'Ow! . . . My lady.'

Eleonora smiled. 'You're a fast learner. Not so loud or they'll hear you downstairs. If you dare kick, I'll call for an audience.'

She tilted her head, appreciating her handiwork, studying me closely. She stroked the whip into my arse crack and ran it up and down. I pleaded, but it delighted her; no matter what I said she wouldn't let me free.

She bent her knee up between my thighs and pressed it on the inside of my legs. The sparse light picked out shiny creases in the leather. She pushed me flat and straddled my arse, riding my cheeks as if fucking me until my backside was wet with her juices. My cock stiffened despite myself as it rubbed against the sheets.

Her breathing quickened. I heard her sigh and felt her shudder.

Then – oh, but I won't go into it – she . . . no, I can't say . . . What am I telling you this for, anyway?

Finally she left me kneeling, my cock sore from her quick, expert tugs, because she didn't like the way I kept growing soft. She had flicked my come out of me and it was helplessly dripping off my chest.

I felt as if I had been milked, and my arse was . . . raw.

She said, 'I'll send word around the party to come up and view you.'

'No!'

'Yes. They would laugh to see the Messenger so . . . compromised. Oh, and your wife's downstairs, isn't she?'

'Please, Eleonora.'

Smack!

'Ow! Please, my lady.'

She lowered her mask onto my face and pulled its string tight, restricting my vision to a few centimetres of rucked sheet and my breathing to a warm hiss. She sighed with a beautiful facsimile of sadness, 'Now you're used up. I'll have to leave you on your knees until you're ready again.'

'Again?' I whispered, muffled.

'I'm taking your clothes, so even if you bite yourself free you won't be able to leave the room. Unless you want to join the party naked, on a leash?'

'No!'

'I will leave the door unlocked. Anyone could come in . . . I'll leave it to chance.'

She slipped out of the range of my vision. Music leaked in from the party, then the door clicked shut. Rays filtered through the curtains. Flies buzzed in the open window and landed on me. They puddled their sucker mouthparts on my skin. The tracks of their feet tickled me infuriatingly as they crawled, but I was too abandoned in my shame to shake them off. I felt squandered . . . And I felt beaten . . . I was tricked. Deceived. Eaten.

Hours later Eleonora returned, dropped my clothes on the floor, and untied me without a word.

CHAPTER 17

I flew reconnaissance flights over the seemingly never-ending procession of troops. Far below me, the Peregrine General Fyrd were marching into the gate. Behind their line came the Summerday Select Fyrd, clad in dirty brigandines that had once been saffron yellow. They were driving oxen pulling room-sized espringals on wheels, capable of shooting a vireton spear through the Insect Wall. The Summerday Select were excellent at demolishing Insect paper and they knew the whole front well.

Behind them came the Shivel Select, mustered weeks before for the advance. Their columns were in close order between the lines of outriders and, further off in the distance, another body of men whose colours I couldn't see. I winged closer and looked down to the road. After the leaf-green of Shivel rode the crimson column of the Imperial Fyrd.

The Emperor had kept cohesion in their formation and the five hundred men rode perfectly spaced. All the other fyrds had become one mass, trailing baggage carts tens of kilometres behind.

I glided lower and saw the Emperor. He was leading, on his black stallion, and the diffuse sunlight gave his figure an unnatural luminosity – he was wearing full plate. Two spearmen rode behind him on either side, each steadying with one hand his pennant in his saddle rest. Reflections darted from their helmets. Their banners with the Castle's red sun on yellow flickered forward above them.

I wheeled away and found Tornado with a division of horsemen patrolling the road's north verge. I half-folded my wings and came tearing down helter-skelter a hundred metres in a few seconds, rocking and side-slipping, legs dangling, to the ground.

Tornado looked down from his enormous, ivory-clad saddle. His worn armour had a raised design that replicated the stitches and hemming of denim.

I said, 'The Emperor's in sight.'

'How far?' he boomed.

'About five hours away.'

'You tell Lightning that I will go to escort him.'

'Of course.'

'The Imperial Fyrd will be looking to me for their lead.'

I heard the excitement in his voice; he was absolutely prepared for some unspecified apotheosis. 'You want to stay close to San in case he conjures up god, or something.'

Tornado smiled. 'My place is at his right hand, whatever happens. No Insect or madman will harm him in Lowespass, where I was born and bred. He'll be safe like he was inside the Castle's walls. And you, Comet; you'd better make sure everyone hears his words. And, like, acts on them.'

'Lightning and I will come out, too.'

'I'll be first to San's side . . . I'll be certain to witness any revelation.'

'What revelation?'

'Any revelation!' His shire horse started forward.

Great, I thought. Now we begin to jockey for position in serving San. Nothing short of god returning would quench our bloody egos. I knew Lightning likes to see himself as San's second in command but now he was anxious that the Circle had failed, and Tornado's grim-faced but calm faith and certainty of his role gave him a rock-sure composure. He doesn't understand that it is often the beliefs we hold most adamantly that turn out to be wrong, because we never examine them.

I sped back to town. More sprinting along the streets, knocking on doors, a few breathless words at each one. Lightning, with Cyan unwillingly in tow, was at the top of the gatehouse.

The large square windows in its overhang were a good vantage point. Lightning and Cyan were watching Insects running among the straggling troops, dropping into quarries. They scurried, carried on their long legs over the uneven ground. They bit experimentally at abandoned carts. When the wind gusted in our direction, we could hear them crunching as they chewed up the wood's surface in long lines. They methodically gathered balls of grey pulp in the palps behind their jaws and then rushed away to plaster it along an edge of the Wall.

They tugged at bodies on the ground, cutting them up and carrying them to the lake. The lake glimmered brown as if the wet land had been scraped flat. Dark patches of carcasses and vegetation floated on its surface. On occasional gusts we smelt it; and it turned my stomach. The rotting, waterlogged corpses stank, a bloated, gutsy miasma as thick as gravy. Above the lake, the atmosphere was so solid with the smell you could slice it. It intruded into everything and was destroying our morale.

The wooden room at the tower top always smelled of tar. I leant on the windowsill as I told Lightning the news. He rubbed his eyes and said, 'Ask Wrenn and Lourie to increase guard on the road and I'll send them mounted archers. We'll go out to greet the Emperor.'

A stablehand brought our horses and we set off from town. The last of the Peregrine General Fyrd were coming into the gate. 'Those are my men,' Cyan said.

'Not yet, they aren't,' Lightning told her. 'I called them up with Micawater and I integrated them with my battalions.'

'Why are they all archers?'

'You will mainly field archers. Every man in Awia from eleven years old drills in archery every Sunday. I had that law passed centuries ago. Select longbow men train every day, shooting volleys together.'

'Awndyn doesn't,' Cyan said.

'Only Awia trains so thoroughly. The General Fyrd from Hacilith don't drill at all because Aver-Falconet doesn't want proficient soldiers in the city.'

Cyan's oval face was wind-burnt and coppery and, despite herself, she had an interested shine in her eyes which I found compelling. She kept watching the troops. A small gap and the next set started past, bleary-eyed from sleeping in camps, and with moustaches and beards, not like clean-shaven Awians. She peered at them. 'Who are these?'

Lightning said, 'Can't you see their standard?'

'Yes ... just. So?'

'So who is it?'

'Green, with a white splodge.'

'It is a silver star on a field vert. A green flag means it's Plainslands, and a silver star is ...'

Cyan swung her feet in her stirrups and bounced them off her horse's ribs.

'Shivel. By god, what has Swallow been teaching you?'

'The harpsichord, mostly. And the violin. She said I have no talent whatsoever. She said even you're better at playing music than I am.'

'I daresay,' Lightning said, with a smile. 'I was unaware your education was inadequate. I did give Swallow funds to hire the best tutors for you.'

'She just brought in the old codger from school. I complained but you never checked ... because you can't abide the thought that she could do anything wrong.'

Lightning said nothing.

'Because you keep pretending you love her,' Cyan added.

'I do love her! With all my heart.' Lightning shifted his position in the saddle. 'She is the best musician the Fourlands has ever produced.'

Lord Governor Anelace Shivel greeted us as he passed. Then his Select cavalry vanguard followed on, all in green brigandines and small star badges stamped from pewter.

'Look at all these men!' Cyan gasped.

'Yes, and they've been in the Castle's pay ever since they left their manor boundary,' Lightning said. 'That will dent the treasury badly.'

'As if whether we can pay matters any more,' I said, and turned to Cyan. 'You haven't seen anything yet. This is only half of Shivel's Select, from Coutille and Pinchbeck musters. Basilard and Spraint musters are a day or so behind – and all his General Fyrd are yet to come.'

Lightning added, 'Governor Shivel has the title "lord", so he is able to raise twenty thousand troops or more, and from the sight of these I would say this is the first occasion he has mobilised them all. You see, my dear? Your manor will easily raise enough for you to be *Lady* Governor.'

'Good incentive to look after your people,' I said. 'Encourage them to multiply and they might replace those we'll lose here. Pregnant women don't get drafted. If they have a large family they can choose who to send.'

'Hark at the cynic,' Lightning said.

'The villages are empty,' I told him. 'San will never do this twice.'

'I think I should lead my fyrd,' Cyan said thoughtfully.

I had thought she wanted to renounce her manorship. I glanced at her, seeing her expression resolving into determination; she was reconsidering her identity yet again.

'Certainly not,' Lightning said. 'You don't even know one standard from the next.'

She sat up straight in her saddle for the first time. 'Well, tell me. How do I organise them?'

'I can't believe she doesn't already know this,' I said.

Lightning sighed, 'I blame myself. I'll do something about it as soon as we get back. However, no reason not to start now. Mm ... let me see.' He hovered a hand at the weary men riding past in loose formation. 'These are Select troops. Select have the same ranks as the General Fyrd and they are also used as officers for the General Fyrd – except for the lowest ranks where you can make shift with veteran General Fyrd if you have to. All Selects are trained using the same methods so different manors can fight side by side.

'You will see, after that gap – that's supposed to be a gap – a new battalion starting. The fellow on the smart black courser is its warden. The warden leads a battalion of a thousand men. Beside him is the vice-warden, and behind him comes the captain of a division, that one on the stallion.

'The captain leads a division – that is, a morai – of five hundred men. The division is comprised of companies – or lamai – of fifty men apiece, and each company is led by a sergeant. A company is split into squads of five to ten men, depending on what you need them for – and squads are led by a corporal.'

'I know that one,' said Cyan.

'At least!' Lightning slapped the reins on his saddlebow in mock exasperation.

I said, 'The fyrd has more or less stayed the same since the time of the First Circle.'

'It's an ugly Morenzian word,' said Lightning. 'Each officer has a deputy; you can see the vice-captain walking past us now. The one with the beard. Give him a nod.'

Cyan gave a cutesy nod, and the vice-captain grinned and nudged his mate.

'All right,' said Lightning. 'Don't get carried away. As a governor you can fine anyone, General or Select, who refuses the draft or goes absent without leave; and depending on the circumstances you can confiscate all their property. Your manor's bureaucracy takes care of that sort of thing.'

Cyan was watching, wide-eyed, realising what she had been missing all this time. 'I want to take part.'

Lightning shook his head. 'No, blood of mine. Not yet.'

'You try to stop me doing everything!'

'It is for your own good.'

'You want me to stay inside playing instruments!'

'No – I'm glad you want to fight. At last you've given me a clear clue as to what you want to do with your life. But you need experience before I give you command. We can't waste Zascai lives. You have no idea what to do, you don't even know the manoeuvre codes. You don't appreciate how terrible the confusion can be in the battle's heat.'

'Tell me and I'll remember.'

'You have no practice yet, my dear. If something changed or went wrong you wouldn't know how to improvise.'

'Of course I do. When you visit Awndyn, your work – battles and hunts – is all you talk about!'

'Have you ever seen an Insect close to?'

'Not closer than the ones we've just been watching.'

'And you want to lead men into battle? Everyone would be killed beside you! Our name would be reviled. When the push starts you must not leave town, do you hear me? Continue to learn archery and in a few short years you may lead your fyrd.'

Cyan spat, 'Archery! I'm sick of people foisting their obsessions on me. Every time you visited me all I had was hours of shooting lessons. You just assume I'm interested. Well, I'm not and I didn't want to take part in your tournaments – or Swallow's music. But this suits me –' she waved at the mounted soldiers '– I like this on my own terms, not just to please you. Why should I do archery or music when I'm not interested? I need to find something of my own. Something that's really *me*.'

Lightning sighed. 'You are proficient with the bow, and at riding, but you can't jump straight in.'

The soldiers were staring at Cyan now and she was heat-hazed with embarrassment, but even more determined to make her point. 'You don't know me at all. Even the presents you bring are the same as when I was a little girl. I liked them then, OK, but I'm grown up now. I'm not a kid! You won't let me fly.'

'What? Only Jant and Insects can fly.'

'I mean metaphorically! I want to be at the centre of things!'

Lightning nodded. 'That is your noble blood showing. Very well, but you must learn poise.'

'Must learn poise,' Cyan repeated, making fun of his deep voice. 'Typical. What about you, with that thing you keep doing with your hand?'

Lightning looked down and seemed surprised. His right hand was closed and he had been touching the scar across his palm. He snorted disparagingly, then pulled his gloves from under his belt and wiggled his fingers into them. He said, 'We might be redundant soon. I have more important things to think about.'

Cyan persisted: 'What is it with your hand?'

'A scar from my wedding.'

'Savory? All the poise in the world didn't save her.'

'Ah!' Lightning looked at Cyan sharply. 'You have no right! You know nothing of what happened!'

'Well, tell me.'

Lightning took a breath as if he was about to speak, but hesitated and drew into himself. 'Whenever I smell pine I remember her,' he said quietly.

I spoke up. 'Cyan's half-sister has filled her head with all kinds of lies.'

'I can speak to my sisters if I want.'

'Your half-sisters are envious,' Lightning said dismissively. 'They do not have your prospects and they must come to terms with Ata's unpopularity.'

Cyan and Lightning, like a peregrine and its prey, were trying to gain height on the other in the flight of the argument and it was an unsettling spectacle. I told him, 'Cyan's little more than a squab, but I can find her some work. Otherwise she'll just wander around insulting Eszai. If she was my daughter I'd find her something to do.'

He shook his head with a stony expression. 'Jant, if by some freak of nature you had a daughter, you would want to keep her safe. You saw what happened to Swallow. I've seen her lamed in battle – and Cyan's mother herself slain. The same will not happen to her.'

Cyan raised her three middle fingers at the troops watching her. She did remind me of her mother, who was more of a rebel than I could ever be, because she had been capable of seeing the whole system and knew how to put her immortality to use. I ameliorate myself to the system, with drugs, because I can only see my own small part, as a Rhydanne does who's used to hunting alone.

Yells broke our sullen silence. Pangare raised her head, ears forward. Riders were galloping up the line, passing by the queue and racing towards us at a mad speed. They were at one with their wild skewbald mounts. Their tack and clothes blazed with colour; their flowing black scarves and loose cotton trousers rippled. Red and green pompoms bounced on the bridles, the thick woollen tassels strung along their reins and the fringes over the horses' foreheads.

'Here's something different,' said Lightning, and twisted around to shout at Cyan. 'Look! The Ghallain gauchos!'

They sped past us and barged into Shivel's column at the gate. Annoyed shouts drifted back. More gauchos charged past. Their saddles were low and minimal, with gaudy numnah rugs underneath, and hoppers full of feathered javelins hanging on both sides. They had gathered transparent Insect wings and lashed them to their cruppers. They had tied on Insect heads by the antennae; and dragged the rest of the carcass behind them on lariats.

A man with a wide scarf around his face rode at their fore, his white trousers tucked into leather chaps. He pulled his horse round so tightly it reared. It pranced up to us sideways, spitting foam. It was so high-spirited it looked like it was about to fly.

'Vir Ghallain!' I shouted.

'Salutations, Comet. Lightning, long time no see.'

'Good to see you,' Lightning managed in Plainslands.

'And I you! And I you! Here are my cavalry, owing to San. Do with them what you will. If you can!'

I said, 'What about your infantry? Where are your draftees? They must be weeks behind!'

Governor Vir pulled his scarf fully down from his mouth and said in a singsong accent, 'They are! My steward, he leads them! Has Brandoch arrived yet?'

'Not by a long way,' I said.

Vir turned to an excitable man in a loose headscarf who turfed his horse to a halt beside us. 'Ull, you see, we beat Brandoch. That's fifty pounds you owe me.' He pointed back up the queue. 'San is here. For San to be here this must be the motherfucker of all battles, we said.' He jigged up and down in his worn saddle. 'We can't miss it. Let's see which of us lives!'

'You're a nutter, Vir Ghallain,' I said.

'Nutter enough to Challenge you one day! And put some clothes on. Hey! Hey!' This last to his horse, which bounded forward and he had his back to me before I could take my next breath. Yet more hurtled up the line, churning the muddy ground either side of the road.

'Incredible,' said Cyan.

'Ranchers,' I said.

'There are thousands.'

'Hundreds. He isn't a lord governor,' said Lightning.

I said, 'If you ask me, they're all little kings within the bounds of their manors. They –'

'Hush, Jant! Look!'

On the road, Shivel's green livery was thinning out, and behind them, all was scarlet.

'By god, the Emperor. In armour.'

'I can scarcely believe it.'

The last few lines of Shivel men kept glancing back. They saw the Emperor mounted on black Alezane, with the banners licking the air above him like forked tongues. Shivel men slowed down, walked their horses off the road and stood watching.

As they parted, the Imperial Fyrd rode through, and more of Shivel's infantry gave way before them. I glanced at Lightning; he nodded, and we urged our horses through the crowd.

The Emperor saw us and reined his horse in. Tornado, a step behind him on his right, the standard bearers, and the whole Imperial Fyrd slowed to a halt.

Lightning dismounted and threw himself at the Emperor's feet, on both knees. I heard his greaves grind on the cobbles. I stepped my leg over Pangare's saddle, hopped to the ground and knelt beside him. A couple of quick jingles behind me told me Cyan had done the same.

Seeing us, all the Shivel fyrd dismounted and knelt in a great swathe either side of the road.

Lightning and I looked up to San's face, clean-shaven and expressionless. He wore an open-faced sallet helmet that pushed his fine white hair close to his hollow cheeks, but the wind blew the ends that protruded from underneath.

Every plate of his armour was lustrous – enamelled white with no ornament but the fastenings of a billowing white silk cloak. Suns were damascened on the bare steel scabbard of his ancient broadsword which hung with his shield from the saddlebow.

I managed one glance and bowed my head again.

Peach-coloured shafts of sunlight shone between our horses' sinewy legs. Their musty, sweaty bellies and withers hemmed us in, their hair brushed against the grain in dark streaks, their hocks covered in drying mud. Their shadows were no more than small patches directly beneath them. Pangare flipped her docked tail and pawed the road too close to my head. I looked up to the underside of the Emperor's horse's long chin, as it chewed its bit imperiously.

The first company of the Imperial Fyrd raised a cheer, then the second company, then the third, and when all ten companies had cheered separately, the five hundred men cheered together; a great, deafening wordless roar that went on and on until San raised his free hand. The cheering straggled into silence.

'My lord,' said Lightning, so dry-mouthed I could hear his tongue clicking. 'I'm sorry – we are – that it's come to this. Please ... And we'll ... We will bring the Insects under control. We will mend our error.'

San rested his reins on his scrollwork saddlebow. 'Lightning, Comet, to your feet. Every second we stay the numbers in our rearguard diminish.'

San's long limbs were encased in armour and, once I'd recovered from the shock of seeing that he actually did have legs, I noticed how thin they were; no muscles on his shanks at all. He must be wearing the cloak to make himself look bigger. I risked a closer glance and saw beads of sweat on his neck. He must be feeling the exertion of wearing armour and riding after fourteen hundred years in the Castle, but it did not tell in his noble bearing. He showed no sign of strain on his face: his self-control was absolute. He conveyed the same majesty under the open skies as he did sitting at the focal point of the Throne Room.

The pennant-bearers behind him were whey-pale and poker-faced, their jaws clenched, their mouths firm lines. They were telling themselves this wasn't happening. Their set expressions were partly pride that such a role had fallen to them, part anxiety from riding for days in far too close proximity to the Emperor, but mostly the blank-eyed denial of men determined to carry out a job they really didn't want to do.

The Emperor asked Lightning, 'Have Insects flown again?'

'They flew every day for three days. There have been no more flights since.'

'Good. I must talk with Frost immediately.'

I stammered, 'Er, Frost has changed. She's . . . well . . . she's somewhat stressed.'

'Is she still the best architect?'

'Um . . . I think so.'

'She will be the Architect until she loses a Challenge. I will make a new Lawyer, Artillerist and Master of Horse from the best in the town to complete the Circle. We will need them in the coming days, but when times are easier I will open their positions to worldwide competition.' San gestured for Lightning to ride on his left, level with Tornado. The Strongman was calm-faced and expressionless, looking straight ahead, his hands invisible under the circular vamplate on his axe haft.

Lightning beckoned to Cyan with a smile, asking her to join him, but she turned her face away. She seemed overwhelmed.

San said, 'Comet, ride ahead and announce our entry to the town.'

I don't remember climbing back onto Pangare but I must have done because the next instant I was on a level with the Emperor's face. I gave a quick nod and with shaking hands I unlaced my dented post horn from the saddle, where it shone like a New Year's decoration. I gave Pangare a single word and she leapt down the road.

Behind me the whole Imperial Fyrd and Shivel fyrd began to move again, with the jingle of tack and clop of hooves.

The Emperor San here! I thought as I rode. The Emperor San in armour! I had seen his white panoply before; it was displayed, by tradition, in the Castle's armoury but nobody ever thought he would actually wear it.

When a new Armourer joins the Circle it is always his first honour to make a perfect suit of armour for the Emperor to the highest specifications, copying the measurements of the last. Sleat had put so much effort into creating San's perfect armour that I am surprised he ever made anything again.

I heralded San's arrival into Slake Cross. People lined the roadside, leant out of windows, clustered in the hoardings, stood on the new earth ramparts. I slowed and cantered Pangare through the gatehouse arch, and hundreds of people dropped to their knees in a great swathe as I passed. I could get used to this.

CHAPTER 18

I rose before dawn and went to the washroom to have a powder bath. Those of us who have wings moult and re-grow flight feathers continuously, one or two at a time, but in the last few months I had lost six or seven, leaving me with great gaps in my wings. It made flying more laborious and I was at the stage of exhaustion when, no matter how much I ate, my meals didn't provide energy any more. San had asked me to sleep in a pavilion in the canvas city because he thought my presence might curtail the fyrd's drinking (ha!), the inter-manor rivalries, brawling and petty theft breaking out there.

As I rubbed handfuls of talcum powder between my feathers I reconsidered the problems of the last few days. I had been gathering information for the Emperor, everyone was bombarding me with questions, and I had to think one step ahead. The Rachiswater fyrd vied with Tanager, and the Carniss fyrd stole things from everybody. The Awndyn fyrd had been arriving all night, stomping past my tent. The carpenters had been hammering, by firelight, while the Emperor slept – presumably – in my bed. It was bloody bizarre. On the positive side, he had waived most of the formal courtesies, so I spent less time kneeling on the floor.

The powder relieved some of my itching. I took a shower, preened and oiled my feathers into a glossy iridescence. I tied back my hair in wet black rat-tails, lit a cigarette and returned to the hall feeling much more relaxed.

The hall had become a small, austere version of the Throne Room. Most of the Eszai were listening attentively as the Emperor, with Tornado and Frost beside him, discussed our situation.

Tornado was so huge that usually his very gravity pulled everyone's attention towards him, but now he managed to look humble and our concentration focused on San's gaunt figure. Nobody dared question the Strongman's self-styled role as San's bodyguard, testimony to his profound faith although I thought he was overdoing it.

Frost, on the other hand, looked cadaverous. She spoke clearly although much too fast: 'M-my lord – I have estimated the number of eggs in the lake. Given the parameters my approximation is, of necessity, rough. Rayne dissected an Insect and and and she thinks they're hermaphrodite. I have calculated the capacity of air w-which one Insect needs to fly, then figured the dimensions of the flight, and therefore the number of Insects in that volume of air, and what percentage reach the lake, and since they seem to contain between ninety-eight and one hundred and fifty eggs, assuming all eggs are v-v-viable, I –'

'Frost,' the Emperor said gently.

She bit at a crooked finger. 'Um ... between seven million, eight hundred and eleven thousand, six hundred and twenty-one, and –'

'I see,' said San. 'Seven million Insect spawn.'

'Nearly eight, yes.' She gave a quick nod and continued. 'I estimate three hundred thousand five hundred and twelve adult Insects in the v-vicinity of the lake. They defend it so vigorously that no lancer has m-managed to reach the shore. My only suggestion is that we open the d-dam gate and d-drain the lake.'

The Emperor said, 'Does anybody have an alternative proposal?'

Silence around the room. Most eyes were downcast, including mine. 'Very well,' the Emperor continued. 'We shall march to the dam. Frost, what do you need?'

'Twenty draft horses – to be harnessed in two teams of ten – and and and sufficient troops to clear the way.'

'Very well.'

Frost sat down again, muttering, 'Two, eight, five hundred and twelve, one hundred and thirty-four million –'

'Comet?' said San. It was my turn to rise. 'Yes, my lord?'

'What new troops do we have? What manor is currently arriving?'

'Fescue, my lord. Lord Governor Darnel Fescue came in last night with the musters of Fiorin and Melick, both Select and General. They're mostly infantry and shield fyrd, with a few thousand archers. I've put some on escort duty. Marram muster is coming in now and the others will be arriving all through today.'

'How many men?'

'Twenty-two thousand. Behind them, probably after dusk, will come a division of felons under guard from Hacilith's jails. I'm lodging them in Lowespass Fortress. We can discount some manors from our plans: Cathee takes six weeks to raise troops, and Brandoch's infantry will be coming in last, if at all. When I visited, the governor was away touring his musters for the biannual assizes. I had to go around all his reeves' halls till I found him. But I'm expecting the remnants tomorrow.'

'Is our provisioning adequate? Where is Cloud?'

Trc Cloud stood up, in the front row. He was an energetic, sinewy Grass Islander who never seemed to need any rest. He pulled his cloth cap from his crew-cut head and twisted it between his hands as he spoke. 'The rationing will have to continue. I have requested grain throughout the Fourlands. All our depots in Lowespass are empty and the bastle farms have mostly been ransacked. I've ordered all the goods being unloaded to be sealed so their scent doesn't attract Insects. The carts coming up from Rachiswater all have armed protection, and my agents are licensed so no one can defraud us or buy in our name.'

'What about lodging?'

The Cook shoved the cap into a pocket in his striped apron. 'We're extending the encampment. The barracks in Whittorn is full. I sent men there until the reeve sent letters back saying he couldn't accommodate any more. I'm glad it's unseasonably cold because the towns are overcrowding. We can't keep so many people together for much longer. Not to mention the lake, it's a potential pool of infection.'

He continued, very self-assured. After all, he had won his Challenge by provisioning these forts – with the world's best cassoulet which the troops much preferred to the previous Cook's pork stew.

While he was speaking, a movement on the steps caught my eye. Cyan had crept down from the upper storey. She peered around the stone newel post, but Lightning was the only one to acknowledge her. He swung his arms unfolded happily and gave her a smile. She straightened up, glided towards me, and settled beside me on the bench.

'We must determine the order of the advance,' the Emperor said. 'Tell me your suggestions.'

Tornado said, 'Infantry. Lots of infantry with axes and so on. That's our best bet.'

Wrenn said, 'I agree, but swords are lighter to wield for a day's march.'

'A swift cavalry charge,' said the new Master of Horse. 'That way we'll break through 'em.'

'No, no,' said Wrenn. 'If I only had the pick of the resources, I'm sure my approach would be best.'

'Well, you don't have the pick of the resources.'

Lightning rolled his eyes: here they all bloody go again.

Lourie Hurricane, the Polearms Master, spoke. Lourie was usually so silent that on the few occasions he opens his mouth everybody listens, knowing he will say something well thought out and worthwhile. 'The advance should be led by a pike phalanx as best adapted to open ground. We have ten thousand trained pikemen from Rachiswater, Litanee and Eske. My Lord Emperor, they will provide maximum protection to the rest of the host following.'

San asked Tornado, 'Do you agree with Hurricane's suggestion?'

Tornado considered it. 'Yes, my lord.' I could barely see his eyes, shadowed as they were in a deep mass of wrinkles. The rest of his round face was smooth with no wrinkles whatsoever – perhaps they gathered to make a determined assault on his eyes. He reminded me of one of the massive columnar stalagmites in the caves below the town. The signs of constant physical endurance had worn into his face just as surely as water carves clefts in rock; I could imagine him formed of living flowstone. By a slow, cold process, in a cavern stifled by darkness, water that looks clear but is saturated with dissolved rock drips to the ground and precipitates, building a sullen soldier from the feet up. Trickles run down the outside of the column depositing a trail of wet stone, that over millennia grows lumpen and irregular to form his paunch and buttocks. The hollows in the sides of his elbows and knees are smooth solution pockets. Random drips of hard water give him a physiognomy and knuckles. Then with a great heave he tears one foot and the other free of the bedrock and walks off to fight Insects. Tornado could be crystallised loyalty. With a beer gut.

'Lightning?' said the Emperor.

Lightning had been smiling at Cyan and he jumped. 'My lord?'

'Do you agree with Hurricane's proposition?'

'Yes.'

'What arrow-power can you supply?'

'Well ... We have forty thousand archers, ten thousand crossbow men. I will not use crossbows on the field because they cannot shoot indirectly. We will shoot blind over the pikemen's ranks and eliminate Insects immediately in front of the advance. I'm sure the Polearms Master and Javelin Master will agree. However, we need Tornado's infantry to flank us. We have long used this technique with sarissai, akontistai and hastai ... I mean, pikemen, javelin men and heavy infantry.'

Cyan was frustrated. She leant to me and asked, under her breath, 'What are the plans? What does he mean?'

I gave an irritated little gesture to quiet her.

'I want to take part,' she said. 'I'll lead my fyrd as a great governor should.'

'Well, listen and you might learn something.'

'Just what I'd expect from a glorified errand boy.'

Lightning said, 'The Armourer informs me we are holding nearly a million arrows and we can secure the same again. That includes two-thirds unmade arrows, and the off-duty fyrd are making them up.'

Cyan rocked from buttock to buttock. Lightning gave her a 'not now' look, and continued, 'The Lowespass, Carniss and Ghallain mounted archers will provide mobile support.'

Cyan cleared her throat and piped up, "Scuse me?'

The Emperor looked straight at her. So did the rest of the Eszai.

Under San's gaze, Cyan had no choice but to rise to her feet. 'My lord ... um ... I would like to lead Peregrine's archers.'

Lightning sent her a sharp look. The silence of curiosity quickly became one of embarrassment. Everyone glanced at each other impatiently.

I tugged her jumper, hissed, 'Sit down!'

Lightning looked from Cyan to the Emperor and spoke calmly. 'My lord Emperor, this is my daughter Cyan Peregrine. She will soon inherit the manor but I am afraid she is a little premature in her ambitions.' To Cyan he said, 'That is impossible for now, my dear. Please sit down.'

'But –'

Lightning beamed around at everyone and spoke louder, for our benefit: 'I'm sure that some of us will be happy to listen to you after the meeting ... for a very reasonable fee.'

A ripple of nervous laughter discharged around the room. We darted quick smiles to and fro.

'But –'

'I will brook no more argument. You don't understand; this is a very important conference.'

The Emperor waited patiently but Tornado said, 'Get her out of here, Lightning.'

Cyan glowered at him. Lightning said, 'She's just trying to be noticed. Find yourself a sense of humour.'

'This is not, like, a cabaret.'

Lightning said to the room, 'See how ready she is to roll up her sleeves and lead the fyrd? Don't you wish she was your daughter?'

We laughed more openly this time. Cyan did not take well to being discomfited in front of the Circle. 'Peregrine manor seems no more than one of Micawater's musters,' she said. 'If I mayn't lead my men, I'd like to win their trust as a captain perhaps.'

The Emperor looked at Lightning, clearly requesting him to end the interruption. I was about to chip in, myself, but Lightning, with his hands on his hips and an amused expression, seemed well in charge.

'No,' he said. 'You may not. You may watch our operations from the town walls.'

'I'm joining in, so tough! You can't stop me! When you're engaged, I'll ride out!'

He spoke to her only, with serene persuasion. 'You are being unreasonable, blood of mine. Unless you sit down I must find you new accommodation. Say, the upper chamber of a peel tower?'

Cyan hesitated, trying to figure this out. 'Are you threatening to lock me up? You can't do that!'

He sighed, exasperated. 'These men will escort you safely to your new apartment.' He gave a nod to the Micawater fyrdsmen standing with spears either side of the door. They began to walk towards Cyan.

She glanced with round eyes from them to her father. 'No! I only wanted to –' A guard took her arm but she booted him in the ankle and snatched herself free.

She pointed at Lightning. 'I Challenge you!'

An intake of breath around the room.

Lightning stood still, mouth downturned, transfixed. Emotions welled up one after another in his expression: profound hurt. Bafflement. Pride, too, and anger. The anger surfaced quickly and quenched all the rest. 'Do you?' he said, measuredly.

Cyan stuttered and recovered herself. 'I, C-Cyan Peregrine, Challenge you, Saker Micawater, for the position of Lightning within the Castle's Circle.'

I looked around at all the shocked faces. Even the Emperor had raised his eyebrows. Tornado turned his eyes up to the ceiling, his mouth in an amused twist.

San announced, 'I uphold the Challenge. After the current campaign.'

'Very well . . .' Lightning managed a dry whisper to Cyan. 'Now get out of my sight.'

'But . . .'

'But what? What do you mean, but? Haven't you done enough? Do you *know* what you've just said? Now the words are out, you can't take them back! I'll have to shoot against you now!' He took a step. 'How could you *do this to me*? After all I've done for you. You repay me by . . . Throwing it back in my face! Not a thought of what I've given you. I saved you, on the ship. I reached out! I keep reaching out!'

He spread both hands and shook them towards her. His face and neck flushed so red they were blotched with white. He yelled in fury, 'Think before you speak! How can you Challenge *me*? I *taught* you to bloody shoot! Any man here has a better chance than you do. Any Select archer is stronger than you. What do you want? My attention? Now of all times? You always had my fond attention – now you have my Lord Emperor's and Her Highness's and all the *bloody* journalists' attention as well!'

He took a breath, turned and punched the table. Punched it with the other hand, and leant his weight on it to breathe, leaning over the map, his head bowed and massive shoulders hunched like a lion's. Cyan was too petrified even to cry.

He continued, more quietly, 'Nothing I do is good enough. Is it? Nothing I can buy you. All those days I shirked target practice and spent with you. Look at yourself –' contempt turned in his voice '– cashmere and my sister's ruby pendant. You want for nothing, I made sure of that. You don't know how privileged you are. I protect the farmers grafting in your fields. I look after the ships lying in your harbour. In return, you interrupt me! You try to get yourself killed and borne off to the Wall! Fractious, captious, ungrateful, delusional child! You're just like your mother. She took advantage. She betrayed me, and now you do, too. Oh, you are no flesh and blood of mine!' He collapsed into his chair. ' . . . Fyrdsmen, take her to tower ten.'

Their footsteps died away in silence.

'We will resume,' the Emperor stated. 'Tornado, what is the current casualty rate?'

Nobody listened to the Strongman. We were watching Lightning. He sat, chin on chest, staring at the floor, numbly unaware of his surroundings. Minutes went by and he seemed to have retracted totally into himself.

His shoulders were so taut they drew horizontal creases across his waistcoat's chest; under his shirt sleeves his forearms' pleated muscles were like iron. His hands dangled on the rests covered by his greatcoat, but all of a sudden he relaxed and the breath went out of him. He stood up, and muttered, 'I must have some fresh air.'

As if running on instinct he swept a deep bow to the Emperor and said glassily, 'My lord, will you excuse me?'

The Emperor inclined his head.

Lightning folded his arms because his hands were shaking, and left the hall.

His few enemies in the Circle looked smug; a couple leant to each other and whispered – the Archer humiliated by his impudent, imprudent daughter. I glanced around the room – most of the Eszai seemed determined to pretend it never happened. They never let someone else's misfortune affect them.

'Like mother, like daughter,' I said loudly.

'Shut up, Jant.' Eleonora crossed her legs with slow deliberation. But I had broken the tension and the meeting continued.

I remembered, ten years ago, the Emperor saying that Lightning should listen to the child. I wanted to dash out and offer him my sympathies, but I was obliged to attend to the battle plans. In the past, I would have gone after him regardless of the consequences, but that was many years ago, and I am so very different now. Maybe in one of your romantic novels, Saker, your daughter would have loyally complied with your wishes and fought by your side, but real life doesn't work like that. Real life doesn't work at all.

CHAPTER 19

LIGHTNING'S CHAPTER

My own daughter just Challenged me! In front of the Circle and the Emperor – and my lady Eleonora! I think I'm burning up. By god, by god. What has she turned into? With all I've done for her! Try as I might, rack my brains as I do, I can't think what I could have done better. Does she think I don't love her? – I would have changed the world for her! May the rivers Mica, Dace and Moren flood the world and drown it if she ever had cause for a fraction of one complaint.

I have failed, for her to turn out like this. I don't know how. Yes, I do. I have not spent enough time with her. First there was the swarm and then Tris and – why can't she be patient?

The girl is my just deserts for being a damn fool. I went against my nature with Ata; I didn't really love her. She sent for me and I found her sitting, sobbing at her table on the ship. Such a strong woman should never be driven to tears. I put an arm around her to comfort her . . . fool that I am.

I must have spoilt Cyan. Yes. Yes, that's true. My pampering her desires must have led her to think she can demand the world . . . How dare she? . . . She doesn't realise that worlds are hard to come by.

By god, I haven't been this angry since . . . since my family spilt. We all make errors, there's no need to keep castigating myself about that. Yes, the little mistakes made by princes are devastating on account of our power.

Who has she been talking to, to turn out so badly? It must be the effect of Hacilith and that rotten brood of Ata's. Cyan always seemed all right before, but now delinquency hangs around her like a cloud of perfume. I used to love her innocence. She might have been an accident, but she woke me up. A year feels like a year now, rather than ten minutes. I'm alive again – or becoming so – I'm experiencing more now in a year with her than I did in a century before. She invigorated me . . . more, far more, than even Swallow could. Damn it, I even wished I could be like her.

Do I have to give up my own daughter like I've given up everyone else? No, wait. Take a breath. Step back from this – you know you can, there's been worse – and think. In a way she has played into my hands. I have a ... a legitimate way of dealing with her. She isn't familiar with the procedures of Challenges. I did the right thing; I'm free of her for the time being and I can talk to her later, at my convenience ... I am sure she will be very repentant.

The way she has turned out is not my fault. Events swept me along too quickly to make time for her ... I regret not having the pressure of time that mortals do. Promises are made; time passes and sometimes they are not properly kept. Reality intrudes on the best of intentions: doesn't every arrow that flies feel the pull of the earth? But, damn it, I have my duty; I can't neglect it. I knew she was growing quickly, but millions of things demanded my attention ... Swallow should have been more dutiful herself.

But no. When an archer misses the mark, he should turn and look for the fault within himself. A failure to hit the target is never the fault of the target.

The world is becoming too crass. Oh, that old refrain: everywhere is similar, and becoming more so. In the time that reared me the Grand Tour only took us around Awia, and it startled and inspired us. Now the Tour takes our sons and daughters thousands of kilometres and shows them four lands in the space of a year, and they return unimpressed.

I am fighting to protect the very ideals that Cyan is trying to change, and ... oh, what is the bloody point? I'm sure in the past I never had to justify my every move. There is an informality, these days, that causes uncertainty; nobody knows how to behave any more. It was easier when there were proper codes of behaviour ... I am too old and inflexible to bear this blow. Old armour splits; only soft jackets withstand sword blows.

Don't talk rubbish.

The world *is* changing, though. Changing radically, in ways I don't care to understand. And what will I be left with? A sense of nostalgia, for the rest of my life in long centuries to come. A terrible sense that I have missed the only thing worthwhile. Be steady, keep calm. Where are the nerves of steel I have when Insects are charging at me and I have to wait for my range?

I walked more slowly because a recent, mostly healed, rapier wound in my back was starting to catch. I passed into a deep shadow and looked about me, perturbed. I had come as far as the outer road.

I must have paced across the square and three streets completely oblivious.

The tower of the gatehouse overshadowed the barrack blocks on my either side. Soldiers smoking outside on their steps were staring at me in surprise, curious at the sight of Lightning striding down the street in his shirt sleeves.

I passed them, then I stopped dead. The banner of Morenzia was flying above the barrack doorway. A red clenched fist. The red fist: the marriage rite. The Hacilith fyrd must have assembled, one part of my mind observed, but with the sight of the flag my other thoughts winged far away, to Savory. My Savory. Cyan was wrong to taunt me about her. If she knew what happened she wouldn't dare to mention Savory at all.

The wind gusted and the flag flapped, pulling its cord through its eye hole. It released me from my trance and I looked down, aware I was touching the scar across my right palm, rubbing it with my left thumb and forefinger. I turned and walked slowly back to my room. The civilised parts of Morenzia don't conduct the blood-red hand ceremony any more, only the people of Cathee still do, but the country has kept it as their device. I am so used to seeing it, it hardly registers, but occasionally when I am pensive I look a little deeper and the realisation of what it means takes me back to Savory. And again I am in the marriage hut, waiting for nightfall.

I was in the marriage hut, waiting for nightfall. The hut walls were wattle hurdles woven around living trees; I sat on the floor and looked up to the beams of the round roof, constructed in spirals like a spider's web. Through the smoke hole at the apex I watched folds in the clouds push against one another. The dusk sky was different shades of old gold like the mixture in a bottle of illuminator's ink.

After dark she will call me, if she hasn't had second thoughts, celebrating in the village all day with her friends and family. I heard their laughter as they dressed her up and drank to her, and asked her over and over, as is their custom, if she's *sure*, if she's really *sure*. Soon I will know if they have managed to sway her conviction; if I stay here well into the night and she fails to call me, then without a word I will go to the trader I had employed as a guide and leave the dense forest.

Outside was nothing but pine trees behind pine trees all the way up and over the fir-covered ridges of the vast mountain forest of Cathee. Cathee could not be more different from my hunting woods I loved so well; it was dark; it was trackless; it was wild. For hundreds of kilometres from Vertigo town to the Drag Road, from the clay paddy fields of Litanee to the cliffs of the cape there were only trees. Even at the edges where conifers segued into broadleaf forest it lost none of its impenetrability.

I had fasted in the marriage hut for twenty-four hours, alone, and I was expected to use that time to think about Savory and whether I wanted to marry her. I did with all my heart; Savory, when she called me, would never find the hut door swinging wide and her groom long gone.

Love filled me and uplifted me. I was intoxicated; I floated; I was full of love. After so long I was about to be married! Completed – as I had never felt complete before. I had always felt as if something was missing. I had always felt unfinished, but two people living together as one is to be complete. Savory did not have wings, so we would not be able to tangle our pinions together and I would not be able to bury my face in the warm, feather-scent in their pits, or stroke my fingers along their serried rows. They couple in a vulgar way, do humans, face to face rather than belly to back, but then my cousin Martyn and I used to throw ourselves on each other that way, when she had the key to the belvedere, or with excitement after the day's hunt. The smell of deer blood, oiled armour, dry leaves, the perspiration of our eager flesh … It would be strange at first to have a woman without wings, but then it would be strange, so strange, to have a companion at all.

The beauty of it – waiting outside in a far place, for my love to call me, while sunset dyed the sky strange colours and the light drained out of the forest. I wanted to tell her all my history – the past to be discussed in the future – we would have so much time!

I glanced up as the first wolf howls carried on the breeze. The Cathee grey wolves were dumb lanky beasts with dirty pelts and eyes glazed by starvation. They scavenged in large packs and scratched ancient things out of the villages' middens. The few villages sheltered from them behind circular palisades, but I had my new crossbow and I was not afraid. The worst they could do was give me fleas.

I could hear distant laughter from the village and I felt ostracised, but it would be worth it when they throw open their gates and Savory leads me in, when they accept me as one of their own.

I wondered what Mother would think of that. I found it easy to picture her face, even after all these centuries. *Son*, she would say, *do you know what you are doing? She has no fine blood whatsoever.*

That never mattered to me.

You just picked her out of the ranks!

I always knew I would meet my true love on the battlefield.

She is probably not even a virgin. Some fyrdsman or woodcutter will have taken her en passant.

Oh, let me marry whom I love.

Mother raises her eyebrows: *Ah, but is she your true love or your latest substitute?*

She is my true love, and besides, she has the strong will I admire and she is my equal in intelligence. I am immortal and I need someone of whom I will never tire.

Son, immortal or not, you vex me. What are you thinking of, participating in barbarous rituals?

Truc, I had always assumed I would be married our way, but Savory wanted this, and the way she explained the ritual seemed to be more deeply binding than anything invented in Awia and the Plains. Back home, bride and groom simply stand at the front of the audience and together proclaim, 'We are married.' To undo the union is just as simple a procedure, but there could be no separation when Savory and I are wed. This was to be her last visit to her homeland, and I agreed to the suggestion with delight, although later that night her face seemed strangely clouded. I would not have denied her anything. I was determined to know everything about her, and become familiar with her circumstances, the places that she had known and loved. I wished I had met her earlier, and I knew too little about her and the Cathee, but I thought I could learn quickly through taking part. I fretted; where is she? Surely it's nightfall. Why hasn't she called me?

Powders for preening feathers were not imported this far south, so I felt rather unwashed. I fiddled with the red plaid cloak they had given me, because it kept slipping down. The rough wool was unbearably scratchy and I was not at all sure that I had folded it correctly.

I first saw Savory – the doyenne of hoydens – at the front, sitting on a bench outside a pavilion, waxing her bowstring. I was struck that moment by love's arrows, and they sank their barbs deep beneath my skin. The first arrow was her beauty; it entered through my eyes and from there to my heart, where nothing I could do would extract it. The second was her simplicity, her few belongings, her careless mode of life. Like all the Cathee she lived within her skin as if it was someone else's coat she may well have to pawn for her next meal. The third arrow was my own memory, of Martyn, because Savory had the same fox-red hair. Unbraided, it tumbled on her shoulders, pooled on her lap. Its tips brushed the backs of her knees as she sat with one leg over the other, massaging linseed oil into the risers of her bow. From that instant I was her willing servant; my heart belonged unreservedly to her.

Savory had seen the seasons, slept outdoors and laboured hard. Martyn, on the other hand, had skin as pale and clean as split sycamore wood. Martyn was taller than any forester and Savory did not have her upright bearing, but Savory's sparkling, little-girl lightness shone through her experience of harsh realities – like cultivated flowers in a garden grown wild.

Savory had left Morenzia owing to a blood feud between her family and another in the village. It had whittled down her family until she was the last. The forest had nothing wholesome to offer her, so she joined the fyrd and led a division of Cathee woodsmen, the best archers outside Awia. I pieced this together from her broken language, because I could not speak Morenzian. I yearned for a word that we could share, that might begin our courtship, and for agonising weeks I stayed silent and watched from afar.

She taught me her language over six months, though I remained hesitant and only Savory could fathom my accent. She had heard of Lightning in old legends, but they were rarely accurate and she only half-believed they were about me. I tried to impress upon her how different her life would be from now on but, having never seen my palace, how could she understand? She was strong enough to break through my reserve. After all, it had been a hundred years since I had ...

I loved her the more because she did not hang back, afraid. Her antics made me laugh. She was not so headstrong as to ignore my sincere advances. Neither was she afraid of the depth of my devotion, retreating into reserve of her own. She reciprocated. I would have given her roses if we hadn't been stranded at the front. She would have found herself with half of my estate. So then, I asked her to marry me, as composedly as I was able, although I felt like froth inside, like bubbles in Stenasrai wine.

She hung on my arm and looked up, all smiles as she consented. She did love me as I loved her! If perfection blooms only once in a thousand years, that's enough, because I can pick that bloom and it will live the next thousand years too, and on into forever. Constancy is rewarded, I know that much.

'Saker!' Her voice broke the silence. It rang out with confidence above the rustle of roosting birds. 'Saker Micawater!' She called me to the stone. I rearranged the uncomfortable cloak one last time and hurried out.

Savory stood outside next to the cup-and-ring stone. She was an indistinct figure in the dusk, her hands and face pale patches. As I drew nearer I saw her face was painted with henna: red dots with concentric circles on both her cheeks. Her hair hung in long red braids either side of her face. A plaid cloak pinned at her shoulders reached the ground, and beneath, a short simple cambric dress with a girdle. On her forearms and lower legs she wore half-armour for me. The glittering vambraces and greaves showed her limbs' slender curves. The contrast between the hard, warm metal and her soft yielding skin made me desperate to touch her. All along her arms and legs she had daubed the double black stripes of Cathee war paint and her first two fingers were still stained from where she had dipped them and drawn them over her skin.

The dark and glossy smell of wet pine needles was all around, acidic and medicinal, almost like liquorice. The trees' straight boles stood close together as if at attention. Above them, a crescent moon hung like a cutlass in a sky so dark blue it appeared purple.

The cup-and-ring stone was as tall as my chest, a natural rock pushing up from the soil and penny-coloured fallen needles. It was rough-grained and uneven at the edges. The cup-and-ring had been carved on its sloping top many centuries ago, Savory had said, perhaps even before the Empire was established. Though privately I doubted that it could be so old.

In the centre was a shallow round cup, surrounded by five concentric rings, the pattern you see if you drop a pebble in the lake. The carvings had long since taken on the red rock's patina. From the cup in the centre a channel had been carved, deeper as it cut through the rings, to the edge of the rock. The cup was therefore a tiny basin with a drainage conduit.

I did not study it for long. I only had eyes for my painted warrior bride, and she smiled at me but we must not speak a word. My heart beat fast and I was suffused with warmth and exultation. I would take her from here to the Castle to kiss the Emperor's hand and then we would live together forever!

Savory drew her skinning knife from her belt scabbard. It had been polished and it gleamed. She raised her right hand, the fingers spread wide, the vulnerable palm showing. She pressed the point to the ball of her thumb and it slid under her skin. A dark stripe sprang up. Blood ran shining, down her wrist. Savory fisted her hand and dripped it into the hollow of the cup.

She passed the knife to me with a solemn nod. I did not take it: the occasion required a grander gesture. I drew my short sword and held it horizontally. Savory's eyes widened. Hastening to reassure her, I grasped the blade in front of me and slid my hand along it. I felt it bite. My signet ring zipped on the surface; my hand became warm and slick. A trail of blood shrank on the oiled metal into a thin line of crimson beads. I did not let the pain show on my face. I curled up my hand as she had done and let the drops fall into the cup until our blood, mixed together, breached the level, ran down the conduit and began dripping on the ground.

Quickly we held our wounded hands under the flow and felt drops patter on our cut palms.

Still separate, still without speaking, I yearned to hold her. The strength of my desire was close to desperation: *I couldn't go without touching her for any longer.* She produced some cloth and bandaged my hand tenderly, and I bound hers.

She nodded. 'Now we may speak.'

'I love you,' I said simply. I spread my wings completely around her. In our feathered sanctuary we found ourselves looking into each other's eyes, and were trapped there. I whispered, 'What would you have me do for you?'

She found it hard to say anything at all.

'Kiss me.'

She tilted her head upward and touched my lips with hers. I smiled and returned the gesture. She took two handfuls of my cloak and pulled me down to the bloodstained grass. We consummated our marriage there.

Savory stepped happily, leading me along the meagre track. Hatchet nicks on tree trunks marked the way. Among the scuffed fallen needles, the forest's myriad little white flowers had their petals closed.

We went through the gate and into the village. A huge bonfire was blazing in the middle of its clearing. The villagers rushed hand in hand in a boisterous, whirling dance around the fire, in and out of the houses in a long, crazed chain, wherever the maiden at the front chose to lead them. Their uncouth music flickered like a flame up and down an insensible scale; it seemed to have no timing, no beginning, no middle; it ended abruptly and started again. Seeing me staring, the guitarist grinned and plucked with his dirty fingers a most ideal arpeggio.

Some men were digging out a pit in which they'd roasted a wild boar. Five hours ago they had built a fire in a cobble-lined pit, let it burn to heat the stones, then put out the fire. They had laid in the carcass and buried it to cook. Now their spades scraped on hot cobbles, they thrust them underneath and lifted up the boar. They cheered and shovelled it out onto a trestle table. I caught a glimpse of golden crackling and flesh as brown and shining as mahogany. Whole branches of rosemary had been wrapped around it which had cooked onto the skin like fragile and blackened embroidery.

A delicious aroma drifted over. A shout went up, the chain of dancers broke and ran towards the roast pig. They crowded and shoved around the table.

Firelight pulsed and merged, making yellow and hollow beasts of their faces. They tore at the crunchy skin and ripped it away to the hot meat. Juices ran between their clawed fingers. They shoved it into their mouths – round black holes – and while they chewed, they flailed both hands to grab more. Boys and women turned away with fistfuls of stringy meat. Still more villagers arrived to join the frenzy. More and more came running and pressed themselves close around the table. Outside the circle of firelight the village lay empty. As the meat stripped away it became pinker, the white fat was bubbling. They dug their fingers into it, split the carcass apart. They dragged it up and down the table, opened it up. With a warm rip they detached a leg and they jostled into two clusters, a smaller group around the leg wiping it this way and that on the table top as they pulled off the shreds of flesh, holding them preciously until they had enough for a mouthful.

I felt awkward. I was ravenously hungry but was I expected to shoulder between them? I couldn't bring myself to. I didn't want to touch them.

The villagers drew back. They regarded the table: the bones lay stripped clean. Women shrugged and walked away, licking grease from their fingers. Such a show made me feel sick – they had taken less than five minutes to demolish the boar.

One man was so drunk he staggered towards the pit without seeing it in the darkness, a blacker rectangle on the shifting grey ground. He fell straight in. Then, finding the ashes still warm, he turned on his back looking satisfied up at the overcast sky and went to sleep.

A woodcutter at the table unbuckled his axe. He cracked open the bones with a few deft blows, and the villagers set to again on the marrow.

Savory jigged up to me, a succulent earthy smell of roast boar on her breath and an oily shine at the corners of her mouth. She had torn mouthfuls of it with her teeth. She looked surprised, then annoyed: 'Didn't you have any?'

'I couldn't get close.'

'Ay! What will they think, that you haven't tasted your own marriage feast?'

She lead me to the edge of the clearing, in front of their log cabins that all face inward. Some bear skins were spread on the damp grass in front of the reeve's cabin.

'Sit down there, my love; I'll go and bring you some. Smoked pig, baked spuds and pine beer! Isn't that a feast for an Awian lord?' She kissed my cheek and ran lightly towards the smokehouse.

I watched the party. A travelling troupe were enacting a raucous play. The villagers still paid me little heed and took it to be as much for their benefit as for the bride and groom's honour. That was of no consequence; I sat and watched happily. I couldn't understand a word, but I recognised it as a familiar play based on an incident I remembered well. Some five hundred years ago, the Castle's Master of Horse was beaten in a Challenge. He lost his place in the Circle but in the following years his devoted wife practised so much that she was able to beat the new incumbent and win immortality again for them both. Such is the strength of love.

In amongst the mummers, children kicked the embers for baked potatoes. I looked around at the few windowless log cabins, thatched with pine branches held down by netting. Big stone weights dangled from them, all carved in the shapes of animals: beavers, cockerels and squirrels. Every doorway had a beaming white plaster face mounted above it.

The reeve's house was behind me and, on either side of its door, bas-relief sculptures of naked women adjoined the wall. They were life-sized in smooth plaster, so white they seemed to glow.

By the woodpile a big cooking pot hung on a thick chain from a tripod. It was smeared with the remains of hide glue, in which boar nets had been dipped to make them stickier. The enormous twine nets were draped on A-frames. All Cathee villages trap wild boar and carry them to Vertigo to be salted, barrelled, and sold as salt pork to the caravels.

The play was ending and, as usual with dramas of that nature, my character turned up to sort everything out. I was smiling at the actor playing Lightning, when from the corner of my eye I saw two men at the far end of the clearing. They caught my attention because they were skulking at the edge of the firelight. They had a similarity; maybe a father and his grown son.

They began to walk purposefully towards the smokehouse. Was this part of the play? Their faces were masked with determination. As people noticed them, they fell silent and it stirred a sense of menace. I felt the crowd's expectation. Should I be doing something?

The men walked behind the bonfire; its rising heat rippled their figures, and where they passed, people turned aside and the party fell silent. The villagers near me watched, fearful eyes most white and nostrils flared. The two men reached the smokehouse, and axes appeared in their hands! They were wearing cuirasses!

The blood feud! I jumped up and dashed into the reeve's house. From the rack I grabbed my crossbow and a bandolier of bolts.

The backs of the axe men were disappearing through the smokehouse door. I frantically wound the cranequin, but my wound reopened and my hand shook badly. I raised the bow and shot at the father. The bolt snicked into the log wall; the man turned and looked at me, then ducked inside. I *missed*. I was struck stock-still in shock. I *don't* miss. I *never* miss. I can't remember the last time I missed!

I lost sight of him inside the smokehouse. There was no time to reload. I started to run to Savory, but a second later the men were out of the door. They tore across the clearing, eyes popping, fists punching in front of their chests. What had they done to her?

They passed some distance in front of me, their axes flashing in their hands. From their other hands dangled longbow strings. I had seen enough of the world to know they are used as garrottes.

I tried to spin the cranequin back but the strength had gone completely from my cut hand, as if it didn't belong to me. *Click-click, click-click* was all I could get out of the damned mechanism as it rocked back and forth on one ratchet. The men had reached the gate. A woman of their family pulled it open. They sped into the forest and it swallowed them.

I yelled and sprinted into the smokehouse. Where was Savory? Hanging hams swung at my touch as I felt my way between the drying racks. My wife's white dress was a spectral smudge. She lay face-down on the pressed earth floor. I knelt next to her. The back of her neck was cut across cleanly with one axe blow. There did not seem to be much blood.

I jumped up and dashed after the murderers. As I passed the bonfire I threw in the crossbow, in a flurry of yellow sparks. Who talked me into using that thing? If I had my longbow, I could have put seven arrows through them in the thirty seconds they took to cross my field of vision.

I dashed through the gate and into the prickly frustration of the forest's edge. Their fleeing footsteps crackled far in front of me, deep between the trees. The cold leather of my sword grip was damp in my hand.

I saw pale flashes heading downhill. By god, the bastards were signalling at me! But it was only the reflection of the bonfire on their back plates and it soon vanished.

I found myself surrounded by a wall of fretted branches, hard cones, bending needles. They clutched my clothes but I pushed further and further in. Shadows and twigs looked like they could be ... but they weren't, when I got closer. I could hardly judge distances, over the nettles and around snarled brambles. Where the trees grew more densely packed, the ground was clear and springy with needles. I couldn't see in the low space under the branches; it was pitch-black.

I ducked down and hesitated, trying to catch my breath. All was silent. The murderers could be anywhere; without faithful Lymer I would never find them. They had gone to earth, and even if I flushed them the forest was their world and they might have picked up longbows. I was more lost than I have ever been. I listened carefully, but I only heard wolf howls muted in the far distance.

The village's bonfire backlit the trees. Numbly, I turned and stumbled to the palisade, to the clearing, and into the smokehouse, to Savory. Those craven murderers knew she could have beaten them, with her skinning knife and the desperation of self-defence, had they faced her. They had cut her down as she knelt to slice meat onto my plate.

As my dear wife fell she had upset a sack of kindling and there were pieces of bark all over her. I cleared them away and I turned her over. She was ghastly cold. I used my cloak for a pillow and closed her glazed hazel eyes gently. I kissed dear Savory.

The pointlessness of it unhinged me. I jumped up suddenly and ran out of the smokehouse, but the village was deserted. Everybody had bolted into their homes and wedged shut the boards serving as doors. 'Savory is slain!' I shouted. 'Help me find the murderers!'

From inside came small sounds that told me they were busy with other tasks. They were hinting that I should stop causing a disturbance, stop bawling and go away. I stared around the clearing: the bonfire burnt down to a red ember murmur; a clutch of boar ribs on the table; an overturned cup on the bruised grass. Nothing indicated that minutes ago this had been a lively party.

I ran from cabin to cabin banging on the blank doors. 'Help! Help me for god's sake!' But I could not speak the language properly; nor they mine. I hammered on the reeve's door. 'You know me, Asart! We must catch the murderers!' No answer from within. I clapped my hand flat over the sun brooch on my shoulder. 'In the Castle's name, I'm her husband! Tell me who the murderers are! I'll bring my fyrd! Damn you all – help me or I'll raze this village to the ground!'

What was I doing here? Here in the back of beyond? I should never have come to this filthy, tree-dark province at all. These folk had no inkling of my power. My palace where one of their daughters would have lived was no more than a tale to them. They valued their murderous traditions more highly than the distant Castle itself. Here I was the foreigner and how could they understand? With all the time in eternity I would not get through to them! I lost my mind and I curled up, faint, beside the fire.

At first light people emerged from their houses and went about their daily chores as if nothing had happened. I lay on my stomach on the wet grass watching abstractedly. They spoke not a word of Savory. They shut the events away and went on with tapping sap and lathing wood. How could they – when the world was shattered?

Years of blood feuds had bred in them a toleration like a collective sickness of the mind. They were quiet and cowed, but acted as if the random murder was fair and justified. She had been, after all, a Savory. Father Savory killed Pannage and was killed by Pannage's grandson. So it went on. So it still goes on today.

Day only truly dawned on the village when the sun rose above the trees and slanted its rays down into the little enclosure. The dew began to vanish, though it remained, grey and sparkling, in the cobwebs, the palisade's shadow and each hovel's woodpile.

Two men, their sleeves rolled back, went into the smokehouse and brought out Savory on a stretcher. She was naked. They had stripped her naked. I felt a jolt as if I had been punched. My legs went weak but I stumbled to her and tried to cover her body with the cloak. The men put their arms out and blocked me. She was a pale sculpture, she lay on her long hair like a pelt, as red as the hair on her legs and sex. I had last seen her naked when – I had kissed her thighs and breasts – their disrespect was too much for me. 'I'll take her back to Awia! I'll place her in my tomb!'

My pleas were cut short by the high squeal of a fiddle and a flute. The door of the nearest cabin flung open and the troupe of mummers tumbled out. They started dancing! They began to dance the old, false story where the King of Morenzia steals the King of Awia's wife and Awia raises its fyrd to bring her back. The dancers whirled furiously around Savory's stretcher, stamping either side as they acted out the battle. The King of Awia was mock-stabbed by the human king, and he fell. The dancers all jumped on the fallen actor, their hands scrambling under his clothes. They brought out real human bones, all dry and painted black, and began to dance with them, clacking them together.

What did it mean? I had no idea but the dishonour was too much. I drew my sword and was about to set among them and slay every last man, when the reeve came out of his house.

He was wearing a mask. It was a human visage, of heavy white plaster, as if his own face had been smeared with thick paste, but for its blind eye sockets, in which were placed cowry shells. Their pursed toothy grooves made blind black lines. In the mouth of the mask real human teeth were set. No, not set: the mask was the front of a real skull, sawn off and covered in plaster. The rest of his clothes were normal and he came towards me walking confidently, as if he could see through some hidden contrivance in the mask.

Savory had introduced me to reeve Asart, the village leader, answerable to Lord Governor Aver-Falconet. He reports to Aver-Falconet's steward twice a year. Why was he part of this abhorrent dance? Did Hacilith know? Did the Castle know? Of course they must, I wrested from myself. I am the only one ignorant of the Cathee, because nothing like this is written in the books of Awia's libraries.

The rest of the village left their work or emerged from their cabins silently, as if at an agreed signal. The women in short shifts and rawhide aprons, the men in their plaids and breeches, they formed a silent queue behind the stretcher.

I stared around the log cabins, and now I could more clearly see their ornamentation. The heads above the doors were real skulls! They were covered in plaster, shells set in their eye sockets, and affixed with paste all around them to the surface of the logs. Their snaggling yellow teeth showed between carefully moulded lips.

I looked to the reeve's house. The sculptures that I had taken to be women were whole articulated skeletons re-fleshed with plaster. It had flaked off here and there; I saw brittle weathered bone underneath. Their curves and features had been shaped, but where the breasts swelled over some woman's ancient rib-cage, projecting instead of nipples from the plaster were the hooked and open beaks of vultures.

The reeve had by now left the gate and the rest were following. I stumbled behind, some distance from the rear of the procession. I had to see where they were taking Savory. The reeve, villagers and mummers still carrying bagpipes, flutes and bones pushed between the trees on a little-worn path, in complete silence.

We were walking uphill, but I could tell no more. All the forest looked the same to me and I could scarcely see it. My eyes were stinging, I was weeping freely, and trying to see through my tears as through an awash uneven glass. Savory was a white blur as the procession wound between the close phalanxes of dark green pines on either side. The twisting brambles at the trackside scratched me, held me back, and snatched loops of thread out of the damn plaid cloak.

At length we came to a clearing, and beyond the screen of trees I glimpsed a gigantic mound, grassed-over equally with the ground. It must be man-made because it was completely circular, some ten metres across and surrounded by flat black stones propped up against its circumference. Three huge undressed rocks at the front formed a portal, one resting horizontally on two uprights, from which a tunnel lined with slabs led into its lightless depths. A single stone, standing a metre in front of the entrance, obscured the passageway from my sight. I assumed this was their crude mausoleum, like my great family tomb, in which they would lay dear Savory, but the procession did not stop.

The villagers cast glances at the knoll as they passed by, with looks on their faces almost as if it reassured them – and even the reeve's skull mask turned towards it for an instant.

The forest was now alive with birds cawing and skitterings in the undergrowth. I took the arm of the last man in the procession, who carried his toddler son on his shoulders: 'What's going on? Tell me, man!'

He shook me away with an angry sneer.

A great cloud of birds burst up out of the trees ahead, cracking through twigs and branches. They separated out; kites and buzzards began to circle but the big glossy ravens dropped back down into the tree tops further on.

A terrible stench of corruption rose with them and hit me with such strength I gagged. It was the fatty smell of putrefying human flesh, which I have often encountered on the battlefield. The villagers showed no concern. I pulled my handkerchief from my trouser pocket and pressed it over my nose.

We came up to a high log palisade, but the silence and the smell told me this was not another village. Its gate had a woman's skeleton plastered to the centre. Its eye sockets shone dully with cowry shells and all its teeth were bared between open lips. Again, its breasts were sculpted with panting beaks instead of nipples.

The Cathee entered an enclosure where the short grass was free of saplings and in the centre a great wooden scaffold stood two metres high: a platform raised on six trunks stripped clean of bark. The top of the platform was not solid, it was a criss-cross of rough-hewn timbers. Shreds hung down between them. At first I thought the shreds were fabric but they did not move with the breeze. A large strip dangled through the grating, tasselled at the end – it was a human arm and hand.

They set down the stretcher next to the platform and gathered along it, standing in ragged fashion side by side. I remained in the shadow of the gate and watched.

The reeve stood by Savory's head. She looked so peaceful, as if she was asleep, were it not for the outrage of her nakedness. The reeve climbed a rough ladder of logs, up to the platform and appeared high above us against the sky. He crossed towards the villagers looking up, but as he did so he accidentally kicked the arm. It was mostly bone, it swung and fell off, and up stirred the rank smell of carrion. My gorge rose and I hunched over and vomited. What were they doing to my wife? I fell to my knees and heaved again and again – till it hollowed me out.

They did not hand up the whole stretcher. There were no ropes nor pulley to raise it to the top of the platform with any sort of dignity. The two bearers just picked up Savory's body, one holding her ankles, the other her upper arms. He grappled with handfuls of her hair. Stiffness had set in and they had to turn her body as they lifted her. I saw in a flash the pink line of her sex between her legs. The masked reeve bent and seized her round the ribs, manhandled her onto the platform and laid her down.

And then he descended and walked underneath the scaffold, beckoning the villagers to join him. They huddled together, bent over, and began to pick bones and teeth from among the grass. The women folded their skirts and gathered them inside, the men cradled handfuls. Up and down they walked in methodical lines as if harvesting, and any man who found two bones still articulated, pulled them apart with a twist and a yank.

They piled all the bones on the stretcher, and in silent procession like before, they carried the stretcher out past me, though I was on my knees and coughing up bile. I shrank from them but I had to follow or in their stony blindness they would have barred me in with the dead. The first few heavy ravens were swooping down with guttural calls from the trees to feed.

I trailed some distance behind the procession to the mouth of the burial mound. They stopped by its portal, in a semi-circle. The reeve and stretcher-bearers slipped behind the stone screen and into the tunnel. They must have intended to deposit the bones in there.

I had seen enough. I spat and turned away, deranged. I ran back to the village, where I took a bow, a quiver-full of arrows and a spade. If any of the Cathee had tried to stop me I would have cleaved his head in two with it.

So they would take Savory, my Savory, and leave her to rot, feed her to vermin, then jumble her bones with everyone else's? So they wanted to obliterate her identity until no one could recognise her remains? So they were content to forget her unique, intriguing life? What did that mean? What sort of people scrub out the honour of their ancestors? Their disrespect tore at my heart, cracked open and bleeding inside me. Savory is still a person, still my love. What is she to the Cathee? An empty vessel? No longer a woman, just an object that's part of their past, that they will place with the rest and tidy away so life can go on? My life could not go on. My life had stopped. I thought of what we Awians do, with our glass carriages drawn by ebony-plumed horses. I thought of the vigil I kept over Mother's lying-in-state, a drawn sword in front of me and my wings spread. How we exhibited the old bat as if she could still feel, in satin on the catafalque strewn with lilac and lavender and rue.

I could not leave Savory there to rot. I was furious with myself, my jaw clenched so hard my head was pounding, my fingers rubbing over the dirty bandage around my palm. I *missed*. I missed my *target*. I fouled a shot with a crossbow. I went over and over it in my head, unable to comprehend how that could be. When blood began to seep through my bandage I welcomed it as a punishment and a reality.

She will not be crows' food up there on that *platform*. I kicked my way into the enclosure and scaled the ladder. Corpses were arranged lying on their backs all over the timber grid: naked old men and women, some babies, and a dried puddle of a foetus. Some were the maimed fragments of fellow warriors that the Cathee fyrd had managed to ship home from Insect battles. They were in various stages of decomposition and most had lost the small bones of their fingers and toes already through the grid. Some skulls lolled back, disconnected and eye sockets staring at the sky. One was bloated, but most were pecked to no more than skeletons pasted with dark red shreds of sinew and muscle. Green algae grew on the cups of their vertebrae. The ravens had started already on Savory's hazel eyes. I quickly picked her up and, hugging her to my chest, carried her down the ladder.

I bore her in my arms to the clearing with the marriage stone. *Savory, it will make shift for the only monument I can give you here. But you will have a monument, my hunting lady. You don't belong with those people any more.* I raised the spade and speared it into the earth with all my strength. *You are not one of them.* I turned over the tangled roots and soil.

I dug Savory a grave where we first made love. The cup-and-ring stone was her headstone, and I did cheat the villagers of their foul ritual. I covered her tenderly and then I lay down beside the grave and embraced my arm over the little mound of disturbed earth. I do not know how many days I lay there.

I do not remember leaving her side. I must have walked east through the forest for days to the coast. I must have lived on the game I shot, but whether or not I could still shoot I cannot recall. I was absent all that time. At Vertigo, the town built against the sheer walls of a deep chasm, someone gave me passage on a ship for Awia. I returned to my house at a gallop and ordered the gates locked and chained. I wrote no letters and spent no time on the archery field. I accepted no visitors and ignored the Messenger's frantic queries. I waited for my hand and a shredded heart to heal.

CHAPTER 20

Some time after Lightning left the meeting, it ended and the Eszai dispersed. Over the next five days I flew errands for them. Each evening I had piles of correspondence to digest and report to the Emperor; mostly badly spelled semaphore transcripts.

I returned to my desk in the corner of the hall. I started writing but I could hardly concentrate. I kept wondering about Cyan's Challenge and Lightning's strange behaviour. I stared at the piles of letters, under the glass jam-jar of worms I was using as a paperweight. The worms didn't seem to be moving very much. I leant forward and peered at them. They were all limp and flaccid, coating the bottom of the jar. I picked it up and shook it, and they put out a pink, braided-together tentacle and tapped on the glass.

The worms arced up in the middle and raised two perpendicular strands. A sagging worm swung across from one to the other and joined halfway up. It looked like the letter H. It collapsed back into the feebly writhing mass. Weakly they sent up another string from which three comb-like projections shot out: E. A single thread with a right angle of worms at the base: L; and it summoned its energies for a thick strand that curled round on itself at the top: P.

I picked up my paperknife and poked some holes in the lid. The worms sprang to life, stretched up eagerly forcing their tiny mouths against the underside. They pushed ineffectually at it, swaying like animated hair.

They dropped down and started swirling around the jar, in one direction like water going down a plughole. They became a whirlpool of worms, riding up the inside of the glass with an indentation in the middle. I thought they were trying to push the glass apart so I gave it a shake and they slumped again. They started throwing up angry tendrils so quickly I could scarcely make one letter out before it was replaced by the next. An L, an E and a T. Let. A U, an S and an O. What? A U and a T. Us Out. Let us out. Y-O-U-B-A-S-T-A-R-D.

'There's no need for that,' I said, and placed the jar back on top of my correspondence. The Vermiform furiously started cycling letters. As it warmed to its task it threw up whole tiny words, the letters made of one or two worms apiece.

L-E-T-U-S-O-U-T

L-E-T-U-S-O-U-T

I signed a missive, blew on the ink, folded the paper. I dropped some sealing wax on it and embossed it with the garnet sun emblem seal which I wear as a pendant.

L-E-T-U-S-O-U-T

LET! US! OUT!

PLEASE

'That's better,' I said, and was about to flip the jar's clips when I was struck by a thought. 'If I free you, promise you won't harm me?'

The worms paused.

'All right,' I said. 'You're staying in there.'

I looked up across the hall and saw Rayne approaching, carrying an envelope. I didn't want her to see that I had stolen her sample of Vermiform worms so I picked up the jar and slipped it into the big pocket of my coat folded under the table.

Rayne looked over my shoulder. 'You're transcribing code,' she observed.

'It's shorthand. What can I do for you?'

She offered me the letter in her clean, smooth palm. 'Could you take this t' Cyan?'

'Are you sure? It's nearly midnight.'

'Jant, think of wha' she mus' be going through up in t' peel tower. She knows she's made a fool of herself.'

'Well, I'm not sympathetic.'

Rayne nodded sagely. 'Neither am I, bu' I do like her. She's a smar' girl. When t' Circle broke three times, we were in t' coach between Slaugh'erbridge and Eske. Cyan consoled me. I'm grateful for tha'. We talked all nigh'. Can you take i' now? I'm up t' *here* with work in t' hospi'al.'

I stood up and gathered my coat. 'Of course.'

The full moon's light basted the surrounding moorland grey and smooth. Like a ball of butter, it rolled along the top of a platter of thick, opaque cloud and lit up the margins from behind with a creamy glow. Silver noctilucent clouds hung in the western sky over the foothills; the last light ebbing from their thin streaks gave enough illumination for me to see Insects hunting by scent in the valley.

Small bats were fluttering in circuits around the top of the peel tower. I could hear their squeaks as they passed me.

I have had planks nailed out from the window ledges of each peel tower's uppermost room. I swept up to this one and touched down on the end. The plank bent like a diving board. I shuffled up to the shutters of the bow windows in the hoarding. The shutters, as large as gates, were closed. I splayed both hands on the splintered and weathered wood, bent down and put my eye to the crack.

Cyan stomped past the slit, lit by a lantern outside my field of vision. She disappeared and then stamped back again. She was muttering to herself and biting the end of a pen.

I knocked on the shutters and she looked up. She rushed over and pushed them wide. They flew open and hit me in the face. A brief whirl of the sky; I flapped my wings powerfully, cart-wheeling my arms. I toppled off the plank, caught its edge with both hands, and dangled there for an instant before I kicked my legs, flexed my arms and drew myself up again.

'Careful!' I hissed. 'You nearly broke my nose!'

'Good!' said Cyan, and drew the shutters to. I pulled them wide and stepped down into the room.

The tower-top room was big, ten metres square. A single bed and side table by the fireplace were the only furnishings apart from empty crossbow bolt racks on the walls. It was ill-lit, no fire burning in the huge stone grate, but lamplight shone up through holes in the floor, through which arrow sheaves could be hoisted. Cyan's lantern gave a pool of colour on the table next to her silver plate and fork and a chessboard that seemed to have stalled halfway through a game.

Lightning's dog rushed up from the bed, barking, then recognised me and sat down by my feet. I closed my wings, the primaries sliding over each other like fans. 'I only have an hour.' I said. 'I shouldn't be here.'

'Well, I've been trying to write to you for hours,' Cyan retorted. 'Where have you been? What's going on? No one's visited me. I haven't spoken to anyone except the guards for five days!' She retreated to sit on the plain bed, leaning on a blanket roll against the wall, and gave me a baleful look. 'Will you let me out?'

'I'm sorry, Cyan; no. The least the Castle can do is save your life.'

'You could rescind Daddy's orders if you wanted, and the guards would release me. Why are you so afraid of him?'

'I'm not.'

Her forehead furrowed. 'After the guards dragged me out, what happened? What did Daddy say? . . . No, don't tell me. I hate him. Old titwart. I can't believe he's done this to me!'

I stalked across the room, pushed my ice axe hanger behind me and sat down on the fireplace surround. I ached all over and I felt sick. The constant undercurrent of panic and sleep deprivation we were all living with was taking its toll. I said, 'I brought a letter from Rayne.'

'One letter in five days!'

'You don't know how hard-pressed we are –' I gestured at the window in the direction of the town. 'Everyone's terrified and San is driving us like pack horses. I've been sending dispatches to position battalions for the advance in two days. I spent the last hour fending off journalists and checking Lord Governor Purlin Brandoch's cavalry slinking in on second-rate nags. In an hour's time I have to collect letters for your father –'

'Huh!' she cried.

'Hand-deliver the important ones and collect replies. I think I'll report that you're still furious.'

'I'm fine,' she said, not looking it.

'Do you have a message for him?'

She glared at me defiantly. 'If the bastard is in a good mood, tell him I'm dying of melancholy. If he's feeling miserable, tell him I'm singing like a lark.'

'I can't fathom what mood he's in. He's bottled everything up, and he seems very detached, as if he isn't allowing himself to think about it.'

I pulled a sheaf of letters from my coat pocket and leafed through until I found Rayne's envelope. Cyan accepted it and scratched the seal off with her fingernails.

'Is Rayne the only person who's thought of me?' she asked.

'Don't be ridiculous. No. Hasn't Lightning given you his dog for company? He's been sending you the best food, otherwise you'd be eating biscuit and salt beef, like the rest of the Zascai.'

'So he hasn't forgotten me?'

'No. He's incredibly busy too.' I sighed, wondering how I could make her understand what was happening. 'This is the biggest advance of all time. When they start lining up in formation, you'll see what I mean.'

Cyan lay back on the bed. 'I tried to write to you but I couldn't concentrate. I made a complete arse of myself.'

'Yes, you did. I wish I'd –'

'Oh, I don't care what you'd have done. I wasn't Challenging you.'

She put an arm across her eyes and said, 'Pissflaps. Will you let me free, Jant; please?'

'Look, Lightning put you in here for a reason. If I let you out, and you get killed, he would shoot me. If through your actions, you get someone else killed, I would be blamed. And I don't fancy that.'

'It's like being in prison!'

I stared at her. Her truculent tone was beginning to pique. 'Trust me, it's nothing like being in prison.'

'Oh, Jant's *angry*.'

'Stop that! Behaving like a ten-year-old is what landed you in here.'

'*Please* set me free. I'll reward you. I'll give you –'

'It won't happen, so don't try to tempt me.'

The deerhound leapt on the bed and Cyan took its head in her lap. 'Good dog, Lymer.'

I knew she had never really seriously considered joining the Circle. Everybody harbours a secret wish to be immortal. Everyone, now and then, wonders what it would be like. But like most people Cyan had never genuinely entertained the thought, and I bet, in her head, she keeps repeating over and over what she did and imagines the Eszai laughing at her.

I knelt down with a cheerful air and began to build a fire in the grate, refusing to be overwhelmed by the awkward situation. Cyan watched me with animal antipathy.

I said, 'I recognise a spur-of-the-moment Challenge when I see it. All Eszai recognise bluster, too. We're often Challenged by people who know they're not capable of beating us but simply want the attention. By the Castle's rules we have to take each and every one seriously, and separately, because you never know when one is a true talent ...'

'I *don't* withdraw my Challenge, if that's what you're driving at.'

I gathered handfuls of the dried moor grass, heather sprigs and sprays of thyme strewn as a floor covering. I used them for kindling and lit some skilfully with the last of my matches. I swung the kettle spit above the flames and began to make some coffee.

'Rayne was recently Challenged,' I continued. 'By a healer, some Awian noblewoman. High Awian is a useless language for science, and Rachiswater university mainly teaches arts. They're not far behind Hacilith though. This woman believed in the properties of precious metals to cure diseases. She made gold mirrors and shone light into the patients' eyes. It was no laughing matter ... her bedside manner was so good many patients were cured by their own expectations. Rayne set her a Challenge at the front, and she learned that no shiny mirrors or soothing music can stuff a patient's guts back in.' I shrugged. 'Only three places in the Circle have never changed hands: Rayne's, Tornado's and your father's. Everybody who Challenges them makes a fool of himself. You're not the only one.'

'It was his fault,' she said. 'He pushed me to it. In front of the Emperor and everything.'

'Cyan, I've better things to do with my free hour than talk with a stroppy cow.'

'Please tell the guards to release me.'

'No. After seeing you make an exhibition of yourself and humiliate Lightning, even though I told you to sit down, I'm surprised I'm here at all.'

'I don't regret it,' she said.

'He's been the best archer for over fourteen hundred years!' I tried to make her understand that length of time. 'Awndyn didn't exist when he was mortal. Or Peregrine. They didn't have highways, they didn't even have coaches. They used to have ballistae and now we have espringals, thanks to the effort of San knows how many Artillerists. Lightning improved bows, from the early awful type they had before the Circle, to the shit-hot bows you use now. He's lived through all this, and been on top all the time! It's as much his day now as it was then. So it's bloody stupid to Challenge him.'

''Spose you're right.'

'He's seen the four corners of the world . . . Five, including Tris.'

'In the past, though. He lives in the past. And Swallow lives in the future – but I live in the present.' She got up and crouched in front of the fire, rubbing some warmth back into her hands. 'He hasn't been a father to me at all. He's been more of a father to you than to me.'

'Not really. I –'

'That's what he is, your substitute father. It makes me sick how you're blind to his faults.'

'Nonsense.'

'Yeah, well why are you defending him so much?'

'I don't need a father. I survived by myself for years in Hacilith. Worse than anything you've seen. And –' I swept a hand, rattling the bangles around my wrist '– for example, these peel towers. I won a battle myself at the furthest one, at Summerday in nineteen ninety-three. Yours truly and Shearwater Mist beat the Insects before Lightning had even ridden out of Awia. We were the only Eszai in command; the brains and the brawn.'

'Which one of you was the brains?'

'Me! Damn it.' I poured hot water into two cups of coffee. 'Mist was bitten through the shoulder and I had to look after him almost as much as the Zascai.'

'I wish I could be involved in something like that.'

I would have laughed if she had led with a trace of humour in her voice. 'You're not joking, are you?'

'No, I'm not . . . I want out.'

'Stay here, Cyan. Insects are running everywhere. These towers provide enough shelter to last a swarm. There are rainwater butts on the roof and enough stores in the cellar.'

She said, 'I've been watching the archers drill all afternoon. I can see everything from up here. Daddy was riding up and down in front of the ranks as if he'd forgotten me. There are two enormous women soldiers guarding me and all the money stored here. Not men, worse luck; "Bitchback and Nobless" from Midelspass.'

'Really?'

'Mm. They don't pass on my messages. They don't listen to me, even.'

'Wonder where Lightning got them from?'

'I don't know but they adore him. They're so desperate that if they knew a man was up here they'd strip-search you . . . And the lake reeks,' she went on. 'All day when the wind was gusting I could smell it.'

She pushed Lymer aside and lifted the chessboard onto her knees. 'Do you want a game?'

'Huh? No, I don't know how to play.'

'In all this time, you haven't learnt chess?'

'No. Can you fend off wolves using only a sling?'

'No.'

'Well then.'

'I'll teach you,' she said.

'It's a stupid game. I can't think of one good reason for it, and besides, my time's nearly up.'

'You mean you don't have the patience.'

I picked a lancer and offered it to her, but palmed it so Cyan found herself grasping at empty air. She giggled. I placed it back with a click on the board. 'Check! Now, why don't you read Rayne's letter? She likes you.'

'Yeah, I like her too . . . but I find her accent a bit impenetrable.'

'That's the seventh century for you.'

Cyan unfolded the letter. 'Rayne must be an amazing doctor to hold her title for as long as Daddy.'

'She is. As time goes on, it seems less likely that she'll ever lose a

Challenge. The mortals' behaviour benefits her, I think.'

'Why?'

'Other doctors all stunt each other's growth. They never share their discoveries because they all want to Challenge her. Rayne's fond of saying that the branches of science wouldn't be so separate if scholars were less secretive.'

'I suppose, living in the university, she's the first to hear of anything new.'

'Yes. She loves it when novices notice something different. She encourages them. Otherwise they'd just follow her and ape her experiments.'

Cyan read the letter for a few minutes while I played with the chess pieces and sorted out my eyeliner, and then she passed me the letter. 'Why not have a look while I write a reply?' She pulled a pillow from the bed and sat down on the floor next to the low table, her long back rounded above it. She began to fiddle with the nib of her pen.

While she scrawled her reply, I perused Rayne's pages of neat, close writing.

Slake Cross Hospital

17th May

1.30 a.m.

To be delivered by the hand of Comet

Dear Cyan,

I know you are trapped and must be feeling miserable. Your father's rage seemed shocking, but I hope at some time in the future you will agree he may have saved your life and that life is indeed more precious than you currently hold it. Lightning loves you with all his heart but you simply refuse to understand how much strain he's under. He does not want to lose you and he must concentrate on reaching the dam. I didn't think he would do anything like this no matter how hard you pushed him, but San has never put us under this pressure before.

In the coach on the way from Hacilith I enjoyed our conversation. How agreeable it was, for an old lady who does not need much sleep, to talk through the night with a young lady who is too excited to sleep. And then when the Circle broke and you consoled me . . . Please turn over in your mind the tales I told you of your father's life, and understand that in Hacilith you were fed a lot of slander. It shouldn't colour your opinion of him now.

Once you realise of how little consequence you are in the immensity of time, you gain a great power, a liberty and you can follow your own path in peace. Bide your time and learn.

You probably don't feel lucky, but let me tell you, you have been living in a time of such equality and freedom it almost seems to me that the people of this era act like spoilt children. People like myself have toiled over decades and centuries so that you may have such freedom. I expect you feel you have little choice in life but in times past you would have had even less. When I was mortal, girls could not be students and few people could read. I guided Hacilith University to develop in the image of the Castle, so it's run by merit, not by dodderers. These days an applicant to the university must have worked in the outside world for two years, so the prospective students are people who know how to put in a day's work and their mature approach recognises the great worth and luxury of study. You never needed for anything, Cyan, so you never needed to learn until now. I urge you to put your time to good use.

Watch your father from the window as he leads the battle. Would you be able to do what he does, so well? As a Challenger you seem to think you could do better. Lightning and the others who surround you are not simply faces, not simply there to grant your wish but every one has a long and complicated history to which his reactions pertain, just as much as they do to you. The road to becoming immortal is so uniquely steep and tortuous that every man travelling it has a story to tell. Your father is no exception.

Lightning and I discovered the privileges and tribulations of immortality at about the same time, though it meant different things to us both. During six nineteen, when the Emperor's First Circle was defeated, I was scrubbing out the washing coppers in Chattelhouse's laundry room. We were aware that San was losing Awia but the intense fighting was happening somewhere far off in the north. We could only keep going and wait until the Insects arrived at the walls of Hacilith. Every day the news came, the atmosphere grew more and more ominous and we lived under a constantly encroaching threat. How Lightning can call it a golden age I don't know.

Until I was about ten years old I lived on the street with no roof over my head, but I hung around the gates of the College of Surgeons as if drawn to them. I was sitting playing knucklebones on the track outside when I saw the cleaner being sacked. She hefted her bags and stomped away in a huff. The porter began to close the gates but I slipped between them and begged to be allowed to clean the floors. He rolled his eyes but he hired me and I became the most lowly servant to the Guild of Barber-Surgeons. Guilds disappeared before the close of the first millennium, but they were very influential when I was mortal.

I dreamed of being a subsizar, a scholar's assistant, but girls were not permitted and, besides, they would never employ an orphan with no clue as to her parentage.

After I turned thirteen, the gentlemen students sometimes offered to let me stay in the rooms they hired in town or in Chattelhouse, the wattle-and-stone residential hall. I'd move in, then be ejected back to be bullied in the deprived and unbearable servants' quarters, until I could find another Chattelhouse room. The boys never gave charity freely; they always pressed for sexual favours in return. Indeed, one of them suggested that I become a prostitute so he could make some money – but I all wanted was to talk about medicine with them!

Many's the time I tried to sleep on a boy's couch and late at night he would loom in the doorway, turn back the covers and slip in next to me, his hands on my breasts and his penis hard. One man in particular would strew his apartment with pornographic pamphlets as a hint, and every morning he would demand . . . Well, Cyan, the things that happened were so awful I will not set them down on paper.

By the time I was thirty, Chattelhouse employed me as charwoman and cook in exchange for board. Some of the fourteen-year-old scholars grew to regard me as a mother far more approachable than the one who sent them away to study logic, rhetoric and grammar. One boy, whom I'll never forget, developed an infatuation and spent his afternoons teaching me to read. He stammered and blushed his way into finding me a better job. At long last I could mop the Surgeons' lecture theatre after lessons. The chalk scrawls left on the blackboard enthralled me. If I made myself scarce during the anatomy sessions I was allowed to lay out the instruments and clean them afterwards. Eventually I had my chance to attend! I placed the scalpels and saws on the bench, and then hid in the equipment cupboard and peered through its slats. If I had been discovered spying they would have cast me out, but I learnt exactly which implements to lay out for each lesson, so nobody had occasion to open the door.

Huddled in the dark with chinks of light shining on my face, I watched the dissections for years and years until I knew the procedures by heart – and here was the strange thing – they never changed. It was as if the professors couldn't add to their knowledge because they had mastered everything – which, I reasoned, could not be the case if patients still died.

The young men on the tiered seats either sat carving their names in the benches or lapped up the professor's witticisms. But I peered at the cadaver. Of course blood couldn't move through the septum of the heart, which had no holes. Of course ligation after amputation would reduce deaths from shock caused by dipping the stump in hot pitch. He told them that dead flesh spontaneously generated maggots, while flies buzzed round his head and laid eggs on the hanged felon's body right there on the bench.

He propounded the myth that Awian hearts are larger than those of humans because Awians have a higher sensibility for love, without considering for a minute that their wings might need a larger blood supply. He told them that Rhydanne children grow rapidly because they are savages, no better than animals. It never occurred to him to ask how else they would survive the mountain winters. It was clear to me that Rhydanne have short pregnancies and small babies because their mothers have narrow hips to make them better sprinters, a trait Rhydanne must needs inherit if their females choose to be caught by the fastest men.

It was unthinkable that a woman should set foot in the Barber-Surgeon's library. With hindsight I'm thankful that I wasn't filled with the books' received wisdom. I had no framework to force my observations into. But I was consumed by my interest in medicine; I *had* to find out more. It was what I was *for*. Cyan, sometimes in life you will have to admit that you are wrong and alter the way you think. Cherish that process. Why do you think I've lasted so long? The entire discipline of medicine we have today owes itself to my belief, then as now, that knowledge can only be recovered from nature by close observation and practice, not through revered manuscripts or bombastic speech.

My dear, I am remembering my aggravation and losing the thread of my story, so let me simply say that I wondered why their wisdom did not accord with my notes. I questioned whether the gentry really knew better than me. Suffice it to add that Chattelhouse's 'long room' latrines were over a cesspit so vastly deep that it was only emptied every two hundred years. And they wondered why they got plague.

Try to imagine me at the foot of a narrow spiral staircase to the dormitory, mopping the flagstones. It was evening so the tiny arched windows high on the walls gave no light whatsoever.

A student bounded down the stairs, making the rush lights gutter in their sconces. He tripped over my bucket and fell headlong measuring his considerable length on the floor. Dirty water sloshed down the corridor. The dice he had been tossing up and down in one hand rolled to a halt in the puddle at my feet and showed double six.

'You stupid beldam!' he howled, rubbing his knees. Although he was a vain Awian, he had adopted Morenzian clothes against the cold and damp – well, the style we wore in the year six twenty. He had a knee-length robe with the cape of his hood around his neck. His hood's pointed tippet end hung down his back. He'd rucked the robe up in his belt, from which a silk purse dangled, the only ornamentation in his drab garb. The tops of his woollen hose were tied somewhere up under the robe with strings, his ankle boots were soft leather, and now they were soaking.

Lightning was dazzling in comparison, the first time I saw him. He had a white tunic with a long toga wound around his waist and over one shoulder, the one pulled back to keep his bowstring drawn and – well, I am getting ahead of myself.

I offered the hearty boy a hand to pull him up but he ignored it. 'Look at my robe!' he said petulantly. 'It's ruined! This cost more than you'll ever see. Now I shall be late for the gaming table!' He squeezed water out of his curly hair. 'You seem to be amused. It's not bloody funny. I shall report you to the Housekeeper.'

I began to answer but he stopped me. 'I do not speak to servants. Obviously you don't know who I am, but –'

'You're from Awia.'

'I am the son of the Governor of Foin – third in line anyway. So you may –'

'Everyone in your country seems to give themselves a title, so I've read.' I righted my bucket and sloshed my mop about. The water was soaking through my shift and making my legs itch.

He retrieved his dice without answering. 'Something you read ... Hm? ... Servant? You can *read*?'

'Yes. Come with me and I'll dry your clothes. I'll make up some liniment for your knees as well. A bruised knee can swell badly since the body tries to cushion damaged joints.'

'You sound more like a prelector than a servitor,' he said carelessly.

'Would that you could write my essays as well.'

'Oh, but I can.'

That night, I did not sleep. I had explained all to Heron and my thoughts were in turmoil. I knew what to do, what I *must* do, and wondered if I dared. I heard the students clatter to the refectory. I opened the shutters and found it was already morning.

I began, behind the scenes, to do Master Heron Foin's homework. At last I could air all my observations, my theories! I wrote the methodologies of his experiments, delineated hypotheses in novel articles. Heron became suddenly famous, and he knew how to use it; he was a consummate self-publicist. He set himself up as the foremost student, the pride of the college. He brought me more books, though he could never fathom why I wanted to learn.

Far from suspecting the fraud, the Chancellor awarded him the acclaimed prizes in anatomy, physiology and penmanship. He was even recommended to succeed Professor Pratincole. Heron's conceit grew deeper. He loathed and resented the fact he was simply an actor, a mouthpiece for my work, while all and sundry told him he was a genius. They expressed surprise that he could pay so little attention to lectures, spend so much time on the playing fields and still make groundbreaking discoveries. He began to believe that he was doing the work, not me. He would throw me a half-remembered essay question. 'And it has to be done tonight! If you don't, I'll tell the Housekeeper how often you hid in that cupboard. Just bear in mind what you owe me, Ella. You're my servant, I raised you from "below stairs", and you'll have to go back there, anyway, because the damn freshmen are hinting at all kinds of relationships between us.'

Thank god I was grown too old for their sexual advances.

Then on the first of July the Emperor came to Hacilith. Governor Donacobius accompanied him into the town square. Everyone poured out and crowded around their caparisoned horses. I left my washing soaking in lye, dropped the shirt I was squeezing around a wringing post, and dashed to the window to listen. The Emperor himself proclaimed the Games. He announced that every man and woman regardless of age or background was welcome to compete in organised tournaments. San would share his immortality with the winners providing they were prepared to act as leaders in the war.

Many students left to try their skill at the Games, but as far as I could tell, they all came back in the following weeks, and very chastened. Life at the guild went on as normal.

Until, that is, Heron disappeared. On my morning visit I found his rooms vacated and I panicked. His landlord told me he'd gone to the front. Heron had been in communication with the Messenger and had suggested that the Circle needed a doctor. San agreed and asked him to come to Rachiswater to be tested by treating the casualties of the ongoing massacre. Everything I had worked for vanished instantaneously – what good was a rich student's famulus without the student? Devastated, I returned to darning socks.

Less than a month later a letter arrived from the front, from my 'grandson'. Its ink had run where Heron's tears had hit the page. He begged me to come and help him. He was completely out of his depth with the number of men slashed and disembowelled. We had never seen an Insect up close and the injuries they caused horrified him. He had never dirtied his hands in the operating theatre and hadn't the first idea how to organise a hospital. The assistants were afraid, he had lost his authority over them, and the Messenger was too busy to listen to his excuses.

Heron had included enough money in the scroll for me to bribe a fyrd captain to ride pillion on his cart when the next draft left town. So I came to the grimy field hospitals of Rachiswater and I soon had them under control. I know when a floor hasn't been cleaned properly and I was not above showing the assistants how to do it. I improved or made comfortable the majority of the patients, organised supply chains of medicine from the capital, and upbraided Heron as if I really was his grandmother.

San noticed the progress and visited the infirmary. Heron greeted him and showed him in, bowing low and explaining the enhancements he had made, whilst blocking San's view of me. The Emperor looked past him and saw me bloodied up to the elbows, trying to stabilise the condition of a maimed soldier. He came to question me and quickly understood that the improvements had coincided with my arrival so, as I worked, he joined me to the Circle and made me one of the immortals. It was my dream, what I was made for! At last I was in the right place!

That night, I was shown to a pavilion that would temporarily serve as my scriptorium. I sat down to write. Heron burst in, stinking of brandy.

He disentangled himself from the tent ropes and slurred, 'I know the rules, you old bag. I've always learned the rules so I can work the system.'

I said, 'Yes, and that's all you do.'

IIc sneered. 'San wants the best specialists. I suggested the Circle have a Doctor, and you walked in. That's not fair. Well, I'm the next best doctor, so if you were to die I'd take your place.' He drew his dagger and dived at me. I tried to dodge but his fist on the hilt caught my eye such a crack that I fell off the stool, onto my back on the grass.

In a trice he was on me. He raised the dagger above my throat. I had a vivid image of myself as a cadaver on the dissecting table. Female, aged seventy-eight, note cause of death; a single deep puncture. Carotid cut, thyroid and oesophagus pierced, sixth cervical vertebra shattered, spinal cord severed. I'd make a fine lesson! I braced myself to feel my blood spray.

The point arced down. A shout made Heron flinch. His dagger deflected and tore through my hood.

'Fuck!' he said, and glanced behind him. Then he turned as pale as if he'd been bleached.

The Castle's Archer was standing at the entrance, bow flexed and an arrow unerringly trained on Heron. He said, 'I only have to let go. And believe me, nothing would give me greater pleasure.'

Heron collapsed into a kneeling position.

Seeing his face, the Archer looked surprised, but only for a second. 'Heron Foin?'

'I'm sorry, my lord prince, I'm sorry.' To my astonishment Heron began to grovel at the Archer's feet. He changed to High Awian and wept apologies into the grass.

The Archer lowered his bow. 'I know of you, Heron Foin. I know your father. Go home to the backwater little manorship you crawled from. If you harm our genius surgeon or even show your face here again, my brothers and I will take your hall apart until it is nothing but a field with stones in. Do I make myself clear?'

'Yes! Yes!'

'Get yourself out of my tent.'

Heron kissed the ground, jumped up and sped out. I never saw him again. I unpinned myself from the grass and dabbed my black eye with a handkerchief. I had never before heard a voice with such natural authority; it made even the professors sound strained. The Archer helped me to my feet, then bowed low and kissed my hand. 'Now,' he said, 'I would be honoured if you would call me Saker. What is your name?'

*

So, Cyan, you see how much I owe your father. Imagine how overwhelming life must have been for him in the early days of the Circle. Before the Games, the First Circle were no more than boastful mortal warriors leading a mass of untrained fyrd with swords and spears. The First Circle had lasted for two hundred and five years since San first drew them from three countries, but they gradually gave ground to the Insects all that time and left northern Awia to the Paperlands.

There was no effective way of fighting Insects then. The nobility and peasant levies simply fed the hordes and although the First Circle fought, manor after manor fell. We thought we were doomed. Your tutor may have taught you this, but don't forget it really happened, and Lightning was there. A million corpses is not some story you tell children at bedtime!

The blizzard winter of six nineteen put an end to the First Circle. Those who weren't eaten died of starvation, disease and exposure in snow holes by the Rachis river. Deep drifts covered the ruins of Murrelet.

San realised that the First Circle's brave but stupid warriors weren't enough. He needed the best to train fyrds. He needed an infrastructure to keep supplies flowing – cooks and doctors; and to keep knowledge from being lost – agriculturalists and armourers. He needed an administration to take decisions on his behalf on many battlefields simultaneously. In short, he needed people who could think in the long term, as he did.

When San revealed he could make other people immortal, everyone suddenly saw him in a new light. Before, he had relied on the goodwill of the governors to raise and lead fyrds; now everyone clamoured to join the Circle.

San also knew that the celebrations and ceremony of the Games would raise our hopes. He let us see our own capabilities. Our fighting spirit soared.

San kept his personal symbol, the Imperial Sunburst, and extrapolated it to invent all our Eszai names. With the First Circle gone, the Castle's Breckan and Simurgh Wings stood empty, waiting for the victors of the Games. It was an exhilarating time. It threw us together, people from every stratum of society across the world and some with naught but the clothes they stood up in. I heard that Lightning arrived with a retinue of eight carriages of belongings and attendants, to discover that the rooms he was allocated by ballot were tiny compared with those he was used to. He divided his treasures among the new Eszai and filled all their rooms.

In the seventh century I discovered that sexism was not a glass ceiling but is present at all levels, in all classes. It was a glass web, and I threaded my way through it, cut by the strands I broke. San was the first to see my merit and your father was the first man truly to see me as an equal.

Since he has confided in me on many occasions, I suppose I am even more indebted to him for his friendship. It is impossible for you to understand a friendship of fourteen hundred years. You discover things about a person that you might not like, but it makes their virtues all the more admirable. I have the measure of Lightning and he has the measure of me.

I hope I have given you food for thought.

Send word with Comet if you need anything.

Love, Ella Rayne

That *is* food for thought. I folded the letter and placed it on the table. Cyan was putting the finishing touches to hers. 'Will you deliver this?' she asked. 'I don't have any sealing wax. Actually I don't have bloody anything here.'

'It's all right, just fold it. I can take it to Rayne unsealed.' I slipped her letter into my coat pocket and said, 'But she might be too busy to reply. I haven't seen anything like the crowds down there in my whole life before.'

'Will you be able to come back at least?'

'I'll try to.'

'You're the only person who's noticed me.'

I patted her shoulder but she shrugged away. She smelt of soap and birch bark chewing gum, reminding me how young she was for her years. Other seventeen-year-olds don't make idiots of themselves by Challenging Lightning.

I went to the window and opened the shutters. In the still night I could hear the clucking of the hens kept by the guards in their room downstairs. Very bass in the distance, the bass toll of the town's gatehouse bell rolled out over the moorland, thinning as it filled the expanse.

'Midnight. I have to go.'

Cyan tried again, 'This is a prison.'

'Honestly, it's for your own good. You should thank Lightning.'

'I'll kill him!'

'Shame. Thought cage birds sang more sweetly than that.'

'Well, if you won't free me, then bugger off!'

'I'll send you up some bread and water ha ha.'

I climbed onto the plank, ran along it and launched myself off. I flapped to the town with broad, uneven strokes, and landed on the hall's roof. I sat down on the ridge, wings drooping, and shook my hair down my back.

Below me the square was bustling with people. Around fifty of Rayne's orderlies with their white sashes were pulling tables out of the tavern and constructing beds. Fyrd squads were sitting on the tables, assembling arrows from piles of shafts and glittering points. The hall was packed with governors, wardens and captains as Lightning briefed them on the advance.

All the oil lamps and spotlights burned fiercely. The stars were dim in comparison, while the thick clouds at the edge of the sky seemed banked up above the town walls, hemming us in.

I unfolded Cyan's letter and read it.

> Peel Tower Ten
> Thursday

Dear Rayne,

Please will you help me get out of here? It's not fair that i'm locked up – it's just not fair. Daddy is cold & distant – like he always has been – and Jant says Daddy is like that most of the time. Will you ask him for me?

Apart from you and Jant everybody is ignoring me. I try to be independent, and i'm punished. Typical. Even Jant says i made a fool of myself. But i have put it behind me & i'm not thinking of it any more.

I don't want to be stranded in here during the battle – i'm not afraid of what may happen. I want to see the advance – i can come to help you at the infirmary. I'm sick of trying to be a good girl, i just want to be free – please, if you're really my friend, send a note to the guards and cancel Daddy's orders. Thank you for writing – please write again.

Yours,

Cyan xxx (Lady Governor Cyan Peregrine)

Dear Cyan,

I'm sorry but neither Jant nor myself can let you out of the peel tower, given what is happening down here at the moment. But please do not despair, my dear. Bear out your imprisonment patiently and in time the awful things that are happening will bring you wisdom.

You are intelligent but you are not yet wise. Do not blind yourself with opinions drawn from your own intelligence, because even the cleverest people can be wrong if they do not examine solid facts.

Wisdom never comes from staying at home and avoiding unhappiness. In order to become wise you must go out into the world and be tossed about in its storms, stripped bare by terrible experiences and confused by good ones. After a long time you learn to see and control the effect those circumstances have on yourself. Then it will never matter one bit where you find yourself in the world, because you will be able to cope with it. The top of a peel tower or a Hacilith bar will be all the same to you if you are comfortably at home with yourself.

Now you are a little uncomfortable you are crying out for help. But you are a Challenger! You can't be Eszai material at all if you are disturbed by a little inconvenience. Every Challenger is prepared to forgo pleasure and comfort in the pursuit of success. You are now a Challenger, so what are you complaining about? Hadn't you better prepare yourself for the competition instead? In a sense it's already underway, your father made the first move and now you are in check.

I thought you wanted to rebel, to put distance between yourself and Lightning. Then why on earth have you Challenged him as if you are yet another good archer? Everyone expects Lightning's daughter to have a modicum of archery. I thought you were trying to re-create yourself. You must know that if you follow the career of a great man like your father, you will have to accomplish twice as much to shine. You won't be able to shine in your own right if you're known as another archer, because everybody knows Lightning is the best archer.

I doubt you have even thought about it – but of course, you don't really want to compete with Lightning, you just want to escape from his shadow. Consider this – every Eszai and Challenger must submit to a much greater authority: that of the Emperor. None of us can escape San: not even Lightning. You rebel against your father and come under the power of a more authoritative man. Oh, Cyan, when you become wise you'll realise that freedom is a teenager's aspiration and illusion, and the world actually consists of varying degrees of compromise.

You say that Lightning is cold and distant. My dear, nothing could be further from the truth! He is passionate in the extreme! He must hide from his passions because they're so strong. I could give plenty of examples, but I only have time to tell one, a secret to which Lightning never refers, and the other Eszai are too polite – or afraid – to mention.

Eighteen nineteen was a year in which everything changed. It was the year after Jant joined the Circle. Lightning was married and widowed in the same night, and his grief for Savory threw him into an almost catatonic state.

There had been no letters from Micawater. I taught doctors in the university. I sat in my room and read books. I did my daily rounds of the general hospital and came home tired but only in body; I was wondering how Lightning was. He was missed in court and at the front, at the King's table and in the hunting stables. He had sequestered himself, to the exclusion of the real world. I am very much of the real world and, as his closest friend, I decided to pay him a visit.

Eighteen nineteen passed into eighteen twenty. On a freezing January night I arrived at your father's palace to find the Lake Gate locked. The stone winged hounds stood rampant on the gateposts, rain dripping from their paws. I peered through the fine drizzle, but saw no lights shining in the bulk of the palace beyond the river.

I left my coach and followed the estate wall in the dark, until I came to the tradesmen's little arched entrance. I hurried through and across the soaking lawns. I passed the grand staircase and instead knocked on the door of the kitchens in the basement.

Lightning's steward brought me in and gave me supper. As well as his white apron, he wore a black crepe armband. He gathered a candelabra from the dresser and took a taper from the stove, talking all the while. He bent close to light the candles and whispered, 'M'lord scares us. He sits alone for days, no meals, no sleep. He doesn't bother to open the curtains and we don't dare light the lamps in Main. Doctor, he's wound up in himself and the manor go hang. Thought it best to warn you.'

*

He guided me, up out of the Covey cellars and through the silent, unlit palace. I think even you would find it discouraging, the building so majestic I felt it extending on both sides of me as we ascended to the main floor. The steward pressed on, past the drawing rooms.

Mourning cloths covered all the statues in the niches, reducing them to featureless, barely human shapes. The portraits had been turned to the wall; their blank backs faced us. I wondered at them, when there had never been any changes in your father's house before; now I believe he wanted to rid himself of the mute, accusing glare of his ancestors.

The rooms leading off from the corridor were in impermeable darkness, but when light from the candelabra flickered in I glimpsed the furniture and objects of virtu standing in shades of grey. Dust sheets had been thrown over them, as when the servants expect Lightning to be absent for years on business. The chandeliers hung in thick wraps. Black linen masked the deep-framed mirror in the salon. The great gold clock had been deliberately stopped.

The ceilings may have been painted by the world's greatest masters, but we walked past like thieves without looking up. A glimmer of candlelight shone under the door to the dining hall. The steward hesitated and looked at me anxiously. I nodded to reassure him; he gave me the candelabra and showed me through, then bowed and made a hasty retreat.

Lightning sat at the very end of the long table, halfway down the hall. He was leaning forward with his head down, resting in the crook of his arm. His reflection was blurred in the polished marble.

He was not aware of my presence. He picked an orange desultorily out of a bowl with his free hand and rolled it down the table without looking up. It rolled through the small gap between the legs of the silver centrepiece, out the other side and on for another five metres until it dropped off the end of the table beside me.

I put the candelabra down but Lightning did not acknowledge me. He picked another orange and sent it trundling straight down the middle of the table, through the centrepiece.

He was wearing a silk dressing gown and, over it, a very dirty and bloodstained Cathee plaid. He had wound it around his waist and over one shoulder with an automatic gesture from back when he used to wear a toga.

The rear of the hall was invisible in the gloom. I looked past Lightning, and at the edge of the darkness stood his grand piano, wreathed in paper music. Its keys were smeared thickly with dried blood.

The centrepiece was the same then as now, the small statue of a girl reclining on a couch. Lightning rolled another orange between its legs with an accuracy that was both considerable talent and long, long practice. The orange fell off the end of the table and joined several others on the carpet.

'Talk to me,' I said, but the room was so sombre it came out as a murmur. I pulled up a chair and sat down. His breath misted the table top. I touched his arm. 'Come on, Saker. Speak to me.'

'That chair . . . is two hundred years old.'

'I'm not going to break your chair.'

He said nothing else.

'What happened?'

'I was married . . .'

'I can see that.'

'I was . . .'

'Saker . . .'

'. . . Married.'

'I really think –'

'Do you really? Leave me, Ella, please.'

He was still looking away from me. I put my hand to his cheek and turned his head. He complied, though his eyes were blank.

I said, 'I'm –'

'Going to leave me alone?'

'Saker, please tell me the matter.'

'Savory was killed. I tried to shoot the man but I . . . I missed my shot . . . I missed.'

'It's been three months,' I said gently.

'Three months is nothing. Nothing.'

'Long enough for Challengers to prick up their ears.'

'*Challengers,*' Lightning sighed. 'How you worry me. My heart is torn from my body and I'll never heal. Ever. No matter how long I live. I weep every day. Savory was real, she was strong. In an ugly, unworthy world I had seen a hundred thousand and found just one to love . . . And everything I'd been through seemed worth it.'

His washed-out voice continued ' . . . When I close my eyes I see images of her. Smiling in the village. Shooting at the butts. My mind flicks through still pictures shockingly quickly, as if I'm constantly waking from sleep . . . It seems odd that I was really in Cathee.'

'Yes.'

'How could Savory have come from among such a people? They
... I should ... well, in a hundred years the birds will have eaten
them every one ...'

For all my fourteen centuries I hadn't lived long enough to know
what to say. I tried, 'You're missed at the Castle.'

'Already?' He looked away abjectly. 'I feel that if just one more
thing goes wrong, everything will fall apart. Just one tiny thing
and I'll go mad. There were hundreds of things I should have told
her and never had the time.'

'I'm sure she already knew. Sentiments sound crude when voiced,
precious when understood in silence.'

'Oh, Ella. She was perfect, and I'm such a fool.'

'You are no fool.'

'Maybe I have been ... but now I have some of her blood in me. I
can carry it for the rest of immortality.' He began to stroke his palm.

'Let me see your cut.'

He extended his hand to me and opened it. I saw the wound
shining, encrusted with dried blood. He had kept it open to the
white fan of bone.

So, Cyan, you must see Lightning as a person, not just as your
father. There is no point in thinking about death because no amount
of thinking will arrive at an answer. He had to return to the Castle.
He still has not properly recovered from Savory but the Circle needs
him. The Kingdom of Awia needs him, too; who's to say that without
Lightning's generosity and sense of order their aristocracy wouldn't
have dissolved into something akin to the pack of wolves who run
Morenzia.

Cyan, I must go now. I have been writing this letter in between
giving orders to prepare for tomorrow's advance. I apologise for
my deteriorating handwriting: it is about four a.m.

The Eszai and soldiers will be exhausted for days after this – I
have seen men in full armour come in off the battlefield and sleep
where they fall. For twenty-four hours straight they're even
oblivious to the cries of the wounded and nothing rouses them
except extreme physical danger. So, Cyan, if nothing seems to be
happening directly the dam gates open, and if Jant doesn't visit
you, be patient.

I shall give this letter to him now and go to check the preparations
in the hospital.

Yours with love,
Rayne

I collected the letter from Rayne with a stack of last-minute dispatches. The rest I gave to my couriers to deliver.

Rayne's scale of organisation was incredible, and only one part of the preparations heaving the town into action. She had called all her surgeons and doctors drafted with the rest of the fyrd and given them their chain of command. Anyone else in the fyrd who had medical knowledge – first-aiders and nurses – reported to the doctors.

She was preparing to take over the hall as well as the hospital and tavern, because as soon as San is out of the hall tomorrow morning it will be the overspill for intensive care. The medical supplies had been divided into each site and guards kept a sharp eye on them.

Her hundreds of stretcher teams had received their orders. She was stocking the two enormous pavilions inside the canvas city's gate to be used as triage. Dressing stations were being set up on the road behind the troops, as the battalions were already starting to assemble. She had girls at every station to count the casualties coming in, or record dog tags and remove the dead.

The dawn air was cool and fresh. The first light of a new day rose pale gold on the horizon. A last word with the Emperor as the Imperial Fyrd were arming and I swept up into the air. One hundred and fifty thousand men were marching out of town to take up their positions.

I helped direct each battalion into the enormous formation. From the air, the ground filled with men like a fluid jigsaw, pouring into squares of colour. The battle array was one of our many familiar standard plans – Insects are predictable so we have honed the perfect ways to face them in different situations. But this was on a massive scale, taken to an extreme. We had never fielded anything like these numbers before. The front of the host was three kilometres long. It was incredible, just incredible.

I was busy keeping the multitudes in line, with some difficult flying between the enormous host, the town and the canvas city. While one battalion was being eased into place, the next was lining up behind it, then decanted up along the flank to fill their patch. I ordered, threatened and encouraged the wardens depending on their personality. I wove an aerial web linking the Eszai to one another. In the distance I could always see the lake and the dam. The lake was silted and filthy, coffee-coloured brown, with fuliginous shapes and rafts of detritus bobbing in it like broth.

Sirocco the Javelin Master's ranks were filling in behind Lourie's pikemen. The Javelin Master arranged his battalions with great expertise so, while the last ranks were aligning, the front didn't lose coherence. I had a spare second, so I swept away to the edge of the field, and Cyan's peel tower.

The shutters were hooked back wide. Cyan was leaning out, her bare shoulders high as she propped herself with straight arms on the ledge. She was watching the movement of people on the entire ground: from the fresh earth embankments of the canvas city into the extreme distance the road was solid with tight companies of lancers trotting past archers on foot, trailed by dogs pulling diminutive arrow carts, whole divisions of infantry sitting on the verge awaiting their turn to march.

I dropped down, feet together, onto the plank. The draught of my wings tangled Cyan's hair.

'What do you think?' I leant back, sweeping my arm at the colourful, clinquant steel expanse of troops behind me.

'It's exhilarating! The Empire's sheer might.'

I nodded. 'Here's a letter from Rayne.'

A gust of wind snatched it out of her hand, but I caught it. 'Don't drop it! And for god's sake don't let anyone else read it. If I were you, I'd burn it when I've finished with it.'

'How do you know?' asked Cyan.

I boinged up and down on the end of the plank. 'I just imagine it's full of Rayne's advice. You don't necessarily have to listen to her. Other people's advice is from their own experience and you won't reach your full potential following it.'

'Not more advice.' Cyan gave a mock grimace. She shrugged and her ruby pendant rolled down the cleft of her breasts in the bodice.

I pointed at the dam. 'Watch for the great wave when we open the gates!'

'Will you come back and tell me the news?'

'Your wish is my command!'

'I *wish* that was always the case.'

I grinned at her and raised my arms, bouncing on the end of the board. Two more jumps, higher, and I sprang up, arced out backwards, hugged in my legs and described two perfect somersaults.

Falling high above the road, I stretched out my arms in a swallow dive. I opened my wings and curved out over the soldiers' heads, gliding so fast I didn't have to beat my wings once.

CHAPTER 21

The five kilometres to the dam had never seemed so far, there were so many Insects scurrying about between us and the winch house. It would be hours before we could cut our way there and open the gates.

Our skirmishing cavalry had been out since first light, preventing the more adventurous Insects getting too close to the mustering troops. The Ghallain prickers' horses were skittish, being not used to Insects. The men were unruly, but disciplined by long experience working together. They dashed and wheeled in small charges, hurling javelins at attacking Insects. Those with the swiftest horses offered themselves as bait to break up larger groups, luring them in different directions, and their comrades swooped to surround them. Their seemingly effort-less efficiency was a pleasure to watch. I swept over, hearing them calling scores to each other.

'Thirteen!'

'Fourteen! . . . Hey, Jant, away! You Eszai will get your turn later!'

'You're crazy, Vir Ghallain! There's Insects enough for everyone here!'

He laughed. 'There won't be when I've shown Summerday and Lowespass how real men can ride!'

I shook my head and headed back to our lines, wondering how long he would wait before Challenging our new Hayl. The wind was beginning to shift to the south. Lightning would appreciate a good tailwind to add force to the arrows but it was also blowing our scent towards the swarm near the lake, stirring them up.

The main force was drawing up into two deep blocks of roughly equal size, one about ten metres behind the other. The first block would have to break through the Insects, with the reserve formation offering support and engaging if those in front started to waver. In such a large force the Select units were interspersed with the inexperienced General Fyrd to provide an example and keep them fighting.

The centre of the first body was a solid phalanx of pikemen led by Lourie, stationed astride the road to the dam. They stood sixteen deep

246

and, once engaged, their lowered pikes would present an impenetrable forest of points to the Insects, who would simply impale themselves on the barbed shafts trying to get at the men. They wore greaves and breastplates but trusted in the six metres of ash and steel they wielded to fend off Insects better than any shield. Behind them came a triple rank of javelin-throwers commanded by the Javelin Master, in their front line. They would hurl their missiles over the heads of the spearmen should they be hard-pressed by Insects. They were unarmoured and when their ammunition was exhausted they would pull back to the munitions carts following the troops at a safe distance to rearm.

Guarding both flanks of the phalanx were thousands of heavy infantry: solid blocks dripping with chain mail and shining plates, with tall rectangular shields and spears. In addition each carried a mace, axe, or Wrought sword to destroy any Insects who broke through their shield wall. They were a patchwork of colours as they drew up by battalion, each with its standard flickering in the breeze, and within that by division and company. Each square seemed tiled with smaller squares, in five hundreds, and smaller patches still, in fifties. The commanding Eszai stood in their front lines: Tornado and Serein on the left flank nearest the reservoir, the Macer and Sapper on the east flank by Cyan's tower.

The second body of troops were lines of archers, predominantly Awian, and more shield men in reserve, mostly Morenzian. The archers were on foot, their captains and wardens mounted, with Lightning clearly visible on his white horse in their centre. Those on horseback directed the shot of the footmen, who would be loosing blind over the heads of the ranks in front. In the open, archers cannot be left to face Insects alone so they shot high and indirectly, relying on the sheer weight of arrows to impact into the Insects' backs. The Awian ranks were typically orderly, each soldier turned out in blue livery and gleaming helmet, but more spacious to allow each man sufficient room to draw his longbow. The Morenzians were a motley contrast; only their officers and the richer fyrd were armoured. But a sea of banners fluttered above them, proudly proclaiming the village or Hacilith district from which they'd been raised. Each man in their jostling ranks held a shield and spear provided by the Castle and wore a sword, from Wrought. The Armourer and the Blacksmith led this infantry reserve.

Slightly to the rear on each flank of the second block of infantry were the armoured lancers. Eleonora held the left with the Tanager and Rachiswater lancers; and Hayl held the right with detachments from Eske and Shivel. They rode in discrete wedges, ready to intervene quickly if Insects threatened to envelop the archers and infantry.

The aristocracies of Awia and the Plainslands found it increasingly fashionable to arm as lancers, but I thought it an unnecessarily hazardous way of fighting. I couldn't help but remember how the last mass cavalry charge I had witnessed at Lowespass turned out. Still, the casualties probably helped keep inbreeding amongst the nobility under control.

Finally, directly behind the reserve block, the Imperial Fyrd rode onto the field together: a bright red square. They took position in the exact centre of the line, and in the centre of that, the Emperor on his midnight black stallion. Above him flapped the Sunburst, the largest banner on the field. Frost, mounted on an immense destrier, trotted to his right surrounded by the company of her bodyguard, Riverworks's foremen and navvies. She was to take command of operations when we reached the dam.

The whole host was centred on the metalled road leading to the dam's walkway, though only a few men in the deepest part of the mass were actually walking on it. It emerged from under the leading pikemen's feet, and stretched ahead of them, bisecting the expanse of ankle-deep mud that they would have to cross.

Occasionally tiny gaps opened in the battle lines, where a man was having a piss, and his fellows on either side were trying to shuffle out of the way of the splatter, because none were allowed to leave the line for any reason. I curved up, gaining height to about five hundred metres, until the whole host was arrayed in browns and splashes of colour below me; pennants, padded jacks and white armour bright against the mud. There were the many-shaded blue backgrounds and individual devices of Awian manors; the greens and devices of Plainslands manors; the red hand of Morenzia. All the fyrds of the Fourlands bar Cathee, Brandoch and Ghallain's infantry were represented.

Behind the fighting troops, auxiliaries of all kinds trailed through the canvas city back to Slake Cross, industrious as Insects. A constant pony cart relay brought up supplies of arrows and javelins to stockpiles behind the ranks. Wagons laden with stacks of stretchers swayed through the mud to the forward dressing stations, where orderlies fussed over them. Water-bearers staggered under dozens of canteens they would carry to the men once underway. Swarms of boys tried to sell apples from barrels to the stragglers. Whores were doing a roaring trade in the tents with young fyrdsmen who didn't want to die as virgins. A party of artillerists tried to lever a cart-mounted repeating ballista out of a ditch. Squads of Gayle's mounted provosts brandished their truncheons as they trotted between the pavilions and alongside the road, scaring skivers back to their units.

I heard Lightning's horn calling thinly into the sky. Each Eszai carries his or her own signal to call for the Messenger but it has taken me years of selective deafness to convince them that just because I can fly I can't answer them all at once. Now they have learnt only to use them in truly important cases. I wheeled back over the tumult.

Lightning had ordered his Select to bunch up, clearing a strip of ground for me to land on. It simply looked brown, but as I dropped closer it looked like someone had decided to plough a pond.

I came to earth in front of his horse, peeling off the top layer of mud in a sliding flurry of feathers, probably just as Lord Melodrama had planned. 'This had better be good! Even if I can get airborne from this muck, I'll be carrying half the field around with me all day.'

'Hush.' He looked around and then, sighing, dismounted to stand next to me. His riding boots squelched into the slurry and stopped being so damn clean. In a low voice he said, 'I do not want the fyrdsmen to hear. I am worried.'

I whispered back, 'Look, this is the strongest we've ever been. It looks glorious from the air. Half the Fourlands is here. The Insects can't even outnumber us by more than three to one.'

'Yes, that is exactly my concern. Nobody here has experience of handling a host this size. Forget the governors, even most of the Eszai have barely commanded a force bigger than a battalion in the last two hundred years, and then mostly on the defensive. The Emperor hasn't directed a battle for almost eight times as long.'

I shrugged, annoyed. Trust Lightning to be so perfectionist he finds fault where there is none. 'So?'

'Nobody has proper control over this field. A developing situation could get quickly out of hand. The mud will slow the dispatch riders. Most of these troops are untried and barely trained – we have many men but not many soldiers. Originally we just expected them to make a great show for the press and then spend the next month demolishing cells.'

'Look, all the Select is here. You know nearly all the Awians drill regularly. The entire Circle is here. The *Emperor* is here. The green troops will either be straining their best to impress or be terrified of us. Don't fret. Oh, and I checked on Cyan this morning; she'll be safe.'

He scowled. 'That wasn't what I was thinking about. Jant, you're the only one who can watch everything as it happens. If you see anything start to go wrong, tell me immediately.' He looked down the first line. 'Damn! Ata had a proper head for this, so had Dunlin. Or Sarcelle. And the last Hayl.'

I was shocked. Had he really so little confidence in us?

'What about San?'

'You must go to him if he summons you, of course. But remember that he is here to inspire and observe. He hasn't taken formal command from any of us. They are forgetting –' he waved an arm towards the front, in Tornado's general direction '– that San created the Circle to do this for him.'

I looked Saker full in the face. Behind his usual expression he had a weariness I wasn't used to seeing.

I nodded. I pulled my damp feet from the ooze, ran soggily, and leapt into the air. A whole division of Morenzians ducked as I flashed over their spear-points. When I looked behind me again, Saker was still standing where I had left him, patting his horse's neck abstractedly.

I could see my couriers converging on the Imperial Fyrd and its captain turning around in his saddle to speak to the Emperor. San raised his hand. The standard bearers of the Imperial Fyrd sounded their horns and the buglers of every division responded, till the air vibrated with a single note. The advance began.

Lourie's phalanx started to elongate as the men in the front line began to march; then those towards the middle. The lines separated slightly and narrow gaps opened between them as those at the back, and the infantry behind them, waited for their space to move.

Their pikes jutted ahead, held straight out from the first few ranks, and directly upwards in the others. They looked like a hairbrush. I looked down into the spaces between the spears; they seemed to bristle as I soared over.

Hurricane's polished glaive was clear among them, a wider blade in the centre. He was setting the pace deliberately slowly, to prevent men stumbling in the adhesive mud or advancing too far ahead of the archers.

The prickers fell back as planned. Around the flanks, exhausted men headed their horses to the rear to rest. As they retreated, Insects began to venture forward. The strong south wind gusted, spreading a ripple of interest through the Insects gathered around the lake.

I watched the forward movement surge through the infantry and reach the archers. Over the roar of airflow and the rhythmic swoosh-and-batter of my wings I could hardly hear their horns but I saw thousands of men bend their bows in unison. Their shot arced high, arrows pausing at their zenith, turning and falling at a steeper angle, thicker than rain or snow, spraying out in front of the first spearmen.

Their barrage was so thick they were catching Insects in a broad strip in front of the host. Insects writhed and fell. The closest rushed powerfully up against the first pikes. Some were killed outright, others slowed down until the pike points buckled into and cracked their hard carapaces.

Hurricane let the arrow barrage come down some fifty metres ahead of the pikemen – he kept the distance with incredible skill.

The pace was so slow it was a quarter of an hour before the wave of movement reached the last ranks of the Imperial Fyrd. It was midmorning already but we were only ten minutes behind schedule. It is absolutely impossible to keep men walking abreast in perfect rows, and they were stumbling and dragging in the mud. Every formation was warping slightly; growing thinner and longer. The archers' line bent forwards at the ends as the men there walked faster, spreading onto open ground where the infantry hadn't churned it up.

I stretched out in the air, way in front of the pikemen, with the storm of arrows coming down behind me. I was watching Insects charge in up the slope from the lake shore, where they were ranging all over the mud in great numbers, but nowhere so densely packed as to be a serious threat to the infantry.

I turned and flapped upwind in an ungainly fashion, resting now and then because the gusts were strong enough for me to lean against. All the spearmen could see me poised stationary like the figurehead of a ship.

Back towards the town I saw the dual lines of Thunder's immobile trebuchets drawn up in front of the walls. The machines weren't operating but were still manned, just in case – they seemed no bigger than my thumbnail and the crews no more than black dots.

Better go see if anyone needs me, I thought. I swept out wide and came in under the tunnel of arrows pouring up from Lightning's ranks. I flew down the tunnel and out of the end. Then I gained height so as not to frighten the horses, and cruised over the Imperial Fyrd, looking down on their sun banners. It was easy to see the Emperor's billowing white cloak against his horse's back.

I was worried that San was on the field. His presence was foremost in everyone's minds. We couldn't risk him getting hurt – if he was, none of us knew what would happen to the Circle. At least he's well protected in the rearguard.

Back on the other side of the arrow storm, Insects rushed towards the spearmen. The spears thrust out or down. Little dents formed in the first line where shield and spearmen had to stop and make sure an Insect was dispatched before walking round or clambering over it. Eleonora's and Hayl's lancers trotted forward to guard the archers' flanks.

The fyrds walked steadily for three hours, cutting a wide swathe through the Insects, with some attrition of the spearmen and heavy infantry, and horses as the cavalry fended off Insects coming round to our rear. The host trailed bodies like rag dolls, curled up and sinking in the shallow liquid mud.

We had reached the gradient leading down to the lake – the slope helped the men walking but was too faint to speed up the lines. Hordes of Insects were racing from the shore, skittering over the road and pouring towards us. The curling breeze carried the stench of the lake.

I was turning, intending to tell Lourie how many Insects were approaching, when an almighty shouting broke out from the spearmen. The front of the phalanx nearer the lake ground to a halt, but the rest kept going a few steps downhill, staring left at their fellows, wondering what was happening. They pulled the whole of the phalanx front out in a long concave curve.

The first pikes started rattling side-to-side and jabbing at the ground. The men in the second line were also trying futilely to bring their weapons to bear, stabbing the mud. A shout went up to call Sirocco's men into action. They started casting their javelins. Already? I thought. What's going on?

I pulled my wings in close and dropped steeply downwind, air screaming past me. I hit my top speed in seconds, blinked and tears forced out of the corners of my eyes. I swept my wings forward and up, either side of my face, and braked hard. I had to keep above the arrows. I circled, lying in the air, my wings beating quickly, and looked down through their storm.

The men in the first few lines were dropping their pikes. Throwing them down. Their long shafts lay all over and already men were tripping on them. Some had drawn swords and appeared to be digging them into the ground.

The men on the edges of the phalanx flung down their weapons and turned to run. The ones nearer the centre began to follow suit. Unable to force back through the tight ranks behind, they had to run the whole length of the line to get round the flanks. Some fell as they fled and didn't get up again. Bodies struggled and contorted in the mud but I couldn't see that they were fighting anything.

Men in the centre of the first ranks turned around completely and tried to beat their way back into the middle of the phalanx. They came face to face with men behind them who also turned to run but could go nowhere. Time seemed to slow down and I felt a rising nausea. Shit. They're going to rout. The fastest way to die in battle is to break formation in front of Insects.

'Lourie!' I shouted. I couldn't dive lower – I couldn't land. The air beneath me was thick with missiles. The wind took my words. I screamed at the top of my voice: 'Hold the line!'

I saw helmets moving into the centre of the phalanx then falling under the crush. The square's middle was thickening and the edges flaking off, men running back. Lourie and a body of soldiers around him were left isolated on the road out in front. He was bent double, shouting, but no volume could make his troops take the slightest bit of notice.

The javelin-throwers following had now also stopped, their front rank mingling with the last line of the phalanx. They couldn't see forward and were even jumping up to try to see over the pikemen's heads and find out what was happening. Fleeing pikemen began running into their ranks at the sides, pushing them towards the middle, making the crush worse. Sirocco blew his horn, then every Eszai with the infantry began to sound theirs. I glimpsed Tornado looking up to me and frantically waving, mouth moving in a silent bellow. Then I was past, over the vast formation grinding to a halt. Men crunched up together as they walked into each other; the flanks rode on by a few metres as the centre collapsed into itself. The reserve block realised that the men walking ahead had stopped and came to a halt themselves.

Lacking further instructions for the cause of the delay the archers, piecemeal, suspended their barrage. As the last arrows hissed to the ground the screams of the ever-worsening crush below seared up clearer than before.

Finally I could descend – and suddenly all the ground ahead of the pikemen seemed to be in motion. Tussocks and rocks poking through the thin layer of muddy water over the waterlogged soil were advancing of their own accord.

I had no idea what they were. Lower still, I could see shapes, seething in the mud, half-crawling, half-swimming. I judged the scale against the men – they were about half a metre long and mottled brown, very hard to see. They were moving close to the surface of the soil, like little Insects. I saw one lifted up on a man's spear, writhing. It had a longer, narrower abdomen than an Insect. I saw its legs opening and closing as they waved in the air. Its thorax and triangular head were flattened, but they had the same high-gloss goggle eyes.

I looked towards the lake and saw them emerging from the water, climbing up on the lake shore. They were scurrying, slower than

Insects, but faster than a man could run. I couldn't see the ground between them on the shore; there was no end to them. They weren't Insects. I hadn't seen them before – they were monsters!

The waters' edge was slick with glistening wet carapaces. The tops of their eyes emerged first, then their leg joints, combing through the ripples. They crawled straight out, head, thorax and the strange long abdomen; rivulets running down between their hard segments.

Oh no . . . These are the hatchlings. Young Insects. Insect *larvae*.

Lourie's troops had dissolved into a tussling, hopelessly entangled mob of men, crushed by their own confusion and swarmed over by the larvae. They were pressed so closely together they were suffocating. I saw armoured fists raised. Men used sword pommels to club each other out of the way. None of the infantry could see the lake. To them, the creatures were closing in from all sides equally, so thick on the ground that one man could do nothing. They had no idea what they were facing. The great length of pikes was useless against creatures close by and tight against the mud, and the small sword or misericord most carried was too short to be effective without bending down. The larvae were crawling up the legs of the armoured men, biting in between their plates, hanging off faulds, curling around men's necks. As they stabbed at one, another bit them. Men wrenched them off, leaving chitinous legs trapped between their armour's plates, but as they pulled one off, more swarmed up.

The heavy infantry by now were seriously worried, even though few had even seen the larvae yet. On the wings I could see their step beginning to waver and corporal looking to sergeant; sergeant to captain; captain to warden; warden to governor or Eszai, all wanting to know what to do.

Lourie and those with him – already no more than a company – were now nearly surrounded. Larvae flowed towards them like a tan wave. He knew it was safer to keep fighting than to run. Anyone who ran was borne down by clinging hatchlings, or tripped as several lunged at his feet, or he slipped in the mud and they overwhelmed him.

Lourie was spinning his glaive and stabbing larvae before and behind him. He was making his way steadily backwards but his path was blocked by the jostling crush – the remains of his own ranks. Bodies were beginning to pile up on the edges. The men in the middle were heaving their own dead out of the way to give themselves more room, but the armoured bodies only hemmed them in and gave the ravenous larvae a feast.

I chose a spot some distance from Lourie, slightly ahead of the front of the advancing larvae, and landed. 'Hurricane!' I yelled.

Lourie's sallow face turned towards me for an instant. His legs were muddied up to the hips. He had taken his helmet off and his cornrow-braided hair glistened with sweat.

I yelled, 'Run! There's a way out, here!'

Lourie ignored me. 'The Emperor,' he said loudly, looking down. 'I'm not running in front of the Emperor.'

'There's nothing you can do! Come on!'

Lourie said something derogatory about Rhydanne. He spun the glaive high and under his arm, accurately stabbing a crawling larva. He lifted it into the air. It flicked its tail under it, spattering mud.

They were sweeping towards me quickly, jetting water out of their tails to propel themselves through the liquid pooled over the churned earth, swarming on their short legs across the drier ground. Their hunger seemed even more desperate and insatiable than the adults'. I readied myself, trying to make out the nearest. It had a narrow, cylindrical shape and a long abdomen made up of segments that came to a point.

Familiar, but smaller, six jointed legs were bunched together under its thorax. The flattened head was hunched and joined to its body by a thick neck. It was dark brown with paler sandy and black spots along its sides. The crook-backed carapace was thinner, with many more joints and far more flexible than an Insect. Thick spines edged and topped its sinuous abdomen. Tiny wing-buds lay tight against its thorax like a backpack; much smaller than Insects' undeveloped wings but these were recognisably a different stage in the life-cycle of the same creature.

I had seen enough. I swung my ice axe at it, missed, and the pick passed close to its head. It reared up onto its two back legs, spread out its front legs and opened its jaws threateningly. Another made straight for my foot. Its jaws shot out and grabbed my ankle. Fucking shit! Its jaws shoot out! It bit straight through my boot and suddenly a pair of hooks twisted in my ankle. I slammed my axe down through its neck, with the speed of pain. It was impaled, but it didn't let go. It flexed the joint of its extendible jaw and pulled its body towards me by the fangs anchored in my boot. I levered them out with the axe pick. It curled up, convulsing – its mandible folded limply back underneath its head.

I took steps backwards, smashing the heads of larvae around me. Pleased with my prowess I looked up – the whole kilometre of ground from myself to the lake was swarming with them! I ran, limping, in the opposite direction and took off.

Dank though it was, the air had rarely felt so welcoming. Unfortunately I couldn't stay up here, I had to stop the rout spreading. I could feel my bitten foot bleeding into my boot. My flight path took me over the left flank; Tornado's halted formation. I'll tell him first.

I came down in front of the heavy infantry. Their nervous eyes peered from helmet slits. More mud splattered into my flight feathers as I slid to a halt. I couldn't keep doing this or I would soon be grounded. Tornado exploded out of the ranks before me, over two metres of confused belligerence in chain mail.

'Jant! What the fuck's going on?'

'Insects. Larvae, I think. Loads of them, coming this way.'

'What?'

I stopped, took a breath. 'It's a new type of Insect, coming from the lake. They're smaller but there's millions of them. Hard to see cos they keep very close to the ground. I killed a couple; they're softer than adults. But they're fast and they can swim. Lourie's cut off! Pikes are useless against them. His men are running.'

'No! No one runs! Not now!'

I had never seen him look so furious.

'Tornado, this is something new . . .'

'What about spears? Are they any use?'

'Short ones might be, if you stab down with them. Long swords, maces, axes maybe. Their jaws are on a hinge, like an arm! They shoot out *this* far in front! One bit me in the ankle! I saw them reaching through gaps in armour.'

He called, 'Signal the advance! Fyrd! Follow me! Your Emperor is watching! Runners! Tell Serein to keep his men close to us – don't let any spaces open up!'

'What are you doing?'

'My job. These soldiers are the Select of the Plainslands and they're not trying to wield a pike like a tree-trunk. You can tell San that we're going to rescue Hurricane and then we're going to reach our objective. If you can kill them, so can we.' He spoke loudly, for the benefit of the front ranks. They cheered. He looked at me levelly, though without malice.

'Look –'

'That's all, Jant.' He turned away.

'Excuse me!' But the bastard didn't pay the slightest bit of attention. I muttered as I took off, 'I'll go find someone intelligent to talk to.'

Now with a better view I could see the central phalanx had disintegrated into a bloody shambles. Those who could were splashing away, shoving through the archers behind them, discarding weapons and armour. The captain of a Rachiswater division tried to halt them. She grabbed a man but he kept running with such force that he pulled her from her horse and they both fell struggling into the mud. The surrounding infantry began to form up into shield walls, whether out of fear of Insects or their own routers I couldn't know.

Sirocco was trying to stage a more orderly retreat with what remained of his command but he was now faced by solid ranks of shields and spears in the hands of panicking men.

Lourie's diminishing band were standing in a circle, completely surrounded as, hundreds of metres away, the left wing began to wheel ponderously towards him. Tornado's men were fighting already in fresh swarms of nymphs. The right wing was still halted in confusion, not yet in contact with the larvae: cavalry rode up and down trying to see what was going on even while the ranks nearest the slaughter were peeling away and breaking up. The ground was heaving as larvae, attracted by the blood, funnelled into our centre from the left, from the lake. The sky was alive with horns, shouts and screams. Shit. Shitshitshit! I glided low, heading for the Micawater standard, until I picked out Lightning.

I leant against the wind and soared lower and lower to horseback-level, then pulled my wings in and dropped to the ground. At that very moment the Circle broke.

Lightning gave a great cry of rage: 'Lourie!'

I furled the blades of my wings and staggered to my feet. The mud here was atrocious. Lightning's horse was smeared in it up to the breast.

'Hurricane is dead.' Lightning looked down from the saddle. 'What in San's name is happening out there? Do I shoot or advance?'

'I don't know for sure,' I said. 'The sarissai were attacked by Insect larvae. They routed and the akontistai are caught up in it . . .'

'Insect *what*?'

I briefly described the new kind of Insects. 'Little, long Insects. So big –' I held my hands apart. 'But their jaws shoot out *this* far on a kind of jointed appendage. They're intent on eating. And they're going to keep coming because the ground from here to the lake is solid with them.'

Lightning looked to his steward, who was on a brown horse beside him, acting as a division captain. The warden of the first Micawater battalion was on horseback just beyond him. Lightning said, 'We don't know what these things can do. We haven't seen them before and they're not Insects; I don't know what it could mean. Abort the march. We will return to town.'

I said, 'Tornado and Wrenn are already advancing. They are – were – trying to relieve Hurricane. They're in amongst the larvae all up there –' I pointed towards the centre.

'What! Into my target zone?'

'Yes. The larvae look small and easy to kill but they don't know how many there are.'

'Why are they advancing independently? Why didn't you stop them?'

'Tawny wouldn't listen. He's been throwing his weight around ever since San arrived. But there are millions of larvae. They're bound to get cut off.'

Lightning rubbed his hand over his mouth and gazed at me. 'A battlefield is no place for heroics, Jant. The fate of the First Circle is all the proof we need. San's presence is causing us to act like fools.'

'What can we do?'

'I can't see Tornado's and Wrenn's positions. I can't cover them now without hitting them. And bloody Tornado's advance must have left all my archers following him exposed to attack from those *things*.'

'Yes.'

'Right ...' Lightning shook his head and focused properly on me. The crisis had revitalised him. His depression had lifted. He said, 'We're pulling out. We're not going to have a second massacre at Slake Cross.'

He called up four dispatch riders simply by pointing at them, said, '*You* go to Sleat. Tell him to get his fyrd to form a shield wall in front of the archers on the west flank. The archers must shoot at will to support them. *You*, go to the Sapper and Macer on the east flank. Tell them to sound the retreat and retire *in order*. Advise them we are facing a new type of Insect and they should avoid engagement. Tell them the Emperor commands this. *You* tell Hayl the same and then command the reserves on the east wing to follow the hastai as they pull out. *You* go to Thunder. Inform him that we will be retreating and ask that he prepare to cover us. Suggest that he tries flaming projectiles – they may scare these larvae. Then tell the Slake Cross garrison to man the walls.'

The dispatch riders galloped away, spraying muck over the front rank of archers. Lightning turned to his steward. 'Harrier, speak to the Blacksmith and organise the battalions here into a proper defensive position – because when the Insects finish off Hurricane's men they'll be up against us. We will retreat in unison with the west flank.'

'Yes, my lord.'

Lightning sighed, looked at his saddle pommel then up again. 'Harrier. Make sure the fyrd know that the Emperor is watching them and they must stand firm. But if anyone runs, they must be shot. Tell the wardens this. And have the provosts form up behind us. We can't afford another panic.'

'I understand, my lord.' He paused, nodded, then sped away.

'Jant, go to Eleonora. I mean the Queen. Say her lancers must charge straight up the flank and pick up as many of Tornado's and Wrenn's troops as they can, then retreat to camp.'

'Consider it done.' I prepared to take off.

'And you must inform the Emperor of what I have ordered.'

I stared at him. I had to tell San we were *retreating*? 'Yes, but ...'

'Do it. I will meet you at the Imperial Fyrd once I have finished here.'

Back in the air I could see the formations below beginning to reorganise themselves with glacial speed, drawing together more tightly. I shuddered at the thought of being land-bound, encased in metal, clumsy and slow in the face of the darting nymphs.

The Queen's cavalry were gleaming on the extreme west flank. As they were not treading in the infantry's tracks they had escaped the worst mud and, being upwind of the Insects, the horses were calm. At the point of their wedge I could see Eleonora's upturned face calmly watching as I circled down to land nearby.

She spread her wings in greeting, called, 'Why, Jant! You honour us with your presence!'

I approached her. She sat confidently astride her steel-clad thoroughbred, armoured in her usual mix of shining metal and self-assurance. She held her helmet beneath one arm and lance in the other hand, a pale blue pennon lazily waving from it. Her dark hair was immaculate and I even imagined I could detect a trace of rose perfume. An oval shield and a selection of weapons were slung from her saddle. She looked just as formidable on the battlefield as in her boudoir. 'Such a shame to bring you down here, when you look so ... graceful in the air.'

I had no time for Eleonora's crap. 'We're being attacked! 'Leon, there's a new kind of Insect coming out of the lake. Lightning has ordered a retreat. A total withdrawal! Tornado and Serein's hastai will soon be cut off at the front. Lightning commands you and your lancers to charge, rescue them, and carry as many as possible back to town.'

I described the larvae. Eleonora frowned, then changed to an overhand grip on her lance, pointing it at the ground like a spear.

'Tell Lightning I accept his command.' She turned, shouted, 'Lancers of Awia! Follow your Queen!' She glanced at me and pulled her helmet visor down over her smile. I staged my own tactical retreat.

I flew to the Emperor and tipped my wings to him. He raised a hand and the Imperial Fyrd walked their horses aside to let him through. As he did so, Frost on her dapple stallion emerged from behind the last riders on the corner of the square. She urged it into a trot and began to advance, even as the call to retreat was going up. Her bodyguard trailed her. I circled, trying to keep her in view. She's an experienced Eszai, she should realise how serious this is. What was she playing at?

I glanced down, acutely aware of San watching me. Frost could look after herself. I descended. The horses of the Imperial cavalry tossed their heads and held them high, their white-edged eyes watching my great wings beating. The horses were actually shaking as their riders struggled to still them.

The riders and mounts acted as a windbreak, and I had no current to balance on for the last few metres. I fell down heavily and landed in a crouch. My coat-tails flopped to the ground. There was a smash and tinkle of broken glass in my deep right pocket. Crouching in the hoof-printed mud I wondered what it could be. Shit. The jar with the Vermiform worms.

I hadn't thought about it at all up until this instant. I looked down, and worms were wriggling out of my pocket.

CHAPTER 22

Worms, bursting from my pocket, squirmed down my coat in rivulets and dropped off onto the ground. They scattered in all directions and began sinking into the mud, wriggling and twisting around my feet as they burrowed their way down. I scrabbled frantically with both hands, trying to catch hold of them, but they disappeared right under my fingers. I went after others, and the same thing happened. They were too quick; the ends of their tails vanished into the mud. In a few seconds, they had all gone.

I looked up at the Emperor, who was leaning forward over his horse's neck, watching me curiously. I said, 'Ah, my lord . . .'

'Comet?'

I stood up. 'Lightning sent me to say he's halted the advance and is recalling the men to camp.'

'So I see. Why?'

'There are millions of little Insects with extendible jaws, coming out of the lake. They killed Hurricane; now Tornado and Wrenn are surrounded. Lightning's sending the Awian lancers to their aid.'

'Little Insects?' the Emperor queried.

I felt something tighten around my ankle. I looked down and so did the Emperor. A thick tentacle of worms was pushing from the soil like the fat stem of a vine. It had wrapped twice around my ankle and the tip was halfway round another loop.

The Emperor's eyes widened but he said nothing. Apologetically I tugged my leg. The tentacle paused, tugged back, then yanked me off my feet. Before I could hit the mud the tentacle shot out of it, a thick column, hoisting me up. I dangled helplessly from my ankle as it poured up, past the Emperor. It kept going, bursting from the ground like the trunk of a tree. Its surface had a linear texture; millions on millions of worms streaking into the air.

The Emperor and all the square of horses shrank quickly below. I could see the whole battlefield now. The Imperial Fyrd's faces looked up, pale and shocked. On all sides of the square they were turning their horses and taking flight. Those in the middle were stepping this way and that trying to push a way out. San, in complete control of Alezane, was looking up at me calmly.

Further off, the canvas city; the pavilions and interlaced ropes – I swung round and caught a glimpse of the clash of lancers and dazzling armour against the Insect larvae, and behind them the lake's brown mirror.

I yelled and yelled. My other leg flailed, knee bent, and my bitten foot was throbbing. My arms dangled, and my coat swished somewhere below my head like a slashed leather curtain. My letters dropped out of my pockets and started fluttering to the ground. My keys and hip flask plummeted after them.

The blood was rushing to my head. My wings slipped open and settled down past shoulder level, loosely spread. My ice axe bounced around, hanging in the space between them. I waved my arms about but couldn't find anything to grab on to. My ankle was agony – the worms were squeezing it tight and my leg was stretching.

I did a sit-up to see the thick snake of annelids wrapped around my ankle, a branch from the solid column stretching to the ground.

'Hey!' I yelled at the stem. 'Let me go, you fucking thing!'

I felt something give and I plummeted a metre. It went taut and held me again.

'No!'

It let me go ... caught me. The worms moving over and clinging to each other gave an elasticity, so I bounced slightly. My joints stretched to popping point. It let me go, caught me. I automatically flapped my wings, looking like a hawk hanging upside down in a snare. I wouldn't have time to turn and fly if it dropped me on my head.

'No! *Don't* let me go! Please don't drop me! Let's talk.'

It just shook me, furiously. My jaw clattered, my bangles jingled and my hair, streaming out under me, swept against my coat skirts.

I stomach-crunched up again and tried to grab the tendril but it just twirled me around. The mud and horse-backs streaked round and round beneath me.

'Aeee! No! Talk to me! Vermi–'

Three more branches spurted out of its stem; the tips pointed, quested towards me and coiled around my wrists and other foot, faster than I could move them. I felt my limbs gradually drawn out with a strength I couldn't resist, until I was spreadeagled like a starfish.

The Emperor's horse backed off until he checked it. He was still looking at me, emotionlessly.

The worms kept pulling me taut. My shoulder joints cracked. I screamed, 'Oh, god, no!'

They stopped pulling and suddenly whipped me the right way up. I was standing in the air, twenty metres above the battle. I had never been upright and stationary in the air before, and the chaos was going on all around me.

Among the rivers of soldiers streaming past in retreat, people were pausing, making a slower flow of steel helmets and heads looking up. Some had stopped completely to gawp and the flow went around them; there were collisions here and there. An enormous, clear space had formed where the trunk went into the ground. Nobody was prepared to approach it. God knows what they were making of a clearly recognisable Messenger stretched like a spider in a vast flesh vine.

Worms slid over worms, providing a greater strength by far than muscle fibres – another tentacle snaked out from the mass. Its tip came to within centimetres of my face and seemed to look about, then it flattened, turned upright and formed into a stylized female face, like a mask, with no eyes in the almond-shaped sockets. I could see down to the mud through them. The well-sculpted lips moved quickly but the Vermiform's polyphonous voice was not in synch; it harped out from both the mask and the main trunk: 'What have you done? How could you bring this on yourselves?'

Wonder and despair vied in its voices but I was panicking too much to care. 'I'm sorry I put your worms in a jar. It was wrong. I –'

The Vermiform pulled my limbs smoothly. Bands of shredding pain flamed up my back and across my chest from shoulder to shoulder. I shrieked. There was something experimental in the pull, as if it could haul much harder if it wanted to.

It said, 'Not that! The water . . .' It swung me from side to side and pushed its mask close to my face. 'Where did the lake come from? You stupid, stupid people! You've made a hatching pool!'

'We built the dam to flood the Paperlands,' I said.

'You have caused the death of this entire world!' It sent out thread-thin but steel-rod-strong strands and jabbed me all over my body, which was as effective as a slap. 'You gave the Insects a place to breed! They lay their eggs in still water! Didn't the Somatopolis tell you anything?'

I looked to San; his face raised and eyes narrowed to see me against the bright sky. His horse was trembling and so dotted with sweat his cloak was sticking to it.

Lightning galloped in, standing in his stirrups, his reins tied down and an arrow at string on a longbow. He drew and loosed. The arrow passed clean through the trunk – the worms seethed aside making a hole, then resealed.

He came to the Emperor's side, nocked another arrow, his face white. His horse paced back and forth, stomping the mud, pawing and snorting, head lowered, but he wouldn't let it bolt. He kept beside the Emperor – his spurs drawing blood from its white flanks.

'The Emperor . . .' I gasped.

'*Where*?'

'Down there.'

The Vermiform snapped its mask back into the trunk and started retracting. It carried me down, still stretched out – I saw the mud rushing up closer and closer. It brought me to the Emperor, though San didn't give me so much as a glance. It stopped, jerking me to a halt a metre off the ground.

The top of the curving trunk overhung San's head but the surface nearest him extruded its mask and brought it close to his face. He returned its gaze equably, without moving a muscle.

Lightning aimed at the mask and loosed. His arrow passed harmlessly through it – the worms parted again. The arrow whistled past me and through a sudden gap in the trunk. With the slightest ripple the holes closed and the mask regained its composure.

'Comet,' San said, without moving his gaze from the female visage. 'What is this?'

'It's the Vermiform. And arrows are no good against it.'

The Vermiform addressed the Emperor: 'So you are the one whom Dunlin has told us about?'

San tilted his head as if asking the Vermiform to continue. It said, 'Ourselves in the soil see that larvae are already coming out of the lake. Why? Why did you do it? Do you all have a suicide wish? Do you even *know* what you've done?'

'What have we done?' the Emperor said emotionlessly.

'Created a breeding pool for Insects in this world! Was there a mating flight? Do you know they lay a hundred eggs a minute? Have you any idea how many more are to come?'

The Emperor said nothing.

The Vermiform threshed, furious. 'Are you going to miss this warrior?' and slowly drew my bonds tighter and tighter. I tried to pull back but it was hopeless: agony flared straight through my shoulders – my arms and legs were riving out. I started screaming – I could feel the suck of the cup-joints in my hips stretched to the point of dislocation.

The pauldrons of San's armour moved infinitesimally, as if he shrugged. He did not look at me, only at the mask.

The Vermiform said, 'Dunlin is a better commander than you ever were, San. He is marshalling an army in several worlds that is much better than anything you've managed to establish here.'

San said, 'I thought that would happen.'

'Dunlin will be infuriated when he hears it's come to this.'

'That is the least of my concerns ... Could you put my Messenger down, please?' he added, although he said it as if my shrieking was irking him rather than if he cared that I was being torn limb from limb. I was released abruptly. I fell in a loose tangle, hit the ground heavily and curled up in the cold mud, hugging my shoulders.

'These are just the first nymphs emerging,' the worms choired. 'There will be hundreds more of these waves. Larvae are so ravenous that if they all hatched together they would devour each other for want of food. Countless worlds have fallen this way.'

The Emperor said, 'It is an extremely long time since I was last in the Shift.'

The Vermiform continued, 'The older larvae will shed their skins and become Insects, and begin dropping food in for the new larvae. Five moults later, those adult Insects will take flight too – and you'll have yet another generation of millions of larvae emerging. Once that started happening in the Somatopolis we didn't have a chance. You certainly don't have one, with the stupid pathetic weapons you still wield. We can taste saltpetre, aluminium, tungsten, uranium in the earth yet you still fight using wood and iron! You'll be overwhelmed. Every body of standing water in your whole continent will soon become a hatching pool. Every pond, every lake –'

Lightning nocked another arrow to string.

'Dunlin is more active than you are!' the worms said. 'He understands that Insects are a mortal threat, but you don't seem to!'

'We are doing all we can.'

'Even when Insects were building bridges here, you did not respond seriously enough. They have overrun our world completely, and many others we have seen. Worlds take thousands of millions of years to form and Insects can destroy them in a decade! But you ... it is as if you were deliberately trying to keep a stalemate with them. You never take an inch against them. We know why: without their outside threat, the Fourlands wouldn't need your Circle, your rule, or *you*. But your plan for keeping the Insects at a manageable level has all gone wrong. First there were swarms, then bridges, now they're breeding! The balance has tipped. You will never hold them in check now.'

The Emperor bridled at the accusation. 'We keep the front and push them back when we can. There are far too many to defeat. This is a stalemate of necessity, not intention.'

'No. Dunlin told me this was a world where a few Insects appeared at first. When that happens, the residents can easily exterminate them. Awia could simply have wiped them out. When they began to spread you could still have made a concerted effort and killed them all. But you let the situation get out of hand in order to get into power, didn't you? They needed you as a leader once the swarms started. And you kept them needing you ever since.'

San shook his head. 'False. We were all ignorant of war before the Insects arrived. We had no way to fight them. They are more difficult to kill than you say. We had no knowledge of their habits. We didn't know they were going to expand so quickly.'

'And when they did start spreading, you let them so the people would put you into power!'

For the first time ever, I saw the Emperor lose his temper. 'We fought tooth and nail! Yes, when Insects first began to proliferate, if we had made a concerted effort we might, *might*, have killed them all, but more were always following! We were embroiled in a civil war –'

Which you ended by dividing the Pentadrica as a prize, I thought.

'– It was all I could do to stop three countries tearing a fourth apart and then turning on each other. We had no proper weapons, no strategies; we had no idea how to kill Insects.'

The Vermiform fermented with fury. Eight thick worm-pillars thrust out of the ground in a two-metre circle around San's horse. Like the first trunk they tapered towards the top. As they rose, the main trunk thinned, worms disappearing into the earth to shoot up as the new pillars. They grew to its height, bending over San and his horse. They looked like gigantic octopus tentacles waving around a boat. His stallion reared, but he rode it.

The tentacles joined together above him, caging him in. The mask extended into thin strings and pushed towards San's face. Worms separated and flowed onto his skin, spreading to crawl all over him.

They snaked down his breastplate collar, under his helmet, into his hair, in the folds around his eyes, circled his lips and slithered into the wrinkles on his neck. The Emperor did not move as worms turmoiled out of his armour's joints at armpits and waist, from his wrists to slip between his fingers holding the reins. They wriggled under the plates on his thighs and shins to the shining laminae on his feet. Lines of worms formed a moving, living pink net all over him.

Lightning yelled. He spurred his horse over to me, dismounted and helped me from my Jant-shaped hole in the ooze. I poked around among my sodden letters, found my hip flask and took a long swig.

'What's happening?' Lightning said wildly. 'What are these maggots attacking San? What must we do?'

'It's the Vermiform. From the Shift.'

'How can I kill them?'

'You can't.'

The worms stopped writhing over the Emperor, poured up to his breastplate and webbed its surface. From the centre, a rope of worms spouted out and dived at the ground. They pooled on the mud and gathered themselves into a semblance of a man, building from the feet up. All the worms peeled off the Emperor, and onto the man's shape. It gained height, thinned, worms represented hair hanging down to the shoulders, pinched cheeks, a thin nose, a body flanged or curved, closely portraying plate armour. It became a perfect imitation of San.

'We have tales of god coming back!' Lightning cried. 'And this thing appears!'

'It isn't god,' I said. 'It's a Shift creature.'

The effigy of San chorused, 'You told them what? You told them there's a god? You ...' Its contempt knew no bounds. 'You gave them the idea of god?'

'There is always a god in the minds of men,' the Emperor said quietly.

The Vermiform said, 'Have you used that for your own ends too? No wonder this world is about to be lost to the Insects, if you are waiting for god to help you. Your people will all die as they wait!'

'We are not waiting,' San said. 'We are fighting.'

The mask bobbed. 'They're being slaughtered! Do they know of the Shift?'

Lightning muttered, 'Is this mountain of livebait saying there is no god but the Shift exists?'

'God isn't here but a Shift creature is,' I said.

The Vermiform said, 'San, your Fourlands are lost. Your Circle will break and your Castle will fall. I must warn Dunlin that this world does not have much time left, and I must arrange defences. The Insects here will soon build bridges to other worlds. We hope they will act with more intelligence than you did.'

'Leave the Empire, you foul thing,' said San calmly.

The eight tentacles that joined together above the Emperor, caging him in like the struts of a tent, sent out a thick strand into the air. We could see worms streaming up to its tip, which looked truncated; they were vanishing there. The thick rope was pouring into nowhere – an area as big as a buckler that looked the same as the rest of the sky.

The trunks thinned, the caricature of the Emperor dissolved as worms left it and joined them. The trunks shrank to strings, then their bases lifted up from the earth as if being reeled in. They looped into the hole in thin air, twisting together into a rope as they did so. The end of the rope vanished. The Vermiform had gone. I knew it would be appearing like a cable in another world.

The Emperor looked directly at me accusingly. So did Lightning – he had been gaping at the worm-arc, as had all the soldiers standing or on their knees in traumatised silence around us. Streams of retreating riders and men-at-arms coming off the flank were passing us, back to town. The Emperor looked at them and sighed.

Lightning said, 'That was a throng of earthworms, wasn't it?'

'Yes,' I said.

'Mmm. From the . . .'

'From the Shift, yes.'

'Right. Uh-hum. It said flying Insects will lay eggs in every lake. Not in Micawater lake they won't.'

I accidentally put my weight on my bitten foot and yowled. Lightning shook himself. 'Are you injured?'

I honestly could not tell whether I was seriously hurt or not. I had my arms crossed, hands clasped desperately around my shoulders. I said, 'I'll go to Rayne.'

San began to turn his horse but Lightning ran across and grabbed its bridle. The horse, true to its training, stood still. San glared down at the Archer. Lightning, from force of habit, lowered his gaze, then rallied and looked the Emperor straight in the eye. 'My lord,' he said. 'Where are you *from*?'

I knew what he meant, and so did San, but he didn't deign to answer. The thought of a Shift world full of potential Emperors was enough to make me shiver worse than the horses.

'Where are you from?' Lightning repeated. 'Not from the . . . From the . . . You're not like that thing, are you?'

The Emperor closed his eyes and shook his head gently. 'I am from Hacilith . . . From the place where Hacilith city now stands. I am a man. A man like any other Morenzian. Believe me, Archer.'

'My lord.' Lightning let the bridle go.

A thought occurred to me. '*When* are you from?'

The Emperor ignored me, but Lightning took up the question, frowning. 'Yes. That thing said millions.'

San gave the clear impression that he neither knew nor cared what the Vermiform said. He was regarding Lightning closely. He stated,

'No, I am not that old. Yes, I am older than you think.'

Lightning swallowed hard, pressed, 'Then how old?'

San was still scrutinising him. 'You must dine with me tonight, Archer.'

We were astounded. 'Yes, my lord,' Lightning mouthed. 'Yes – certainly.'

'Now you must return to your fyrd. You have my full authority to supervise the withdrawal.'

Lightning bowed, white-faced. San glanced at me. 'Messenger, put aside your pain. Find the Architect. We must discover a way to drain the lake. Everything depends on this now, it seems.' He looked slowly around him. 'Everything.'

I struggled into the air. My wing muscles were tender from the assault and the constant take-offs. If I kept using them now I knew I would be grounded for days. But I had to carry out San's request, and I was anxious to escape from the curious queries of the fyrdsmen still gawking at the air where the Vermiform had vanished.

I soared up above the devastation and circled, looking for Frost. The Imperial Fyrd were now toy soldiers beneath me. Lightning was tiny on horseback as he galloped away from them. The host's advance, seemingly so inexorable only an hour ago had stopped and it was ebbing away.

I searched in vain for Frost. I looked among the east wing that she would have to pass through. It was a wide stream of men in full retreat. If Frost was heading the other way, her small group would be battling against the current and I'd see the flow of men dividing round them like water cleaving around a rock. But they seemed in good order with no stragglers – Hayl's cavalry was carefully screening the withdrawal. From the lack of agitation in their ranks they seemed to be still ignorant of the larvae.

I climbed, widening my search. The reserve had formed into a solid shield wall with archers in tight-packed shooting positions behind them. Lightning's orders reached slow actualisation in the movements of tens of thousands on the field. The archers resumed shooting and arrow volleys sailed by below me, rippling the air. Already the rear echelons were beginning to form into columns, ready to pull out following the east wing. The real battleground was in front of the shield wall. But I didn't have time to look – I had to find Frost and, even in her recently *disturbed* state she wouldn't have been stupid enough to go that way, surely?

I circled again, and cast my gaze towards the periphery. A motion caught my attention, so fast I thought it had to be Insects. I angled towards it, and saw it was the orange Riverworks banner accompanying Frost. Her horsemen were out on the east flank, far beyond the retreating troops and moving at a full gallop, something I wasn't expecting in the mud soup. I dived towards them and saw they were heading rapidly towards the river bank, following a narrow supply road of quarry chippings. It was a causeway over the sodden ground, built at the same time as the plunge basin. Frost knew the valley like the back of her hand and was taking a quick detour around the chaos. I scanned the route ahead. Near the diminished river the track met the road, wide enough for wagons, that climbed the ramp to the dam and formed the walkway on top.

I shed height quickly and checked for larvae. Along the entire length of the lake margins they were crawling up the shallow slope, long bodies twisting from side to side. Their claws pushed trails in the gravel. Some turned on each other, and on the carcasses of Insects littering the lakeside.

Scores were emerging onto the dam's face where the lake lapped up against it. In ragged lines they climbed its nearly sheer wall, finding purchase where it would be too steep for an adult Insect. Ripples broke over them, but they hung off its cobbles, moving up with mindless persistence; six legs and hooked feet scrabbling slowly.

Nearly all headed directly to the carnage before them; downstream of the dam the shore was reasonably clear. The adult Insects were likewise occupied. Frost would only have to worry about stragglers as long as the shambles in front of her continued to offer an easy supply of food.

I bit my lip, realising I was thinking of Tornado's and Wrenn's battalions only as bait to draw Insects away from Frost. Guiltily, I decided to take a closer look.

Tornado's men had advanced barely a few hundred metres after I'd left them before becoming trapped. There was no end to the nymphs emerging from the lake. The infantry divisions were concentrating on chopping as many as possible, but they were already an island cut off and disappearing under a chitin tide. They had formed into isolated schiltroms, standing in circles of shields shoulder-to-shoulder, presenting their weapons in all directions. Larvae were chewing through shields, running up them and over the heads of men so I saw waggling larvae crossing the circles. Two larvae replaced every one dispatched. The circles were visibly shrinking; the air was heavy with screams. I picked out Wrenn, a Wrought sword in each hand, slashing and cutting the nymphs to shreds but there were too many. It was like trying to sever snowflakes in a blizzard.

The Queen's lancers were whipping their mounts through the swarm. Each rider stopped only to pull a desperate foot soldier up behind him before turning and spurring back. They stabbed with their lances but the best weapons they had were their horses' iron-shod hooves. The chargers' long barding frustrated larvae trying to climb it but they could crawl under and they shot their jaws into the horses' pasterns. Casualties were beginning to tell. Some mounts threw their riders in terror. I never saw any get up again.

I put the terrible sight behind me and turned back towards Frost. My course took me over where Lourie's soldiers had fallen. I was shocked to find myself staring at what looked like an ancient battle-field: skulls grinned under pot helmets, bones shone through the gaps in battered armour. Every last scrap of flesh had been consumed. The bone-mounds were covered in gnarled, motionless larvae sitting with heads looking up and long tails pressed to the ground. Their thin carapaces were translucent. Some were missing legs or heads. The back of every thorax was cracked and open.

Shit. They weren't dead larvae, they were empty shells. They were growing, shedding their carapaces within only a few hours of emerging. Five moults, the Vermiform had said. Surely all the moults couldn't take the same length of time? At this rate, by the end of the week we would be up against a swarm of Insects greater than any we had ever seen.

I found Frost leading her group, galloping flat-out up the curving road. Gaps appeared as the stronger mounts pulled away. She lashed her horse mercilessly, obsessed with reaching the dam. The horses were dripping sweat and wide-eyed with terror at the smell of Insects.

I waved. 'Come on! The way's clear if you're fast!'

They pounded on, only a couple of minutes from the dam. But as they drew closer, nearby larvae began to converge on them.

'Look out!'

Frost ignored my warning and carried straight onto the dam's crest, pushing her horse through the larvae as if they weren't there. The rest followed her. I could see larvae hanging on horses' legs by their jaws, working their way up the sides of the screaming animals. The riders flailed at them with swords, maces, gauntleted fists.

I saw the trailing horse eaten as she staggered; larvae swarmed up her legs and took her apart, stripped the skin from her side in great swathes until her guts fell out. Here and there, they laid her bare to the bone in seconds. She died squealing, trying to free her hooves from the close-packed spiny nymphs. The rider, flailing at the beasts working through his armour, threw himself over the parapet and plummeted to his death rather than being eaten alive.

With a terminal burst of speed, Frost reached her destination: the winch tower. She leapt off her horse, just short of the portcullis, shot the bolts of the iron maintenance door and disappeared inside the tower itself. The majority of her company were following. Abandoning their horses to occupy the larvae, they sprinted to safety, finally swinging the door shut behind them when it was clear there would be no more survivors. A minute later, the Riverworks Company banner jerked up the flag pole and unfurled in the breeze.

CHAPTER 23

I focused on the banner, soared round and set down on the roof of the winch tower. I slipped to the parapet, between its beacon and enormous warning bell. I looked around; the timber fence along the walkway had completely disappeared. Insects had chewed the stakes down to pulpy stumps.

I looked down the faces of the winch tower. Both its portcullises were down, blocking the walkway on both sides. Both tracks were covered with larvae; they clustered around the grating trying to get through, but it was thick metal mesh and the gaps were too small. Adult Insects on the side nearest the Paperlands were chewing the bars fruitlessly.

A rhythmic clanging echoed from inside the tower. I listened carefully; it was heavy and sharp, metal against stone, and muffled as if coming from a distance, which was strange because it was directly below me.

I shimmied over the parapet and kicked a louvre through. I swung one leg inside, ducked my head under the top lintel and sat straddling the ledge, hunched half in, half out of the tower. I looked down.

The tower had no floors – it was one great, hollow dark space filled with machinery. Some candle lights flickered far below me on the ground. The scale of the crowded shafts and cogs interlaced with each other completely took my breath away.

I soon distinguished the mechanisms. On the walls below my window and opposite were fixed those needed to work the two portcullises – spindles wound with the last couple of loops of rope, and greased metal runners. The larvae's short, whisker-like antennae poked between the bars of both gates and their jaws flashed out, tearing at the air.

The mechanism to raise the dam gate was even more impressive. Only Frost's dedication could have designed it, and only the effort it took to have drawn it together could have made her love it as much as she did. The shafts were painted black, but their naked steel working surfaces shone with oil. The inside of the tower looked like that of a windmill in which all the wheels and beams and pegs had turned to metal.

The square floor was paved and on either side were circular, stone-rimmed holes from which thick cables ran, like ship's ropes. They were tarred and very taut. They led up to a horizontal brass roller and were wrapped around it at both ends. It looked like the spindle used to raise water from a well, but on a massive scale. The roller was braced with girders attaching it to all four walls, secure at head height. Its vertical wheel meshed with a complicated system of gears onto a horizontal capstan carrying a chain. Lots of tackle to harness horses lay tangled, attached to the free end of the chain.

Frost was down there, dwarfed by the machinery. I could see her rounded shoulders and bandanna; she had taken her helmet off. I shouted down but she couldn't hear me. She was bent double, peering into a square hole in the floor. Its trapdoor was open and it was big enough for one man to fit down at a time. The clanking resounded from deep underground.

Several soldiers were distributing gear piled by the walls. A big man beside Frost held a rope around his waist with both hands. The end disappeared into the shaft, and he was lowering it.

I climbed down the rough wall and ran to her. 'Frost?'

'Jant!' She stood upright and stretched, her hands in the small of her back. Her face was streaked with dirt and her brigandine jacket hung open. She had stuffed her brown velvet rabbit under its fastening flap and its head nodded comically at her bosom.

'Jant, we lost our horses. We couldn't bring them in. We had to leave them outside and the Insect young just ripped them apart.'

'I saw it,' I said.

'We needed horses to raise the gate and open the dam. Now we can't.' Without looking she slapped her hand onto the weighty rope. 'See?'

'Shit!'

'Yes. Shit. But I think I've figured a solution.'

'What are you going to do?'

She pointed down the maintenance shaft. A line of brackets bolted to the wall formed a ladder leading into the depths. A murky flicker of lamplight came and went down there.

'Climb down and I'll show you.'

'I'd rather not.'

'Come on. There are ten men crammed in the gate chamber but you can hang on the ladder.'

'No, no. I don't have time. I have to get back to the Emperor and tell him what you're doing.'

The rope around the soldier's waist tugged twice, pulling his hand, and he began hauling something up. Frost said, 'Now we've made a start, I can rig a block-and-tackle to make raising the spoil easier. This is your last load doing it the hard way.'

'As you say.' He grinned at her. He seemed in good spirits.

'What are you doing?' I asked again.

She stamped her steel-toed boot on the paving stone. 'If you went down into the chamber, you'd see the top of the gate emerging from the floor, with the ropes attached to it. Millions of tonnes of water are pressing on the gate, keeping it shut. So we are digging down on either side of it.

'We are going to provide a new passage for the water over the top of the gate, then down into the original outlet pipe. Of course we're digging on the downstream side first to open up the passage to the face of the dam. Then I'll ask them to excavate the other side. Water will burst up, fill the chamber and drain away down the downstream side, out through the face of the dam, like it's supposed to. We will drain the lake, lads! You'll be heroes!'

The men broke out in optimistic smiles.

I said, 'Really? Won't the water gush back up the shaft?'

Frost's lips set thin. 'No.'

'But –'

'Sh!' she snapped. 'I'll put a lid on it, or something.' She took my sleeve and turned me away from the toiling fyrdsmen. 'Not in front of them. Don't ask any questions, just spread the news as to what I'm doing.'

I said, 'The downstream face is covered with larvae too. I expect some will have crawled up the passage.'

She stared at me, then nodded. 'Oh – when we break through? Yes, some might crawl into the chamber but we have our pickaxes. And the water will flush the rest out. I left a few stores here but we don't have many spades. Fly thyself to the town and bring us more supplies.'

'There's a limit to the weight I can carry.'

'Yes, of course. Bring what thou canst, thou wilt have to make a few trips. I want water, clean fresh water –' she gestured in the direction of the lake ' – because my men can't drink that muck and this is thirsty work. They're afforst from the ride, and forspent already.'

'Frost, the first law of communication is to speak the same language as the person you're speaking to.'

'Sorry. You know what I bloody mean. Bring some more lanterns, another couple of spades because we don't have enough to go around, and some food.' She dithered. 'Oh, and can you bring me some coffee too?'

'Sure.'

'I can make it on the stove. It's going to be a long night and I think I'm going to need it. We'll keep digging until we make the breakthrough. The men have to remove all the cladding from the floor of the chamber with muscle power alone; there's no way we can use acid down there.'

I shook my head. 'You're mining out the core of your own dam?'

'No. I'm just making two little holes, one either side of the gate.'

'But whoever's trapped in the chamber will –'

'Will be able to climb to safety up the brackets,' she said firmly. 'Now, do you have a pen and paper? I need to write a message to the Emperor. Go and fetch the water bottles, and when you return I'll have it ready for him.'

I nodded to her, then quickly scaled the tower wall, slipped through the window and felt the pull as my wings took my weight. I flew back to Slake Cross.

The town was a collage of hideous sights. It was incredibly crowded; people were still coming in from the battlefield but they were also drawing back behind the town's walls out of the canvas city. We had no chance of holding the palisade and camp against the approaching larvae. They could climb, and they could swim, too, so the moat was useless. The tower tops bristled with soldiers ready to repulse them.

I ran towards the centre square and the water pumps, passing stretcher-bearers carrying horrifically injured men. They left trails of blood through the streets already slippery with mud and horse dung. Exhausted soldiers crowded the staircases and corners, trying to summon the last reserves of energy. Some were chewing handfuls of hazelnuts, their iron rations. The walking injured leant against walls waiting for their friends to bring them pannikins of stew. Soldiers bare to the waist were queuing endlessly outside the shower block. Its doors were wide – men too tired to undress were standing clothed under the flow of water.

More queues of thousands: up to the enormous cooking pots on a table under an awning. Under the Cook's cornucopia banner, his assistants were doling out tremendous quantities of bean stew to whoever was well enough to take it. Soldiers were waiting in line holding their bowls.

As I passed them, Tre Cloud darted out. 'The Swordsman's lost his leg!' he cried. 'Featherback lancers just carried him in.'

'Is he conscious?'

'I'd say. He's bawling blue filth.'

I set off sprinting to the hospital. I could hear the screaming from a street away. I skirted round wounded men laid side by side on stretchers in the street against its wall, and entered onto a floor slick with red. Gore was spattered up the walls to above head height. Doctors were concentrating on their immediate patients and yelling for assistance, dressings, fresh water. Nurses carrying pitchers or bandage rolls shouldered past each other, dashing through the maze of beds.

All around me men were lying, moaning, crying. One reached out and grabbed my belt. I looked down at him, and as I did so, he died.

I slipped on blood, distracted by the tremendous variety of injuries. There were lots of empty eye sockets, or men with bandages over their eyes, because larvae had pulled their eyes out. There were plenty of men with cloth wrapped around bloody stumps; adult Insects had lopped off arms and legs. There were wounds to the throat, to the groin, to joints that were less protected by plate. Along the walls slumped hundreds of men with extreme exhaustion and dehydration – every one being given litres and litres of salty water. One porter with a mop was ineffectually stirring the pools of glutinous blood on the flagstones. It reflected the camp beds along the wall.

Lying in a corner there was a man whose face had been chewed down to the bone on his forehead and cheeks – I could see into his mouth. And in another corner – something so terrible I quickly blotted it from memory.

I saw Wrenn – lying by the wall, on a stretcher bed extending towards the middle of the room. Three lancers in plate were holding him down, one on his either shoulder and one on his leg. His other leg was nothing but a bleeding stump, bitten off below the knee. He was kicking it in the air and drops of blood were spattering on the soldiers. He was yelling, his mouth a black oval, his cheeks stretched and eyes slitted. Where his shin should be, I saw the white ends of neatly severed bone.

They had stripped him down to his padded gambeson but he still had armour on his uninjured leg. He was covered in many smaller excruciating wounds, bleeding heavily through tears in the jacket. Most of them were deep punctures, where larvae's fangs had slid in like curved smooth thorns, but they were nothing compared to what had happened to his leg.

Rayne was resuscitating a man with a crunchy broken jaw and a mushy nose. She left him to her assistant and dashed over, leaving sticky footprints.

She gave Wrenn an injection into the crook of his arm, pressed a cotton pad on the place, withdrew the needle. She quickly dropped some clear liquid on a white tile, and mixed it with a drop of blood pricked from one of the three soldiers who looked most like him. The mixture did not go grainy but stayed smooth, so she patted the windowsill for the lad to sit up there, and she rigged up a waxed cotton tube that would transfer blood down from his arm into Wrenn's.

Wrenn was yelling all the time. 'No! Put me back on the field! Leave me there! I want to be left! Bitch!'

She grasped his hand and he tried to fend her off, but he calmed a little as the scolopendium took effect. 'Leave me! I can't be Eszai any more! Let me die!'

'Let him die unbeaten,' I said.

Wrenn glanced in the direction of my voice, with unfocused eyes, and smeared blood across his cheek with the back of his hand.

Rayne was furious, 'Ge' ou' of t' way, Jant!'

'He can't be the Swordsman now. He'll die anyway. Let him die without the indignity of being beaten by a Challenger.'

'There's more t' life than tha'!'

'I've never had pain like this before!' The fear was stronger than the agony in his voice. 'And . . . and . . . Oh, god, I'm so bloody cold.'

He turned his head and spoke to empty space: 'Skua? You can't be. You died . . . I lost Sanguin. I left it out there . . .' He stared, glazed-eyed, and then passed out.

Rayne pointed to a tourniquet on his thigh, and looked at the soldier on the window ledge. 'Did you pu' tha' on?'

'Yes.'

'Good. You did t' righ' thing.'

Wrenn's stump was bone surrounded by meaty pulp. The end of the artery dangled, swaying loosely and dribbling blood. Rayne pinched the end and expertly wound turns of silk thread around it – four, five, six times. She tied the thread and then smeared on an ointment of turpentine and phenol, with tansy extract. Then she bound a poultice loosely around it. The poultice, a pad of spongy elder pith wrapped in linen, had been steam-cleaned then infused with a lot of rose honey.

She stepped back and surveyed her work. 'I can feel him pulling on t' Circle. This could've killed any other Eszai bu' Wrenn. He's such a figh'er. Wha' are you doing here? Have you brough' a message?'

'No. I'm passing through. Do you have anything to tell Frost or San?'

She shook her head. She was untying the tourniquet from Wrenn's thigh. 'You're no' encouraging, Jant. Saying "leave him"! How dare you!'

'But how can he swordfight now?' I protested. 'Even if he survives, he'll lose his place in the Circle to the first Challenger who comes along.'

'I've deal' with maimed Eszai hundreds of times. I know I'm righ'.'

'I'd hate to be forced back to obscurity,' I said. 'Wrenn is the same. Do you expect him to win duels on a wooden leg?'

Rayne said, 'Stranger things have happened.'

I huffed. 'A Swordsman with one leg? How likely is that?'

Rayne said, 'Look. There are all kinds of freakish abilities in t' Circle. We even have a man who can fly. Tha's pret'y damn weird.'

I took her point. She continued, 'He migh' go on for a year or even more before get'ing bea'en. He may well have t' come t' terms wi' being mortal again. Bu' a' least he'll have more life. He can change his outlook. He can change from being t' Swordsman t' someone else. I am giving him time t' think. Once he thinks abou' i', he'll thank me for no' let'ing him die. They always do. As long as they can continue t' live wi' digni'y, and have the chance t' die peacefully in bed surrounded by grandchildren, i's bet'er than dying on the field. Isn' i'? Dying in shi' and confusion means nothing. You gain nothing. He'll prefer living and growing old t' dying in bat'le. If he wan's to die in bat'le he can do i' later. He needs time t' clear his mind. No ex-Eszai has ever told me any differen'.'

'He's gashed here as well.' I pointed to a deep, narrow cut above the knee of his severed leg. The black tip of a broken Insect mandible stuck out.

'T' poleyne plate mus' have come off his knee. Tell Sleat those clips don' work. A shard is still in there. I'm going t' take i' ou'. T' soldiers tried t' pull i' ou' and i' broke.'

Insect mandible shards are much worse than their leg spines. I know many people living with Insect spines embedded in their bodies. If Rayne can't extract them without causing further damage, she leaves them in. But jaws are highly septic, considering what Insects eat, and broken pieces will rankle in wounds and cause fatal septicaemia. I helped Rayne as she began to operate to extract the shard.

She eased the blood-hardened cloth away from his skin. Then she took a scalpel from the steamed-clean tray and made a cross-shaped incision at the point where the mandible had gone in, widening the cut. She squirted spirits of wine into the wound with a syringe, and grasped the end of the triangular shard with forceps. It had one very sharp edge, and to prevent it cutting Wrenn's flesh when she drew it out, she took a little hollow steel cylinder like a straw with an open slot along its length. She slid the tube onto the shard's sharp edge. Then she drew it out firmly and smoothly along its path of entry. In time with his heartbeat, blood welled up, overran the camp bed and pattered on the floor. Rayne rinsed out the wound and put a dressing on it.

Then she detached the tube from the arm of the soldier who was giving Wrenn his blood. He looked very pale and weak by this stage. She nodded to him. 'You can go. Take a sip of juice, over there … Then go and ea' mea' and drink a lo' of water, and have a res'.'

The dazed soldier wandered off. Rayne crooked her thumb at Wrenn. 'Even if their blood is incompa'ible you can risk i' once, but a second time would be fatal.'

She felt his pulse with a couple of twiggy fingers on his neck. 'No' a' home.'

'When will he wake up?'

'Could be any time. Migh' not. But if I know Wrenn, he'll wake as soon as he can. Tha' one never gives up.'

'We'll see.'

'And i' makes a difference from having t' cure him of VD.' She smiled without any trace of humour. Invisible flies were buzzing around my head. I hunched my shoulders and an avid pain ran between my wings; I stretched them against the stiffness.

Rayne wiped her hands on a cloth. 'I have Tornado in here as well, you know.'

'What's wrong with him?'

'He lost an eye.' She pointed across the room to where Tornado was sitting on another stretcher bed, with his head in his hands. Bandages covered his eye. He was stripped to the waist – you could reconstruct the battles of eight centuries from the scars on his body.

'What! By a larva?' If they could wound even Tornado, the Vermiform was right; we were finished.

'No. In the crush someone's spear went into his eye. Don' talk t' him. He's very pissed off about i' – he's embarrassed, too.'

'I told him not to advance.'

'If you remind him of tha', he'll punch you. Fescue's jus' lef' here, dead. And Vir Ghallain has been mauled. From wha' I've seen, they've los' him too.'

'I'll speak to his Select.'

Rayne beckoned a doctor. 'Watch over Serein and remove his armour.' Then she turned to her next patient. She wouldn't be diverted until all that could be done had been done.

I set off towards the water pumps where containers were stacked. I filled as many as I could carry and slung them around my body on two crossed leather straps. As I left, the last of Tanager's lancers raced in. They didn't seem to be bringing many survivors – some injured men rode pillion, but others were little more than chewed parcels, slung over saddlebows.

I flew bottles of water, packets of food and enough coffee to keep Frost going out to the dam for the next two hours. I even managed a couple of spades for which Frost was even more grateful than the coffee. Each time, the spoil heap by the portcullis had grown. By the fifth or sixth time I climbed through the window of the winch tower, it had completely blocked the portcullis and was slumping through to the walkway. Inside, a chain of men were passing buckets along and the one at the end threw the dirt onto the mound.

I sat on the ledge and hooked the supplies on a winch that Frost had rigged up. One of the soldiers lowered them, hand-over-hand, while I climbed down the wall.

Soldiers stood around the machinery, leaning on it to eat the latest packet of bread. They had all kept their helmets on for protection underground, and they were filthy; their faces black with dirt and glossy with sweat. They were surprisingly cheerful, though; I took their measure as I approached Frost.

She was sitting on a pile of burlap sacks, intent on her writing. Her jaw was clenched so tightly she had dimples in her cheeks. Tears ran down both sides of her nose.

She had a climbing rope wrapped around her waist, through a metal loop and coiled on the floor. She had obviously found it easier to abseil down the shaft, and the soldiers looked as if they would be happy to belay her anywhere.

I touched her shoulder and she jumped. 'Jant? Wait, I'm finishing this letter. For the . . . will of god . . . and the . . . pro-tect-ion of the Circle,' she pronounced as she wrote, and signed it. 'Arch-it-ect for the Sovereign . . . Emperor San . . . and Chief Eng-in-eer of River-works Com-pa-ny.' She blew on the paper, then folded it and dripped candle wax along the fold.

I said, 'I brought more bread. It's all I can carry.'

She nodded, and bellowed down the maintenance shaft, 'Change of shift! Come up, the kettle's boiled!'

She tittered hysterically, hyperventilated a few breaths, and checked herself. Her teeth were edge-on-edge, her forehead furrowed.

I offered her a muddy loaf. She wiped the tears away with her brigandine cuff and shook her head contemptuously. 'No! No more time off!' She sat down on the sacks. 'Will you take the note to San?'

'Yes. Are you OK?'

'I'm fine. There's no problem. I don't know why you think there's a problem, because there isn't.' I could hear the steel in her voice. She was showing both her personalities at once. Her extreme stress had laid them bare in front of me and it was like talking to two different people. I didn't know whether to speak to the tearful, emotional woman or the single-minded engineer; whether to give her a comforting hug or a quadratic equation.

She took her bandanna off – her hair flowed loose, matted with mud. She blew her nose on the bandanna and stuffed it in her pocket. 'Right! Comet, we have broken through into the downstream passageway. We've made a big hole in the maintenance chamber floor that the water will drain through. Now we are digging on the other side of the gate where the tunnel's full of water. If we can keep up this rate, I expect to make a breakthrough sometime in the early hours of the morning ... and the lake will start to drain ...' She turned to the men preparing to take the place of the even grimier diggers climbing out of the shaft. 'Do ye hear that? The faster you shovel, boys, the more lives you will save! People out there are being savaged! Your fellow fyrdsmen are dying in whole battalions! Insect spawn are crawling all over the town and more of the ... *horrible things* ... are coming out of the lake every minute. Accept victory, and we will win. We will do what we set out to do!'

The men cheered.

She gave them a smile, then drew me aside to the spoil heap. Her eyes were bloodshot and brimming. 'My last p-project. Riverworks's final contract will be successful. The Emperor must then c-complete our plan and advance the t-troops over the lakebed ...' She caught a breath. '... And kill all the larvae we leave stranded in the mire. You must give him this –' She handed me the letter.

'Of course.'

She looked at me levelly, she seemed to have swung round to a calm phase. 'Describe to the Sapper exactly what I am doing. Tell him the Glean Road will be passable but the Lowespass Road will not. The waters will take two days to subside. Will you tell him that?'

'Of course.'

'I never – ah – oh, Jant, I never built the basin for a hydraulic jump this huge ... It's ...'

'*Are* you all right?'

'Yes, yes, I'm fine. You must also send a semaphore to Summerday ... Tell them to evacuate.'

'Most of the Summerday people are here,' I said. 'The governor has been fighting.'

'I know. But some are left in the town, and you must evacuate them.'

'Why?'

She glanced over to the wall, on the other side of which was the lake. She breathed out the breath she had been holding for a few seconds, and tittered. Then she panted another breath. 'When the lake drains, their ... streets might flood.'

'Might?' I had never known her to be so unspecific.

'Mm. Tell them to get out, immediately. And tell Mist to move the ships he has in the river mouth. I don't remember who Mist is at the moment; I mean, what his real name is ... So many come and go. But if he's the Sailor, he'll be able to do it.'

'I'll tell them.'

She nodded slowly. 'Then goodbye, Jant.'

'See you, Frost.'

I turned to go, but she clenched my hand. 'Goodbye. Goodbye, Comet.'

Tears rolled unnoticed down her cheeks. She bit on her bottom lip, then smiled at her workers gathered around the hearth. 'Oi! Shift B! Did I give you five minutes or five hours? Go back down there and *dig faster!*'

I climbed up the wall. As I slipped through the window, one leg in, one leg out, I looked down to see her sitting on the sandbags. She had taken the brown velvet rabbit from her lapel and was holding in both hands, looking at it as if in silent conversation.

Dusk was obscuring the gruesome remains. Larvae were crawling everywhere, covering the uneven ground sickeningly swiftly, and gathering in hordes around any flesh they could find.

I only saw adult Insects in the distance towards Plow – they were already moving on. I wondered why and then I saw larger larvae among the rest – the second moults. They moved nearly as fast as adults, eating their smaller brethren. Maybe the adults were leaving because they feared their own growing spawn turning on them.

I noticed one about to shed its skin and circled low, watching. It suddenly raised its head and froze. I could see through its shell; a slimy bulk was moving inside, pressing uneasily against the surface as if struggling to get out.

Its thorax split down the midline. A pale bulge pushed out through the crack and arched up: the new thorax. The nymph pulled back and withdrew its head from inside the head of the empty carapace. Its chitin was almost white; its legs looked soft as it clasped its empty shell, standing on top. It had a dented, unfilled look but it arched its back and pulled its abdomen free of the casing. As I watched, it began to harden, turning darker brown. The hollows in its abdomen filled out and rounded; its short antennae began to move.

I hastened to the town. The Emperor was sitting in the hall, surrounded by a crowd of people, giving out commands to Eszai and Zascai alike. I pushed through them and gave Frost's letter to him. He read it, then nodded gravely. 'Thank you for bringing this, Comet. There is no need for you to visit the dam again. You should have your wounds seen to now.'

I repeated Frost's words to the Sapper, who received them with his usual glum acceptance. I gave her message to the semaphore operator and watched him begin to pull the levers to move the semaphore arms that would send the order to evacuate, hundreds of kilometres down the valley to the governor's steward.

I returned to the hospital, where a doctor cleaned and bandaged my bitten foot, though it was so swollen he had to cut the boot off. He checked my wrenched limbs and said I would be all right if I looked after myself. Not a chance. I am growing experienced enough to realise that if you wait, the pain will go. Long life gives you an ability to weather anything.

I told the journalists that no news was to be given out in any form. Then for hours I did the rounds to see if anyone needed the Messenger. Rayne just shooed me away.

Tornado was too humiliated to speak to anyone. Lightning had been the last to leave the field and he was organising archers on the ramparts. That reminded me – what about his daughter? Nobody had taken Cyan any news. From her confinement in the peel tower she would have seen the whole battle taking place.

I missed a gust and had to wait for the next. Go! Now! I took off from the gatehouse and looked back once I had gained height. It was one a.m. and, through the pitch dark, hails of incendiary missiles poured from the towers. Larvae covered the walls. Men on the walkways were tussling with them. The lamps on the curtain wall only illuminated a few metres of churned mud, the moat and the innermost fallen tents.

Cyan had put a light in her window to guide me in. I landed on the plank and stepped down into the room. Cyan bolted towards me and threw her arms around me, sobbing into my chest. 'Oh! Terrible ... it was terrible.'

'It still is,' I said, trying to disentangle myself.

'I saw everything.' She pointed out to the sea of mud. 'I watched it happen. I felt so powerless. I saw all those people dying – I tried to look away but I just kept watching!'

She thumped my chest. I caught her wrists gently. She looked up at me as if seeing me for the first time. She began to cry in earnest. 'The Insects ... they ... They would have killed me, too!'

'Yes. Hey, shush! Sh-sh, little sister. Crying doesn't suit you.'

She stepped back, wiped her eyes and glared at me. 'I'm Lady Peregrine. I can cope with it.'

'Remains to be seen.'

'Is Daddy all right?'

'I think so.'

'Not that I care, of course.'

'Oh no. Course not.'

'What's happening down there now?'

'Well, the larvae are growing. The Eszai are picking mandible shards out of each other. The mortals are shrieking and dying.' I told her what had happened to Wrenn, Tornado and Hurricane, and Frost trapped inside her dam, digging into its rubble core. Cyan grew more and more alarmed. I said, 'But this is the safest place to be. We've lost the canvas city already; the larvae are scaling the town walls. I don't know if they will crawl all the way up this tower but if they do, look – here's my axe – you can cut them off the walls as they come up to the window. Don't let them get close because their jaws pincer out.'

Cyan sat down, on the bedspread smudged with old sleep. 'Oh, god, Jant ... if I had been down there, I ...'

I sat beside her and spread my wing around her. 'You shouldn't have watched.'

She turned and hugged me, her face pressed to my throat. 'I don't need protecting,' she whispered, and I felt her lips move against my skin. She looked down at my trousers, ripped and scratched and plastered with mud, Insect and human blood.

'Oh god. What happened to your foot?'

'It's nothing. Don't worry.'

She kissed my neck and I smelt the hot, comforting scent of her little body. Her hair was so silky it was like putting my hand into a cool stream of water. She began to stroke my feathers. 'Is it all right now?'

'No, it isn't.'

'Can't you regroup and ...?'

'There are too many. We're totally fucked; I don't know what the Emperor can do.'

I knew I smelt overpoweringly of fresh sweat. That, or something else, was having a strange effect on her. The ache of my muscles and the stinging of all my little scratches began to feel triumphant. I was so tired I felt light; she started caressing me and her touch loosened the tired muscles in my back. The world closed down to this room; this bed and Cyan. Nothing else existed.

'Mmm ... mmm ... I need to do this ...'

'It's the crisis ... Mmm .... think nothing of it ... Oh god; touch my wings.'

'Your body's so taut. You're like a racehorse ... With too many limbs ... Shit. I didn't mean to say that. Comet ...'

'Most girls call me Jant. It's useful to have two names.'

I felt my cock straining at my underwear. I shuffled to free it and it pointed straight up inside my trousers. Cyan saw the bulge and said, 'Oh. I ...'

We were both minded how much her father would hate us to do this, and that made us want to do it more. 'Do you want me?' I asked.

She wouldn't meet my eye. 'Yes ... but I'm inexperienced.'

I blinked. I hadn't expected her to be a virgin. I don't know why; I suppose because she had seemed so adventurous – she'd always been surrounded by admirers.

'I'll be careful ...'

'Yes, OK.'

'There's just this, here.' I guided her hand to my crotch and she felt the stiffness through the cotton. Her fingers moved up my cock as if she was trying to find an end to it. I took off my trousers and briefs and let her take it tentatively in her hands. 'It's smooth,' she said.

'Yes. Not like that; like this ... ah ...'

Her bodice lacings had come loose and her undershirt was open.

Her breasts had fallen a little outward, pressing against the stiff panels, caged in by the criss-cross lacings. I could see their curves but their nipples were hidden.

'I'm good at giving pleasure. I'll make you feel amazing. You'll feel like you're floating.'

'Oh.' She remembered. 'It's not safe.'

'You're safe with me.'

I pushed her gently down until she was lying on her back. I put my head under her skirt, into the darkness between her thighs and kissed their soft skin. I licked the silk of her panties. I poked my tongue around them and started licking her. She gasped and flinched but I calmed her with whispers. I soon found out that she was on her period, a little string sticking out of her. That explained why her scent was so beguiling. Women are most sensual when it's their time of the month.

I pushed her skirt up, her panties down and kept licking. She wasn't used to it; she wriggled and whined and kept looking down at me, one arm across her face, biting her shirt sleeve. I must be giving her so much pleasure . . . and soon it will be my turn.

The muscles in her legs tensed. Her thighs became more and more rigid, until they were like steel. She grunted and her body stiffened. She clamped her thighs around my head so tightly I nearly suffocated. Then she cried out and all her tension released at once.

I looked up, bedraggled with her juices. Cyan gasped, with an expression of wonder, pure bliss, and started laughing. Her face was open and unguarded for the first time; it was so wonderful I started laughing too. At that moment the chessboard beside the bed slid off its table with an almighty crash.

The chess pieces rolled all over the floor. The floor began to shake. No, the whole building was shaking; I could feel the vibrations. 'What's that?' Cyan shrieked.

The lamp on the window ledge flickered. 'What's happening?' She sat up and drew the blanket round her.

She said something else, but I wasn't listening. I was backing into the doorway of the staircase leading to the roof – the spiral steps wound up into their turret behind me. It's happening again. This is nineteen twenty-five all over again, and the ground's giving way. It was that night when –

I woke, and lay in my camp bed in the dark tent, listening.

'Jant!' Cyan was yelling at me. 'Jant! Don't go crazy! What are you doing?' Her voice took on a hysterical edge. 'Snap out of it!'

I snapped. I dashed across to the window and grabbed the lamp. If the earth really was falling in and we were locked in the tower I couldn't see how we could survive.

We both looked round as one of the vixen guardswomen appeared in the doorway. She threw something I couldn't see. It bounced off my foot and by the time I had located it on the floor she had disappeared. It was a key.

The crashing roar grew and grew. It was composed of hundreds of other noises: a gravelly sliding crunch. A landslide ... I knew this had to be a landslide ... There was the din of rock cracking, thuds as individual stones tore loose and fell. The long hiss of earth shifting; the tremendous roar of water.

Through it we heard the bell on the top of the winch tower clanging; madly, unevenly. *Dang ... dong. Dang! Dong!* No one was ringing it – it was tolling of its own accord.

We strained to see. From far out in the darkness came a sense of motion, commotion; gigantic shapes moving. It was like listening to a ship in distress, beyond the mudflats, sinking in the dead of night.

The lights on the tower seemed to tilt, rush forward and down; then they vanished. The deafening roar of a mighty, mighty wave thundered towards us. We could see nothing.

The roar swept past us, obliterating all other noise. The churning of foam and swoosh of falling water resounded on every side.

'The dam!' I yelled. I felt crushed and hopeless – a sensation I recognised – the Circle was breaking. Frost – what is she *going through* out there? It started slowly creeping up – came on in a rush.

I felt the Circle go dead. Frost's link had gone and I was loose again. We were aging. I felt separate and lonely without the other Eszai to back me up. Mortals must feel like that all the time ... I had forgotten what it was like to feel mortal.

The Circle reformed, gently. I could almost feel the Emperor soothe it back into existence. Why had he left us falling apart into nothingness for so long, like beads slipping off a string? Had he been asleep? Was he deliberately reminding us of mortality?

I was kneeling on the floor. The shock had dropped me to my hands and knees and I was looking at a patch of floorboards covered in dried herbs. Their crispy leaves were sticking to my palms.

I had felt Frost dying. By god, what had happened to her? I couldn't tell if the overwhelming, crushing sensation of darkness had been her experience, or if it was my imagination.

'Get up!' said Cyan.

The roar of the wave went on and on. It passed us and we heard it receding into the distance. Another noise followed, the same volume, still loud enough to shake the tower – the rush of water swirling in spate, out of control.

Cyan stepped squarely in front of me, shouting, 'Jant! What's wrong with you? Stand up!'

'The Circle broke,' I murmured.

'Daddy!' she screamed, and started crying in terror. 'What's happened to Daddy?'

'Sh! It wasn't Lightning. He's in town.'

'How do you know?'

'It was Frost. I knew what she was doing . . . She broke the dam.'

I felt different, and I realised that I was actually feeling the Circle. It was the Circle that had changed. Its sensation was subtle, just background; then it had gone. No one can feel the Circle or distinguish individuals in it unless its equilibrium was disturbed. I realised I was so used to its ever-present sensation that I had taken it for granted, and now I was feeling it's slightly altered shape. Frost's qualities had gone, and the combined effects of everyone else's, whether enhancing or cancelling each other out, had settled into a new equilibrium.

'Frost was in the Circle when I joined,' I said. 'I was always aware of her without knowing.'

'Look!' She pointed down. The spent flood waters, hissing and edged with foam like a wave running onto a beach, poured up to the base of the tower and broke around it. We watched the level start to nudge up the wall.

Our lamp reflected parts of the water's surface rushing past. It picked out eddying lines as flickers of silver and eel-like flashes. It was moving so fast it was backing up its own bulk into peaks and troughs of great, corrugated standing waves.

Continuous rapids hurtled over where I knew farms had been, now reduced to rubble. The rock outcrops were drowned metres deep. We looked out to Slake – the wide expanse of churning, crinkling flood waters between us and the town reflected its lights.

There was nothing left but water. Everything had been swept away. Everything in the path of the massive wave had vanished and we could hear nothing over its roar.

'"The waters will take two days to subside,"' I repeated.

'What?' said Cyan.

'That was Frost's message. She worked it all out.'

Cyan sought out my hand. She sighed, head bowed, looking at the gushing torrent. We stood next to each other, hand in hand in the warm night, and watched out of the window until the faintest light of dawn began to splinter onto the floodwaters.

CHAPTER 24

TROOPS ADVANCE INTO DEVASTATED VALLEY

Exclusive special report by our own correspondent in Slake Cross

I stand on the observation platform of Tower 10, a sturdily built peel tower close to Slake Cross. Beside me stands a veteran artillerist of the Lowespass Select, calling out directions to his trebuchet team in their bombardment position – a makeshift construction of logs and sandbags providing a stable platform on the soggy ground. Another barrel of burning pitch jerks up into the sky, joining half a dozen more, as they crash down on a distant ridge of paper.

Two days have passed since the dam collapsed and the waters have now receded sufficiently to allow infantry to advance. I am further forward than any journalist has been so far. Only the cooperation of the enlightened artillerist has got me past the provosts, passed off as part of his battery. At such elevated points alone can any real picture of the situation be gained; the land is an otherwise flat quagmire, nearly devoid of vegetation and dotted with thousands of dirty pools. Divisions advance cautiously over this ground, pioneers laying brushwood tracks for the fyrd to follow.

A Plainslands unit clears the way north of us, their spears audibly 'popping' eggs that have been scattered by the dam collapse. To my left flamethrower crews are moving forward under the guidance of the Sapper. Occasional bursts of fire mark their encounter with a clutch of undeveloped Insect larvae still wriggling in a pool. The same scene is being re-enacted all the way along a twenty-kilometre front. It is strangely orderly because it is, with few alterations, the plan envisaged years ago.

The intention then, though, was to drain the lake gradually. The Castle has confirmed that Frost sacrificed herself deliberately to destroy her own creation. The gates could not be opened with Insects freely swarming over the dam. Frost's terrifying calculation was that only by engineering a collapse from inside the dam could the lake be emptied. In a single catastrophic torrent, adult Insects have been drowned, their eggs have been left to wither in the sun and their hideous young have been smashed by debris or washed into the sea's fatal salinity.

The mood of the troops, though, is sombre. This promised bloodless advance has proved to be anything but. Their mood stands in stark contrast to the optimistic banter when they, the largest force mustered in the Empire's history, prepared to attack three days ago. Many dwell on lost comrades, the casualties of the recent battle greatly exceeding those of the famous defeat one hundred years ago. Their exact numbers will not be known for weeks; the remains have been swept away by the inundation, complicating the sad task. The immortals have also suffered heavily, adding Hurricane and Frost to their losses, with Serein critically injured.

Still more wonder what the recent changes in the Insects portend. Whilst the horrific larvae are now lying dying or dead, many are openly sceptical of the Castle's assurances that the mating flights were caused by the dam. The Castle has abandoned plans for any such future constructions and claims there will be no future flights. So far it is too early to tell. Surely there deserves to be a full public inquiry as soon as possible?

Reports from the surrounding areas are still sketchy as the signalling network was badly damaged and large parts of the Lowespass Road have been washed away. Comet has flown reconnaissance missions as far as Summerday. He reports the town walls saved it from the force of the break wave but with the surrounding country it is inundated, with thirty centimetres of water in the streets. Thousands of farmsteads and fortifications along the entire valley have been destroyed and fatalities are high. Few casualties are reported in Summerday owing to the successful evacuation efforts.

Rayne, fearing outbreaks of disease, has requested that the inhabitants of the region do not return yet. Only fyrd are permitted into the devastated area; priority is being given to hunting surviving larvae, most of which have been spread over a wide area. In the meantime the civilians are facing a bleak existence, cast on to the charity of others.

Of the dam itself, nothing remains apart from two low mud hillocks scarcely a man's height. The sluice gate was discovered in the ruins of a peel tower forty kilometres further down the valley.

Tomorrow, the Emperor will lead a ceremonial advance to the drained lake bed, land lost to the Empire for a century. There he will formally reclaim the ground as far as the river and annex it to Lowespass manor. Two hundred square kilometers will be reclaimed from the Insects. Most General Fyrd units will remain for two months to secure the area and rebuild defences. Only then will standing garrisons take over and the fyrd be disbanded. If the land can be kept, and the Insects' aversion to running water raises the hope it can be, it is the first successful advance in over three centuries.

Perhaps this, then, is Frost's ultimate triumph. How reasonable was her brave notion that the Castle could defeat the Insects? For the second time in a decade a plan has met with a bloody check in the mandibles of our enemies. Frost, in her ambitions and her actions, had overstretched herself – but that is no more than the world expects its immortals to do.

Kestrel Altergate,
Eske, June 13th

You are cordially invited to Micawater Palace for the Challenge of Cyan Peregrine to Lord Governor Lightning Micawater, which will be held in the palace grounds, on August 12th this Year of Our War two thousand and twenty-five.

The Challenge will be preceded by two days of events and feasting.

All other Challengers for the position of Lightning this quarter-year may submit their Challenges in advance so they may shoot in competition with Lightning preceding the Challenge of Cyan Peregrine.

RSVP to Lightning at Micawater Palace

CHAPTER 25

Two months later, I was standing on the roof of Lightning's palace, feasting my eyes on its fabulous vista. I slid down from its ridge to the balustrade, knocking off a couple of tiles. The groundsman, far below me on the terrace, waved his fist; so I gave him a cheerful salute. The view was so amazing, and the summer sun so hot, that I wanted to see Lightning's majestic tournament from above.

I leant against the slope of the pediment, in the shadow of the gold ball on its point. The tiles beneath my feet were hand-made to look like feathers; the chimneys behind me were collected in refined plain pillars.

Everybody who was anybody was here, and some people who were nobody at all. Coaches were arriving continually, through the Lucerne Gate and down the Grand Walk to the front of the palace. The Walk was wide enough for three coaches abreast to drive between the double rows of pollarded elms. In the middle each coach reached a marble statue on a plinth of Lightning's mother with a winged stag. They trotted around it on either side and parked next to each other on the vast gravel semicircle in front of the portico.

I walked along the balustrade, onto the end of the portico and peered over. I could just see Harrier on the front steps, welcoming in the latest batch of visitors. His age was showing; he had grey hair above his ears. He gave each guest a key on a ribbon and ushered them into the cool shadow of the exedra porch. They entered under the pediment, between its four fluted columns with drooping plume capitals, into the house.

The Austringer and Eyas Wings stretched out on both sides of me, perfectly symmetrical. I returned, along the top of the balustrade, to the back of the palace. Pavilions covered the whole lawn down to the lake.

The celebrations started yesterday, with archery competitions in the main ring adjoining the blue and white striped awning of the long stand. Notable archers shot at novelty targets like a dove tied to the top of a pole, or a hazel wand upright in the ground. There had been promenades and pleasure boats on the lake. Lightning had laid on no contemporary entertainments like jousting; instead he had had chariots made and a track built on the other side of the lake. He had stepped into one of these brass-clad contraptions, taken the reins of a pair of coursers and showed us how to race them. His youngest brother had been a champion charioteer. Tern and I had watched the races, very tentative at first but people quickly got the hang of how to drive them.

Then last night Lightning had held a ball. We had found costumes laid out in our rooms. The women looked beautiful in their draped gowns, and laughter echoed along the corridors as the men tried to figure out their togas. We were surprised but we took it as good entertainment. Everything, from the ancient harp music to the sickly mead, orgeat and boar roasts served in archaic style, was a reconstruction of his memory of the original Games. Lightning was beside himself with joy. He was home at last!

Down on the lawns everyone was scattered around the enormous stand along one side of the archery ground, roped off from the rest of the grass and outlined by hay bales. The other side was open, towards the lake and bridge. Beside it stood a cloth-of-gold pavilion for the Challengers and, on the other side, servants carrying trays of chilled Stenasrai wine came and went from a refreshment tent.

The pavilions were an ancient round design, not triangular, and the lines of bunting surrounding the archery ring were the same as those topping the walls of an amphitheatre. The whole scene belonged in the pages of a picture book: Lightning was indeed reliving the founding of the Circle.

A series of tall flagpoles flew long, dark blue banners with the Micawater mascle. My Wheel flag and Rayne's red oriflamme pennant were there too. We were acting as witnesses for the Challenge. At least two Eszai witness every Challenge; mortals are never used as witnesses because Eszai are less likely to be corrupted. We have a vested interest in keeping the Challenges fair and we would fiercely resist any less than the best being admitted as to do so would tarnish our own status.

I looked out into the distance. The avenue ran straight on the other side of the lake, between beech plantations to the crest of a low hill. A folly stood there, a scaled-down replica of the entire palace, placed exactly opposite it at the end of the vista. It was so ingeniously decreased in size that it skewed the perspective – making the avenue look longer than it was. Everyone who saw the folly for the first time believed it was a palace exactly the same size at a great distance. I knew it housed only a single ballroom, but its trick of the eye was so exact I imagined that I could see a tiny Jant leaning on the pediment looking back at me. I shuddered.

Lemon trees and spear-like cypress grew on the brow of the hill clear against the sky around the folly and, beyond it, livestock grazed on smooth-turfed grass like a carpet. I could just see the beginnings of the hills rising up to Donaise in the distance. Tiny, spidery vine frames climbed them, and their lower slopes were lines of immaculately planted grey-green olive groves and coffee plantations.

I suppose the landscaped garden isn't really designed to be seen from the roof. The guests on the terrace will have the best of it, or those strolling along the avenue, from which smaller pathways led and opened up new vistas. The perspective presented statues that seemed far off, suddenly near at hand. Gaps in the woodland revealed winter gardens, espaliers, great pillars, all meticulously landscaped for kilometres around.

Beyond the beech wood two smaller avenues crossed the main one in an asterisk, and of course Lightning had had time to watch over the trees as they grew and matured, so now centuries later, they were looking their best.

I stood on tiptoe and looked down the length of the Austringer Wing; over the roof of the Austringer building at the end. I could just see a dark green pattern of tall hedgerows – the labyrinth. It was enormous; lemon hedge on one side of the path and box on the other, so if you got lost you could smell your way around it to the great trellis and pergola in the centre. They are covered in vines drooping fat clusters of purple grapes. The tendrils hang down like a screen of falling water, and it is wonderful to push through them to the hideaway inside, where you can sit among statues in its shade.

Past the maze grew the long, unkempt grass of the 'wilderness' – nothing of the sort but a well-designed meadow where Lightning held garden parties. I'd rather have kept it natural than have it look so through artifice and expenditure. Beyond that rose the belvedere, once copied by the Rachiswaters in their circular style. I wondered why it was that the richer people became, the more sequacious?

At the end of the Eyas Wing, in the other direction, a slope went down to 'the farm' by the river, a few kilometres distant but the clutch of aslant roofs looked more like a small town. Most of the estate workers lived there, tending beehives, kitchen and herb gardens, a phasianery for peacocks and pheasants, a rabbit warren, brick kilns and a dovecot. Lightning calls the estate office 'The New House', although it is four hundred years old. The Alula Road passes through to Micawater town itself, which was disguised behind another well-placed copse. Lots of townsfolk were here, watching the festivities and loving it. They were the sort of Awian citizens who hold street parties on their lord's birthday.

People were converging on the archery stands. From up here, parasols over women's shoulders looked like little circles. I noticed a knot of people heading from the refreshment tent and in their midst I recognised Eleonora's confident stride. Beside her was my little, dark-haired, vivacious Tern. The Challenge is about to start. I had better go join them.

I stepped off the balustrade and tilted out in a long, slow glide. I swept over the terrace onto which the palace's doors opened; then the water gardens below them, a round central spring framed symmetrically by four limpid pools.

The ground dropped away and steps led down to a parterre, with the sky-blue roses of Awia in flower beds bordered by low hedges. More box hedges looked like embroidery, clipped into lacy flowing designs, scrolls and plumes against the rich, loamy earth. From that level stone hounds guarded a balustraded double staircase descending to the avenue. People walking on the paths between the flower beds looked up as my shadow sped over them.

I focused on Tern and Eleonora and the courtiers surrounding them, who were settling on the lowest seat of the stands nearest the archery ground, reserved for the Queen's use and covered with samite silk. I came in above the rounded end of the awning and veered wide to the arena's grass, flared wings and touched down. My landing drew a little tentative applause from the crowd.

I hopped over the ropes and Tern came forward to meet me. 'My love,' I said over her shoulder as we hugged. 'My dear, dear love.'

'Isn't this exciting?' Tern exclaimed. 'What a magnificent day!'

Eleonora nodded contentedly. 'It's a Lakeland summer all right. Three fine days and a thunderstorm. It's like clockwork.'

'Well, the sooner we get this over with and on to the party the better.' She passed me a glass of sparkling wine. 'I pestered Lightning to give us some real Stenasrai. "You must have had Stenasrai in six twenty," I told him. "It's better than that ridiculous mead." It's a wonder anyone in the seventh century had any teeth.'

I was enjoying the party but I still had a lot to do. Since the slaughter of the battle there had been more people hiding from the draft. There was a groundswell of sentiment against the war and criticism of the

Emperor, which the Emperor was ignoring until it gradually subsided.

Eleonora had covered herself with glory and was full of pride. We hadn't regained so much land since the Miroir battles of the last Tanager dynasty. No wonder the Rachiswaters had been so keen to match them by making advances in Lowespass, but Eleonora had taken more than any of them. Our shared knowledge of how awful the battle had been brought us together in this warm sunlight, whereas Tern, who could never understand, just kept talking. 'I worried about you when the Circle broke,' she said. 'Although worry is quite an inadequate word for what I felt.'

'I was fine, my love. I saw the flood. I never want to go back to Slake Cross though. Every time we go there we get massacred.'

Tern said, 'Some people are talking about an odd phenomenon. My warden says god appeared to the Emperor on the battlefield.'

'Really?' I said casually. 'In what shape?'

'A very strange one. A tall column of smoke, and trees made of worms.'

'Mass hysteria.' I shrugged. 'People report all kinds of visions under battle stress. It's terror that causes it. Lowespass generates more folklore than it can use.'

'Well, I don't see why it should have to export it.'

I said, 'Some fyrdsmen say that you can still hear the winch tower bell, tolling underwater in the river. Fyrdsmen will tell you any old crap.'

I was interrupted by three flights of whistling arrows being loosed on the other side of the lake in honour of the victor of the chariot races. Eleonora shook herself. 'Lightning slept through the dam breaking,' she said. Tern and I laughed. It's a joke that Lightning is such a sound sleeper Insects could be eating him and he wouldn't wake up.

'You dare wake him, Jant,' said Tern. 'Why didn't you?'

'Um . . . I was busy.'

'And the Emperor asked Lightning to have dinner with him. At least, I heard so . . . Is it true?'

'Yes. That *is* true.'

'But it's unheard of! For Lightning, for anybody! Well, come on. Tell me. What did they talk about?'

'I asked Lightning, but he wouldn't say.'

'I would never have thought anything like a one-to-one conversation could ever happen.'

'It was in the hall at Slake,' I said. 'No one else was there.'

'Couldn't you have spied? No, stupid question.'

Eleonora spun the key to her suite around her finger on its ribbon.

'This place is quaint. I like the marble bathrooms. But it's not as big as Rachiswater. Or as grand as I've planned Tanager to be. It's odd to think it was the capital once.'

'It's not bad for five four nine!' Tern said.

'Lightning's town was even bigger than Hacilith back then,' I added. 'Hacilith took a hundred years to overtake it. He never wanted to extend it; he wanted to preserve it and the palace too.'

Eleonora spun and spun her key. 'What a shame. Lightning rattling around in the house alone for fourteen hundred years. One hundred and forty bedrooms and no woman to share any of them with. It's enough to turn a man's mind. Why hasn't he ever married? Does he bat for the other team, or what?'

Tern laughed. 'No-oo. He's just looking for the perfect match.'

'Well, we'll have to do something about that.' The two women looked at each other. 'He just needs to relax. Perhaps his Queen could ... command him to.'

'I think he wants some kind of red-haired huntress,' Tern said as we settled ourselves in the stands.

'Nonsense. He just needs the attentions of a woman *au fait* with her desires.'

From here was a much better view uphill to the palace. It was all warm, shortbread-coloured Donaise limestone, from the rusticated stonework on the lower storey to the rich carving in the great pediment; many strips of decorative mouldings surrounded a smooth bas-relief of the winged hounds bearing the lozenge coat of arms. Each column led up to a statue on the roof as if supporting it. Between the columns two levels of windows proclaimed how many rooms could house Lightning's guests. The Eyas and Austringer buildings at the ends of the two wings had enormous windows with round arches giving on to the ballroom and stateroom respectively. It was built in the most regular manner rare in the country today; Awia has gone straight from Micawater's classical to neoclassical, and now Rachiswater's art nouveau, without ever having been through a rustic phase like the Plainslands.

'It's all right for some,' I said.

'What do you mean?' said Tern.

'Well, Lightning walked straight in to the Circle. He never had to wander around the world the way I did, before I even found out the Castle existed. He didn't have to plot and scheme like an Awian prince, either, because he had the Castle and his immortality instead. No wonder he can pretend this noble liege fantasy.'

'It's how he had time to bring us together.' Tern laid her hand on my knee.

'I call that plotting and scheming,' said Eleonora.

Tern said, 'I paid him a routine visit and he mentioned I might be interested in Jant. I remember taking my coach to see Lightning one morning and I told him how Jant's courtship was progressing. "He came to see me last night – I love his appalling timing. And do you know – his boots were covered in manure!" How we laughed!'

I snorted unhappily. Travelling from the Castle to Wrought to court her had been the start of my drug-taking. I stayed awake for two, three nights at a time, driven to extreme exhaustion by a fear of inadequacy. And apparently Tern had already decided to marry me before I started and there was no reason for me to have used scolopendium at all.

She had flicked open a pamphlet. 'Ha!' she said. 'Lightning has a grotto. He never told me.'

'A what?'

'A grotto. How exciting. I've been coming here for nearly a hundred and twenty years and he never showed me. Listen.' She read from the book: ' "Who would have thought that a cavern of such delightful artifice would lie at the end of the path? A passageway leads to a charming rocaille grotto with a small waterfall. Niches in the walls form shell-adorned seats, and above them is the inscription: *All time not spent in loving is lost*." Ah, isn't he sweet?'

I said, 'The grotto's on the other side of the secret garden. We can visit it later. What's that?'

'It's a programme for the party and a tour of the grounds. All the sculptures and so forth.'

I let her chatter on, dwelling on how beautiful she was – the gentle contours of her face, her manicured hands. I thought how lucky I was that she found me equally wonderful.

Tern loved the summer sun, though her manor had a much more dismal climate. Wrought is in the rain shadow of Bitterdale; all the clouds that come in from the sea rise over the hills, drop their rain on her manor and leave the inland manors clear.

I looked down to the glistening lake. Far on our right towards its centre an artificial island was covered with trees. The pink marble pediment of the dynasty's mausoleum, its engraved frieze, and the pinnacles of other memorials showed between the tree tops.

The still water reflected them, but further off by the sluice gate bridge, the stirred-up water scintillated as its silica flecks reflected the sunlight. Many people were promenading along the bridge, and I don't blame them because Micawater Bridge is one of Frost's finest legacies.

It spanned a little man-made river flowing out of the tail-end of the almond-shaped lake, once natural but artificially enhanced since Esmerillion's time. The bridge carried the avenue through its roofed and arched arcade, and below it had square windows along its length above the span. Their shutters were closed; all were honey-coloured varnished wood to match the stone. From flagpoles along the length of the parapets, blue pennants draped down almost to the water.

There were rooms inside the bridge: all well-furnished and painted, and there was even a tiny theatre for music recitals. Lightning's friends sometimes use it as a summer house. From the windows they can look out over the lake to watch fleets of swans, dragonflies whizzing over the water's surface beneath them, and sometimes horse hooves clattered overhead along the avenue. So, over the centuries, Lightning has shaped the landscape much as Frost did, but for beauty and convenience. Whenever he had enlisted her help for a feat of engineering it was also a feat of elegance.

'Look!' said Eleonora. 'Here he is.'

Lightning emerged from the gold pavilion, carrying a compound bow so big it looked like a longbow. Cyan was behind him in a black T-shirt, waistcoat, quiver and a bracer on her arm. Lightning strolled up to us and bowed to the Queen. 'I hope you enjoy the tournament.'

'I will,' said Eleonora.

The Challenged Eszai always acts as his own master of ceremonies, conducting the Challenge himself according to his own style. It was a necessary part of the façade of unshakable confidence which is our most effective guard against Challengers. Lightning had asked his five reeves, from his musters of Micawater Town, Bitterdale, Altergate, Tambrine and Foin, to act as functionaries.

Lightning walked to the centre of the area and held out his hands to the crowd. 'This is my standard Challenge, which I set to show I can defeat a Challenger at all kinds of shooting. There will be three rounds. The first is for distance. There will be just one arrow each, unless the bow fails. I wish the Challenger, Cyan Peregrine, to shoot first in each round.'

Cyan stood behind a dark blue pennon on a cane. She looked small next to her father and seemed very aware of the inconsequential figure she cut, with the slivers of her legs and narrow squared shoulders. Her red compound bow looked like a toy in comparison with Lightning's. She took an arrow and nocked it to string and then, with the bow in her hands, she lost her uncertainty and became businesslike. She knew what to do, and I knew how good she was: I had witnessed her skill in the Jacamar Club.

The crowds waited. There was not a breath of wind. Cyan took the string in a pinch grip, the horn draw-ring on her thumb. She drew the string, tilted the bow high for a distance shot, and loosed. Her arrow looped high above the lake, seemed to pause at the top of its arc, turned and came down, easily clearing the grassy far bank. It clattered on the avenue.

One of the reeves went to place a flag where the arrow had fallen. The crowd gave a polite round of applause, which we joined in while Lightning stepped up to the pennon. He held the arrow across the grip, already nocked. He crafts his tournament arrows himself, for perfection; each has azure fletchings and a gold cresting band.

The crowd fell silent. It is an awesome thing to see Lightning shoot. He raised his bow and tipped it back, drew it fluidly full compass until it formed a perfect semicircle and the tang-less pile point drew back into a groove cut into the massive grip. His powerful shoulders and back muscles took the eighty-two-kilo strain. Eleonora looked avariciously at the angle of his shoulder blade.

He loosed – and the arrow sped from his bow, so high it disappeared. It started coming down way past the point where Cyan's arrow had fallen. It passed the avenue, the grass behind it, and fell silently into the beech woods. The crowd applauded and Lightning acknowledged them. Well, he made that look easy.

Minutes passed before the official result could be returned. The Bitterdale reeve came running and announced, 'Seven hundred and thirty metres! Three times the Challenger's distance!'

Cyan was pale. I wondered whether her intermittent self-control could stand such a test.

'Now,' Lightning said. 'We have the speed contest. One minute to shoot as many arrows as possible into these targets.' He gestured at some archery butts scarcely a hundred metres away. 'Reeve Tambrine will time the minute.'

He put his great compound bow on a rack and picked up a smaller one, much like Cyan's, faster to draw than a longbow. He stood beside her and they both pushed a row of arrows into the ground in front of them. The Tambrine reeve lowered his arm and Cyan started plucking up the arrows and shooting them as fast as she could.

Lightning dawdled. He picked an arrow, loosed it, looked in its direction, chose another and turned it over, fitted it to string.

There was a great hiss of indrawn breath from the crowd. We rose to our feet, staring at him. Tern touched my shoulder. 'What is he doing? Why is he doing that?'

'I don't know.'

When the minute was up, Cyan had shot fourteen arrows and Lightning had shot ten. Cyan was panting, then she looked at Lightning's target and her eyes and mouth went wide.

There was silence, then a sudden uproar as everyone turned to their neighbours and started asking what it meant. The reeve was looking, concerned and frightened, at his master but Lightning wasn't meeting anybody's eye. He turned to Cyan and said, 'The heft of that bow of yours warps left at a distance. See, your arrows are tending left on the target? You should shoot a little right for the next round.'

He came over to us and took a drink of water. I said, 'What are you playing at? You lost! Deliberately. Obviously deliberately!'

He smiled at me and the ladies. 'Don't worry. I needed to give Cyan some sop to her pride. There's one round left.'

'You're playing with your life!' Tern shrieked.

'I just don't want to show my daughter up too much. I know what I'm doing. I'm unbeatable at accuracy.' He didn't say it as a boast, it was a plain fact.

Lightning gave me the compound bow and took his customary longbow from the rock. He carried it as fluidly as if it was part of him, an extension of his body. An accuracy target was set up at two hundred metres' distance – a black ring on the outside, then, white, blue and gold in the centre.

Lightning announced. 'We have five arrows each. Whoever scores most highly on the target will remain – I mean, gain – the title of Lightning. Cyan Peregrine will shoot first.'

Cyan came forward to stand on a stone slab set into the grass. She felt for the reassuring ends of the arrows in her quiver, selected one composedly. She sighted and loosed. The arrow appeared in the middle of the cross in the gold, the target's exact centre. She stepped aside and looked at her father defiantly.

Lightning stood on the flagstone. He was the target archer absolute. He made it seem so effortless. He faced the butt with a calm expression, confident and determined. His whole attitude was of command and power over the bow, the arrows and the target. He placed his feet apart with the weight equally on them, in a firm but springy stance. He was balanced and relaxed – a finger above the nock on the string, and two below. He used no marker, he knew it so well. He drew, and loosed sharply, the string free in an instant, and the arrow flew straight and sure.

There was a crack of wood. Lightning's longer arrow had split Cyan's in two. Its blue flights stood out from her white ones.

A roar from the audience. The reeves and servants sitting on the bales jumped up to applaud. Lightning acknowledged them but the noise seemed to daunt Cyan. She wasn't experienced enough to have expected it. She said nothing, just looking out to the target and down to her own gear. She pulled the string and extended her left arm in one movement, and the arrow point came up. She looked directly to the target.

Her arrow hit the edge of the gold. It was Lightning's turn to shoot. His arms were firm and unwavering, his attention never relaxed. Again he split Cyan's arrow perfectly.

The crowd's applause ceased immediately.

'What is he doing?' I said. 'He could have won then!'

Eleonora murmured, 'By god, he's brave.'

'What?'

'One day, immortal, in the far future you'll be able to say you saw this, and the rest of the world will look on you with awe. You will be able to say you were there at the beginning.'

'I don't understand.'

'Just watch.'

Tern edged closer to me and put her arm around my waist.

Cyan shot again, and again Lightning hit her arrow directly, splitting it in half.

She raised her arm and wiped her face on her sleeve. She was desperate, but she stood with an elasticity to resist the force and recoil of her twangy little bow. She was the timeless picture of grace as she drew it with a beautiful movement until it filled her whole frame. She hit the gold above the arrows – they were as snug together as a fistful of sticks, their flights entangled.

Lightning split her arrow.

This was the last one. Cyan was aware of every factor that might make a difference. She shrugged her waistcoat tighter, she adjusted her bracer. She dug a thumb behind her belt buckle. Her little movements were like the wriggles of a worm on a hook.

She raised her bow and shot. The arrow snicked in next to the others on the gold cross.

Lightning's turn: he drew. He loosed.

His arrow went wide – into the black outer ring.

Everyone in the stands was on their feet. He had lost.

He trembled as he lowered his bow. He gulped as if with a dry throat and tears came to his eyes, but with absolute mastery of himself, they weren't shed.

Cyan was walking in a small circle with an expression of confusion. He stopped her, and made her look at him. He kissed her and said something softly. Cyan blinked.

Louder, he added, 'Now I am out, and you are in. Enjoy it.'

He placed the end of his bow against the inside of his shoe, and unstrung it. He wound the string around his hand and slipped it in his pocket. Then he began to walk, past the stands and the dumbstruck audience, leaving Cyan behind. 'But ...' she said. 'But who's going to look after me?'

We stared, motionless. My head felt like it was full of cotton wool. I couldn't think: my mind wasn't allowing me to form any thoughts. There was nothing in my head but a wondering space. I felt light on my feet and nauseous, as if my body wasn't real. Black shadows began to gather at the periphery of my vision – I was about to faint. Everything was blurred. San only knows what Lightning must be feeling.

Tern sat down heavily. Her speech stumbled: 'W-What has he done?'

'I don't know.' I answered too quickly.

'Deliberately. He did it deliberately.'

The Queen's voice quivered at a higher pitch as she made an effort to control it. 'What a way to teach Cyan a lesson.'

There was a scuffle at the end of the stands and Rayne rushed out. She grabbed the back of Lightning's shirt and sank to her knees. She was hysterical; the ends of her open mouth were down in her jowls. Tears were running from her eyes channelled into the crevices between her cheeks and the sides of her nose. 'Saker!' Lightning tried to raise her to her feet but she had no strength; she just sank back.

'Saker, what have you done? Why? Tell me you won' leave! There's no need t' leave t' Circle! You aren', are you? Tell me you're jus' playing t' system. Tell me i's jus' a trick. You'll Challenge Cyan in a year's time and bea' her. Won' you? Or you'll bea' t' next man who's sure to bea' her ... Tell me tha's true! Or ... or you'll Challenge Wrenn and bea' him, and be t' next Swordsman. Oh yes, tha' must be i' – so you can be together wi' Cyan ...'

Lightning supported her at arm's length, his hands on her upper arms. Rayne kept screaming, 'Where will you end up? I's horrible t' be old. I know – i's terrible! You don' want i'! Don' let i' happen! Don' le' time pass, Saker, you're a' your best! A few years and you'll never have security again! You'll die! ... After all this time, why? Why? I can' bear t' be alone. Don' leave me!' She collapsed to her knees, sobbing, and as she did so she pulled his shirt out of his belt. She pressed his shirt tails to her cheek.

'Come with me into the house, Ella.'

'You were my friend!' Her voice was ugly with distortion.

He turned her towards the palace and, speaking to her quietly, led her up the avenue towards the terrace.

I tried to hold Tern's hand but my palms were sweating and my hands had no strength to grip. Uncertain whether I could feel her or not, I pressed too powerfully and she winced.

'I just feel numb,' I said. 'I can't allow myself to think about it . . .'

'You'll have plenty of time for that, immortal,' said Eleonora. Cyan crept into the gold pavilion to escape the crowd's disdain. Nobody congratulated her and nobody applauded. All eyes were watching Lightning and Rayne climb the monumental staircase onto the terrace and go through the tall open doors. They disappeared from view under the great elliptical ceiling of the dining hall.

CHAPTER 26

The feast, that evening, was a solemn affair. We were back to normal food and clothes; Lightning had moved on from needing his seventh-century nostalgia as well as from needing the Circle, but his guests were embarrassed and confused. They didn't know what to say nor how to phrase it. They didn't know how to react, so they made their excuses and drifted away.

Lightning, at the head of the table, tried to make us feel we should celebrate, although none of us could see any cause. We were all wondering at him and frightened on his behalf. So we gave up on the feast and retired to the library.

Lightning sat at his grand piano and played so calmly that Eleonora, Tern and I thought he must be planning to get back into the Circle.

The library's coffered ceiling had panels painted with pastoral and historic scenes. It was so lofty that a man on horseback could wield a lance in the room. The walls were covered completely with three tiers of bookshelves. Baroque wrought-iron steps could be pushed on rails along each level, leading to three rectangular balconies that stepped out, rising to the ceiling.

Eleonora was up on the first of these. She was examining the nearest shelves filled floor-to-ceiling with Lightning's diaries – maroon leather with the dates embossed in gold. A few were of paler hue when he couldn't find a colour to match exactly. She was flicking through one randomly; it would take years to read them all.

Tern was perched on the window seat, idly watching the stream of departing guests' coaches fall to a trickle then sputter to a stop as the great and good of the Fourlands hurried away. Rayne had already left, with Cyan in her care, both of them crying. In two days they would reach the Castle, where the Emperor would make Cyan immortal.

I studied the panels in the stucco ceiling, Mica valley landscapes rendered in oils, more mannered and pastel-toned than the dramatic colours of real life. The same iconic images over and over, and yet again in the ceramic and champlevé enamel vases on the delicate side tables – maybe that's the brake of Lightning's patronage. I picked at my chair's lavish cushioned seat, slowly creating and unravelling a loose thread. I marked imaginary lines in the rock crystal carafe of vintage port before me as I worked my way down it.

Over each lintel around the room were lunette paintings of Lightning's other properties. I could see through the nearest door, down a short corridor lined with small bronzes, toxophilous or booted and spurred for the charge, a sinuous ormolu clock, a walnut escritoire, and through to the Great Dining Hall.

Its doorway was crowned with his coat of arms in marble marquetry, plain, veined or flecked, each from a different part of the manor, surrounded by cipolin stone wreaths symbolising the Donaise Hills. Servants were clearing away the untouched feast from the huge table and, high above them at the end of the hall, portière curtains concealed a musicians' gallery.

I lost track of time; it certainly felt like we had been here for hours, exchanging only pleasantries, all tacitly waiting for some kind of explanation from Lightning while he pretended not to notice. I shifted position and flapped my wings open. I scuffed the carpet with my feet; I wanted to run and shout to break the tension. I considered going for a flight to blow away the fevered stuffiness of the room.

Lightning suddenly changed the music to an expansive waltz and looked at me steadily. 'No, I'm not disappointed with the world. I'm not tired, just bemused. I want to find out more and I need time to think.'

Finally! 'Is it to do with what the Emperor told you, when you had dinner with him?'

'Yes, tell us what he said. We all want to know,' said Eleonora, leaning forward on the balcony railing.

Lightning paused, then smiled. 'He said that you would certainly ask about it, and he would prefer it if I didn't tell you.'

'I'll ask him myself.'

'Comet, you know very well San keeps his past a secret.'

'He told you his past?'

'Yes. The Emperor explained it to me. He told me about the Shift as well. The things he said are just so incredible . . . I need time to come to terms with them. He only told me because he realised, at that point on the battlefield, that I didn't need immortality any more. He realised I had grown out of it.'

Tern spoke up from the window seat, unable to keep the sour note from her voice: 'Did he know you would throw the competition?'

'I expect he considered it. He knew I was leaving.'

'Didn't he ask you not to?' she urged.

He laughed. 'San has known Rayne and I a long time, longer than anyone else in his life. He might only speak to us once a decade, but I suppose that's as close as he gets, to friends. He knows Ella and I well, and he didn't find this too hard to predict. San relies on people wanting to be immortal more than anything else in the world, but if one of us Eszai finds something he wants more than immortality, San can do nothing to keep him. Ten years ago, when Cyan was kidnapped by Shearwater and I set off to rescue her, I must have valued her more than immortality, subconsciously I suppose. I mean, I wasn't aware of it at the time. So, no ... I am free to change, now. I am free to understand your other worlds, feel the passing of time again.'

'Well, aren't you afraid of dying?' Tern demanded.

Lightning lapsed into silence again. He played a little more loudly for a while, until a crunch on the gravel drive outside interrupted him.

'A little coach is coming in!' Tern cried.

'Is it? What are its colours?'

'Green and grey.'

Lightning stopped playing. 'Green and grey is Awndyn.'

The coach slewed to a halt. In the light from the palace lamps we saw the two horses were frothing. A plump woman in a shapeless silk dress and long ginger hair, leaning on a stick and moving slowly, swayed out of the carriage, ascended the steps and disappeared into the portico.

We heard her footsteps resound loud on the Reception Hall's terrazzo floor, then soundless as she passed into the carpeted winter south wing, through the salon and study. The door flew open and Swallow Awndyn barged in. A servant was following worriedly, close behind her. She slammed the door on him and glared at us all.

Lightning stood up. 'Welcome!'

His fiancée took a fistful of her hair and pulled at it in fury. 'What happened – Lightning? Have I heard right? You lost a Challenge? To your vile squab?'

'So it seems.' He relaxed back onto the piano stool. 'I'm sorry you missed it, my love. I sent you an invitation.'

'*You stupid moron!*'

Lightning quoted mildly: 'I love my love with an S, because she suddenly shows a slanderous side. Her name is Swallow and she comes from the strand.'

'I came straight here when I heard!' She ground her walking stick into the carpet. 'I can't believe it! You *never* lose! I never thought I'd live to see it! I can't even imagine it!'

Lightning offered her a glass but she didn't register it. She was incredulous. 'I expected to see you dejected, and here you are slamming at the piano like ten madmen. Are you insane?'

'That is no way to speak to your betrothèd.'

'All my life I've been fighting to get into the Circle and you just throw it away! Like it's nothing! Throw your life to a stupid child like a bauble!'

'The surprise should improve your music. It has become a bit samey over the last few years.'

'You!' She was speechless, and she still wouldn't sit down. 'How dare you!'

'Answer me this first – do you still want to marry me?'

'But ... you're a loser. You lost.'

Lightning closed his eyes for a second. Swallow continued, 'You're going to become mortal. To get older!'

'So you don't want me now?'

She hesitated and Lightning continued artlessly, 'So you were interested in me for my immortality, rather than as a person?'

She looked to the books portrayed in the lush weave of the carpet and the cascades of fruit in the deep wood mouldings on the door jambs. She ground the heel of one hand into her eye. Her red wings opened slightly, pulling her gown tight across her front; she was as flat-chested as a narrow boat. Her face had become lined, and she had plucked her eyebrows into an expression of constant surprise.

Swallow was the best musician of all time, but the Emperor did not need a musician. He didn't need music to rally the fyrd when everyone agreed Insects must be fought. He didn't need music for propaganda when he was offering immortality. She hated the fact that the sole determiner of the value of anything was its usefulness in the Insect war. After fifteen years of the same ambitious refrain the pressure had made her diamond inside, but she wasn't sparkling, however emptily. She was cutting.

'I want to join the *Circle*,' she said. 'How can you help me now? I *am* a musician. It's *all* I do. Just like an Eszai.'

Lightning leant back, his elbow on the piano's music stand. 'Oh, Swallow,' he said. 'You never noticed for one second that I really adored you. But now I'm leaving the Circle you suddenly see me. For ten years I have been offering you a place in the Circle through my love and you were too proud to take it. Do you think I can't tell, after hundreds of years of fending off gold-diggers? You strung me along –

with your pride you believed you could make it into the Circle on your own merit and I was your back-up plan. Even if you had become Eszai, you still wouldn't have married me, because deep down you don't want to. I was just as wrong to court you, but I didn't want to admit it, because I thought you were like Martyn –' He looked momentarily surprised at himself. 'But you are not. Now you are showing your true colours.'

'Ha! At least I still have feelings, not like you, always controlled, living in this fucking art gallery; you're so transparent.'

'On the contrary, you barely noticed I existed. I wondered what I had to do. If you had wanted Donaise you could have had it. I would have done anything. Now it's too late.'

She said, 'You're always deluding yourself. You with love, Jant with drugs; god knows what the rest of the immortals rely on. In a few years you won't be able to draw any of your wonderful bows any longer because you'll be *old* and *weak*.'

'I am sure it will be an interesting experience,' he said brightly. 'I never considered what I would look like when I'm forty. Or sixty. Well, now I'm going to find out.'

Swallow couldn't stand the fact that he was looking on it as an interesting experiment. 'You're a fool! And I've been looking after your nasty daughter all this time! I wish I'd known!'

'Be quiet about Cyan. I *have* just given my life for her. I only regret I didn't do it earlier, so I could have been with her as she grew up. I should have raised her instead of you.'

Swallow exploded with fresh anger. 'And now you're leaving me – where? Your bastard games will have wasted my talent! One day I'll be just a faded memory to you Eszai – worse still! – an old governor! And you won't hear my music any more.'

Lightning smiled and glanced away. He reached around with one hand and pressed a couple of keys, twiddling the first bars of a piece of music. Swallow stopped dead. 'Don't you *dare* play my aria.'

Lightning brought his other hand into play and expanded the music to its full glory.

'Stop it!'

He had turned back to the keyboard. 'What, this? You make your own immortality with every effortless opera. You are the greatest composer in the world, Swallow. What do you really want? Immortality might not give you what you really want. It didn't for me. Ask yourself, and be true to yourself. You already have fame. You have recognition. Your music brings a great response and many friends. But you harp on the same old tune of wanting the Circle. You don't appreciate the magnitude of your achievements, you only see the things you haven't done.'

'It isn't good enough, if I'm still mortal. I don't want to die.'

'Everybody dies except San. Eszai just take longer. Why should you be saved?'

'If I can make music forever, I'll be happy.'

'No, Swallow. Immortals are those who prize success and fame over happiness. They gain what little happiness they ever have from success. Their thirst for perfection and fear of being beaten drives them on. I no longer prize immortality in those terms, and neither should you. Learn from my example. Escape. You don't have to forgo an Eszai's single-mindedness. I won't let anything get in my way, even though the obstacle in my path was immortality itself.'

Swallow made a sound of disgust. She pulled off her engagement ring and flung it in rage. It hit the inside of the piano's upraised lid, dropped onto the strings and we heard it chime.

'I did love you, Swallow.'

'Liar!' she screamed. She turned to me. 'Jant, you'll help me, won't you?'

'All I can, but I doubt it'll do any good. It's up to you, now.'

'You said I was like a sister!'

'I can't change the Castle, Swallow.'

She bowed her head and sighed. 'I sometimes feel that I'm on the edge of some great truth. I get excited. I start scrawling the notes on the manuscript. I see the glow, the edge of the bright light where genius resides. I can never reach it completely. Maybe my excitement makes it ebb. The intense white light retreats, eludes me. I grow cold. I am left on the shore. No genius breakthrough tonight, just another symphony finished and my eyes are sore. It is happening more and more these days. I am getting older, and I no longer write from the heart. I'm getting older, Jant, and I will lose my genius. I'm still running the race; time is still burning down the bridges to things I could have achieved.' She burst into frightened tears.

'None of us can change the Castle,' I repeated.

'You immortals only exist because we allow you to,' she sobbed. 'If you're a ... barrier to me ... I'll make your life hard in the real world.'

Eleonora cut in, with a voice used to command battles and law courts. 'Spare us the vulgar threats, *Governor* Awndyn. There are not even a hundred immortals and you had one more chance to join them than the rest of us. You held out for yet another and lost both. Return to your music. We look forward to your next concert.'

Swallow swept the room with a look of pure hatred, took a step forward, hesitated, turned on her heel and stormed out. Her progress down the passageway was marked by a vase smashing every few metres. A little while later we heard the clop and crunch as her coach departed at a gallop. Silence returned.

Lightning sighed. 'I'd just had those replaced. The third time.'

I smiled. 'Well I'm sure you can afford to have them repaired. Or make some new replicas.'

'I don't think I'll bother this time. Time for a new look.'

'Lightning, are you sure?'

'Never more so. And you will all have to get used to calling me Saker.'

'I think people will still call you Lightning,' Eleonora said. 'And Lightning, I *do* want to escape.'

CHAPTER 27

Next morning I took breakfast in the Orangery. I sat at the round, polished table and pressed my toes into the soft moss that covered the ground like a carpet. An orange tree grew through a large hole in the centre of the table, over which its boughs hung low with fruit. The table was laden with all the foods that pass for breakfast in Awia, a variety far greater than I could actually eat. I had no appetite, I was thinking back to what happened the previous night. I still couldn't understand Lightning's volte-face. I felt an open rift in the centre of my being, as if he was already dead.

The sun shone through the glass wall which curved up to the panes of the ceiling. Black-painted wrought-iron flowers and tendrils spiralled from the curlicued frames, as if the struts of the glasshouse themselves were growing. More orange and lemon trees with smooth bark were rooted in the clean, deep moss all around me. The air was rich with scent.

An arcaded loggia passage connected the Orangery to the palace just behind me. In front, I looked out down the lawns to the shimmering lake. On the nearest end of the island the tops of tall monkey puzzle trees poked up from the dense woods extending to the shore, where a tiny jetty emerged.

The Queen of Awia appeared at the glass portal, kicked off her shoes and walked across the moss barefoot. As always she looked fantastic, elegant in cream suede, with her sword scabbard swapping the back of her legs. But beneath her soft feathers, her porcelain face and sepia eyes, I thought she was just another thick-skinned tart. She sat down beside me, so the orange tree didn't block her view of me. A servant appeared immediately and started loading her plate with kedgeree.

I said, 'The guests have gone. When are you leaving?'

'Me?' Eleonora laughed. 'Oh, no. I'm staying here for a while, Queen's prerogative. I'm going to do all I possibly can to impress him. And I'm well capable of that.'

I wondered how to warn him. I couldn't think how without

incriminating myself. I said sarcastically, 'He'd be overwhelmingly impressed by dressage and the lash.'

'Do you think I can't change? If Lightning can, I can, of course. The Eleonora you saw won't be the one he sees. On the contrary, I intend to marry him.'

'What!'

She continued, 'But I won't hide all of my . . . more wanton side. If I try to act like a maiden, well, he might not like maidens, and that would be a great shame, wouldn't it?'

'Your talents lie elsewhere.'

She stifled a smile. 'You'd be surprised. It's difficult to break through his romantic pose but there's a real man under there. I've never met another with such a mix of strength, intelligence and perfect self-assurance. A real equal.'

'I don't want to know.'

'And he's better hung than you. You can tell from the crease of his trousers.'

'I *don't* want to know! I can't believe it! Imagine: sell all your antiques, Lightning, and redecorate with mirrors – Eleonora's moving in! All the servants must wear leather harnesses and nipple clips!'

She laughed. 'I'm not that bad.'

'Well, I don't *bloody* understand why he chose to lose the Challenge.'

'I think his leaving the Circle is a very clever move. When we marry, it will be the joining of the two greatest houses in Awia.'

'Oh, god . . .' Realisation began to dawn.

'Think what he's doing. When Cyan becomes Eszai, she cannot inherit Peregrine manor, because the Emperor no longer allows immortals to own land. Lightning will keep Peregrine, so reuniting all the scattered lands of his original manor, which has always been his aim. When he marries me he'll regain Avernwater too, and we will possess all the manors of Awia except Carniss and Wrought. Lightning will not only have united his manor, but the whole of Awia. He will be King, as he should have been fourteen centuries ago. He can fulfil the role he had to relinquish when he joined the Circle, and bring the Micawater dynasty back to the throne, that has lain dormant with him so long. That's what he always wanted. It's a long time to wait. We will have a single great manor and Awia will have a degree of stability that has never been seen before. Never!'

'You're founding the first absolute monarchy in Awia.'

'Well done, Jant. You have figured out my aim, at least.'

It did not sound so good to me.

Eleonora added, 'The Emperor would be pleased.'

'Would he?'

'Of course. All the manors would be in Zascai hands.'

'Except Wrought.'

'Don't worry about Tern, I think that would suit San, too. He would like the Castle to keep some degree of control over the weaponsmiths. And with Lightning and I to lead the Awian fyrd, think of all the business they'll be getting! If Wrought is threatened by anything, it's the new industries in Hacilith.'

I felt nauseous, staring into the future of a new dynasty. The thought of Eleonora and *Lightning's* future generations, that I would have to watch, and to serve as an Eszai, for hundreds of years after them, terrified me.

'I feel time-sick,' I said. 'Who knows what will happen?'

'Whatever happens, you're shielded from it. Protected by the Castle's walls, you immortals experience the arrows of misfortune as nothing but a tickle, compared to us. You should even enjoy the experience, because you know you'll live long enough to see the wheel of fortune turn up once more. You might even see the system change yet again, from our dynasty – though I hope it won't.'

'What if Cyan is beaten and Lightning wants to rejoin the Circle?'

'He would bring me into the Circle too. We could stay together forever and I would be immortal as well. I've always fancied it.'

'But then you'd have to abdicate.'

'Yes, but we would crown Cyan Queen. Cyan, instead of us, would restart the Micawater dynasty. Lightning can't lose, really.'

'Providing Cyan complies with his wishes.'

'Oh, I think she will learn humility in the Circle. I think she would make a good Queen.'

'You can't tell what will happen, Eleonora.'

'No. But we welcome the uncertainty! Awia is free to change now. The role of Archer can change, too! Saker is no longer holding them back.' Eleonora took a forkful of kedgeree. 'And he has such a fantastic body.'

I looked at her, and her eyes were shining. It could be love, or it could be all that seafood.

Cyan was right; for all my show of independence, Lightning had been a father to me. Now with this sudden view of the future he daunted me even more. 'Where is he? I must speak to him,' I said, though without much relish.

'At the boathouse.' She pointed through the front windows. I put my boots on at the Orangery door and walked out.

*

On my way down to the lake, I threw up in a random corner of the ivy-clad stone staircase. Great, I thought; the vomit Comet is back.

The ground's spinning. Wow. It's been years since it did that. I felt amazing and I didn't care. I think I've come to terms with sco-lopendium. I've been drinking it for months without increasing the dose, so I was sure I could live this way.

This was the scolopendium I took from the barge – the drugs that Cyan bought. I've been taking a sip every day since I crash-landed; dissolved in wine in my hip flask. How else do you think I could keep going after the Vermiform's assault? I know I told Rayne that I had thrown it in the fire, but I lied to her. I lied to you as well.

But that was my only lie. Trust me.

The glorious palace front was clear-cut against the sky. It looked as bizarre as a building from the Shift. But, I thought, ours was a Shift world as well, one of thousands in the continuum, and it was as strange and beautiful as the rest.

I looked for the window of our bedroom, on the second floor of the Eyas Wing, with its curtains drawn. I pictured Tern still asleep up there, her manicured hand brushing the coverlet.

Two floors below our window, Eleonora was eating breakfast alone, her feet on the cool, mossy ground. She suddenly feels indescribably happy. A beam of light sparkles on the lake, shines through the panes and dazzles the glasshouse. Her country! 'This place is great!' she says enthusiastically, puts down the coffee cup and decides to go for a ride.

On her way out she passes the bow store, where Harrier is sadly placing his master's bows back on their racks. His sense of dis-appointment has left him swirling with the current; Lightning's skill was a tenet of faith with him, because Harrier himself was a Challenger once. He pauses, then takes his own longbow from its case, holds it in both hands and presses it to his chest, thinking, why shouldn't I go and join the archers who'll soon be queuing up to Challenge Cyan? He starts to wipe the longbow down.

A hundred kilometres away, Cyan and Rayne in their coach are crossing out of Awia. Cyan is alternately crying and defiant. She is horrified by what she has done to her father, but she can see no way out. She would see it through to the conclusion. What else could she do? Ornate shadows lengthen behind the coach's intricate fretwork screens. 'Daddy lost deliberately,' she repeats.

'It crushes me, too.' Rayne bites her lip. 'But he gave you t' chance t' step ou' of his shadow and develop your own life. Establish your own name and identity. Isn' tha' wha' you wanted? Don' yield to preceden' and t' power of t' past. You'll forge' him, though I never will ... I'll think of him, sometime in t' far future.'

Rayne, when she arrives at the Castle, will visit Serein Wrenn, who is currently lying in the hospital mourning the loss of his foot and his friend. He glances up when Mist Fulmer comes in, bringing a tray of beer and cakes. Mist cheers him up by telling him he can still take the wheel of the caravel *Windhover*, on the bright ocean out of Tanager.

Mist walks back to his room via the Breckan Wing roof walk, looking out over the parapet across the plains. 'At least I'm still here,' he says. 'In this great place.'

In the chamber below his feet, those of Tornado are being massaged by his new girlfriend. Sleat in his room is busy polishing armour but looks up and sees them, tiny figures in the window of the opposite building. Tornado and his girlfriend disappear, rolling off the bed and pulling the covers with them.

'What was that thump?' thinks the Cook, looking up. Never mind. He checks his watch; he doesn't have much time. He takes his jacket and hastens out of the ground floor of Breckan, across to the kitchens. The clockwork of the Castle ticks steadily, it pushes years around; the slow hand – centuries.

The Cook hangs up his jacket and begins to prepare a fulsome feast for Cyan Lightning. His kitchens are shaded by the towering Throne Room. When Cyan is made immortal, the Eszai will convene inside, where for ever and ever, the Emperor San is sitting on his throne.

CHAPTER 28

Lightning, his shirt sleeves rolled up to the elbow, was pushing a flat-bottomed boat over the grass towards a slipway and landing stage jutting out into the lake. He saw me coming towards him, straightened up and wiped his hands. 'Good morning, Jant. Will you give me a hand with this punt?'

We pushed the boat to the top of the slipway, settling it onto the metal rollers. 'What are you doing?'

He slid a punt pole out from under its benches. 'I'm going to the island. To see Martyn, you know. I am going to visit her one last time and explain what has happened. I will say goodbye to her and take my leave. I do not think I will need to visit her again.' He smiled sadly.

'I must go back to the Castle, for the ceremony,' I said.

'Of course. In two days' time, when I feel the Circle drop me, I think it will be a fraught moment . . . I will need to be alone.'

'Be careful of Eleonora. She . . . well, she . . .'

He raised an eyebrow.

'I think she . . . you, er . . . she said . . .'

'I can handle her. She gave me cause for hope, when Swallow had not. I'd like to pretend I never noticed her while I was engaged to Swallow but time is now too precious for me to hide from myself.'

Could he really be capable of leaving his palace to chance and future generations whether his offspring or not? I raised a hand to it. 'Imagine that ruined, all the treasures gone, the roof falling in. How can you tell they won't squander it?'

'I think Cyan will look after it. But if not . . . Look, Jant; who knows what changes she'll make and what innovations subsequent Lightnings will come up with? Who knows what the discipline of archery will turn into? To think, your Vermiform even laughed at our weapons.'

I understood, though it frightened me. A future without the constraints of Lightning's authority will be uncertain, but it would be more free.

'I'm free to change, too.' His eyes sparkled. 'I have to adapt, and come to terms with these different times. I'm looking forward to the coming of the modern world.'

I pleaded, 'You could return to the Circle. If not as Archer, as Swordsman. Wrenn's been maimed and you're officially the second-best.'

'But I don't feel like Challenging my friend. I no longer feel the lure of the Castle. Isn't it fabulous!'

'I barely understand.'

A breeze gusted across the grounds, cooling my face; followed by the low rumble of thunder over Donaise. Saker looked out at the ruffled water. 'Jant, I remember when you joined the Circle. I was afraid of you.'

'No!'

'Yes. I was living here and I hadn't done anything new for a hundred years. I had settled into a rut. Rayne sent me a letter saying, "Come and look at the man who can fly!" But it's impossible for a man to fly. You stormed the Circle. I remember you standing on the spire to show us all what you can do. You dived off and we gasped. We thought you'd be killed for certain. But you swooped over the bonfire and vanished up into the sky. I was so shocked, so inspired! I thought I'd seen everything, but you reminded me there was yet more. There will always be more. Thank you, Jant. I hope I have opened your eyes in the same way.'

I nodded, speechless. I hoped being tongue-tied wasn't going to become a habit.

'Then I saw you become disenchanted, and we know what you're like now with the drugs. Try not to be disillusioned; it's a fate worse than death. You proved that all your other worlds exist. San knew all the time your drug-fantasies were real.' He shook his head in wonder.

'The Shift?' Yes, I wanted to talk to him about that. I said, 'Remember Dunlin?'

'The last of the Rachiswaters?'

'He is in the Shift. Don't ask me how, because it's a long story. But if you grow old, and at the very end of your life you don't want to die, then you can Shift. Take scolopendium – I'll make it for you – and you can go through and join Dunlin. And if you're mortally wounded while fighting the Insects, I can ask Rayne to give you enough scolopendium to Shift. That's more or less what happened to him.'

There was a long pause. Lightning said thoughtfully, 'Jant, do you know your power?'

'Huh?'

'Rhydanne are such a curious people. You have such a clever mind, yet you never see the bigger picture.'

'What? The Shift? They're just other worlds, a bit different from here.'

'No, I didn't mean that ... No wonder San doesn't want you cornered... but don't you realise the Emperor is scared of the Shift? I can tell you that much. He knows about things which he really doesn't want you to bring back, even if they followed you accidentally.'

'What? The Gabbleratchet?'

Lightning shrugged. 'He didn't say. Besides, I know San doesn't want the truth to be widely known in case people start trying to go there themselves instead of staying here to fight the Insects.'

'There are Insects there as well. And worse.'

'Ah, so many new secrets I'm learning – it's a whole new world ... Will you do something for me, Jant?'

'Yes.'

'Will you look after Cyan? When she becomes immortal, will you guide her the way I have guided you? You've seen so much trouble yourself, you should know how to keep her out of it.'

'That's very clever. She's inheriting your place in the Circle.'

'Yes. When she is in the Circle she'll become part of the establishment and she won't be able to be rebellious any longer.'

I said, 'In fact, she's submitting to a much higher authority in order to escape yours.'

'Well, she hasn't realised it yet. Even if it's just for a short time, it'll do her good.'

In turn, Lightning had cast off the Emperor's authority. This was *his* teenage rebellion, and San knew it was time to let him leave. He looked stronger and more confident than ever.

'All right,' I said. 'I'll look after Cyan.' He had saddled me with the girl, given me a wayward subordinate to look after. I can't sleep with her now, can I?

'Thank you, Jant.'

Incredibly, there had been nine new Eszai in the last ten years. I was one of the older ones now, having to give advice to the new immortals. I hated that, but with a tired resignation I didn't see that I could do anything about it. 'Now *I'm* becoming part of the establishment,' I said.

Lightning grinned. 'It is the inevitable process.'

'I never thought it would happen to me but it's happening at last. I'd never have the guts to leave. I barely understand it.'

'You can't. You're too young.' He stepped up onto the covered stern and I passed him the punt pole. 'When you put another thousand years between yourself and your past, you'll understand.'

'I'll never leave the Circle, Saker,' I said with conviction.

He smiled. 'Look after Cyan. She'll need it.'

'I will.'

He held the pole up and rocked his weight forward, enough to tip the boat onto the slipway. It ran down, spinning the rollers, and splashed into the lake, sending out a wave before it. A cloud of glittering specks rose up from the silt.

Lightning dug the pole in. Standing tall on the back of the boat, he pushed calmly away from the shore without a backward glance. I remained looking out in the direction of the island for a long time after, when he had gone.

ACKNOWLEDGEMENTS

A big thank you to all the people I used to go caving with. Thank you to CU Hang Gliding Club and Blooners 2000 Hot Air Balloon Company for helping me see the Yorkshire Dales and the Chiltern Hills from the air. Thanks to the Yorkshire Dales Falconry and Conservation Centre for days out hawking. Thank you to Dr Jo Cooper, curator at the Natural History Museum Bird Group at Tring, for letting me view the awe-inspiring collections, and to Alison Harding for letting me play with the Ornithology Library. Many thanks to Stella Swainston for details of PSU Riot Procedure, shield instruction and equipment, used in my fyrd shield walls. Thanks to Dr Marco de Boni for memorably explaining hand-to-hand combat in between mouthfuls of pizza. Thanks, John Berlyne. Thank you, Mac and Jenny. Above all, love and thanks to Brian, without whom none of this would have been possible.

M. Trevillion

STEPH SWAINSTON is a qualified archaeologist with a degree from Cambridge and a research degree. She worked as an archaeologist for three years, taking part in the dig that researched the oldest recorded burial site in the UK, before becoming an information scientist. The author of *The Year of Our War* and *No Present Like Time,* she lives in England.

FICTION

10/07

"A more original sort of fantasy."
—*Time Out London*

Steph Swainston returns to the dazzling, dizzying world of the Fourlands with the audacious sequel to her acclaimed novels *The Year of Our War* and *No Present Like Time*. Jant Comet, the messenger, has survived deadly insects, internecine politics, and even his own debilitating, life-threatening addiction. But now he faces a challenge greater than any he has met in the last several centuries, one that could shake the foundations of the Fourlands forever. For the Emperor himself is riding to the front, and nothing is as it seems . . .

"An uncompromisingly classy act."   —*The Guardian*

"[Swainston] has a facility with language and a genius for plot and character which Booker prize winners could, and should, be envious of. . . ."   —*Publishing News*

Cover design by Richard Aquan
Cover illustration by Christophe Sivet

Fantasy

ISBN 978-0-06-075389-4

EAN

9 780060 753894   51395

$13.95   0707

An Imprint of HarperCollinsPublishers
www.eosbooks.com
www.stephswainston.co.uk